Small Treasures

Small Treasures

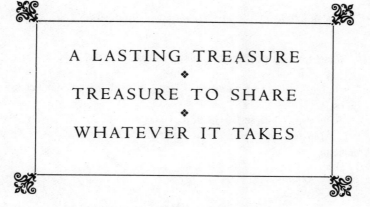

A LASTING TREASURE

◆

TREASURE TO SHARE

◆

WHATEVER IT TAKES

THREE COMPLETE NOVELS BY

Lass Small

SMITHMARK

This edition published in 1993 by SMITHMARK Publishers, Inc., 16 East 32nd Street, New York, NY 10016.

SMITHMARK books are available for bulk purchase for sales promotion and premium use. For details write or call the manager of special sales, SMITHMARK Publishers, Inc., 16 East 32nd Street, New York, NY 10016; (212) 532-6600.

Library of Congress Cataloging-in-Publication Data

Small, Lass.
    Small treasures : three complete novels / by Lass Small.
        p.   cm.
    Contents: A lasting treasure—Treasure to share—Whatever it takes
    ISBN 0-8317-7866-0 : $9.98
    1. Man-woman relationships—Fiction.   2. Love stories, American.
    I. Title.
    PS3569.M286S63   1993
    813'.54—dc20   93-2063
                                                              CIP

Printed in The United States of America
1   3   5   7   9   10   8   6   4   2

To Jennifer and Frances,
with my love.

Dear Readers,

It is especially nice that these three books are being reprinted at this time. It was ten years ago, in April of 1983, that my first book, *A LASTING TREASURE*, was published. That book was honored by Waldenbooks as the top seller of the Second Chance at Love line for 1983–84. Since then, my books have consistently made the best seller lists and have received awards from romance magazines, booksellers, and an Award of Excellence from my publisher, Harlequin-Silhouette.

My background for writing is the School of Fine Arts. I know that sounds odd; it is. I love to draw, and I find it amazing to see the blend and contrast of color. For me, it's magic.

The magic is with words, too. I'm not a writer, I'm a storyteller. The words are carefully selected so that the reader can "see" what is being told. When readers write that one of my books has touched their hearts, my heart is touched. Or when they say a book has made them laugh, I laugh, too. It is wonderful to be able to share my stories.

Books have always been important in my life, so when my youngest child was plagued by allergies, and I was confined along with him, it was no surprise that I began to write short stories.

Each one I sent out was rejected. It seemed logical that if I wrote a book, I would be able to sell the short stories. I had no idea how difficult it was to sell a book. I wrote at least nine books—all were rejected. Then, on the advise of my local bookstore manager, I wrote a romance and it sold.

I'd hit the market when the publishing houses were moving into the field of romance and scrambling for manuscripts. By now, I've sold almost fifty books which are scheduled for publication through 1994.

Writing stories about people is so interesting because they are probably the most fascinating creatures on our fragile planet. Men, particularly, are so strange and different. They are a peculiar combination of lure, oddity, inventiveness, and power, with a touch of compassion and gentleness that throws us every time. Women, of course, are perfect.

I hope you enjoy these three books. I loved writing them and sharing them with you.

With all good wishes,

A Lasting Treasure

CHAPTER ONE

"WELL, ADELINA MARY ROSE KILDAIRE"—Addy smiled at herself in the long, wide model's mirror in the dining room of the big old house—"you're doing pretty well for yourself." She plaited her wheat-colored hair into a single braid and idly considered her rounded body reflected in the mirror. How discouraging it was to have hips and breasts when one was a designer of women's clothing. Why couldn't she have been as flat as a board, like Pearl?

She heard the front door opening and closing and the hum of people talking as guests began to arrive for that afternoon's ladies-only showing of her summer line of lingerie. Gusts of frigid February air blasted into the house along with the guests, and the giant furnace in the basement rumbled into life.

The model's mirror was placed against the window wall. Addy looked out at the woods frozen in a tangle against the winter sky. Not for the first time, she wondered what the block had been like when all the other great houses still stood there on the north side of Indianapolis. Gradually they had been abandoned and demolished. Her own Gown House remained in lovely splendor, the single surviving house on the now-overgrown block. She owned the house, the entire block, and a staggering mortgage.

Miss Pru, her dear friend and mentor, bustled past her, hesitating long enough to scold, "You've braided your hair too tight, Addy. Your eyes are pulled back into slits. You look as if you're auditioning for *Madama Butterfly.*"

"Auditioning?" asked blond model Pattycake as she hurried in, late as usual. "Who's auditioning?" She was bursting with life, bubbly, giggly, irrepressible. She was eighteen and stagestruck.

"Addy's braid is too tight and it pulls her eyes slanted," Miss Pru explained over her shoulder as she hurried away. "She looks like Madame Butterfly."

Pattycake cocked her head and studied Addy carefully. "Your eyes are too blue," she pronounced. "You'd have to wear brown contacts. And you're really too English-looking. Your nose is too straight and your mouth is a good two inches too wide. You'd have to change all that . . . and take voice lessons."

Addy gave her a droll look and laughed, then loosened her hair and began to braid it again.

Each year she held two ladies-only shows on the afternoons before the summer and winter showings. At both the afternoon and evening shows today they would model the summer line of gowns, dresses, jackets, and raincoats. Almost one hundred people had requested tickets for one of the shows. That evening there would also be some male guests. Only the afternoon shows were restricted to women.

The hum from the drawing room grew louder, and the models rushed around getting ready. Addy surveyed the chaos and grinned. She loved it. She checked her dress in the mirror and knew it fit her well and was attractive. The long-sleeved, soft woolen shirtwaist in blue-gray made her eyes even bluer. They sparkled with excitement.

In spite of the models' nervous whispers and giggles, Addy knew everything was under control. She could easily have kept them all calm, but their excitement would communicate itself to the guests waiting out in the drawing room.

Once her braid was finished, she looped it up the back of her head and pinned it there tightly, then began to search for her daughter, three-year-old Grendel. No one ever thought she and Grendel were related, because Addy was so fair, and while Grendel was pale-cheeked, she had dark button eyes and straight black hair. She was the postage-stamp print of Paul Morris, who'd taken off when Addy had learned she was pregnant. That had left lasting scars.

Stretching to see over the models' heads, Addy called softly, "Grendel?"

"I saw her just a minute ago," offered Pearl, one of the models. She was six feet tall and incredibly thin. When she'd come to work for Addy and had said her name was Pearl, Addy had squinched up her face and asked, "Pearl?"

Pearl had just grinned and replied, in a marvelous imitation of Pearl Bailey, "Us black pearls, honey, are rare."

Pearl moved to the mirror and posed dramatically.

She wore tangerine-colored pajamas that were smashing with her chocolate skin. To Addy she said, "Aren't you glad I'm naturally this color and you didn't have to paint me in order to make the contrast between this rag and my glorious skin?"

Addy grinned and tried to pinch Pearl's nonexistent rear end. Pearl stood up straight and sent a smug look down on Addy, then snaked down a long, skinny arm and gave Addy's round bottom a sassy pat.

"You have a mean streak that wide," Addy told her. Her hands measured off two feet. "And since you're only this wide"—she put her hands about six inches apart—"you can see the over*whelming* ratio." She turned haughtily away from Pearl's grin.

"Grendel?" Addy called again. She stopped next to Miss Pru, who was making last-minute alterations on a chemise. "Have you seen Grendel?"

Miss Pru smiled indulgently and replied softly, "She's checking the house. I think she's becoming a real professional." She spoke around several pins held in her mouth, which Addy forbade *anyone* to do. But she allowed Miss Pru certain privileges. Whatever would Addy have done without her? She was middle-aged and deceptively starchy-looking, and she was all that had sustained Addy during a long, trying time.

The word "professional" made Addy pause. "Do you think it's okay for Grendel to model?" she whispered. She had been worrying about that lately.

"Of course, Addy, you know Grendel enjoys it," Miss Pru assured her in a quiet voice. "She doesn't show off as much as she shares the fun." She snipped a thread.

"Grendel's no problem," agreed redheaded Dale, who was looking contentedly at herself in the mirror.

"That's right," Pearl agreed. "She's a doll."

Addy slid her a look. "You're prejudiced," she said, which made Pearl roll her eyes at the ceiling in exasperation.

Just then Grendel hopped into the room. She skipped among the adults and grabbed Addy's hand. "Mommy," she hissed in a loud whisper, "'most every chair's tooked." Three was not known for lucid speech, Addy thought. Only those familiar with Grendel could plausibly interpret what she said.

"Taken," Addy corrected as she curled down to her child's height and pretended to straighten her gown. Grendel wore a summer nightgown of white seersucker with scattered blue flowers. It was sleeveless, with a large flounce of white eyelet around the bottom. Grendel's eyes were snapping with excitement, and Addy's heart clutched at seeing how perfect she was. It always amazed her that Grendel was real and by far the most charming and brilliant child ever born. And that wasn't just maternal prejudice, Addy assured herself. She had looked around and compared impartially.

Linda, the brunette model who was paired with Grendel whenever she modeled, also entered the room. Grendel looked like Linda's child. It made Addy almost jealous that they went so well together. Linda arranged her peignoir and bent over Grendel, checking her makeup. They both had such white skin that they needed rouge under the very strong lights to keep them from looking washed-out. Linda examined Grendel critically, added a dab more rouge on her nose and chin, and leaned back, peering at her but not frowning. Addy had reminded her often that frowns cause wrinkles.

As Pearl put it, the models were blond Pattycake, brunette Linda, redheaded Dale, and one black Pearl. The others had named Pearl as their outstanding model,

and, since she was so tall, she groaned and rolled her
eyes at their play on words.

Miss Pru modeled older women's clothes with elegant
style, but Addy considered her own rounded figure unsuitable for modeling. While she seldom showed anything herself, she would end the afternoon session today
with a lovely, subtly naughty robe.

It was time to begin the fashion show. Miss Pru started
the music tapes. Addy took the contrived three steps up
to the tall, curtained double doors between the dining
room and the drawing room and stepped into the lights
beamed on the entrance. She grinned at the women sitting
on folding wooden chairs, which Pearl's father, Marcus,
had borrowed from his church. Marcus was Addy's security. He could fix anything.

The runway was five feet wide and twenty feet long,
contrived of planks set on sturdy trestles, with chairs on
either side. The sides of the walkway were draped with
cloth.

The walls of the drawing room were covered with a
neutral burlap that had been pleated vertically from the
chair rail to the ceiling. It would suffice until Addy could
afford to have the walls replastered. It made a nice tex-
tured background for the showings. The room had been
cleared of its customary furniture and rugs.

More than fifty women were present for the fashion
show. All of them were customers. The first year there
had been fifty women also, but thirty-eight had been
friends pulled in to fill the chairs. When Addy welcomed
the guests, her chatter conveyed a natural friendliness.
She felt very comfortable with women. It was a snap for
her to narrate the ladies-only show.

After she'd greeted the women, she stepped off the
ramp to sit on a high stool placed at the left of the runway
out of the spotlight. That way the guests wouldn't look

at her but at the models as she described what they wore. In order to give her four models enough time to change, Addy made it a practice to describe the material, any unusual aspects of the garment, and how it was constructed. She also explained where she'd gotten the trim and material.

"Dale's panties are mostly cotton for coolness," she told the guests. "We usually use a blend from Texas or North Carolina, but this material is from Egypt. Did you know that Egypt has been exporting cotton for over two thousand years? They probably did it before then too.

"Dale's robe weighs only four ounces because the cloth is so fine. Gussets have been put under the arms so that there's enough room to reach easily without straining the fragile cloth."

Dale turned and moved, and the robe floated out like a soft, green-tinted mist. Her body looked lovely in the fine lingerie. The summer underwear and nightgowns were sheer and revealing, but the models weren't self-conscious.

It pleased Addy to hear a constant hum of comments during the showing. It was all very relaxed and informal. As usual, there was a pleased murmur for Grendel, who came out dancing and laughing, and several oohs and aahs rose from the women for some of the robes and nightwear.

For the last segment of the show, Pearl took Addy's place in order to give her time to change into the robe she would model. She disappeared through the hall rather than back over the ramp. She could hear Pearl describe her own robe. "Since this makes me look like I have a figure, you can tell Addy's a genius..."

Addy changed, made sure her hair was slicked back, discouraging the little wisps that tended to curl around the edges, and returned to the ramp in time to hear Pearl say, "And so to bed. Me, I just wear basic black." They laughed, as always. "But Adelina has something you'll like. She's going to describe it to you herself."

Addy slipped through the drapes into the lights, standing in a deceptively simple, pale peach robe. She assumed a formal, aloof pose. She wore tiny pink pearls in her ears. The robe was a soft lawn, sleeveless and fitted to the hips before it fell to the floor in soft folds. Over the shoulders and around the low-scooped neck there was a soft four-inch bias ruffle. The robe was very feminine.

Addy turned, moving slowly, showing it off. "Actually, being manless, I wear an old flannel bathrobe to bed." They tittered. She could see clearly only those women close by, because the rest of the room was in shadow. Some of the women had been her first customers, and she'd become very fond of them.

"There's braided horsehair in the bottom hem to weight it down so it'll swing nicely," she explained. She twirled around, and the skirt swung in a lovely circle.

"In the olden days," Addy went on, "Coco Chanel weighted her suit jackets with a gold chain in the hem. When you stood up or moved, the weight of the chain would straighten the jacket and keep it neat. Gold, being the price it is, is not in the hem of this robe, just the horsehair.

"Ginger Rogers once wore a weighted skirt to dance with Fred Astaire so that, when she turned, the skirt would wrap around her. As she paused, it would slowly unwrap. It was so heavy that it almost toppled poor Fred. He had to change his steps to stay out of reach of that heavy skirt.

"Now this skirt won't knock any man over." She looked up at her audience and grinned. "At least not by itself." They laughed. Addy turned, letting the skirt flare, then cautioned, "Don't do this on a stairway. You might really break a leg—not just in the show-biz sense."

She stood still, demure again and formal. "Now, no woman, wearing a robe like this, is going to style her hair this way." She indicated her slicked-back braid, then pulled out the pins, slid off the elastic holder, and easily unbraided her hair. She rumpled it with both hands and peered through it vaguely. "Is that more like it?" There was a chuckling murmur of agreement.

She ran her fingers through her hair, controlling it but leaving it marvelously, carelessly tousled as she continued telling them about the robe. "This material is very soft, but it's built so that it will stay up—if you want it to." She grinned a little wickedly. "If you undo this top hook"—she put her hands up to her chest and did that—"it will still stay up, but the shoulder strap tends to slide off." She showed them, allowing one strap to slide slowly down. "If you undo the second hook, both shoulder straps give up." Addy undid the hook, and both shoulder straps dropped away from her shoulders. She assumed a sweet expression, and in a hammed-up version of a Southern accent asked, "Don't I look like my name's Daisy June?

"But even with the second hook undone," she continued, "your bosom will stay covered." She showed them as she moved, turned, and leaned over. She gathered her hair at the top of her head before she said, "The third hook will bare your bosom, but," she advised, "you let him do that." She laughed with the guests as she allowed her hair to spill over her shoulders... and her eyes lifted to the silhouette of a man just inside the door of the entrance hall! What was *he* doing at a ladies-only show? But he *was* there. She stared. He was a powerful wedge of wide shoulders and narrow hips. His feet were apart, his fists on his lean hips, and his head was thrust forward, completing his aggressive stance.

Addy felt like a slave girl on the block exhibiting herself to bidders. The man looked as if he was about to make a bid. Her lips parted as she waited for it, and an absolutely remarkable sensual sensation ran up her thighs, through her stomach, and up into her breasts.

She blinked and jerked her head as she realized where she was. She sketched an abrupt nod at the clapping and chattering women, then whirled and stepped down through the drapes. "There's a *man* out there!" she hissed at Pearl.

"A man?" Pearl was astonished. "What's he doing here?"

"Acting as if he's in a slave market eyeing the merchandise."

"Watch yo mouf, white chile."

Indignant, Addy huffed, "Pearl, blacks aren't the only ones who've been slaves. Why, right this minute in—"

"Calm yourself, Addy, I'll call Papa." Pearl hurried away as Miss Pru bustled out front.

Addy snatched up her blue woolen shirtwaist and clutched it to her chest like a shield. He'd watched her do all that. Who was he? "Pattycake," Addy whispered, "go see if he's still there." She fumbled out of the robe and jerked the blue wool dress over hear head.

Pattycake sighed with exasperation. "Okay, okay! But it's not as if you were *exposed* or anything!" She went off, not over the steps via the runway but around through the hall.

Addy raked back her hair, furiously braiding it skintight. Her cheeks were hot. Was she blushing? She hadn't blushed since she'd told her family about Grendel. Twenty-seven, an unmarried mother, and she could still blush? How weird. Why would she blush? It had to be anger. Why was she angry?

She'd been fully dressed, but she hadn't expected a

man to be at the lingerie showing. She must be feeling hostile because he'd watched her as she'd moved, and he'd listened to what she'd said. She'd acted out of character because she'd been sure there were only women present. Women say things to other women they'd never say to men, she reasoned. If she'd known he was going to be around, she'd never have modeled that robe at all!

She fidgeted, waiting for Pattycake to return. For some reason she really didn't want to face that man—not after the way she'd behaved up on the runway. Thinking of him as he watched her up there, she felt a strange sensation touch her stomach again. She'd never felt that way before. What was it?

Standing in the doorway, he'd looked so . . . formidable, as if he'd carelessly pay the asked price, whatever it was. She shivered a little, but she wasn't cold, and the shiver wasn't from fear. It was more as if she was . . . excited.

She reminded herself that she was a grown woman. She could handle anything. She'd been on her own and self-supporting since she'd first gone to college. She'd worked at every kind of honest work she could find, and she'd survived. She'd survived it all.

She stared out the window at the gloomy winter snow and frowned. Why was she reluctant to face him? Of course, with Miss Pru and Marcus to protect her, she hadn't had to deal with any man except in the most casual way. She didn't have the leisure time for a full social life, and she didn't really miss it. She'd dated enough to know men weren't important to her. She loved her work, Grendel, her house, Miss Pru, and all the rest. She didn't need some man moving in and disrupting the careful balance. Moving in? What did she mean by assuming he wanted to move in? Other than standing militantly in the door, what exactly had he done? She tried to decide.

Pattycake came back and said, "He's gone." She sounded disappointed.

"Good."

"But he's coming back tonight. He got some tickets from Miss Pru for his mother."

"We don't have any left!" Addy objected. "How could she give him tickets?"

Pattycake raised her eyebrows and said with slow emphasis, "His mother is Elizabeth Turner Harrow."

Addy eyed her excited face. "What's that supposed to mean?"

"You're obviously not an Indy native."

"Is anyone?" Addy asked.

"Elizabeth Turner Harrow is a civic leader."

"Hooray for her."

"Now, Addy, she's a very nice lady. And she's also involved in the theater!"

"Ahhhhh." Now Addy understood. Pattycake had theatrical ambitions. "So you're going to do Little Nell on the runway tonight?"

Pattycake's eyes danced. "I'd considered Lady Macbeth."

"Of course, the Scots tartan," Addy guessed, naming a summer dress to be modeled that evening.

"But I decided that's been overdone." Pattycake posed, arm out, head thrown back.

"It's generally underdone—as in half-baked," Addy remarked dryly.

"So I thought Blanche from *Streetcar* would do it."

Addy nodded in understanding. "The smoke-gray chiffon evening dress."

"Umm-hmm. It's perfect." She fell into the role, deliberately awful. "Oh Stanley you beast."

"I don't remember that line."

"I'm improvising." Pattycake gave an excessively sweet, eyelash-fluttering smile.

"Don't."

She grinned naturally. "I wouldn't."

"Thank God."

"But I was tempted!"

As Addy groaned, Pattycake commented with eighteen-year-old tolerance, "Oh, Ad, you're so easy to tease. You take everything so seriously. You didn't think I'd *really*—"

"Nothing people your age does surprises people of my age."

"I'll find your cane," Pattycake promised as she flitted away.

That left Addy free of distraction, and her thoughts of the man came winging back. He was very attractive. But she hadn't really seen him. How could she find him attractive and so distracting? He'd be there that very night. And he'd be watching. Why would he care one way or the other? He wouldn't. But if he did come back that evening, there she'd be, doing the narration.

Of course, she wouldn't be looking at the guests. She'd be sitting in the shadows to the side, looking at the models. Even if he glanced at her, there'd be nothing to hold his attention. It was no big deal. Why was her silly mind running around that way?

But as soon as everyone left, Addy cornered Miss Pru and went to some lengths to coerce her into doing the narration that evening. "That's perfectly silly, Adelina," Miss Pru protested. "You've practiced it and know it all by heart. I'd have to read it."

"Practice now," Addy coaxed.

Miss Pru scowled at her. "Why can't you do it?"

"My throat's gone." Addy choked a little. "It's very sore."

"Let me see."

"Stay away! You might get it too." Addy backed away.

"You're acting very strange." Miss Pru assessed her, frowning. "I've never seen you like this. What's the matter?"

"My throat," Addy croaked, raising a protective hand to it.

"Nonsense!" Miss Pru studied Addy with narrowed eyes. "That man this afternoon, Dr. Samuel Grady..."

"Samuel Grady? That's who that was?" Addy's hand dropped from her throat, and her voice sounded perfectly normal. "Who's Samuel Grady?"

"He's a consultant for pediatricians," Miss Pru answered, a knowing look coming into her eyes.

"How do you know that?"

"He gave me his card when I asked him what he was doing here," Miss Pru explained.

"Why *was* he here?"

"To pick up tickets for tonight's show for his mother."

"We didn't have any more. How'd you find any? Where would we put anyone else?"

"I gave him five." Miss Pru began to needlessly straighten dresses hanging on nearby racks.

"Is the chandelier going to hold five more people?" Addy gestured wildly.

Miss Pru wasn't worried. "Marcus will find a way."

"Where's the card?" Addy wanted to see it.

"In your office." Addy started to hurry away, but Miss Pru laid a hand on her arm to stop her and added shrewdly, "Is it because he's coming back tonight? Is that why you don't want to do the narration?"

"No, no!" Addy made her voice husky. "It's my throat. Do you think for one minute I'd let some man boggle me?"

Miss Pru didn't reply, but Addy could see from the way she tightened her lips that she had to bite her tongue to keep from saying more.

CHAPTER TWO

WHEN THE AFTERNOON ladies finally drifted away they left behind a very nice number of orders, enough to give cause for high glee. Addy's response, however, was somewhat subdued by the thought of Dr. Samuel Grady's imminent return. She shooed Grendel and the chattering models upstairs to various rooms to rest before the evening show at six. Then she went to her own room.

Instead of lying down, she stood at the window thinking. Sometimes she thought the shows every three months were too much for them. Not for the models so much as for the seamstresses—and for Marcus and his crew. She knew she was lucky that the models were so accommodating, and she appreciated it.

Things were looking up, she thought as she gazed down at the snow-covered yard. Not very far up yet, but up. The overhead was staggering. The inventory of materials and equipment in that barn of a house was vital. Her four full-time seamstresses were jewels and worked very hard. It also helped to have several other women who did piecework at their homes—gussets, zippers, and the tab fronts of shirts.

And thank God for Marcus, Pearl's very large father. He'd volunteered his help when they'd first moved into the house. He could be dictatorial, but he kept her car going and the ancient furnace in the basement rumbling. How could she keep the sewing machines going without him? He was a magician when it came to motors—or to convincing someone they wanted to leave her property. He was intimidatingly huge. Next to Marcus, Pearl looked like a munchkin!

How old was Marcus? She knew he'd been married several times. Hedda was Pearl's stepmother. Addy speculated on what had happened to his other wives and wondered if Hedda might have hurried along her predecessor. Hedda looked as if she could do something like that.

Then there was the house. Addy touched the peeling paint on the windowsill. It constantly needed care. She was forever getting notes saying she owed Marcus for some repair. She called it blackmail. "Why don't I just turn all my income over to you and you give me what's left!" she often told him.

"Don't get biggity," he always said loftily.

"Biggity?" she huffed. "Me?"

"Your grammar's dreadful," he would reply.

She looked around her room. Of course, in that old house, with twenty-four rooms—counting the four in the attic—there was bound to be something going wrong all the time. Then, too, Marcus charged her a hundred dollars a month for "grounds upkeep." With the help of his ever-changing team of young, otherwise unemployed men, the walks were shoveled in winter, the grass mowed in summer, and the gravel drive kept weeded and raked. "Marcus, why don't we get a rider-mower?" she'd asked. "It could be converted in winter to a snowplow, and we'd save money in the long run."

Marcus had barely acknowledged her as he'd directed a young man to trim around the curbs of the basement window wells. "No," he said, "the young men need something to do."

There just wasn't any answer to that, and Addy had to admit they did a good job. Her block always looked well-kept.

Then one day Marcus had brought a sleepy-eyed, shyly smiling young black girl named Emmaline to the Gown House. "You need another seamstress," he told Addy.

Addy resisted. "Well, not right now."

"You can pay her by the piece—while she's learning," Marcus had pronounced.

Miss Pru had put Emmaline to work. Addy had huffed, "I don't know why I'm even consulted! Everyone does exactly as *he* wants to around here!" But Miss Pru had ignored her.

Later she'd told Marcus, "Emmaline isn't a seamstress, she's a sore thumb! She does half the work of the others in twice the time. She's useless!"

Marcus stopped barely long enough to reply, "She still has to find herself."

"Emmaline wouldn't know where to start looking!" Addy snapped. "She's a dreamer. She isn't in touch with reality."

"Now, now." That was the closest Marcus had ever come to placating her. "Don't worry. Emmaline will work out."

"Work out?" Addy sputtered. "She isn't familiar enough with the word 'work' to make use of it!"

After that Addy privately called Marcus the Godfather. Not her godfather, but everybody *else*'s godfather. The Godfather of the Black Mafia.

Of course, without Marcus and Miss Pru, she would never have made it. She knew that full well. And she knew Marcus was scrupulously fair. He didn't do anything that didn't need to be done, and he charged very reasonably.

His men had painted her house. She'd instructed that it was to be white, and Marcus had nodded at her directions—then painted it antique-blue with a French-vanilla trim. "But I wanted it white!" Addy had been outraged.

"Come over here." Marcus lumbered off across the yard and across the street with her trailing along, waving her arms and objecting. He'd ignored her, then turned and gestured. "See? It's just right." Not waiting for her reaction, he'd started back. She'd seen that he was right. That was the most frustrating thing about Marcus: he was always right.

When they'd had their first show Marcus had said, "My wife, Hedda, will do the catering."

Addy had replied politely, "Thanks, but Miss Pru and I will do that."

"No," he'd said. "You'll be too busy. The afternoon ladies want something dainty and sweet, and the evening bunch will want something different. Hedda will fix it."

"But, Marcus . . ."

"It's the eats what makes the product look good."

"The . . . eats?" She couldn't believe she'd heard right.

"Don't sass," he advised.

"How can you criticize my grammar, then come up with 'eats'?"

"Watch yo mouf."

"Good grief!" She'd laughed. Then she'd looked at him, getting serious, and said, "You know, Marcus, you could make a fortune fixing motors."

"I do," he told her. "You need another sewing machine. You need a backup. A couple of them are running on my genius alone, and even genius can't keep metal from wearing."

"Why don't we set you up a repair shop in the basement? You'd make a bundle."

"People who get things fixed that way are either very poor or very rich, but rich people who are that frugal don't buy designer clothes. It's a different clientele entirely, and not what you want."

"I worry about the time you have to spend on my things and how many people you find work for, but I don't figure you get any of it. You give it all away."

"I have sufficient income," he assured her.

"From 'eats' to 'sufficient income'?"

"Hedda will do the eats."

And Hedda had and still did. She was magnificent, large, but not large in a fat way. She was simply a tall, magnificent woman. Her skin was very black, and her lips were black too, and perfectly formed. Her eyes were very white with ink-black irises. She was intimidating. She rarely smiled, but when she did it knocked you backward. And she never spoke. If Addy or Miss Pru said something to her, she listened and either shrugged, nodded, or shook her head.

Hedda was a magician when it came to food. The tea cakes for the afternoon showings were traditional English fare, but her hors d'oeuvres were imaginative and delicious. Once Addy had told Hedda, "I don't know if they come for the showing, or if they come for your hors d'oeuvres and stay for the showing to be polite." And Hedda had nodded.

Hedda wore African, or quasi-African, dress. It was really Hedda dress, and it was so exotic that on anyone else it would have seemed ostentatious. It looked right on Hedda. With her nodded permission, Addy had copied a brown and cream version of Hedda's wiggles and dots and stripes to make a summer cloth that had been very popular.

Addy knew that fabric design could make or break a dress, as could trim. The wilder the print, the simpler the dress should be. When she did her own designs, she signed them. She'd had several extremely successful simple summer dresses that were perfect because of their unusual fabric.

When Addy worked in the attic with waxes, pots, and color baths, Emmaline would sometimes lean against the doorway and watch. She drove the busy, driven Addy to frustrated distraction. Addy would shoo Emmaline back to her sewing machine. To Addy, Emmaline was a zero. Pearl and Heda were worth every cent, but that Emmaline kept turning up like a bad penny.

Addy was distracted from her thoughts when Miss Pru came into the room and scolded, "Why aren't you lying down?"

"I'm not tired," Addy protested before she remembered her fragile throat.

"Lie down," Miss Pru commanded. "I have a vinegar cloth to put on that throat."

"I don't want a vinegar cloth on my throat. It won't do any good. Vinegar cloths are supposed to help headaches." But she lay down anyway, and Miss Pru put the cloth on her throat, patted her cheek, and left the room.

Addy lay there grimly with a vinegar cloth on her non-sore throat and considered how Miss Pru, Marcus, and Hedda ordered her around. She decided the reason the strange man worried her was that he might try to pry away her last vestige of independence. But why would he want to do that, and what independence did she still have? She faced the reality: she had none. She'd lost control of her whole life. What in the world was she doing lying there in bed with a vinegar cloth on her throat?

She removed the cloth and tip toed up to the attic to fiddle with the silk-screen frame, which had loosened, hoping not to run into Miss Pru or Hedda. From the top of the grand staircase she had heard Miss Pru rehearsing the evening's narration. Addy practiced subtle coughs from her unscratchy throat. Life was sometimes very demanding.

A while later, Grendel scrambled up the attic stairs, having awoken from her nap. *"Mommy!"* she greeted her mother with great joy. Who could resist? They woke up the models, and all of them trooped down to the kitchen for a light snack of Hedda's perfect hors d'oeuvres. Then the models went about making sure their changes were in the right sequence for the narration. Addy could tell that Miss Pru had the narration down pat. Addy had been trying to mimic the silent Hedda and limit her conversation to head nods and shakes to disguise her normal throat, but she was distracted by the thought of seeing Sam Grady, pediatric consultant, and every once in a while a word slipped out.

Would he come? Maybe he'd just taken enough tickets to give to his mother, Elizabeth Turner Harrow. If she was his mother, why wasn't there a Grady in her name? If he didn't show up, Addy would have wasted a lot of trouble getting out of doing the narration.

Listening to the front door opening for the first of the

guests, she was very surprised to realize she'd be a little let down if he didn't show up. She fidgeted and paced around needlessly and listened as the crowd gathered. Would he come?

He did. He and an older woman and three younger ones finally arrived. Addy glimpsed him discussing the hors d'oeuvres with them. He smiled and licked his fine lips discreetly and turned his handsome head, which was set on a strong throat atop wide shoulders that led down to a perfect, muscular body that was selfishly concealed from view by an extremely expensive and well-fitted suit. What a show-off he was, standing there quietly, speaking inaudibly, and drawing every feminine eye to himself. . . .

What in God's name was the matter with her? She was antimale and had been for four years. She never wanted anything more to do with another man. She was completely immune, not only to males, but to male doctors who were pediatric consultants. She was a mature, independent woman, pursuing a fine career and in control of her own life. Anyway, those three young women didn't look like Sam or each other, so they couldn't be his sisters. One or all three of them must be his wife, ex-wife or mistress.

"I'll do the narration," Addy told Miss Pru coolly.

"Your throat's all right again?" The question was so placid that Addy lifted her chin when she replied that it was.

"It must have been the vinegar cloth," Miss Pru said smugly.

Ignoring her, Addy walked deliberately past Dr. Samuel Grady, but she did it very quickly, as if she was in a hurry, and when she was sure his back would be to her. When she was past them, she turned and nodded politely, giving his group a slight smile, although her eyes didn't focus on anyone. Even unfocused, he was devastating. Her stomach quivered and her thighs tingled.

How on earth could she feel such a reaction to a man she'd never really looked at? He was probably actually ugly. She was building all this up impossibly. Three glimpses of a man and her silly mind had woven a romantic version of Sir Galahad. What did she know about him? He had a great silhouette. He was excessively masculine in impact. He was a pediatric consultant, and he had a mother. Lots of doctors had mothers. The whole thing was ridiculous. If she got a good, clear look at him, she'd be disillusioned. She turned at the end of the room, stood still, and focused deliberately on him.

He was watching her. He smiled just a little and looked amused. She'd been wrong. He wasn't devastating, he was ruinously gorgeous. Not gorgeous meaning beautiful, but a gorgeous, rugged male.

She flitted blindly away and left the room by instinct. She told herself that in spite of his deep, pleasant voice he probably had a high-pitched giggle. Then in the hum of the crowd she heard the rumble of a man's laugh and knew in her bones it was his.

Gradually the guests filtered into the drawing room and sat down still chatting. An air of hushed anticipation settled over the room, and Addy found that her palms were wet with perspiration. What a relief that she knew the narration by heart. Her thoughts were winging away in all directions. When the crowd laughed at her patter, she was startled.

Pearl had the temerity to lean over from the runway and suggest with a flared-eyed snarl that she slow down a little. Addy thought Pearl would turn out to be just like Marcus. With Hedda for a stepmother and Marcus for a father, what chance did Pearl have of being docile? Addy's mind went spiraling along, but her mouth did slow down, giving the models a little more time to change.

After the showing, the guests seemed to linger longer than usual. Everyone appeared to know Elizabeth Turner Harrow, and apparently she was in no hurry to leave, so there was nice, leisurely visiting. Mrs. Harrow kept the general conversation on the show and the materials, and she ordered two dresses, a suit, and a raincoat. She chose a thin, flowered material in delicate colors for the raincoat and asked for an umbrella to match. Addy accepted the order without a flicker of an eyelash. She'd never made an umbrella before, but she'd figure out how. She could always buy one and recover it. Was that legal?

Addy smiled rather tightly as she took orders from the three younger women and set up the dates for their fittings. That their names were all different only made it more reasonable that they were all Sam's great and good friends. She noticed he was easy and familiar with them in an intimately teasing way that suggested long acquaintance.

Busy as she was, Addy still managed to study all three women. They were very smooth and good-looking. They'd lived pampered, untroubled, proper lives that were well-spent, not frittered away. They were so confident and comfortable with themselves that Addy's mouth went a little sour.

A quick glance showed her that other women were leaving orders with the models and Miss Pru, and Grendel was grinning and being darling as she stood by one or another of her "family."

Just then, next to Addy's ear, his deep voice light and silky, Sam said, "So she's your daughter?"

Addy nodded stiffly. "Grendel." She stared no higher than his perfectly made lapel.

"Grendel?" Humor laced the name as he said it.

She shot him a hostile glance. "Yes."

"You look like the Grendel; she looks like an Addy."

Thrills went through her at hearing him say her name, and she examined her thumbnail, finding it fascinating, then said primly, "We like our names."

"I do, too. Where is . . . Mr. Kildaire?"

She decided he might as well know. "I'm not married."

"That's nice to hear."

Nice? When she considered all the agony not being married had brought her? Nice wasn't a very good word. . . .

"Grendel looks like a healthy little girl." He made the observation in a friendly way.

"Do you always consider a child's health?" she asked in a less friendly way.

"Don't you look at clothes?"

She glanced up briefly and smiled just a bit as she admitted, "Yes." He grinned down at her, his eyes still amused, and sensation washed through her, taking all the starch out of her body, leaving it weakened, softened, and not too reliable.

Mrs. Harrow approached them and said she must be going. "I'm already late for a meeting, but they'll be so slow getting started, making coffee and gossiping, that I'll still make the important part of the evening's business." She exchanged a smile with Addy, then asked, "If I gathered fifty women, would you arrange another showing?"

Still feeling weak, Addy found the offer stunning. A dream! "Oh, yes!" she said.

"May I call you about the day?" Mrs. Harrow asked kindly. "It would be all right?"

"Oh, yes. I'd love to." Addy frowned a little.

"I know how tight your time must be," Mrs. Harrow apologized, "but I have some friends who simply must

see your show. You're a very clever designer, and your
things are lovely."

"Oh, it's no problem," Addy hastened to reassure her.
"I was frowning because I ended the sentence with part
of an infinitive and Marcus..."

"Marcus?" Sam questioned, scowling. "Who's Marcus?"

Mrs. Harrow's grin was exactly like her son's teasing
one as she asked, "Now why would that worry you?"

Addy ignored Sam's question and laughed with Mrs.
Harrow. As the three young women who'd come with
them walked over, Sam touched Addy's elbow and said,
"I'll be seeing you." She managed to give him a quick
glance as Mrs. Harrow shook her hand.

The three women claimed Addy's attention. One said,
"Your designs are just marvelous."

Another said, "I'm so glad we could get tickets. It
was an excellent show—and so well done."

The third exclaimed, "How did you ever get Hedda
Freeman to cater?" When Addy gave her a blank look,
the woman grinned and said, "You must have clout.
Hedda quit catering five years ago."

The three women had to relinquish Addy's attention
as other people came up to say good-bye and comment
on the show, but Addy was distracted. Sam had left, and
she felt blank.

She wasn't aware of all the others leaving, but eventually she looked up and found they had gone. She glanced
around the empty rooms and noted that Miss Pru was
turning off the lights. She helped, then followed her up
the stairs and murmured good night.

Not paying any real attention, she automatically prepared for bed, climbed in, stretched out, and gave herself
over to her thoughts. The evening had had a different
flavor, and she decided it was because Mrs. Harrow was

such a vivacious woman. She was Samuel Grady's mother and a little awesome. Handsome, too. She would be a terrific advertisement for Adelina Kildaire's clothes. People would ask her where she had found that dress or suit, and Mrs. Harrow would say, "At the Gown House." She was a gracious lady, and she was Sam's mother.

Addy allowed herself to consider Sam. He was being obviously friendly and interested. Well, it wouldn't do him any good. She was through with men forever. She'd slept with a man, and she hadn't liked it at all. It had been painful and embarrassing. She never wanted to go through that again. And she wouldn't have to, because she had Grendel. There was no reason to have anything else to do with any man. And that included Samuel Grady, M.D.

CHAPTER THREE

JUST TWO REASONABLY normal days later Miss Pru came
to Addy in her workroom and said, "Dr. Grady is out in
the reception room and wants to see the robe you modeled
during the lingerie show."

"Oh? Ask someone else." Addy went back to work.

"There *is* no one else." Miss Pru was patient.

"Isn't anyone here?"

"If anyone was, would I say there was no one else?"

Addy was intrigued by the expression on Miss Pru's
face. It was a quizzing kind of look. Addy would have
liked to spend some time exploring why Miss Pru should
look that particular way, but she was too boggled by the
prospect of seeing Samuel Grady again. "You do it," she
told Miss Pru.

Miss Pru huffed in an incredulous way and snapped, "Don't be ridiculous!" She left the room.

Addy looked down at herself and decided the sweater she was wearing was too snug over her chest. She ran upstairs and put on a starched, mud-colored shirtwaist with a cream neck scarf and added high heels so she'd be less intimidated by Sam's height. Then, looking into the mirror, she skinned back her hair into its stern braid.

But her attempt at disguise wasn't successful. The dress was actually very flattering, even though it was mud-colored. It was nipped in to show off her waist, and the skirt flared out over her hips, drawing attention to her legs. Nervousness made her cheeks pink and her lips red.

Breathing deeply to steady herself, she walked down the grand staircase in a stately, businesslike manner. Then, carrying the robe, she walked into the reception room. The runway had been removed and the customary furniture and rugs had been replaced. She nodded to acknowledge Sam, although she didn't really focus on him.

The power of his attraction made her hands fumble, and she licked her lips and swallowed. Then he said good morning, and her eyes couldn't settle on anything.

By being very formal, maybe she could overcome her nervous reaction to him. "You wanted to see this robe, sir?"

"Very much."

"Here." She thrust it toward him.

"Well, since I'm not sure I saw it properly, I would like to see it modeled." He paused when she said nothing, then added, "May I?"

"I'm sorry. None of the models is here right now."

"Couldn't . . . you?" Was that amusement in his silky voice?

"Well, you see . . . I . . . uh . . ."

"Please?" His voice deepened and softened.

My God, she thought, and knew those three women must be his slaves. They probably wouldn't even mind that sex was revolting and messy just so long as it pleased him. She wondered which one was the favorite who was going to be gifted with that robe.

Filled with a turmoil she didn't understand but, even more incredible, filled with a need for him to see her in that robe again, she nodded brusquely and went through the house to a dressing room. She'd been oblivious to the women working there. She changed into the robe, tossing her freshly starched dress into a heap.

She didn't have the courage to take down her hair, but she took off her shoes and made her way back to him barefooted. Her palms were wet, her lips dry, and her tongue was stuck to the roof of her mouth.

Halfway back through the big rooms, she said to herself, What are you doing, Adelina Mary Rose Kildaire? Just what *are* you doing? She stopped to consider her conduct. Then she hunted out Grendel and took her hand and walked sedately back to Dr. Samuel Grady, with a three-year-old child as protection.

Addy stopped just inside the draped double door, clutching Grendel's hand with both of hers, staring at Sam's chest. Grendel balanced on one foot, her other foot on her knee. She examined Dr. Grady with a lively expression and beamed a smile at him, which he returned. Addy thought that her eyes couldn't be totally useless if she could see all that.

Sam said to Addy, "Could you . . . uh . . . turn?" He stood watching with great interest, drawing a circle with his hand to show her what he meant.

She nodded and released Grendel's hand as if it were her first time on ice skates and she was being forced to release the rail that had been supporting her. Stiff as a poker, she walked forward, turned, and walked back to where she'd been. She picked up Grendel's hand again. Grendel blinked up at her, squirmed her hand free, hopped over to a table, and disappeared under it.

Sam said, "Lovely," in a way that sent prickles down Addy's back. And then he approached and walked slowly around her, examining the robe—and her—in such a way that Addy was reminded of the first time she'd seen him. Her feeling then, of being on an auction block, flooded her senses in an alarming way.

Sam um-hmmed a couple of times, then said, "I believe there are . . . some hooks?"

Addy's hands slapped instantly against her décolletage as if she'd concealed her life's savings there and he was pointing a gun at her. She said something that resembled "Awwk." The blood drained out of her face and thrills shot up her body at the thought of him fumbling with the hooks nestled between her breasts.

He loved it. She sneaked a peek and saw sparkling humor in his eyes and a quirking of his lips. He raised his brows and said again, "The hooks?" He waited.

"This is . . . the only model." She'd had to swallow between the words.

"Just the first two," he suggested.

Addy knew any woman who wasn't as antimale as she was would have been winding around him like a cat in heat and inviting him to undo all the hooks. She was proud she'd resisted and felt very pleased with her strength of character.

He lifted his hands as if to help, but she took a long step backward, smack into the wall. Trapped there, red-faced, and acting like a high school girl with her first college man, she bent her head and carefully undid the first hook. The shoulder strap slid down slowly in a very wanton way. Her face went scarlet. Why had she ever devised this wretched thing? She took a deep breath to say the gown wasn't for sale after all.

"Very nice," Sam murmured, his voice vibrating in the pit of her body. "And the second?" He appeared to expect her to continue.

Mindlessly, her obedient hands went to the second hook. They automatically undid it, and both straps went down. Sam stepped back and just looked at her. She was standing against the wall, her arms straight down at her sides, the palms of her hands pressed against the burlap surface, her breath held.

"I'll take it."

He sounded as reasonable as if he were buying a car, but the incident brought back the runway episode with its impression of a slave market, and Addy wasn't sure if he meant he'd take the robe . . . or her.

"May I take it with me?"

So he *did* mean the robe. "Don't you want one made to . . . her specifications?" Why was that so hard to say? "Another color?" she added lamely.

"This is perfect."

"But I've worn it. At least let it be cleaned."

"I'll do that. I haven't time to come back, and later it might be gone."

Was he going to give it to . . . her . . . today? A black depression descended over Addy like a cloud. He asked the price, and she added half again as much, explaining, "Since it's been worn," as if she was cutting the cost.

"That's all?" he asked. He seemed surprised.

She clamped her teeth together and wished she'd doubled it. She flipped aside the drapes, undid the robe en route, and called for one of the women to box it as she stepped out of it and tossed it aside.

"Box it? But it's been worn!" the woman protested.

"Just go ahead and box it!" Addy said through gritted teeth.

The woman frowned, then shrugged and obeyed.

Dressed in the crumpled shirtwaist she'd retrieved from a heap on the floor, Addy smoothed her hair, grimly put on the high-heeled shoes, and went back to accept Dr. Grady's check.

He was squatted down with Grendel standing between his knees. Her tiny hands rested on his gray-suited forearms, and she was laughing with him. At first Addy was only fleetingly conscious that Grendel lived in a female world and must miss not ever being around men. Then slowly her consciousness was drawn to how alike they were—their coloring, their grins, their humor. The only dissimilar thing was their skin. His was tanned, while hers was delicately white. How strange that Grendel would look so much like a total stranger. Samuel Grady was nothing like her father.

Addy plopped the boxed robe down on a nearby table, and picked up his check. She held it up as if to verify the amount and signature, but her eyes were blind to it.

Sam rose effortlessly from his squatting position. Good leg muscles there. "I appreciate your showing me the robe," he said. "That was very kind."

"I sell clothes," she said tersely.

He smiled, appearing relaxed as he asked, "I wonder if you and Grendel and Miss Pru would be my guests for an early dinner on Friday."

Addy took three breaths, her lips parting each time, but no sound came as she looked at him, round-eyed and unbelieving. He'd asked her to dinner!

Grendel bounded around and exclaimed, "Yes!"

Addy's eyes were pulled to the movement, and her tongue stumbled awkwardly as she said, "Well..." There was no way in this world she was going to get tangled up with a man like Samuel Grady. If you walk on the track, you get hit by the train. Finally she managed to reply, "I'm afraid we have other plans for Friday."

"Oh." He looked at her kindly, but his smile faded in his obvious disappointment. "Well, perhaps another time?"

Grendel scowled and demanded in the way of children, "We can't? Why not?"

Her mother looked down at her, wishing her as silent as Hedda, and said, "Perhaps another time." As she said that, she realized she'd echoed Sam's words. It sounded as if she were agreeing to the idea.

Very smoothly he suggested, "We could go sledding on Sunday." That was a calculated offer, Addy decided. As he'd probably known she would, Grendel squealed in agreement. He cast a smugly confident look at Addy and asked, "Sunday, then? How about late morning, then having lunch?"

"Well . . ."

"Oh, *yes!*" squealed Grendel. "Please!" She hopped around and clapped her tiny hands.

How could she deny Grendel the outing? For Grendel, Addy would do it . . . once. "All right." Again she was stiff and ungracious. He'd get discouraged.

"Fine." He grinned. "I'll pick you up about ten thirty?"

Addy gave a short nod, aware that Grendel had to skip around in order to get rid of her excess excitement. "When's Sunday?" she wanted to know.

"In five days."

Grendel stopped dead and her face fell as she exclaimed in disbelief, "Five?"

Yes, lots of things could happen in five days, Addy thought, and then they wouldn't be able to go. She watched Sam pick up the box containing the robe.

To Grendel he said encouragingly, "Only five days.

And it'll be worth the wait." His glance slid back to Addy.

"Five?" Grendel said again and made her little face look pitiful.

"Cut it out, Grendel," Addy warned. God knew where she got her dramatics. "Say, 'I shall look forward to it, Dr. Grady.'"

"You a doctor?" Grendel asked.

"Yes."

"Like *my* doctor Je-wam-ee Tin-keh?"

"Oh, is Jeremy Tinker your doctor?" He lifted his eyebrows in question to Addy. She didn't reply but she didn't deny it, and Sam said, "I was in medical school with him. He's a good friend and a fine doctor."

"He makes faces," Grendel supplied.

"Faces?"

She nodded seriously. "When I get a shot. He make terrible face. Once I cry"—her tiny, mobile face looked very pathetic—"he howl. Like a dog."

"That's good old Jeremy all right." Sam bit his lip and added, "He has wolf blood."

Sam escaped while Addy was trying to explain that to Grendel.

On Saturday Grendel awoke with a 104-degree fever. Addy reported it to Dr. Tinker's answering service. It shouldn't have been such a surprise when Dr. Samuel Grady, pediatric consultant, turned up at the Gown House. But it was.

"What are you doing here?" Addy asked in astonishment as she let him in the front door. "Do you make house calls?" She glanced at him as they went upstairs to Grendel's room.

"I'm taking some of Jeremy's calls this weekend," he replied smoothly. "And I was going right by here"—he grinned at Grendel—"so I decided I'd best see why my sledding partner was lying around in bed and not feeling very well." His eyes turned to Addy in such an accusing way that she wondered if he suspected her of deliberately making her child sick in order to avoid going out with him.

Grendel obviously felt so rotten that she didn't have to pretend, as Addy knew she did on occasion. Sam stayed with her for an hour, sponging her off and sympathizing with her while he gave her a shot to stop her nausea. Watching him, Addy decided he must have majored in bedside. She squirmed uncomfortably, appalled to realize she was envious of the concentrated attention Grendel was getting from Sam. Grendel felt too poorly to appreciate it, Addy was sure. When Grendel was really sick she was a sober, cooperative, uncomplaining patient, like now. It scared the living daylights out of Addy.

After the hour was up, Sam said he'd be back later, which made a gelatin mass of Addy, who followed him down the stairs on ramshackle legs. "Is she that sick that you have to come back?" she asked anxiously.

"Oh, no! Why did you think that?" He sounded surprised.

"Well, to have to come back here, and I thought, with you being a consultant and all, that she must be . . ."

"No, no, no." He shook his head. "I'm at loose ends, and I'll be in the area a little later, so I'll stop in just to see how she's getting along."

"And she isn't dying or anything?" Addy's chin quivered.

"No, she's fine." He peered at her. "Are you all right?" He felt her head. "Open your mouth."

She complied automatically, until she realized what she was doing and snapped it closed, then said shortly, "I'm too old for you."

"No," he denied, "you're just about right."

"Are you implying I'm a child? Childish?" she said a little huffily.

But he only chuckled. He shrugged into his coat, picked up his bag, and opened the door. "Don't give her anything by mouth until I come back." He started out, then turned back. "Unless I'm longer than four hours. In that case give her a little weak, sweetened tea, a tablespoon at a time."

Addy said, "Yes," then added automatically, "Thank you for coming."

He only grinned again and left. She watched him go surefooted down the icy steps and out to his car. She wondered who had gotten the robe and how he'd shown her about the hooks. The thought made an odd, powerful twist go through her. She tried to figure out why she was so depressed and thought it must be that Grendel was feeling so awful. Poor baby.

Almost two hours to the minute, Sam Grady returned. He brought Grendel a box of green Popsicles. He mashed one up in a bowl and fed it to her with a spoon. She watched him with big, sad eyes and complained because she wouldn't be able to go sledding the next day. She even managed to squeeze out a tear in such a way that Addy was cheered. Grendel's being so dramatic had to mean she was getting better.

By then it was approaching dinnertime, and the delicious aroma of Miss Pru's roast beef and hot bread was wafting up the back stairway, mouth-wateringly seductive. If Grendel was good at drama, Sam was no piker. He straightened his back wearily, inhaling deeply with great appreciation while he said woefully, "That certainly smells good." He made it sound as if his nose were pressed against the outside of a windowpane as he stood barefooted in the snow.

What could Addy do? She was trapped. He'd come to see Grendel twice. Even though she dreaded his bill, she was grateful he'd been there. So she asked, however reluctantly, "You wouldn't want to stay to dinner, would you?" It wasn't even a question, just a negative statement, accompanied by a shaking of her head. It was as left-footed an offer as possible, and she expected him to refuse it.

"Why, how nice of you!" he exclaimed, doing a good job of sounding surprised. "It's terrible to be a bachelor, because my apartment is never filled with the fragrance of home cooking. It's a cold, impersonal place I just use to store my things and to sleep in a cold bed."

"That's too much, you saying that so pitifully," she scoffed.

"I thought I'd done that quite well!" he replied with asperity. "I got invited to dinner, didn't I?"

"If you want a home life and home cooking, you can get married, or hire a cook."

"I'm working on it."

Her stomach clutched at his words. Was he . . . courting someone? Would he marry someone? "Where do you live?" she asked.

"I'm staying at Windridge. I've a condo there. Do you know it? It's on Emmerson off Fall Creek, about five miles east of Meridian Hills. It's very attractive, but you have no idea how much a home-cooked meal can mean to a bachelor."

Addy suspected she'd just been maneuvered. She narrowed her eyes and studied him. He was tricky. She'd have to be very careful. She watched him perk up as if he were a new puppy just adopted, and he and Grendel chuckled and chatted. He was tricky all right, and she had just better watch her step.

CHAPTER FOUR

GRENDEL SAID HER tummy wasn't hungry for a meal, so after Sam promised her another Popsicle in an hour, he and Addy went downstairs to help Miss Pru. Miss Pru smiled a welcome at Sam and scurried about her work. She was sixty-three and looked forty-eight. She tinted her hair in a clever way, her figure was excellent, and, although her lips were thin and seemed prim, her smile was wide and friendly.

Miss Pru handed them platters and bowls for the table. The back hall, beyond the kitchen, was wide and long. They'd set a drop-leaf table there and had their family dinners either there or in the solarium at the end of the hall. With a white cloth, candles, and yard holly on the table, it was lovely.

"Are you a surgeon?" Addy asked Sam.

"Passed my Boards last—"

"Then you can carve."

"Is she always so rough-tongued?" Sam complained to Miss Pru.

Tactfully, but with a private, sharp, censuring glance at Addy, Miss Pru replied, "Perhaps she's just worried about Grendel."

"No need," Sam assured her. "Grendel is as healthy as a horse."

"But a very small one." Addy's voice was thin.

"She really is all right." Sam gave Addy a direct serious look of reassurance, and for the first time her eyes clung to his. His lips parted slightly in a soundless gasp, and his expression changed.

Addy's chest was a maelstrom of sensations, and she blurted, "Grendel is illegitimate."

His eyes stayed on hers, and he leaned only an inch toward her as he said in a low voice, "That must have been very, very rough for you."

Addy jerked her head to one side, pulled her napkin onto her lap, and said huskily, "I never would've made it without Miss Pru." Her eyes turned to the older woman. "I owe her our lives."

"Nonsense," Miss Pru denied. "It was Addy who changed my life."

"I had to give up my apartment in Bloomington," Addy explained, "and I moved into Miss Pru's boardinghouse. She sold it to put the down payment on this house. She did the first sewing..."

"Now, now, it wasn't all my doing." Miss Pru turned to Sam. "She began designing and sewing dresses to sell when she was a sophomore in college, so she had a tidy sum saved for herself."

"And when I didn't know what to do about Grendel . . . and he . . . had . . . and my family was still in such shock that they didn't know what to say to me or how to advise me, it was Miss Pru who supported me . . . in my keeping Grendel . . . and being practical. Planning. Helping get things done and solved. Miss Pru and then Marcus."

"Marcus?" Sam's voice was intent, his face suddenly still.

"That Marcus." Miss Pru chuckled and clicked her tongue.

Addy's own tongue went on. "Miss Pru found this house. She brought me to look at it, and it was a pile of junk, the boards loose. It was awful."

"The location was excellent," Miss Pru told Sam. "Loose boards could be nailed back and weathered siding could be painted."

"I wanted it white, and Marcus painted it blue," Addy added. "Next he wants to paint it royal blue with lime-green trim, and after that blood-red with mustard trim and—"

"Who's Marcus?" Sam demanded.

Miss Pru and Addy exchanged amused glances. "He lives across the street," Addy told him. "When we moved here, we couldn't figure out a name for the business, and our first blundering choice was the House of Delilah. Everyone knows Delilah was a successful woman, right? Well, the only people who came were some tenacious men who were sure it wasn't really a dress shop. They'd stand on the porch at all hours and swear they weren't the police and all they wanted was a little fun. 'It ain't a raid, baby, honest,'" Addy mimicked in a carefully steadied voice.

"Then we called it Kildaire's," she went on. "But apparently men thought that sounded like a bar, the house standing alone on the block this way. We spent a lot of time arguing through the door in the early morning hours. They'd say, 'Aw, c'mon, honey, open up.' And we'd swear it wasn't a bar and we didn't serve liquor. They'd say, 'Jes' one li'l one? C'mon, Kildaire, we'll drink to Ireland!'

"After that we called it the Gown House." Addy glanced at Sam, but he looked so grim she explained, "The Town House—the Gown House."

"That was very dangerous," he said finally. "The neighborhood in transition and two women alone that way. Anything could have happened."

"Oh, no." Miss Pru waved a dismissive hand. "Marcus always came over and ran them all off."

Addy laughed. "He'd come over the porch rail, looming like a mountain, and say, 'Git!' in that thundering voice of his, and they'd *git!*" She laughed again. "The first time he did that he scared us as much as *them!*"

"Who *is* Marcus?" Sam's voice was tight, and he glared at Addy.

"He's my security," she explained.

With Sam's question supposedly answered, Miss Pru changed the subject. "What exactly does a pediatric consultant do?" Addy was sure Miss Pru knew that answer perfectly well and was just giving him a chance to talk about himself.

Reluctantly Sam turned his attention to Miss Pru. "When a GP or a pediatrician gets stuck, I review the diagnosis and what has been done to see if there's anything that's been ignored or forgotten or if there's anything new or different he or she might try. Therefore I keep up with all the current medical research. I'm rather like a court of last resort."

As he spoke Addy watched him, his manner, his level look, his large, capable hands, and she thought how much the doctors must appreciate his calm, his authority, the fact that he was there to turn to. Baffled, they would find support in him and his knowledge. They would know they'd done the best they could.

"That must be emotionally wearing," Miss Pru said softly. "It must be terribly serious before they come to you."

"All of life is precious, but there are times when it's best to let a child go. Stupidity is the only intolerable thing."

"Jeremy . . . ?" Addy had to ask.

Sam's eyes were steady on her. "He's one of the best." He paused, then asked, "Are you dating Jeremy?"

"Good heavens, no! I've no time for that."

"You don't date at all?" he asked quickly.

"No!" she replied shortly as she began to collect the empty plates.

"Who's Marcus?" he asked yet again as he rose to help her clear the table.

"I told you. He's my security."

"Police or blanket?" he growled.

Addy laughed. "He's married to Hedda, who I think is a female witch doctor. I wouldn't tangle with her under any circumstances, particularly since she caters for us now and then. On top of that, I'm sure he's the Godfather of the Black Mafia."

"Marcus Freeman?" Sam looked very interested.

"Yes, how'd you know?"

"I've heard about him," he said in a thoughtful way, but he didn't elaborate.

They had a trifle for dessert. As Sam licked his lips discreetly, he offered, "I could board here."

"You've been lucky with dinner this time," Addy scoffed.

Miss Pru agreed. "We generally have tea and toast."

"I don't believe that."

"With canned fruits Hedda puts up in the summer," Addy added. "Marcus sells them to us at double the chain-store price." She grinned at him. "Along with being the Godfather, he's also a pirate, so you can see how formidable he is." Now she could handle quick peeks at Sam, but she still couldn't do it calmly. She thought it was smarter not to look at him directly. Even not looking at him, his presence carried an impact that made her too self-conscious, too aware of herself as a woman. Paul had never affected her that way. Sam was so vital and so very attractive, so excessively masculine, that it was just as well he dealt only with children.

After they'd helped Miss Pru clean up the kitchen, they brought another Popsicle up to Grendel. As they climbed the steps, Sam asked, "How's your family now? Concerning Grendel, I mean."

"It was terrible for them," she admitted. "We're from a very small town where the Kildaires have lived forever. Both my parents were very strict, and I shocked them horribly. I had a hard time convincing my father I hadn't been raped or at least forced. My mother was mostly concerned about my two younger sisters. She said it wouldn't have been so bad if it was just me, or if my sisters had been boys, but how could the girls ever say no—and be believed—when everyone knew what their sister had done. Both my parents cried. It was terrible. They love Grendel, but they have problems over her still. I'm sorry about them, but...but I'm so glad I have Grendel."

"Is that why you don't date? You think you're ...ruined?"

"No. I don't want to." She spoke firmly.

"You think your life is over?"

"No, no," she corrected. "I have all I want. I don't have to get involved with another man." She made her mouth prim and lifted her chin, but she didn't look at him.

She felt his eyes on her as he argued with gentle cleverness. "Grendel should be around men enough so that she doesn't get warped." Having planted that thought in her maternal heart, he went ahead of her faltering steps into Grendel's room and began to talk to her cheerfully.

Addy stood in the doorway and listened to their conversation, to the timbre of his deep voice, to how Grendel tried to get her voice down to his level, to how he made her sick child respond.

Addy watched his mouth as he opened it unconsciously as he fed Grendel the mashed Popsicle, how he closed his lips around a nonexistent spoon, and how he licked his lips when Grendel did. She saw how he smiled at her daughter. . . .

Early on Sunday morning Sam came back to see his patient and give Miss Pru a thank-you bouquet for Saturday's dinner. He pretty much ignored Addy, who hung around listening as he explained the button cards he had brought to Grendel which had a big, blunt needle, thick thread for little fingers to control, and buttons with big holes that could be sewn on the cardboard.

In the afternoon he came again and gave Grendel a book that had all sorts of cloth in many textures — velvet to burlap. They identified the different ones together. Grendel, who was her mother's child, could name each and every cloth. She loved the book, but she mourned the missed sledding. She was markedly better, and Sam assured her there would be other times.

When he suggested a trip to the Children's Museum on Wednesday, Addy regretfully said she couldn't, that she had appointments. Sam said that was all right, he hadn't thought she'd be available anyway, but he was counting on taking Grendel. While Grendel whooped and bounced, Addy felt a great wave of disappointment.

Mrs. Harrow, Sam's mother, came for her first fitting on Tuesday and brought a woman with her who had a camera. She was about Sam's age and utterly beautiful. Her name was Diana Hunter, and she was a professional photographer. She asked permission to take some pictures of Grendel, who had recovered fully from her flu by then. Addy gave Diana a distracted go-ahead, assuring her that Grendel would love it because she was a dreadful ham.

At first Addy felt very stiff with Mrs. Harrow, but she relaxed under the older woman's easy manner. Mrs. Harrow had contacted her friends and wanted to confirm a week from Saturday at noon for the showing. Addy said all her models were available and it was all arranged. Mrs. Harrow was very pleased. Addy was even more so.

On Wednesday Addy was in bed with Grendel's flu. She felt rotten and knew she looked worse. Sam came to her door and stood by her bed to tsk. "You're a malingerer," he told her, but he smiled nicely.

Addy was indignant. "I am not! Get out of here!"

But he sat down on the edge of the bed and said, "You look lovely lying there in bed with the covers up to your eyes."

She was hostile and embarrassed. She knew she looked absolutely ghastly. "You'll get the flu."

"Do you have any fever?"

"The way I feel, it's a hundred ten." She was appalled to hear a self-pitying waver in her voice.

He clicked his tongue once, as if impressed, and said, "That high, huh?"

"Yes."

Then he leaned over and kissed her forehead, and her temperature shot up even higher. "Why did you do that?" she gasped.

"To see if you have a one-hundred-and-ten-degree fever."

"Do I?"

"Almost." He took her hand and held her wrist as he gazed at his watch.

She knew her heart was racing. He'd know, too. She twisted her wrist, trying to wrest it free. He smiled and told her to be still. "It's the three-day flu," she said, "and I don't need a doctor."

He felt the glands under her chin and then down her throat. Then he pulled back the covers and put his head on her chest. "What *are* you doing?" she exclaimed.

"I left my bag in the car, so I don't have my stethoscope with me, and I've got to listen to your heart and how you're breathing."

"And you're doing it that way?"

"Well, of course! How do you think they did it before we had stethoscopes?"

"It was never a problem before. I think you ought to take your head off my chest."

"This is really very nice. I wonder what fool invented the stethoscope?" He sat back up and looked at her, amused.

"You're going to get the flu," she warned him again.

"I'm never sick. It's one of the requirements when you apply for medical school. They have a question on the application, 'Are you ever sick?' If you say no, then you're admitted. If you say yes, you're rejected."

"I can imagine what you put down when they inquired about sex."

He grinned. "What do you think I put down?"

"Either 'yes' or 'often,'" she guessed sardonically.

"I put down 'over.'" He looked down his nose at her.

"That doesn't surprise me. I'm sure you needed the room on the back to fit everything in." She was disapproving.

He ignored her comment and told her she had the three-day flu and didn't need a doctor. She replied stiffly that she'd known that already. He patted her head and told her to stay in bed and be a good girl. She glowered.

Then he took Grendel, who waved from the door, and just left her there. Addy sulked all morning, telling everyone to leave her alone and refusing to drink the mysterious purple stuff Hedda sent over. So Miss Pru and the seamstresses drank the home-canned grape juice instead.

Addy heard Sam and Grendel return in time for Sam to be invited to lunch. Grendel had brought her a pinwheel to put by the hot-air register. When the furnace blower went on, the pinwheel turned madly, its bells ringing. "With all that racket," Sam said, "it will encourage you to get well, if only to get up and make the damned thing be quiet."

Addy gave him a long-suffering glance.

He'd brought her blue Popsicles. He mashed one up and insisted on feeding it to her with a spoon. She sniffled once and said, "I think I'm catching a little cold along with the flu."

He got a cool cloth from the bathroom and wiped her face and gave her almost too much sympathy, then smiled at her and asked, "Do you need to be rocked?"

"Rocked?" she asked incredulously.

He nodded. "Could you wait until after I eat? I'm starved from running after Grendel all morning at the museum, and I need nourishment before I tackle you."

"There's no need for you to 'tackle' me!" Addy stated.

"But I want to!" he protested. "It's what's kept me going all morning."

Just then Miss Pru sent Grendel up to tell Sam lunch was ready, and he had to lean over and kiss Addy's forehead again in order to see if the Popsicle had made her fever go down. But how could it go down when he kept sending it spiraling upward?

It seemed to take two hours for the next thirty minutes to go by. Finally Addy heard Miss Pru and Grendel in the hall. She was propped up on an elbow, straining to hear Sam's voice, when the door opened and he walked in.

"You didn't knock," she accused him, embarrassed.

"Doctors never knock. It's one of the perks."

She pulled the covers back up to her nose and lay back down. He sat down beside her, his face kind, his smile amused, as usual. She asked politely, "Did you have a nice time? Did Grendel behave?" It was awkward to make conversation with a man who was sitting on the side of the bed, especially such an attractive man. Drawing-room conversation seemed inappropriate under the circumstances.

"She was perfect," Sam said. "She's been raised well."

The words "I wondered..." were torn from Addy, but she stopped, and her fingers played with the top of the quilt.

As if he could read her mind, he said, "I had something else in mind for you."

Her eyes flew to him. "What?" she asked, as if she hadn't really heard him.

"There's a Bluegrass concert Saturday. Do you like that kind of music?"

"I love it," she said without thinking.

"Will you go... with me?"

"Oh, yes," she said, so quickly that she didn't think

what she was saying. Then she qualified it with "Well . . . if I'm healthy enough," which left it open so that she could beg off later.

But he said casually, "You're already committed."

The concert began rollicking and ended sentimental, and the whole performance was very satisfying. Addy had worn a red, scoop-necked, long-sleeved wool dress with a black velvet cape, and she looked terrific. He'd told her that. Her high-heeled short boots were black velvet with red lining as was her muff. He said she was good advertising for her Gown House, that all the women were jealous of her and wondering where she'd found such a smashing outfit.

Addy blushed with pleasure, but she didn't say what she was thinking, that he was partly right—the women were envious of her, but only because he was her escort.

When he took her home, he walked to the door with her and kissed her good night. It shattered her. She behaved disgracefully. She kissed him back and gasped and clung to his shoulders, and her blood turned to molten fire as sensual thrills surged through her body. To be kissed by him . . . to be held . . . to feel his lips on hers and on her face. To be held to him, close to his body! She dropped her muff and didn't even realize she had until he stooped and handed it back to her.

He smiled down at her, his eyes seeming to spark with fire as he leaned over to give her a gentle kiss on the cheek. Then he opened the door and helped her over the threshold and said good night.

She wasn't capable of replying. She stood in the open doorway, letting all the heat out of the house as she watched him walk to his car and drive away.

His kisses had been so different from Paul's. Paul's had never made her feel this way. Her whole body was in an uproar—and wanting more! She'd never had such kisses.

Obviously she was experiencing a sexual response to Sam's kisses. This was what the biology books talked about and what romances proclaimed as being worth all the trouble. She groaned as desire licked through her body at the thought of Sam's kisses. It was a strange kind of agony, but not unpleasant.

Addy's legs were getting cold, so she finally closed the door, wandered up to her room, undressed, and crawled into bed all in a trance. But she wasn't so far gone that she didn't hear the furnace laboring to replace the lost heat.

The next day she'd regained control. When Sam called, she replied in a casual way that should have put him off a little. "I enjoyed the concert," he said, "but I enjoyed our good-night better."

Deliberately pretending he meant his leaving her, she replied, "I realized you must be tired. I too had an early night." He laughed. Only then did she remember it had been almost one o'clock when they'd parted, which didn't qualify as an early night. Calling it that revealed how short the evening in his company had seemed to her.

The three young women who had accompanied Sam and his mother to the special showing came at various times for their fittings. Addy felt sure they were Sam's mistresses, because none was named Mrs. Samuel Grady. Later she learned they were his half-sister and two step-sisters, whereupon her attitude toward them changed remarkably.

A week after Diana Hunter had taken the pictures of Grendel, she returned with the prints and showed them to Addy. At first Addy thought Diana was selling her the prints, but gradually she realized Diana was talking about hiring Grendel as a photographer's model. "Grendel?" Addy asked, surprised.

"She's a natural model. She can look any way I suggest! Just look at these!" Diana gestured to the variety of expressions shown in the scattered pictures.

"Well, she is a ham. . . ."

"How about it? We pay standard fees, and she could save up the money for college." When Addy still hesitated, Diana asked, "What's the trouble?"

"I'm afraid she might turn into a smug little mirror-conscious prig," Addy admitted.

"Not Grendel. She thinks it's fun. Like acting stories. We'll be quick enough, and treat her ordinarily enough so that she won't feel so special. I promise."

"Well, we could give it a try, and if we see signs of her being spoiled, we could stop," Addy said, relenting.

"Good enough. I'll pick her up and deliver her home. And, Addy, we'll be careful of her. I promise that too."

"She's so young and little."

Diana laughed. "She's a sturdy little tease. She's a survivor."

Thinking of all they'd survived so far, Addy agreed.

CHAPTER FIVE

THE FIRST PICTURE of Grendel appeared in the *Journal*, and Addy received some nice compliments from people who saw it. The toy advertisement didn't mention Grendel's name but, later in the month, after her picture was used again, there was an article on photographer's models, and a picture of Grendel was included as someone new to the field. It said her name was Grendel Kildaire and her mother was a designer of women's clothes.

Grendel modeled four times that month for an hour each time. Diana treated her in a businesslike way. She set up lights and backgrounds ahead of time and took the pictures rapidly while Grendel acted out a story. Grendel loved it, and Addy was a little shocked by how much a three-year-old could earn in four hours.

On the day of the showing Addy arranged for Mrs. Harrow, Sam arrived with his mother's group. He was the only man in the room. Most other men would have felt ill at ease, Addy thought, but not Sam. He sat in the front row, and when she came out onto the platform in a two-piece wool tartan, he winked at her.

After that she went into some sort of time warp. Her eyes retained the image of Sam and, although she sat on the stool and her eyes were directed toward the models and her mouth gave out her memorized narration, her real self contemplated Sam's image clearly imprinted in her mind. She mused over it. That mouth had kissed hers. Those arms had held her close. Those eyes had smiled down into hers. She'd been pressed against that body.

In her bemused haze she watched as her daughter danced out onto the runway. Grendel put her chin on her chest and pulled her mouth down in concentration as she showed the ladies—and one man—that she could undo her own buttons. All of her clothes fastened in front with buttons that were big enough for her tiny hands to handle. Grendel's modeling sold a lot of children's clothes.

Of course, that day Addy didn't model. She wasn't about to get up in front of Sam's mother on a runway. Not that she was interested in Sam, or that he was interested in her, or anything like that, so it didn't matter what Elizabeth Turner Harrow thought one way or the other. But, Addy decided, there are times you did things and times when you'd rather not, and modeling for Mrs. Harrow and her friends that day was one time she'd rather not.

Even in her daze, she considered her attitude silly. Her business was clothes, the showing and selling of them, and she suspected for some strange reason that she was being pretty dumb. She should straighten up and behave and not let some devastating man, whom she had no use for at all, interfere in her business life.

As she straightened up on the stool, she knew his eyes were riveted on her, watching every move. Good grief! How perfectly ridiculous. It was just like her to be paranoid that way. Why would he look at her? She continued listening absently to herself speaking, then carefully turned her head a bare notch and, glancing as far to the right as she could, peeked at Sam. He *was* watching her!

She'd been right. She wasn't paranoid after all. Her heart thundered, her palms grew moist, her breath caught, and she had to swallow in the middle of a word, though her mouth was so dry she had nothing to swallow, and it sounded awful. Her tongue darted out and licked her lips, and then things went more smoothly.

At last the whole ordeal was over. The ladies had loved it. Addy could hear the one man's heavier clapping and his low voice amidst the twittering of the women. She felt she'd run the mile in less than four minutes in high heels.

Hedda had arranged cakes in the parlor, and Miss Pru poured the tea and served the dainty food. The ladies milled around, calling cheerfully to one another, exclaiming over materials and ordering copies for themselves. They weren't in any hurry to leave. It was a real party.

Sam eased up to Addy and said, "I came specifically to see you model the robe again." He chewed his lower lip, and his eyes spilled laughter as he watched her blush.

"You bought the robe and another one hasn't been made up yet," she replied rather tartly.

"Make it red," he suggested.

She frowned. "Red?"

"Men like red."

"I'm not selling to men."

"You sold me." Had he said it that way deliberately?

"Did she . . . like the . . . robe?" Addy forced out the question despite her agony. Whom had he given it to?

"I haven't given it to her yet."

"Oh." She looked off sadly, then had to ask, "Why didn't you let us clean it?"

"I'll take care of that," he assured her. In a whisper he added, "I can smell your perfume in it."

The most erotic thrill flooded her as she imagined him holding the robe to his face and breathing of it deeply, inhaling the scent of her. She imagined him allowing the robe to slide down his naked body as he inhaled the essence of her. Good lord!

She pursed her lips and straightened her backbone and asked primly, "Would you like some cake?" He said he wasn't quite through with the one he had. She looked stupidly at his hands and wondered how the plate and fork had so magically flown into them.

She excused herself formally and went to the kitchen and held a tea towel under the cold faucet until it was soaked and her hand was turning numb from the cold. Then she squeezed the excess water from the towel and put it to her face in gentle pats so as not to disturb her makeup.

Hedda leaned around her and frowned questioningly into her face. Addy wondered if Hedda really couldn't speak or if she just didn't bother to. "Yes. Headache," Addy told her.

Hedda reached into a voluminous pocket in her long purple skirt and took out two black pills. She handed them to Addy, who took one look at them and knew they were voodoo. The black of the pills was probably dried chicken blood. It was African witch medicine. She peeked cautiously at Hedda. Her expression was serene. It would be. She hadn't had two strange pills thrust at her with an enigmatic, watchful face seeing if she had the courage to swallow them.

Addy looked at the pills in her palm with a good deal of anxiety, but at last she popped them into her mouth. Hedda stopped her abruptly and frowned furiously, then chewed elaborately. Addy chewed obediently. They were after-dinner mints soaked in licorice. So much for voo-doo.

Having swallowed the mints, Addy stood leaning against the sink, looking out the window at the winter-scape and thinking that a psychological remedy for a psychological headache made sense. Maybe her imagination was getting out of hand. Sam was just a man, a man made up of muscle and bone and hair. But it was all arranged in such a maddeningly attractive manner.

She wondered what God had been up to to make a man like Sam. It really wasn't fair. Sam ought not to be allowed out among ordinary mortal females. Any sane woman wanted the best of men, and Sam was the best. So did she want him? How impossible! She shook herself, put down the glass, and gently burped licorice. Come to think of it, she didn't much like licorice. She frowned at Hedda, who gave her a black look and then ignored her.

Addy went back to the milling, chatting women and stood around being polite and pretending not to know exactly where Sam was the whole time. Almost half the women there were his age. Addy had him figured for being somewhere in his late thirties. She watched not Sam but all the young women who talked to him easily and in a friendly manner. He replied to them in kind. And not wanting him and with no chance of having him, Addy was jealous.

As he was leaving, Sam found time for a minute with

her and said, "Would you come out with me tomorrow with Miss Pru and Grendel? We could go to brunch at the Marten House."

She nodded. Even knowing she was foolish and had no business walking on the railroad track and pretending she could avoid being hit by the train, she nodded. One more time would be all right. That was what she told herself. One more time.

Several days later, when Sam suggested they go see a play, that was what Addy told herself again—one more time wouldn't hurt. But she looked over her entire wardrobe and found nothing right or pretty or suitable. So she dropped everything else and sketched a gown, selected the material, and, ignoring the knowing glances of her staff, appropriated Emmaline's machine and sewed it herself. The material was velvet—and it was red. She wasn't dumb. He'd said men liked red.

The gown had long, straight, slightly flared sleeves, with wide filigreed braids at the wrists, which were hell to sew. The neck was square, and that too was bordered in the braid. Addy didn't know one single client she'd have done all that work for, but she did it for herself, humming contentedly. The dress was fitted and the skirt was long. She wore a pink velvet coat with a fur-trimmed hood and a fur muff. She had pink, high-heeled ankle boots. Her lipstick matched the red dress exactly.

She knew the play was funny because everyone burst out laughing and exchanged amused glances with the people next to them. She smiled with the laughter, staring at the stage, conscious only of the man to her right.

During intermission the laughter continued, and the buzz of talk was animated and noisy. Sam got them glasses of wine and, as they stood sipping, Addy said, "It's funny."

Sam grinned. "I haven't been paying much attention.

You're so gorgeous I can't concentrate on anything else."

"Addy!" a male voice interrupted.

She turned blank eyes and saw a nice-looking young man she hadn't seen in several years. "Oh, hello, Jim." She introduced the two men.

Jim was perfunctory in his response to Sam and kept his eyes on Addy. "How great to see you! So you're dating now?"

What could she say? There she was, all dressed up and obviously with a date. She nodded reluctantly and said lamely, "A little."

Jim grinned and said, "Good! I'll call you." Then, ignoring Sam altogether, he touched Addy's shoulder in an intimate gesture and walked away.

There was a pause, then Sam said, "Who was that?" in a carefully neutral tone.

"Jim Hardy."

"I see. And what business does he have ogling you that way?"

"He didn't." She shrugged.

"You couldn't see the way he was eyeing you?"

She shook her head. Why was he questioning her this way? He had no right at all. He bought women robes with *hooks* on them and now he was hostile over an old friend for saying hello to her. He had a lot of nerve.

When the play was over, they were silent among the chattering crowd as they left the theater and walked to Sam's car. They drove through the cold streets before he spoke. "If that guy calls for a date, tell him you have one. Then call me and you will. I don't like the look of him at all."

"Oh, Sam, that's not—"

"Yes, it is. Do you understand? Just tell me when."

She sighed in exasperation as she watched the road. The houses were dark, only the yellow streetlights shining on the snow. He turned into the driveway of the unlit Gown House and brought the car to a stop. When she started to get out, he touched her arm. When she looked around to see why, he kissed her.

She made it easy for him. He pushed back her hood and undid the two buttons at the neckline and opened the coat so that he could put his arms around her velvet-clad body and pull her close to him, then closer as his kiss deepened.

Her heart pounded and her blood surged, roaring in her ears. All this couldn't be very good for her body. Getting all excited like that had to affect her blood pressure. She'd probably have a heart attack. But she didn't stop kissing him back, distracted by the wondrous sensual writhings licking inside her body. It would be worth a heart attack to feel that way. Why hadn't Paul's kisses ever done this to her?

Even with her mind soaked in erotic sensations, the thought of Paul caused her to get hold of herself. She might not have been particularly interested in having sex with Paul, but she was definitely interested in a much closer encounter with Sam. That really shocked her, because she *knew* what it was like, and it hadn't been much fun.

But there was no way in the world she was going to get caught in that trap again. She tried to turn her mouth away from Sam's, but his just followed hers. She took her hands from his hair and tried to wedge them between their bodies, but there wasn't any room. When she wriggled, he just purred.

Finally, when he turned his attention to her throat, she managed to gasp, "I've got to go in now." She'd meant to say, "Stop it this minute!" but it came out "I've got to go in now." Then she could have bitten her damned tongue, for he paused. She hadn't meant him to obey quite so fast. In fact, he could have ignored her for another minute or two, couldn't he?

He appeared reluctant to release her as he slowly lifted his head and loosened his arms. He stroked his hands over the soft velvet, not speaking, then said, "It's been a great evening. Thank you."

"No, thank *you*. I enjoyed the play. It was so funny."

"What was?"

"The play." How could she tell what had been funny about it when she hadn't paid attention to it?

"What did you like best?"

"Oh . . ." She searched furiously for some fragment of the play for a clue and finished lamely, "The whole thing."

He apparently accepted that. "Remember, if that guy calls you, you're busy."

"He won't."

"Yes, he will. I know that look."

"What look?"

"The way he ogled you."

"That's silly." She opened the door and swung her dainty pink boots into the snow.

"Quit rushing," Sam growled as he put a staying hand on her arm. Then he swung open his own door, slid out of the car, and came around to her side, offering her his hand. As she headed toward the porch, he stopped her and gestured with one gloveless hand at the woods. "It's beautiful."

She gazed at the still, moonlit tangle of black limbs against the snow. She parted her lips to remark on how it looked like lace, but he bent his head and kissed her again. They clung together in the snow and freezing cold, warmed by their heated blood.

Eventually Sam released her, and she found herself inside the house, watching him drive away. She stood in the entrance hall, lit by an Edison lamp, and contemplated her passion-racked body. The train was coming closer.

With so many of Mrs. Harrow's friends ordering copies of her summer line, Addy had to add two more seamstresses to her regular staff. She again told Marcus that Emmaline was not pulling her weight, and it was a good thing she only paid her by the piece, because she'd go broke supporting Emmaline on hourly wages. Marcus said not to fret, that Emmaline would work out.

Addy waved her arms around. "Two other women could use Emmaline's machine and never interrupt her."

"How's her work?" Marcus asked, unmoved.

In exasperation, Addy admitted, "Beautiful."

"Well? Then why are you fussing?"

"Oh, Marcus, she puts too much time into everything. It's *too* perfect. Her seams will be perfect after the material has rotted away! They'll still be perfect in a thousand years when they dig up central Indiana!"

"Addy," Marcus scolded patiently, "you do tend to get a little hyper. Give her time . . ."

"That's her problem! She takes too much time. She drifts around as if she's on another planet and not quite in touch with this one."

"Be patient."

"I'll be patient all right. A mental patient!"

To protect herself from Sam, Addy stopped answering the phone. She heard the train whistle every time his name was spoken. But it didn't particularly surprise her one day when she and Grendel were at the Children's Museum and who should come along with a great smile to lift a squealing, welcoming Grendel up above his head but—of course—Sam.

Addy tagged along, watching as the large man and

the fairy child explored and exclaimed over the general store and the farmyard, and rode the merry-go-round. The rapport between them was so obvious that one middle-aged woman, standing next to Addy and watching them, said, "You can sure tell who her daddy is." She laughed comfortably and added, "There's no blaming that one on the milkman."

Addy slid a horrified glance to Sam, who was beaming a smug grin at the woman, taking full credit for Grendel! Addy's tongue stumbled over the words as she said, "He isn't my husband."

The woman's smile faded. "Oh? Well. There's a lot of you girls keeping the kid now." Solemnly she nodded in agreement with her words as the trio remained silent, then added with a smile, "At least you're friends, and the little one will know her daddy. That's smart of you." She turned to Sam. "Are you married to someone else?"

Instead of explaining, he replied simply, "No."

"Well." She eyed Grendel. "With a little gem like that, you ought to think about fixing things up between you. You look like a nice little family. And she shouldn't be an only child."

Addy stuttered, "Well, you know...he's not...and I'm...she..."

Sam just looked at Addy with concentrated interest, and the woman patted her shoulder and said, "I know, but learn to cook and don't hop into bed with him again until he makes it legal."

Addy could only gasp, "I can already cook!"

Leaving them, the woman told Addy, "Don't...do the other. Got it?" And with a conspiratorial wink, she was gone.

During the rest of the afternoon Sam was filled with laughter. Every time he caught Addy's eyes, his were spilling over with humor. "Good lord, Sam," she said, "why didn't you tell her?" And she said, "Oh, quit that!" and she huffed, "You think this is all a big joke!" Then she ended up glaring into his laughing eyes, not saying, but thinking, Oh, Sam, you're so gorgeous. I wish you *were* Grendel's father. I wish it had been you.

But as they were leaving they saw the woman again. She gave them a knowing glance, and Sam said to Grendel, "Come along, honey, Mommy's waiting." And it sounded . . . it sounded as if . . . The woman gave Addy an encouraging nod and a cautioning shake of her finger.

CHAPTER SIX

ALTHOUGH MISS PRU denied it, Addy decided Sam must be in close contact with her, because Addy kept running into him every time she went someplace, and he couldn't possibly have time to spend spying on her to find out where she was going. Her stupid heart was exhausted from going from normal into a thundering high at the sight of him. Her lungs were tired of panting, and her body was going into a decline from longing. She wasn't eating well, and she was a little vague. Her designs turned dreamy and romantic, with ruffles and lace and soft materials.

Miss Pru sent her to match some thread, and there in the fabric shop was Sam! He said hello as if astonished to find her there. She eyed him suspiciously. "Did Miss Pru call you?"

71

"Does she need me?" he asked.

"What are you doing here?"

"I'm matching some thread for Mother." He picked up some black thread. "Why else would I be here?" His expression was serious, but there was a betraying sparkle in his eyes.

"Why didn't she get it herself?"

"Oh, you know Mother. She's at another meeting and didn't have the time."

"But you did?" Addy mocked.

"Hey, it's a good thing I ran into you. I have an extra ticket to the hockey game. You can have it."

"You're not going to use it?" Occasionally people gave her tickets and she passed them on to Marcus, who found someone to go to the event.

"Nope. Here." He took the ticket from his breast pocket and started to hand it to her, then looked at it again and took it back, saying, "That one's mine."

Then he reached into his pocket again and said, "This one's yours." But instead of giving it to her, he just said, "I'll pick you up at six, and we'll just have hamburgers first so you'll have room for hot dogs later during the game." He leaned over and kissed her cheek and walked out—to the blast of train whistles coming closer.

Several nights later, feeling as if her body was being rushed helplessly into a sort of Armageddon over which she had no control, Addy found herself sitting about ten rows off the ice watching a bloodthirsty hockey game.

It was astonishing to her how the crowd was filled with bloodlust. They made no pretense of practicing good sportsmanship or of being fair-minded. They yelled and booed and cheered and shouted, vitally involved with every play. In Roman times they'd have been for the lions.

It was all very noisy and exhausting, but mostly Addy was waiting to go home. It wasn't that she was bored or not feeling well or anything like that. It was that when he took her home he would probably kiss her again. She sat there, her eyes obediently following the play while she thought about Sam kissing her. The excitement of anticipation licked her stomach.

He often looked at her and smiled, jammed next to her in his seat, their shoulders rubbing, his thigh alongside hers, shifting and touching. Her body reacted to his. When everyone leaped to their feet and she responded automatically to the move, he put his arm around her shoulders or his hand on her waist. His touch filled her with shivers of sensual pleasure, and the game was wasted on her. She was conscious only of Sam.

He brought her hot dogs and watched her eat them. He licked his own lips as she licked hers. And he laughed down at her and appeared to relish the game and being there. When they left in the closely packed, slowly moving crowd, he went first, holding her hand securely behind him and keeping her close as he made a protected pathway for her.

Outside, as they walked to his car, their breaths frosted in the air. Addy shivered in the cold car as they waited for the traffic to ease so they could pull out into the stream of traffic.

"The heater will warm up in a minute." Sam grinned down at her. "Would you like to go to a dirty, crowded, noisy, smoky old bar? Or should we go to your house and make some hot cocoa?"

What could she say to that? That she wanted to go to a crowded, dirty old bar? She couldn't hide a grin as she said, "The cocoa." When he laughed, it was so intimate that anticipation wriggled inside her. If he came inside, he'd be rude not to kiss her. Or she could kiss him—

casually, of course—as she told him she'd enjoyed the evening. It would be just a light, friendly kiss, nothing steamy or sexual or anything like that, just a pleasant, casual kiss. Preoccupied by her thoughts, she was startled at how quickly they arrived at her house.

She unlocked the door and, after they'd moved inside, she closed it carefully. The house was so big that any sound seemed to reverberate. Feeling awkward in the entrance hall alone with Sam, Addy called his attention to the red crystal lamp that hung in the stairwell. It was Art Nouveau, swirled in silver, and had an original light bulb from Edison's day that still burned.

"It's occasionally mentioned in the *Journal* as an interesting item, and now and then someone comes by and asks to look at it."

Sam looked up obediently and said, "Ummm."

"There are sealed bets as to how much longer it'll last," she told Sam in hushed tones.

"What do you bet?" He took off his coat.

"I don't know." She hung it with hers in the cavernous closet under the stair landing. As she emerged from the depths, closed the door, and turned, he took her into his arms and kissed her. She melted against him. Her first thought was how nice that he'd done it right away without making her wait until he was leaving.

After that, sensation took over, and she simply leaned against him and allowed her body to absorb all the waves of marvelous thrills his kiss produced in her. She was disappointed when he finally lifted his mouth and looked down into her face. Feeling bereft, although still locked in his arms, she made a discontented sound and lifted her mouth as if seeking his.

His pleased chuckle made her eyes pop open as she realized what she'd done. She swallowed and pushed against him until he slowly released her. He allowed her to leave his arms. She wasn't sure why she'd insisted, so she smoothed her hair and tugged her clothes into place. She shot a glance at him and saw him watching her with an amused smile. Why did he think she was funny? Was he laughing at her? She supposed she *had* fallen very quickly into his arms and returned his kisses in a very unladylike manner.

She turned blindly and groped in the darkness beyond the lighted entrance hall. She blundered into a table, then into the wall, her attention on Sam as he followed her. He took her arm and led her. She babbled in a whisper, "You must eat your carrots, you see so well in the dark."

He said he was part cat. She said, "Oh," as if that explained everything, thinking about panthers who were blue-eyed and beautiful and fascinating even if rather frightening.

In the kitchen Addy switched on the light and closed the door to the back hall. Then she opened a cupboard, and three pans slid out onto the floor with loud clangs. She froze, listening, then gasped, "Miss Pru will think there are burglars."

"Why do you call her Miss Pru?"

"I couldn't call her Prudence, and she's such a lady that I had to call her something with a title. But Miss Walker sounded so formal with all we'd gone through together. So I settled on Miss Pru. Now everyone calls her that."

"Miss Walker?" Sam asked.

"She never married. I believe there was a tragedy back during World War Two. I've never had the courage to ask." She removed the lid from the cake dish. "Hedda left some lemon tea cakes here. Would you like some?"

"Sounds good," he agreed. "Are we going to eat in here? I could set the table."

"There's a little parlor in the front of the house. It

was always kept exclusively for company in the olden days. Since we use the drawing room as a reception or showroom, we keep the little parlor for visitors. There's a fireplace. Would you like to go in there?"

"Umm-hmm." He smiled.

She led him from the kitchen to the parlor through the dining room. She turned on lamps so that he could light the firewood while she went back to the kitchen. There she got out a silver chocolate pot and a silver bowl for marshmallows. First she filled the pot with hot water and set it aside to warm so that it wouldn't chill the cocoa later. Then she lay a lace doily on a plate before lifting the tiny lemon cakes onto it. She put forks and spoons and linen napkins on the tray. She emptied the water from the chocolate pot, poured in the cocoa, and put that on the tray too.

Sam came back to the kitchen just then, his jacket off, his shirt-sleeves turned up, and his collar unbuttoned. He looked as if he planned to stay awhile. Addy sneaked a cautious eye at the clock. It was only a bit after eleven. She promised herself to be careful and not let things get out of hand. That is, she would stay out of Sam's hands.

Sam's smile was self-satisfied, but there were no canary feathers clinging to that panther's mouth . . . yet. Resolute, she nodded when he asked if the tray was ready and went ahead of him into the parlor. Step into my parlor, said the spider to the fly. Was she the spider or the fly? The fire was going nicely, but what caught her eye was that Sam had moved a small sofa and a marble-topped occasional table in front of it. The sofa only seated two people. Addy sat gingerly on the edge of "her" sofa pillow, clasping her hands, her knees—and her lips— tightly pressed together.

With fluid ease, Sam sat down on "his" sofa pillow and sprawled over onto hers, his muscular thigh against her hip. Sensations burst through her from his touch. All that just from the touch of his thigh against her hip! She probably should plead a headache and go to bed.

He'd probably agree, go with her, and examine her—*sans* thermometer and stethoscope—and then he'd probably decide she needed an injection. She'd better settle down and get control of herself. She turned to him. "Marshmallows?" she asked politely, thinking that was what she was with him, a helpless marshmallow.

"There's no other way," he began seriously.

Her head floated. Her eyes met his and her mouth parted. No other way? Did he mean . . . ? "W-what?"

"The only way to drink cocoa is with marshmallows," he said reasonably.

"Oh." Her head jerked up, but she brought it down slowly. As her eyes came down level with his again, she noted that he was watching her quizzically, with the same amused gleam in his eyes.

Reminding herself how much trouble one brief encounter with a man had once been for her, she schooled herself to regain control, poured the cocoa, added the marshmallows, and remained sitting forward on the edge of the sofa.

Why was she such a shambles and he so calm? They always said men were the ones who were avidly sexual and women aloof. What was wrong with her? She had never been this way with Paul. The only reason she'd acquiesced to Paul at all was that he'd been so upset . . . and anyway, everyone else she knew was either sleeping with someone or living with someone.

It had been embarrassing with Paul, and she hadn't liked it at all. She'd been so disappointed that she'd cried. He'd said all virgins did that, and he'd gone to sleep, leaving her to wonder if she was weird. Other women liked it. They said so. Had they lied?

"You're awfully quiet." Sam's voice was intimately low and husky.

She gave him a quick, prim smile and sipped her cocoa. She found herself wondering if . . . it . . . would be different with Sam. She blushed and lifted a piece of lemon cake to take a bite, but decided her mouth was too dry, she wouldn't be able to chew or swallow it and she'd choke, and he'd pat her on the back and be darling to her and . . . She put the cake down on the tray.

"Not hungry after all?" he asked.

"Uh . . . well . . . we had a big dinner . . ."

"We just had hamburgers and later hot dogs," he reminded her.

"Well . . . I had a snack this afternoon. With Grendel. She's modeling for Diana Hunter. Isn't it marvelous that her family named her Diana . . . you know, having Hunter for a last name, and Diana is the goddess of the hunt and all? She's a professional photographer." Addy ignored the fact that he was nodding agreement at her every word. "And Grendel thinks it's such fun. . . ." She wound down and then stopped completely.

"Mother told Diana about Grendel. She's an old friend."

"Oh?" Addy looked at him, her jaw falling.

"Of the family," he explained. "Her mother and mine were sorority sisters."

"Yes, I see." And of course, she did see. That's how Mrs. Harrow contrived to matchmake. "I'll just bring Diana over with me. Will Sam be there?" Addy *had* liked Diana. How tricky of her to be likable.

"Hurry up and finish that damned cocoa," he growled at her.

Naturally he would growl, being a panther. He wanted her to lean back so he could . . . lick her feathers off . . . and then he'd purr. She would like to make him purr. Why, Adelina Mary Rose Kildaire! she exclaimed to herself. No wonder you were an unmarried mother! Then she argued back to herself: Only one man and it was hardly depraved behavior. Then she concluded: it's all mental, and he'll never know how he affects me.

"What in the world are you thinking?" Sam asked. "Your lips are working, your head is making tiny movements, and your breathing is fast, as if you're arguing with ghosts."

She turned again to look at him. He was lying back with relaxed grace, the firelight playing over his marvelous face and body. She thought of his words, "arguing with ghosts," and said, "You're not far from the mark."

"Tell me," he invited.

But she shook her head and turned her face pensively to the firelight. If she'd been slated to make a big mistake, as she had once in her life, why couldn't she have waited and made it with Sam?

"Is this old house haunted?" he asked unexpectedly.

"Once a woman came here to buy a dress and said this was a very busy house. I thought she meant our business and smiled at her, but she said spirits roamed here."

"Do you believe that?"

She shrugged. "If there are spirits, they're friendly."

"Why did you decide to keep Grendel after she was born?"

"Perhaps I'm basically selfish." She was looking into the fire. "I sought out all the advice, and the professional people were amazingly kind and didn't burden me with guilt. Their attitude was to allow the past to be past and learn from it. They all gave good, solid information on the pros and cons of keeping her or giving her up. They leaned toward giving her up. But then when she was born, I couldn't.

"Miss Pru just listened to me. She'd been tnere all along, and she never once said what she really thought. My family was still shattered. Talking to them was such an ordeal for them that it was kinder to leave them alone. They were even torn over whether or not I should keep her.

"It might have helped if she hadn't looked like Paul, but she's very different from our family. We're all blond and blue-eyed. In our town, when they talk about a certain redheaded child, their eyes are knowing, as if they think his mother was unfaithful. She was one of our family, so she escaped being shunned. If she'd been an outsider, her life would've been hell. Then an old cousin of my grandmother's came to visit and saw the child and said, 'So the red strain finally popped up again. It's been so long we thought it was lost.' And she traced it back two hundred years.

"Paul, being of French descent, with his olive complexion and brown eyes, was truly foreign to them. They met him once."

"Has he ever seen Grendel?"

"I haven't heard from him since I told him I was pregnant. He turned and walked out of the apartment and never came back. He doesn't know if I kept the baby or if I lost it, or if it was a boy or girl, whole or afflicted. Nothing. One big zero."

"That hurts." Sam's low voice was very kind.

"I hadn't wanted the relationship. I had my life planned, and marriage was far in the future. I'd been strictly raised, but it seemed to me that everyone had a relationship going and *that* was normal and I wasn't. It wasn't peer pressure. No one cared what I did or didn't do.

"He said he loved me madly and couldn't survive without me, that he'd die if I didn't sleep with him. And he did look awful—thin, eyes sunken, nervous. I felt sorry for him."

"So you moved in with him."

"No. He lived in a dorm. I had an apartment, and he just didn't leave one night. I couldn't throw him out, and we argued until I was exhausted. Then he...It was awful."

Sam rubbed the back of her neck in a soothing way, massaging the tense muscles. His long fingers were strong and gentle, and Addy began to relax. After a while he observed, "You've never forgiven yourself, have you?"

She didn't reply for a while. Then she said in a very low voice, "I broke the rules."

"And rules are important because they save a lot of trouble and grief. That goes for traffic rules, health rules, or sex. But having been in a wreck doesn't mean you have to agonize over it for the rest of your life."

"There's Grendel," Addy reminded him.

"She's a darling little girl."

"Oh, I'm not sorry I have her, but what about her? Will she hate me when she's old enough to know all about it?"

"You could have had an abortion," he told her, "but you didn't."

"No." She'd never considered it.

"There will be people who disapprove of everything you did. They won't change. And we need people who value rules, for they don't allow the conduct of civilization to become too lax. But there will be those who can adjust and accept you for the caring woman you are. They'll recognize your struggle and understand it. You didn't keep Grendel as a whim or plaything or a doll

substitute. You aren't on welfare or making the govern-
ment support you. You're self-sustaining and you've made
it."

"Miss Pru was essential. I couldn't have done it without her."

"Yes, you could have. You're very strong."

"I don't feel that way."

"You're invincible. You might worry and fret, but
you'd make it." And she knew he was right.

They were quiet for a while, watching the fire, listening to it crackle. "So the spirits in the house are
friendly?" Sam asked.

Addy replied, "Yes," but she was distracted. Her whole
body was responding to Sam's long fingers working lazy
circles on her shoulders.

"I'm a friendly spirit too," he said. Then he tugged
her body back and turned her expertly so that she was
pressed against him.

Her eyes almost pleaded with him. For what? Did she
want to be taken or released? She didn't know. He arranged her comfortably, taking his time, touching her
lingeringly, until she was nestled just right. He lifted her
hands to the back of his head and ran his own up her
arms and across her shoulders as his hot eyes examined
her eyes, her face, her mouth. And then he kissed her.

His hands moved on her, down her back, to her hips,
up again to cradle her head against the pressure of his
kiss; as the kiss softened and opened, his hand moved
to her waist and up to press the softness of the side of
her breast. He shifted his body, released her mouth, and
planted kisses along her throat, the pressure of his mouth
nudging her head back over his arm, exposing more of
her throat. Then he turned her just a little to allow his
hand to cup her breast.

Her body reacted to his stroking, touching, and to his

kissing. The surface of her skin became excited, and waves of sensations skittered over her. Deeper, sensual curls of awareness licked up through her body to her brain and sent her blood reeling. Her hands closed around his head, and she pressed him closer, and the secret places of her body tingled and shivered.

When she made no protest, his hands and mouth became more urgent. His lips sought hers again. His tongue began a gentle intrusion, flicking, touching, seeking. She groaned and sighed and lay pliant in his arms.

"I want you." His voice shook, and his breathing was erratic.

"I know." She lay there as if helpless.

"Make love with me," he urged.

"No." She could barely make her languid lips form the word.

"No?" He seemed to have a little trouble realizing what she'd said.

"I don't dare," she replied with a sad sigh.

"Addy, I have protection."

But instead of his words comforting her or reassuring her, her eyes popped open and she looked at him, offended. "Oh, you do!" She sat up, turned, and perched huffily on the edge of her sofa pillow, straightening her hair and blouse.

"Hey!" he protested in a soft voice, looking confused.

"So you carry protection around just in case . . ."

"That's not true."

"Oh, no? Then why do you have it with you? You thought that just because Grendel's illegitimate, I'd be a pushover!"

"Now, Addy . . ."

"Well, I'm not! I've learned my lesson *very* well! And just because—"

"You're paranoid about Grendel! You think you have

illegitimate child' written all over you—and backwards on your forehead so it can be read in the rearview mirror!"

"No. But you just want me to let you sleep with me . . ."

"Okay. I'm willing!" He was very irritated.

"Well, I won't!"

"You weren't objecting all this time." She resented his pointing that out.

There was a short silence. Then she bowed her head, and said in a thin voice, "I know. I'm sorry. But it wasn't like anything I'd ever . . ." She fell silent.

But his ears had caught that, and he perked up considerably as he urged, "It wasn't?" She shook her head and kept her face turned away. "Addy, look at me." He put his arm around her stiff body, while his other hand turned her face slowly to him. But she kept her eyes down. "Addy, when I saw you on the runway, showing that robe, you knocked me sideways. Every time I've seen you, you've made my head spin a little more. I brought along protection tonight in case you invited me to spend the night. When I've touched you, you haven't seemed disgusted."

"You thought I'd . . ." She looked up indignantly.

"I'd rather have it and not need it than need it and not have the courage to leave you alone."

"But you thought . . . you thought . . ."

"I hoped." When she didn't reply, he added, "I didn't think you'd be unwilling."

"I don't think we should see each other anymore. I will *not* get involved."

"Addy . . ."

She stood up. "I'll get your coat." She marched out to the entrance hall, took his coat from its hanger, and stood there, holding it for him. All the time he was rolling down his sleeves and putting on his jacket, she didn't say one word or look at him. He took the coat from her hands, watching her as he put it on, then said in a low voice, "Good night, Addy. I'll be in touch."

She didn't reply as he left.

CHAPTER SEVEN

IN THE DAYS that followed, Addy's designs changed again. She'd been creating wondrously romantic gowns, soft and feminine, for the fall show due in two months, but now she drew suits in somber colors with high collars of sturdy material. They were fabulous but stark.

"A marvelous contrast, Addy," Miss Pru commented. "I don't believe you've ever had such an interesting variety in one show before." Miss Pru was choosing which model would wear what for the showing. The seamstress would then sew it to that model's measurements. She was trying to discourage Pearl, who was begging to wear the vertical-black-and-white-striped robe. "You'd look twelve feet tall!" Miss Pru protested.

"That's only two feet taller than I already am," Pearl boasted. The seamstress whose sole work was to make up the samples for the shows also exclaimed how unusual the designs were. To herself, Addy called them B.I.H. and A.I.H., for before and after ice-hockey night. Why she chose to blame the ice hockey for the steamy confrontation by the fireplace in the parlor was not something she dwelt on.

Sam had no regard for her rejection at all. He'd dropped by to see Grendel a couple of times, and once he returned her from a photography session. Addy was filled with jealousy at the thought that Sam had seen Diana Hunter. Diana really was a huntress, she concluded, an insidiously clever one who was charming and very nice-looking, who hid her predatory ways behind a friendly facade. On dark nights she probably smiled with pointed teeth, and her fingernails grew into claws. She was a leopard who could change her spots, a fit mate for a panther.

Sam also came with his mother for her additional fittings and chatted with a tongue-tied Addy as if they were old friends. He might feel comfortable, but she was a basket case. She darted peeks at his mouth and remembered . . . She glanced at his hands and thought . . . She stared at his hard, wide chest and knew . . . She struggled to keep her breath steady and her chest from swelling and her hands from trembling. She was in agony.

Sam met Marcus, who eyed him noncommittally and said, "You the one got in the ladies-only show that time? The watcher saw the doctor's tab on your car license plate and let you in."

Addy gasped. "What did you do to him?"

"He watches closer now."

Sam regarded Marcus with intense interest. "I know all about you, Mr. Freeman," he began pleasantly. But

Marcus shot him a glance that stilled his tongue and made Addy very curious.

The models met for fittings for the fall show. Patty-cake danced in to exclaim, "I've got a part in a play! It'll open this fall!" She was so excited no one could get another thought through to her.

Dark-haired Linda informed them, "I found an extra job as a go-go dancer. I'm making more there than as a legal secretary!"

Naturally they all waited to hear what news redheaded Dale came up with, but she had no news at all. They all scolded her for being dull and claimed that her life was too prosaic. She just smiled lazily.

The blonde, brunette, redhead, and one black Pearl had their fittings and loved the new clothes. They moved in front of the mirrors and told Addy the clothes were smashing.

But their compliments gave her no particular joy. She was pale and said "Thank you" in a nice, polite voice, but they weren't paying any attention to her and didn't see that she was suffering.

Sam saw and was tender with her. "Quit being so kind to me!" she snarled at him under her breath.

"Why?" he asked.

"I can't handle kindness." She hadn't had much prac-tice.

"I can use a lot...any you might have lying around ...even crumbs." His voice was low and coax-ing...and kind.

"Cut it out!" she snapped, flouncing away from him.

At another fitting a few days later, Mrs. Harrow said to Addy, "Sam is a very nice boy, and my favorite son. Of course, he's the only son I have." Addy recognized that old chestnut and smiled politely.

"Addy, why won't you date Sam? He's harmless."

Which just showed how little Mrs. Harrow knew about her own son! Harmless? Sam? Balderdash! He should wear a warning sign. "Mrs. Harrow," Addy replied carefully, not looking at her, her face feeling pinched with the effort, "Grendel is illegitimate."

"My third daughter almost was," Mrs. Harrow told Addy conversationally, "but the divorce became final, and I got married to her father just in the nick of time."

Addy could only stare.

"Of course, her father stood by me. He was excessively possessive, and I had a married name at the time. But everyone knew who the father was, and that's why my first husband was so asinine about the divorce. He wanted things to be awkward for me out of revenge. My second husband, Tom, never told me how much he paid my first husband to let me have the divorce. I was sure at the time that everyone in Indianapolis was pointing at me and whispering behind their hands about me. It was an extremely nerve-racking time.

"She's a darling. I'm so glad we have her," Mrs. Harrow went on. "She was worth all the mess. We named her Cyn, which shows you Tom's humor. It was so long ago and I've been married so many times and have so many children and stepchildren that the scandal is almost buried. Only my oldest enemies remember and recall it. Times change. I wouldn't worry about it if I were you."

"No wonder Sam is so understanding about it."

"Oh, Sam." Mrs. Harrow flapped a dismissive hand. "He's a pushover for babies. Always has been. Baby *anything*, but human babies especially. That's why he's chosen the field he has. But he's never been serious about a woman. I've been pushing and prodding, but he says for me to be patient, he's working on it." Mrs. Harrow eyed Addy in a penetrating way, then she smiled and spoke of other things.

* * *

A day or so later, when Sam came by and invited Addy to dinner, she groused, "You certainly have a great deal of free time."

"That's why I'm a pediatric consultant. Do you realize I went to school until I was thirty-two? That's a lot of years to study, but the rewards are large fees and no office hours."

"No office?"

"No. The patients I see are almost always in a hospital. Occasionally I see some who aren't, but then I meet them in their home or at their doctor's office."

"How do they get in touch with you?"

"I have an answering service that always knows exactly where I am. I rarely have emergencies." He paused and smiled at her. "Addy, come to dinner with me tonight. I'll take you wherever you want to go."

"I can't. If you walk on the track, you get hit by the train."

"I'm a train?"

"Something like that." She examined her thumbnail. "Sam, give it up. I'm not interested."

"You don't kiss 'not interested.'"

"Well. Yes. I don't know why that is, but . . . you are very good."

"That's a start," Sam told her.

She was scornful. "It's all men want. Sex."

"You've known the wrong men."

"Man. One man."

"One?" He could only stand and look at her.

By that time she'd given her thumb as much attention as any thumb deserves in a month, so she flicked a glance at Sam and said good-bye and walked away from him.

* * *

Two days after that, in the late afternoon, Miss Pru came to Addy in her attic studio and said Sam needed her. Irritated, Addy set the timer and told the loitering Emmaline to remove the material from the color bath and rinse it when the dinger sounded. Emmaline nodded in her lazy, slow way, and Addy sighed in exasperation and clattered down the stairs to the second floor and then down the grand staircase and through to the front parlor.

Sam looked as if he'd been on a three-day drunk. He needed a shave, he was hunched down on the sofa with his elbows on his thighs and his hands hanging between his knees, and he was staring at the floor. He hadn't taken off his coat. His hair was tousled, as if his hands had raked through it a hundred times. He didn't respond when Addy spoke to him.

She walked slowly toward him and stood in front of him, but he didn't look up. She knelt down and put her hands on his knees, peering into his face. Wearily he met her eyes and sighed as he almost shook his head. It was as if he'd started to but didn't have the energy to complete the movement, or that he'd shaken it so much that the muscles were exhausted.

She touched his stubbled cheek, her heart filled with compassion as she asked in a whisper, "What is it?"

"It's never easy." His throat sounded raw.

"No?" she encouraged.

"We lost a hard one. Something should have worked. It shouldn't have happened. We did nothing wrong. But we lost."

"Oh, Sam . . ." And she kissed his cheek with infinite tenderness.

"There are so many things I don't understand. God is going to run when I get to heaven, I have so many 'whys' to ask him. Everything has a reason. The universe is logical. But I can't figure out this one. It's another one in which there is no sane reason why we lost him. That little tiny life just . . . snuffed out. And there isn't one good reason for it."

As Addy listened, she gently pushed his coat off his shoulders and pulled the sleeves from his arms. His rumpled suit coat followed, then his tie. Miss Pru arrived with an omelet and a glass of warm milk with vanilla and nutmeg mixed in it. "I imagine you've had too much coffee," she said.

Sam nodded. He ate, chewing, waving the fork, going over the diagnosis, the treatments, exactly what had happened and when, and asking why it had. Addy listened.

Then when he yawned and sank into a stupor, she took his hand and led him up the grand staircase. She gave him a terry-cloth robe and showed him the bathroom, saying, "Hot shower." Then she made up the bed in an empty room and turned on the electric blanket. Outside it was snowing again.

He came into the room, heavy-eyed and rough-looking, his hair wet. She got a fresh towel and sat him on the edge of the bed and dried his hair. He wrapped his arms around her and leaned his head against her, moving his face tiredly against her soft breasts. She told him softly to stop it. He ignored her.

His hands turned hard and demanding, and he pulled her down on his lap to hold her and kiss her. There was no denying him. Her resistance was only tentative. Before long she was lying on the bed, allowing him to make love to her. Her clothes vanished as if by magic, and soon they were in the bed, their naked bodies touching.

The sensation of the texture of his hairy skin against her sensitive, quivering body sent her mind reeling. He seemed to feel it too, and held her silently so that they could realize the pleasure it gave them both. "Oh, Addy," he breathed in her ear. The sound, almost inaudible, thrilled her all the way down to her toes. He moved his mouth down her soft throat, deliberately, delicately whiskering her, his mouth opening hotly to kiss and lick along her skin, tasting her.

To feel his scalding, wet mouth within that beard-roughened face was thrilling, and it made her gasp and squirm against him. His body jerked and tensed, while hers softened and relaxed. He kissed her mouth, his hands roaming over her, and she buried her own hands in his tousled hair. His kiss deepened, his mouth opening, moving, encouraging her response. Her lips parted, and their mouths fused.

His strong palms slid over her satin skin lovingly, taking pleasure in the feel of her, and her skin tingled at his touch. Her body moved, inviting his explorations. Their kiss deepened even more, and as their tongues met, his fingers sought her secret places and touched her gently. She moaned, and her breasts swelled against him, aching for his attentions.

Sweat filmed their bodies. He slid easily down her, causing her to gasp. His mouth teased her breasts while his hands smoothed and touched her. Her own hands moved on him, though not as boldly. She ran them greedily through his hair and around his head and throat, along his tightly muscled shoulders and down his rock-hard back. She rubbed his hairy chest and clutched his shoulders as she writhed and moved, wanting him.

She wanted him . . . terribly. She pressed against him, and her hungry mouth kissed wherever it could. Their breath steamed in that cool room, and their bodies were wet with sweat from their passionate labor. Still, Sam prolonged it. Finally he slid back up her, his weight on her. And as he kissed her, his tongue gently invaded her opened mouth and his body invaded hers.

He paused, shifted to his elbows, and breathed heavily as they lay coupled, clamped together, fused. He looked down into her face. "I love you, Addy." He was breathing hard; his eyes were leaping fires, smoldering and flaming into hers as his body smoldered and flamed in hers.

He leaned down and kissed her very sweetly, then his weight came down on hers and he began their ride to an explosion that lifted them to an exquisite release. Addy clutched him, as her body tensed against the tide, then she fell back, limp and filled with wonder.

He lay on her, his elbows again supporting most of his weight, and showered tiny kisses onto her flushed face. In a slow, rough, thickened voice, he said, "Fabulous. My God, I've never had it like that. Oh, Addy."

He lifted himself carefully off her and lay beside her to gather her close. "Let me sleep just a minute. I want you again right away. I just have to sleep for a little while. Don't move . . ." And he went instantly to sleep.

Addy lay in his arms, stunned from the amazing experience. It was astounding! So that's how it could be. She could not refrain from touching him. He was so deep in sleep that her gentle fingers made no impression on him. She touched his lips in something like awe. She smoothed back his hair with gentle soothings. So that's how it could be between a man and a woman. It was marvelous. It was a miracle. Why hadn't it been that way with Paul?

He had been inept, selfish, and she hadn't desired him. She hadn't wanted him because she hadn't loved him. And she knew now she was in love with Samuel Grady, this terrible, marvelous man. She lay in his arms, touching him, yearning for him. But after a time, she carefully moved away from him and stood naked beside the bed. She looked down at him, and her heart moved.

She dressed pensively, finding her clothes scattered around the room where he'd flung them. She looked down at his sleeping face many times. She hesitated long in the doorway, then went out, closing it softly behind her.

Downstairs in her office, she sat at her cluttered desk and gazed out the window with unseeing eyes. Miss Pru found her there.

"Adelina, what are you up to?" She didn't say it with censure but with concern.

"I don't know." Addy turned troubled eyes to Miss Pru.

"I'd hate to think you'd be . . ."

"What?"

"Well . . . indiscreet," Miss Pru supplied. "I'd hate for you to be hurt."

"He was so . . ."

"I don't mean to interfere." Miss Pru turned away.

"No one has a better right."

The two women looked at each other, and Addy got up and went to the older woman and put her arms around her. They stood silently, then Miss Pru patted her shoulder and left the room.

At dinnertime Addy checked on Sam, but he hadn't even moved. She looked in on him again before going to bed, leaving a glass of milk with a saucer over it and a wrapped sandwich on a tray in case he woke up hungry. His clothes had been pressed, his shirt was washed and ironed, and they were hung on hangers where he could readily see them.

In the morning he was still asleep. The bed was rumpled and he was in a sprawled position. Addy stood for a while, filling her eyes with the sight of him, then took the untouched tray of food and, leaving his door open,

went down to the kitchen. She left the door to the stairwell open too. Then she fried bacon and put rolls in the
oven. When he arrived a few minutes later the coffee
had just finished perking. She looked over her shoulder
at him shyly.

He grinned at her and said, "Good morning, darling."
She moved from his embrace, embarrassed. "You are an
angel of mercy," he told her.

"For letting the aroma of eggs and bacon and coffee
float up the back stairs?"

"Well . . . It's the second best way to waken a man."

"Second?" she began, then stopped as he grinned.
"How do you feel?" she asked, changing the subject.

"I was out on my feet. Jeremy and I had been with
the parents, trying to help them cope, from midnight
until just before I came to you. I couldn't think about
anything but getting to you. I was used up and needed
you. Oh, Addy, you were so sweet to me."

She hadn't yet solved how she was going to handle
what had happened between them, so she said briskly,
"You start with oatmeal."

"I can eat," he admitted ruefully, "but I'm not hungry
for food."

"I'm not getting involved with you," she warned him.

"Honey, you're already involved with me." She again
evaded his reaching hands and looked up at him forlornly.
"It'll be all right," he assured her. "Just leave everything
to me." He'd been completely exhausted the day before,
but she saw that the loving and the long sleep had restored
him. He was his old self—confident, teasing, and kind.

Grendel bounced in just then, exhilarated to find Sam
there. She asked to be held and exclaimed over his whiskers, so he brushed them against her cheek. She shrieked
and giggled and wriggled in his arms, and he laughed.

Addy envied her daughter. Then Grendel squealed, "Mommy, did you feel his whis-pers?"

"Whis-*kers*," Addy corrected, standing aloof and busy at the stove.

"Did you *feel* them?"

Sam looked at Grendel with a solemn expression and asked, "Do you think your mommy should be whiskered too?"

"Yes!" Grendel yelled, chortling.

"Behave!" Addy commanded. "I'm cooking the eggs." But Sam went up behind her and hugged her, and his touch sent electric thrills all through her. An egg hit the floor with a splat.

Holding her against him, Sam nuzzled her neck as she scolded, "The egg!" That made him laugh, while Grendel squealed and yelled.

Miss Pru entered with raised eyebrows and a hidden smile. "Shall I whisker you too?" Sam offered.

She put up a cheek quite willingly, and he bent down and rubbed his against it in a courtly way. She patted his prickly cheek and said, "Ahhh, that was just lovely."

Grendel disagreed with Miss Pru. "It's *funny!*"

Addy didn't comment about her own reaction. She just bent down to mop up the egg—as Sam reached over and turned off the smoking skillet.

He was full of himself this morning. Every move was one of triumph. He was the conqueror.

Addy couldn't handle the whole situation. She was embarrassed. Making love was extremely intimate, and she was back to not quite looking at him. She couldn't possibly regret what had happened; it had been too glorious. To know at last how it could be between a man and a woman making love was the stuff of dreams. But . . . but she'd gone quite wild. Would he remember? Had he been aware of her conduct? He'd been so intense himself, perhaps he hadn't realized she'd been out of control.

He did remember. His dancing eyes told her so every time she almost looked at him. She kept her mouth prim and her back straight all through breakfast while she longed for him to take her back upstairs, strip off her clothes, take her to bed, and rub her entire body with his whiskery face. She swallowed a lot and licked her lips with quick flicks, trying to keep her eyes on her plate. And when he left to go to his apartment to shave, he said, "Keep my bed turned down, Tiger."

"Now, just a—" she began, but he only gave her mouth a hard, possessive kiss and went out the door to his car, whistling. She stood in the ever-glowing light of the Edison bulb in the entrance hall and leaned her head against the cold pane and wondered how she'd ever gotten so tangled up with Sam Grady. The train was looming ahead, and there was no time to get off the track.

She dragged herself upstairs to the attic, which she'd left to Emmaline the day before, and stopped in the door. On the drying line were four batik cloths, each a yard square. The spidery lines and various colors were stunning. Emmaline looked up placidly, and Addy stared at her. "Emmaline?" she asked uncertainly, gesturing at the fantastic artwork.

Emmaline looked at them vaguely, then smiled and went back to spreading wax on another cloth, not bothering to reply.

Addy examined them more closely. "Did *you* do these?" she demanded, stunned into incomprehension.

Emmaline looked up again and nodded before going back to her new design. "Umm-hmm," she said.

"They're *gorgeous!*"

Emmaline smiled without looking up. "Thanks."

"And I've kept you chained to that sewing machine when you can do something like *this!*" Addy was appalled.

"You don't mind?" Emmaline slid the cloth into a color bath.

"Mind? I'm going to bring the chains up here! Do you know what these could sell for?" She seemed to see dollar signs in front of her eyes. "We'll have to talk to Marcus. We need to set you up in business. You can work here until you get started. Then you can have your own business, and I'll buy from you. Can you give me first refusal? These are *fantastic!*" She was awed. "They're so beautiful, they almost scare me. I'll find Marcus."

"He's out of town," Emmaline offered absently.

"Where?"

"I don't know." She didn't sound interested.

"Probably in Chicago taking lessons from the Mob."

"Yeah," Emmaline agreed indifferently.

Addy went a little berserk. She ran for samples and matched them with the cloths, pairing various dresses with the scarves. She sketched up her ideas, then made a list of women to invite to come see them. "How many can you make in a day?"

"I don't know." Emmaline shrugged.

"Don't press . . ."

"Not 'til they're dry," she agreed.

"I mean don't hurry them. Do them at your own pace." Addy tried to think how to be clear. "Do them the way you do your seams for dresses. Don't hurry."

"All right."

Addy looked to see what she was working on as Emmaline India-inked a Chinese character in the middle of a hand-drawn, perfect circle. Then she took a smaller brush and added the perfect finishing drip mark. Addy was dumbfounded. "Emmaline, where did you learn to do that?"

"Oh . . . on public television. They had a show on people treasures . . . uh . . . the country says these people are treasures . . ."

"National treasures," Addy supplied, remembering seeing the same show.

"And this lady did dresses like this."

"My lord." Addy sat down on a stool. *"You* are a treasure."

Emmaline smiled and scoffed, "I'm too young, Addy. They were all old. Probably thirty-five or even forty."

"You're a young treasure," Addy assured her.

"Aw, Addy, you're always so nice."

And Addy blushed as she remembered how often she'd complained about Emmaline to Marcus.

But the day wasn't over.

The mail had come as usual. Miss Pru sorted it. As happened routinely each day, she put Addy's mail on the credenza in her office. There was rarely anything earthshaking in the mail and therefore no particular need to open it immediately, so Addy left it there until just after lunch.

There was one letter, an ordinary letter. Nothing about it indicated that it was different. It was from California, she noted before slitting it open. It was addressed to her as a personal letter, and it was from Paul Morris.

CHAPTER EIGHT

EVEN THOUGH SHE'D glanced at the signature and read the "Paul," Addy didn't really believe it was from Paul Morris. But her body became very still as she read the note without actually absorbing the words. She had to read it several times before she really understood that it *was* Paul who'd written, and what it was that he'd said.

"I know you'll be surprised to hear from me. I thought about you a couple of times after I left and wondered how you got along.

"I got a copy of the *Journal* a while back and saw the picture of a little girl named Grendel Kildaire. Kildaire isn't a common name, and it said her mother was a designer and that's what your masters was, so I decided to write and find out if you kept the kid and if she's mine.

103

"She's about the right age and she looks like all the kids in my family. You can write me here. Paul."

Addy's emotions ran from shock at hearing from him after such a long time, to indignation that he'd had the nerve to write to her, to fury that he'd dare to ask if the child was *his!* She released an animal roar, a mixture of maternal protection, the humiliation she'd endured, and the burden of worry and loneliness of the last four years. It was a primal crying out against all the injustice of the abandonment she'd endured at his hands.

Miss Pru hurried in just as Addy was tearing the letter apart in the first act of destroying her enemy. The sharp cry of "Adelina!" stopped her. She raised almost mad eyes to Miss Pru, not recognizing her. The older woman said her name again, but the tone was gentle, reaching out to her.

Addy turned stark, staring eyes to Miss Pru and just looked at her, as if seeing safety in a storm-tossed sea. Miss Pru lifted a slow hand to her arm and asked, "What is it?"

Addy stared down at the ripped page in her hand. As understanding returned, she held her rigid hands out toward Miss Pru, who took the pieces from Addy's stiffened fingers, then went to the desk to fit the pieces together so that she could read it.

When she'd done that, she looked at Addy and said gently, "I won't say anything right now. It will be better if I think about my words first."

Addy stood stock still, every muscle rigid. "She isn't *his*. She's *mine!*"

"Yes, dear, I know. Let me think about this," Miss Pru said placatingly.

"How dare he!" Addy trembled with fury.

"That's true, Addy, but not about the note. It's true of some of Paul's conduct. But let's calm ourselves and not say or do anything rash. Let's just put this aside until we can think clearly."

"I don't need to think! Not about this." She jerked her hand in the air.

Calmly Miss Pru took Scotch tape and repaired the letter. Then, as Addy stood there like a stone statue, Miss Pru read it silently again. She put the letter inside a folder, out of sight. "I'll put this in the file cabinet of business letters, under 'M' for Morris."

"How about 'R' for rat?" Addy snapped.

"Or we could put it under 'W' for weasel." Miss Pru tendered a small, coaxing smile.

Addy would have none of it. " 'B' for bastard!" she snarled.

Miss Pru nodded, raising her eyebrows with a thoughtful expression. "That's a fairly accurate description," she agreed.

Through her teeth, Addy growled, "He thought about me 'a couple of times'!"

"Yes." Miss Pru's voice was soft and comforting. "I know."

"How dare he?" Addy raged. "He takes off, leaving me with the consequences of his lust, and he thinks about me 'a couple of times'!"

"It's been a shock, hearing this way," she offered.

"After all you and I had to go through just because of him!"

"But some good came of it, Addy. We have Grendel. And I found you. My life was so empty before you came to my house."

"Look what it did to my parents. What would have happened to Grendel and me if we hadn't found you?"

"Well, it would have been extremely dull for me, I'll tell you that!" And Miss Pru smiled again.

Addy walked stiffly to the window and stood staring

out at the woods. The temperature was edging up into the low thirties, turning yesterday's brief snow into slush.

"Would you like me to ask Sam to come over?" Miss Pru suggested. "He's very sensible and—"

"No! I've had enough of men. Look what being with a man has done to our lives."

"You don't . . . regret keeping Grendel, do you?"

Addy's head whipped around, and she glowered at Miss Pru. "Of course not!" she snapped. "How could you ever think that?"

"Then you can't resent Paul . . ." Miss Pru began.

"It was ghastly . . . being with him. So embarrassing. So intimate! It was terrible."

"You're primarily upset that he left you," Miss Pru went on.

"That's right! The bastard. I could wring his neck!"

"Addy!" Miss Pru managed to almost frown as she straightened and tried hopelessly to look formidable.

"Sorry." But Addy was sulky and her response came automatically. She wasn't really contrite.

Again picking up the thread of her evaluation of Addy's conflict, Miss Pru said, "You don't resent becoming pregnant and having Grendel as much as you're insulted that Paul would leave you to solve your problem all by yourself."

"And writing four years later and asking, 'Hey, is that my kid?' You're darned right I resent him. Insulted? That's not quite the word. At the time I was horrified, trapped, devastated, embarrassed . . . All those things, and on top of it all I had to face my parents and tell them. It tore me in two. I still haven't healed, and I doubt my parents ever will."

"I know it was very difficult for all of you."

"But you didn't judge me," Addy pointed out.

"My love, don't you see that I was in a unique position? I needed only to judge you according to my own ideas. Your parents judged not only you but also themselves. Don't you see they can't forgive *themselves?* They still feel they failed you. Grendel reminds them of that.

"People are extremely complicated," Miss Pru went on. "Body language is supposed to be a science and you can 'read' someone by the way they sit or stand or move their facial muscles. To me that's too much like Freud, who said the mind was conditioned and driven by sex.

"To say sex alone is responsible for our behavior is like the six blind men touching the elephant. One felt the tail and said an elephant was like a rope. One fingered the tusk and said a heavy spear. Another, handling the ear, said it was like a leaf. And the one who felt the leg said it was a tree. 'No,' said the one at the trunk, 'it's a snake.' And the one who touched the side said an elephant was a large wall. They were all right.

"The mind's that way—very large and diverse. How can we tell what influences the way people react? A person doesn't talk or listen on one level. You listen to another person speak, plan what to reply, are reminded of something else entirely, and your thoughts go along on an altogether different course.

"You may cross a leg one way because of pain, or a twinge of gas, or a body hair caught on your underwear. There are too many levels all working at once to guess why anyone does anything. Our minds are too complex and busy. We try to oversimplify."

"But people go into therapy to find out why they do things."

"We might discover something there, a comfortable reason, and if we do, fine. But the real reason could be lost because it was such a silly thing, so meaningless, so casually said or seen that it doesn't make an individual impression. It just sank into our busy brain and perhaps touched something else, which then influenced how we see ourselves in the mirror, or what part of ourselves, or how we see our children."

Addy capsuled it: "So everyone should just do his own thing and forget about agonizing over how other people will react."

"No, no, no." Miss Pru shook her head and lifted a staying hand. "No one can do that and you know it. I sometimes think you come up with ideas like that just to raise my dander." She studied Addy carefully. "Rules can be silly, but you can count on the golden one, doing unto others as you would have them do unto you. And the big ten are superb guidelines, though most of those are incorporated into the golden one. And, Addy, that one is good to keep in mind as you consider Paul's letter."

Addy's look turned hostile, but Miss Pru smiled gently and said, "I'll file this under 'M.' It doesn't have to be dealt with today." She turned at the door. "Did you see Emmaline's batiks? Aren't they gorgeous?"

"Oh, Miss Pru, and I've treated her so badly."

"See? Body language. You thought she was lazy, but she's a dreamer of beautiful things."

"And the colors! They're exquisite."

"Are you going to use them?" Miss Pru asked gently.

"Oh, yes! I thought I'd do simple frocks of solid colors so that the scarves will star."

"Excellent. Have you chosen any of the samples?"

"Several. A couple will be garish, and we'll have to make sure only women who they flatter buy them. You'll have to do that. Your color sense is staggering."

"Oh? Let me see," Miss Pru said, and they began to leave the office, pausing only long enough for Miss Pru to file the folder under 'M.' They climbed to the attic to gawk and exclaim over Emmaline's art treasures.

So the letter was put aside, but Addy didn't forget it. It haunted her. And her determination to shun Paul and spurn any attempt to contact Grendel was solidified.

Sam arrived in time for dinner that evening. He carried two cases into the house—his medical bag and another small one. He also brought Miss Pru a hostess plant, and she said she'd start a greenhouse if he kept that up.

When Addy gave him a cold stare, he grinned at her in encouragement, but he didn't try to take her in his arms.

At the table, Miss Pru set another place, and Grendel hopped around like a cricket. It was very homey. The great big house, the aroma of good cooking, the bright faces—though Addy knew hers was sour—all created a feeling of constancy and security.

"We have a hard freeze coming up." Sam offered that bit of news. "But it shouldn't last. March came in like a lion and therefore it will have to go out like a lamb."

"I've got a new book," Miss Pru murmured. "I'll just crawl into bed and read."

Grendel went under the kitchen table and growled, pretending to be the March lion. Sam squatted down and asked her, "Are you a bunny?"

"Noooooo!"

He thought elaborately and asked, "Are you a bird?"

"Noooooo!" Grendel had to smother giggles with her hand.

"Well, what in the world *are* you?"

"A fear-OOO-shus *lion!*"

Sam hit his forehead with the flat of his palm and said, "Of course!"

Addy went stiffly about, doing her share of the chores and giving Miss Pru disapproving glances for making Sam feel so welcome. Miss Pru ignored her.

During dinner, Miss Pru mentioned Emmaline's batiks and suggested, "Sam, you'll want to see them."

When he agreed, Miss Pru should have flown backward clear down the hall with the force of the furious glance Addy sent her. Instead she just smiled.

Addy figured that maybe Sam would forget Miss Pru's suggestion, but he didn't. After the dishwasher was loaded and humming, Sam said, "I'd really like to see what Emmaline has been up to. How about now?"

"Ask Miss Pru," Addy said stiffly.

"Why would I climb two flights of stairs when I have a young lady who'll volunteer?" Miss Pru pinched Addy's bottom and hissed for her to behave herself.

Addy led Sam sullenly toward the more formal grand staircase at the entrance. To use the back stairs would be including him too informally. He paused briefly, but she went up the stairs in measured steps as if to a firing squad. He took the steps two at a time and caught up with her. "When Grendel gets married, it'll have to be here," he decided.

She gave him a stern, quelling flick of a stare to show him that how or where Grendel was married was none of his affair. He might still be feeling squashily sentimental after tossing her in bed the day before, but she herself was feeling daggers through her vitals from Paul's letter.

Sam stopped on the second floor and told her he'd be back in just a minute. He had to, as he informed her, "put my shaving kit in my room."

"*Your* room!" she exploded.

But he strode off, entered the room he'd slept in the day before, and came out, grinning at her as he closed the door. "The bed's stripped. Clean sheets every day?"

Carefully spacing the words, she said gratingly, "You are not moving in here."

"Oh," he said, and his face was puzzled. "Well, at least the next time I'd have shaving things here, and I wouldn't have to go down to breakfast all whiskery. Of course, you all did seem to enjoy the whiskers. I could wait to shave them off until just before I had to leave the house."

"There will be no next time. You are not going to stay here at all!"

"No one can predict anything." He smiled at her confidently. Then he glanced around. "Where're the stairs?"

She wanted to settle once and for all that the room was not his, but he took her arm, and she gestured automatically toward the door to the attic stairs. She was gathering the proper argument when he kissed her mouth, and the words scattered off in all directions. While she was furiously searching for them again, she had to try to push down the waves of desire his kiss had exploded inside her.

By that time they were up the attic stairs. Sam reached around her to open the door, leaning so close that she breathed the male scent of him. Her senses were affected in such a swooning, irrational way that she stumbled.

He steadied her, grinned down at her, and kissed her again. Then he looked around, apparently not at all affected by her kisses the way she was by his. She seized on that thought and worried over it. Why wasn't he equally affected?

Sam whistled, impressed with the batiks. "The girls have to see these."

"What girls?" Addy retorted waspishly. All of his harem?

Absently, engrossed in the beautiful scarves, he replied, "My sisters."

"Oh," she said feebly.

"This is Ann." He touched one. "That's Cyn." He

pointed to another. "And...that's Terry." He nodded toward his last choice.

She became indignant. "I want that one."

"No." He was positive. "This one is you. I saw it as soon as I opened the door."

"That one?" She eyed it, astonished.

"It's complicated and subtle, the way you are. And it's beautiful." He turned to her. "The way you are." He kissed her just as beautifully.

That was when she should have jerked back and taken a firm stand about the room he was appropriating down-stairs and his place *outside* her life. It was the best time to present a clear, concise admonition. The knowledge that it was the right time did cross her mind fleetingly. But with his kiss, she lost track of what she was supposed to be firm about. She had a fragmented idea that she could come back to it and get it all sorted out later. After that she drowned in his kiss.

He was really very good at kissing. She excused her participation by thinking that, when you find someone that good, you should appreciate it as you would fine music or dazzling colors. You need to give your attention to such talent and relish and enjoy. She did that.

Finally he paused and smiled, just above her face and out of focus. "Do I get clean sheets every night?" he whispered. She couldn't remember why they would have to go to all the trouble of putting clean sheets down on the studio floor; it was only a little dusty. But before she could start to undress him to make love, he asked softly, "What could I have done or said to make you so cross with me?"

It was like splashing a bucket of cold water over her. Paul rushed back to her mind. She jerked free and tried to recall the words she needed to make it clear that Sam was not going to become a part of her life.

"Sam," she began, but instead of looking serious and subdued, he smiled down at her with great tenderness and reached to take her hand. She jerked it away from him. "You are not moving in here. You go right this minute and get that shaving kit out of that room. That room is not yours. I am not a convenient lay for you just because you need sex and haven't the control—"

"Hey. What's up?"

That flustered her, and she had to straighten out her tongue in order to continue. "I will not go to bed with you, so just forget it."

"What happened? Something's wrong. I'm almost sure I haven't said anything. If I did, I didn't intend to put you on your ear. It has to be someone else. Who said what?" His concern was irritatingly sweet.

"No one said anything. It's just that I don't want to get involved with any man."

"I didn't hurt you, did I? I tried to be gentle with you, but God, Addy, you were fantastic and I—"

"No, no," she interrupted, "you didn't do anything." She looked at him, feeling full of hurt, and admitted, "It was lovely, but..."

"Then did I say anything? Honey, I'm on your side all the way. I can't think of anything I might have said that could've made you unhappy—"

"No, you've been very sweet and I—"

"Then it was someone else." His eyes questioned her solemnly as he promised, "I'll break his neck. Who was it?"

"It's just...Sam, I just don't want any kind of a relationship."

"Is it *all* men or just me?"

"Oh, Sam, it isn't anything to do with you."

"It has everything to do with me."

"I feel terrible about this. I shouldn't have—"

"I don't feel much like laughing myself right now."

"Sam..." She was almost pleading instead of being firm.

"You have to tell me what it is. How can I fix it until I know what's wrong? Tell me who's hurt you." His low voice coaxed her. "Remember, I can damn near fix anything."

She might have told him then except that she and Miss Pru had shoved the threat of Paul into a file drawer so that he wouldn't loom so badly. She just couldn't cope with her feelings for Sam. He was too devastating. Her feelings for him threatened to swamp her at a time when she needed a clear head to deal with the threat of Paul. She'd always handled and solved her own problems. In spite of Miss Pru, Addy felt she was alone in the world and Grendel's only protection.

"My interest in you isn't a casual interlude," Sam told her. "I'm serious about you, Addy. I'm so serious about you that I'm willing to back off and take it easy until you're ready to consider how much I do care. We'll be friends in the meantime. All right?"

Not believing he could be serious, she eyed him cautiously, but his face was very earnest. Their eyes locked, and she knew that, although she might not be able to handle an intimate affair with him just yet, she didn't want to lose him. She held out her hand. He lifted it to his heart and, his eyes steady on her, ventured, "Friends can kiss."

She gave him a wan smile. He leaned forward and very gently kissed her mouth in undemanding sympathy. It almost wrecked her.

CHAPTER NINE

THE NEXT AFTERNOON Diana Hunter called to say that the sleet was so bad she was going to stay at the studio and not even try to go home. Was it all right for Grendel to stay too? Addy said yes. But just after six, when Sam arrived, Diana called again to say that Grendel was running a fever and what did one do with a child who was sick?

Sam said he'd take Addy to Diana's studio and bring Grendel home. On the way there, Addy sat rigidly still, amazed by Sam's skill in driving on the slick streets. When they arrived at Diana's, Sam wouldn't let Addy needlessly risk the walk and made her sit in the car while he went inside. He came out carrying a bundled-up Grendel, whom he put carefully on Addy's lap for the drive home.

He was so skilled on the ice that Addy didn't realize he was deliberately exaggerating the road conditions. When they turned into her deserted street, the car slid sideways for a heart-stopping fifty feet or so. He allowed it to creep into her driveway and slide to a calculated stop. He grinned at her. "Whew! Wasn't that a lot of fun?" He laughed when she grimaced. Then he said, "It's a good thing I left my shaving kit here. I believe you wouldn't turn a knight out on a dog like this." She gave him a hesitant look as he slid out of the car. He insisted Addy stay there while he carried Grendel into the house. Then he came back for Addy.

He hadn't exaggerated the difficulty in walking. It was treacherous. She accepted the fact that he would have to stay the night.

All evening long Addy was quiet, distracted, and aloof, although Grendel's temperature didn't frighten her. They had put her to bed and made her comfortable. Grendel did her best to seem pitiful. She raised a tiny hand to her forehead and let out languishing sighs. Sam predicted a cold was in the offing. He recommended a nice glass of orange juice and cautioned Addy not to overdo the vitamin C. Addy only muttered, "What do you know?" as she mashed up another vitamin C pill and dumped it into the orange juice.

For dinner Miss Pru served sausage patties, baked potatoes, green beans, carrots, and applesauce with hot biscuits and honey. Sam smiled like a large cat that's been stroked and patted his stomach as he told Addy to convey his compliments to the chef, who sat across the table and smirked. Addy decided Grendel had absorbed her dramatics by osmosis from Miss Pru.

They'd almost finished eating when Grendel appeared like a waif in the doorway from the back stairs. She stood there until they'd all seen her, then said forlornly that she was lonely upstairs...all by herself. She assumed the expression of an abandoned child. Addy wondered if the worn teddy bear, dangling to the floor from one hand, was a calculated touch. Surely Grendel was too young to be that deliberately theatrical.

"Maybe you're not lonely," Addy suggested. "Maybe you're just hungry. Perhaps what you need is some applesauce? And how about a nice hot biscuit with some honey?"

Grendel tried to keep her pose, but a grin crept over her face and she said, "Yes!" She scrambled to her chair and climbed up on it while Addy adroitly slid her padded seat under her. Grendel smiled around the table, ready for the party.

Addy watched her child covertly, knowing she was the most charming and delightful little girl in all the world. But she monitored Grendel's behavior, giving her a ready smile, a slight shake of her head, or a cautioning *shhh* in order to keep her from taking over. Grendel was so darling, it would be easy for Addy to indulge her.

Feeling Sam's eyes on her, Addy sometimes sneaked a glance at him. His smile held such approval that her eyes fled from his.

After the meal he helped clear the table as if he was family, choosing what to give Grendel to help carry to the kitchen.

Then Sam picked her up and carried her back upstairs to her room. He hadn't asked Addy if that was what she wanted him to do, and she sent a resentful glare at his retreating back. He'd even used the back stairs.

Not long after that the furnace went off. Addy heard its dying shudder in the kitchen and locked eyes with Miss Pru, appalled. Addy instantly went to the phone to call Marcus.

The Freeman phone was picked up and, since there

was no reply, Addy knew it was Hedda. "Oh, Hedda, the furnace just quit, and Grendel's sick, and it's so cold. But it's so icy outside. Is there any way at all that Marcus can come over?" There was a pause, then the phone was quietly replaced.

Addy hung up and looked around at a sound from the back hall. Followed by the slippered, robed Grendel, Sam had come down the back stairs. "That sounded like the last gasp of the last mammoth. The furnace?"

The women nodded. He looked around the kitchen, then back into the hall. "Where's the basement door?"

"Can you fix it?" Addy asked doubtfully.

He gave her a clear-eyed, surprised look. "It can't be too different from recalcitrant children, can it? All you have to do is kick it and show it who's boss, right?"

"That's how a pediatric consultant works?"

"Is there another way?"

"He was telling me a story," Grendel said in an accusing tone, as if they'd contrived the interruption.

Sam picked her up and promised, "Right after the furnace is fixed, I'll finish. First things first."

With her arms possessively around Sam's neck, Grendel blinked at Addy. "It's about a darling little girl." Her three-year-old grasp of pronunciation made that "dawing widdle gul."

Addy gave her child a patient look, showed Sam the basement door, and followed him down. There he surveyed the monster, now dead, that took up the middle of the central room. It looked like a giant metal squid with multiple arms which reached into the far recesses of the great house. Sam whistled, impressed. "Has the Smithsonian Institution contacted you about it yet?"

"We've taken only sealed bids, so we're not sure."

Sam walked around it, still carrying Grendel, who also looked around with interest from her comfortable perch in Sam's arms. When he returned to Addy, he handed Grendel to her without a word and opened the door of the somnolent giant. "Umm-humph," he said, then turned to Addy and explained, "My first year of med school there was one whole semester of 'Umm-humph' in all the various ways. Vital class."

"Of course," she agreed seriously as she set Grendel down on the Ping-Pong table.

Sam peered again into the dark vitals of the furnace. The sound of a key at the outside door caused them to turn. The door opened, and another giant descended into the basement. Marcus had arrived like a dark knight to the rescue.

"Oh, Marcus!" Addy exclaimed. "You got here!" "Thank goodness you were home," she added.

Sam looked offended and said to Marcus, "I hadn't even begun..."

Marcus stopped and said, "Oh. You fixing it? Good." Sober-faced, he turned to go.

"Marcus..." Addy wailed.

"I'm a *consultant!*" Sam said with asperity.

Marcus turned back. "You intend to check me out?"

Sam sized up the furnace and said, "It can't be too different from people." He waved his arms vaguely. "Body, appendages, heart, lungs..."

"And we're going to operate?"

"Never needlessly," Sam replied, holding up an admonishing finger. The two men exchanged smiles. Then Marcus went over, peered inside, squatted down, and looked closer. He stood up and gave a connection a thumping kick...and the furnace rumbled back to life.

Addy burst out laughing, and Sam gave her a smug look as he said, "See? I told you all it needed was a good kick."

Marcus raised his shaggy eyebrows and explained,

"It's knowing *where* to kick."

Sam reached out a congratulatory hand and said, "Magnificent. It's always awesome to watch an expert."

Marcus permitted an acknowledging nod and offered, "Want me to help in your next operation?"

"I know too much about you to doubt you could." Sam smiled. "You're a dark horse." But the one who wins the race, Addy thought.

Marcus rolled his eyes and sighed. "You honkies never can resist."

That only made Sam grin wider. "I know you're a mechanical genius. You..."

Before he turned away, Marcus cast Sam a quick look and said, "Keep it to yourself." The words in that soft voice were an order.

"After he tells me," Addy said.

But Marcus only gave Sam another stern glance as he went up the steps to leave.

Addy put out a detaining hand in his direction and called, "I need to talk to you about Emmaline."

Without pausing he called back, "That'll solve itself."

"I think it has," Addy replied.

Marcus turned on the stairs and gave her a level look. "What do you mean?"

"She's a genius. You should see what she can do painting cloth, batiks, silk screening. Good lord, Marcus, you have to come and look!"

"I shall tomorrow. We have dinner guests, and I must return."

"I am so sorry," Addy began to apologize.

"No need to fret, child. I probably saved the furnace from dismemberment at the doctor's hands." Then he told Sam kindly, "Remember, I've had a three-year graduate course in that museum piece. I know all its quirks."

"Mr. Freeman . . ." A small voice came from the Ping-Pong table.

"That you, pixie?"

"You didn't say hello."

"That's 'cause you're a pixie. I can't see you all the time."

"I'm here."

"I see you." He nodded once in formal acknowledgment.

"You can't see me?" Grendel was interested.

Gravely, Marcus explained, "It's like fairies and elves. Can you see them all the time?"

Grendel considered that, her eyes moving as she concentrated. Finally she shook her head. Marcus nodded, turned, and left, then locked the door from the outside.

Addy whirled around to Sam, jumping with curiosity. "How old is he? Do you really know all about him? Does he have enough money? I worry about taking up so much of his time, and he really doesn't charge much, and he generally gives it to someone else. How old is he? Pearl is his daughter, and she's twenty, so he has to be at least forty. Hedda's not his first wife; how many has he had? She's not Pearl's mother. Does she speak at all?"

"Hey!" Sam protested. "He just told me to keep my mouth shut. Would you want me to go back on my word?"

"You didn't give your word."

"I sure did. Marcus only looked at me, but I'll do it his way, and he knows it."

"He is large. But I'm dying to know how old he is."

"Why?"

"I keep trying to figure it out. It would make a difference how I speak to him. I treat him as if he's about your age—"

"I'm not forty!" Sam protested.

"—But if he's older, I shouldn't argue with him quite so much."

"Age gets respect from you?"

"Well, the way I was brought up..." She stopped and blushed. She hadn't been brought up to jump in bed with men either.

"How old are you, Addy?"

"Twenty-seven," she said readily.

"I'm thirty-nine."

She grinned slowly as she raised her eyes to his. "So you're not forty."

"No, I'm not!"

"That's when life begins," she commented.

"Oh, it does, does it? What do you know?"

"I know a lot of women over forty. That's a smashing age for women, and at forty men haven't yet reached their peak."

"Speaking of peaks and perks—" he began.

"Have you ever been married?"

"No." He shook his head a couple of times.

"Why not?" How could he ever have escaped?

"I hadn't yet...met the right one." He lifted his hand to her face and leaned down to kiss her mouth very gently.

Just then a plaintive little voice said, "I'm a little cold."

The adults looked around in surprise, and there sat Grendel in her woolly bathrobe, cross-legged on the Ping-Pong table, watching them. "Where have you been?" Addy asked her.

"Just sitting here...waiting." She sighed theatrically.

"I didn't see you," her mother told her.

"That's 'cause I'm a...patsy?"

"Pixie."

Grendel nodded sagely. "Pixies is hard to see."

Sam picked her up and kissed her forehead. "A cool pixie. Are you hungry?"

"Yes," she said like a child lost in the woods for two weeks who'd survived on berries and bark.

"How about toasted biscuits with jelly and orange juice?"

"Orange juice on biscuits?" A three-year-old can be literal, Addy thought.

"No." Sam was patient. "You put jelly on biscuits and drink orange juice."

That made more sense. With Sam carrying Grendel, they left the metal squid humming in the basement and went up to the kitchen. It was only about eight o'clock. Once Grendel's small personal furnace had been stoked, they took her up the back stairs to her room and tucked her in again. She yawned and yawned and blinked and smiled. She wasn't even trying, and she looked adorable.

Addy allowed herself a brief kiss, touched Grendel's forehead with reassuring fingers, and gave her child a dewy smile. Sam watched Addy, who was gazing at Grendel as she hugged her teddy bear, popped her thumb in her mouth, and sighed, her heavy eyelids closing.

In the hall, Addy and Sam stopped and looked at one another before Sam moved to take Addy into his arms. She remained stiff, her mouth tightening.

"How could you be so cold after that tender, warm scene in Grendel's room?" he complained.

"I'm not going to . . . be with you . . . for the night . . ." The words came out in a jumble.

"For the night?" he questioned.

"I can understand a man your age not being a virgin . . ."

"A virgin?" he asked. "A no-woman's land?"

"But there is no way I'm going to allow you to add

me to your list of convenient women when you feel the urge."

"Urge? As in—"

"And you keep your distance. I know the ice is dangerous, and you may stay this one more time, but in the morning you will pack up your shaving kit and vacate! Do you understand?"

"Urge like for ice cream? Or chocolate?"

"Pearl's chocolate. I'm vanilla." She gave him a stern glance.

"I've always liked vanilla."

"Forget it," she admonished.

He was incredulous. "Forget vanilla ice cream? Never speak to my mother? Give up my car?"

"You know very well what I'm talking about."

"You've been reading too many books. Bachelors can only wish their lives were really what people believe them to be. A bachelor is lonely, forlorn...sad. He needs warm love and good food and a sweet woman to hold." He again tried to take her into his arms.

Resisting, she said, "No, Sam, I've just told you—"

"Come on, baby, cuddle with me. It's cold and icy outside, and I'm a stranger in a strange house with no friends." He grasped her pushing hands, pulling her close enough to nuzzle her throat and the side of her face. He blew gently into her ear and chuckled low in his throat. "Now, then. I've just blown in your ear and you'll follow me anywhere." He released her and walked briskly toward his room, hesitated, looked back, and paused. He frowned at her and sighed in exaggerated irritation. "You're *supposed* to come running after me!"

She shook her head, assuming a serious expression. He examined her face with amused eyes. "There's nothing like a challenge." And feeling no need to explain, he offered his arm formally with a slight bow and said,

"Shall we adjourn to the parlor, Miss Kildaire? I am the champion backgammon player of all northern Indianapolis—although Gina Stephens tenaciously keeps challenging me for a rematch—and I shall allow you to take lessons for an hour or so. I'll match you a free house call for a simple silk dressing gown."

"That'll be three free house calls to one silk dressing gown!" she objected, as they descended the grand staircase.

"Done. In a deep blood-red."

"Don't count your dressing gown before it's sewn."

"My child, you have no idea what you're up against." He leered at her smugly.

His words could mean many things, and she wasn't sure if he was still talking about backgammon. "Red again," she said. "You're hooked on red."

"Only because you tend to choose it and I like you in that color."

She turned that color too. She'd been making red clothes to wear with him, and she was wearing a red turtleneck with white woolen slacks at that moment. She'd bought the sweater two days ago, and she'd made the slacks yesterday.

Courteously he inquired, "May I bring some friends to your party?"

They were moving the two-seater sofa to face the fire as she asked, "Party?"

He replaced the marble-topped table in front of the sofa and replied, "Yes."

Squatting in front of the cabinet to find the game board, she paused and turned to ask, "The next showing? May's fall showing?"

He looked at her in surprise. "No. St. Patrick's Day."

"St. Patrick's Day?"

"St. Patrick's Day. Anyone named Kildaire would

automatically have a party on St. Patrick's Day. It would be un-American not to."

She couldn't believe that. "Un-American?"

"Of course. Like not having pizza on the Fourth."

"I'm not Catholic."

"Well, you can wear orange! You don't *have* to wear green. Irish Protestants wear orange! But not around the greenies. They tend to get upset."

"What will ever happen to Ireland?" she asked sadly.

"God knows." He shook his head. "And the irony of it all is it's done in the name of God, like in the Middle East. Now don't get me started on that, because we have to talk about the party."

"I haven't had a party since . . . in a long time."

"Then it's time." They shook the dice to see who would lead off, and he won and said that was a portent and he'd choose the silk for his robe during intermission. "How can you say you've had no parties when you have the showings?" he asked.

"That's business," she replied dismissively.

"But they're great parties. With all the big doors slid back into the walls, which opens up the entrance, and the drawing room, the dining room, and this parlor— it's perfect for crowd flow. How many shall we have?"

"We?" she asked cautiously.

"I'll split the cost and bring the booze. Will Hedda cater for a St. Patrick's Day party? We could have a George Washington Carver one to balance."

"We?" she asked again.

"We ought to be able to handle two hundred."

"Two hundred? I don't know that many people."

"I do." Sam counted points, moving his marker. "It'll be a blast. Next year we'll have to screen applicants for invitations."

"Next year?" Things were going too fast.

"Any parrot blood in your family?"

Realizing she'd been repeating his words, she had to ask, "Parrot blood?"

"Right," he said, then added, "You've lost this game. It's your turn, and you can take it if you'd like to go out bloody but unbowed. However, there is no way you can catch up. You could concede and thus practice conceding to me. You'll have a lot of use for the talent. When . . . you marry, will you allow Grendel to be adopted by . . . your husband?"

"If he wants to." She was taking her turn stubbornly.

"You wouldn't mind?"

"If a man loved me enough to marry me, he'd be a man who'd love children, and he'd be a good father to Grendel."

"I have a great many talents besides backgammon." He lowered his eyelids and looked humorously wicked.

She smiled in defeat.

CHAPTER TEN

ICE WAS STILL ticking on the windows when Miss Pru took a new paperback book up to her room to read in bed. Addy and Sam barely interrupted their hotly competitive game to bid her good night. Addy won the second game. Sam said that was only for her morale. He couldn't allow a student to get too discouraged.

"How did you know I liked backgammon?" she asked, curious.

"A glint in the eye, a quickness of the hand, the outthrust of the jaw..." He waved one large hand in small circles as he listed the symptoms.

"You make me sound like a pirate coming on board ship with a cutlass clasped between my teeth."

He nodded and agreed. "Very similar." Then he asked,

129

"May I have a key to the house?"

That startled her. She said, "A *key?*" as if she hadn't heard him correctly. "I've *told* you, Samuel Grady, that . . ."

He looked at her with tolerant patience and said, "If I'm called on an emergency, I'll need to be able to get back in."

"Oh." That was logical, so she got up and went to the jar in the entrance hall and brought back a key and handed it to him.

Putting it on his key chain, he said, "You wouldn't want me to sleep huddled in the car, freezing to death, not being able to get back inside, would you?"

She frowned. "If you could get back here, you could get back to your own apartment."

"You are the most inhospitable woman! You won't even let me sleep in your room on the floor! You put me clear down the hall in a separate room!"

"You really have no need for that key," she exclaimed and held out her hand. "Give it back."

He smiled.

"Sam."

"The way your lips move when you say my name boggles my mind."

"That's because you're an old roué, a practiced, forty-year-old—"

"Thirty-nine."

"How many years have you been thirty-nine?" She raised supercilious eyebrows.

"Vicious. You won one game and look at you! It's turned you into a smug, predatory, snarling wolverine. I'm terrified." He stretched and yawned. "Tell me about your life and times."

"Are you an old roué?"

"I'm a young, thirty-nine-year-old, innocent boy."

"Hah."

"Now, Addy, you know anyone who's been out in practice five years is still wet behind the ears. I had my nose to the grindstone, studying, from age six to thirty-two. That's almost thirty years! Think about that. I was in school longer than you've been alive."

"What do you know?"

He laughed, then said, "Well . . . a thing or two."

"Can you sew a gusset?"

"It just so happens, madam, that I am quite good at needlework. You should see me do a three-cornered skin tear." He raised his chin and looked down his nose at her. "What would you do with a ruptured intestine?"

"I'd call Marcus. He can fix anything."

Sam frowned at her and said, "So can I." Then, still frowning, he leaned forward. "Come on, I've got to beat you another set to make sure you realize I'm the winner, and then I'll choose the silk for my dressing gown."

She fought to the final roll, but she lost. She gave him a grim, grudging "Good game."

He acknowledged it. "You're an interesting competitor." Then he smiled. "You move so nicely, and when you shake the dice, you jiggle entrancingly—"

"Sam," she began.

"—and I beat you with one hand tied behind my back."

Disgruntled, she said through clenched teeth, "You had the use of both hands."

"No, if you will notice I never moved my left hand off the arm of the sofa."

She looked at his arm and knew he was telling the truth. "Which shows that a one-armed man could play backgammon?"

"Actually, it shows that the skill doesn't involve the use of both hands. It's not like making love. Then you need all four."

"You have four hands?"

"Haven't you ever dated any one of us? We do try to be subtle, but passion brings out all four hands. It's like our third eye."

"Third eye?"

"There's that echo again! The accoustics in this house are remarkable. The third eye is for keyholes. That way your brain is centered as you watch and you're not using only one side—and your nose doesn't get in the way, and your head fits under the doorknob easier."

A chuckle rose inside her as she said, "So you four-armed, three-eyed guys are a bunch of sneaks?"

He nodded gravely. "Would you like to see my third eye?"

She gave him a cautioning look.

"It's in the center of my forehead. It's quite small, so you'll have to look for it very closely. It's small because, of course, keyholes are small; and to look fully you need the entire eye."

Her chuckle escaped and she laughed. "You're really crazy."

He denied that, shaking his head as he explained, "By admitting that we have the third eye, we make people disbelieve us and go undetected." He gave her a small smile and coaxed, "Wouldn't you like to see it?" He reached out his arm and put his hand on the nape of her neck to gently urge her toward him.

"I'm afraid."

His voice went husky and a little rough. "Now why would you ever be afraid of me?"

"It's the threat of the four hands." She suspected that the look of pure innocence she gave him was a little spoiled by the humor she could almost feel dancing in her eyes.

"I'll keep one behind my back," he promised.

"Two," she bargained.

"I'll try," he hedged. Gently he drew her close. She was mesmerized by his mouth. "It's on my forehead," he said. Her eyes moved up to his broad forehead, then caught on his stare, and they smiled at each other before he kissed her.

It was very nice, lying against his sprawled figure, her soft body against his hard one, her mouth being kissed sweetly and his hands moving on her. He used all four. After a time he lifted his mouth and asked, "Did you see it?" His voice was low and intimate and rumbled in his chest.

"What?"

"My third eye."

She shook her head and grinned, amused.

"What did you see?" His hands all moved on her in slow strokings.

"Some comets," she replied lazily. "Colors."

"That's it!"

"Comets and colors?" She was confused.

"I didn't say it was an ordinary eye. When you see it, you see comets and colors."

"How nice," she said vaguely. Then she reminded him, "You said you were going to keep two of them behind your back."

"Two of my eyes? How could I?"

"Two of the four hands."

"No, I said I'd *try*. And I did. It was a terrible struggle, but I was distracted from it by some soft, lovely woman who snuggled against me and kept kissing me and running her hands under my sweater."

"I did not!" she protested. "My hands have been right

on your shoulders and along your head the whole time!"

"You're one of *us!* You have four, too!"

"Good lord!"

He continued teasing flippantly. "Do you know how our species make love?" His eyelids lowered halfway, and he gave her a scorching glance.

She nodded seriously and replied, "Marvelously."

"Oh, Addy." He buried his face in her throat. "Come to bed with me."

"You promised..."

He lifted his face and frowned into hers. "Whatever made me do a stupid thing like that?"

Her hand went up and smoothed back his hair. "I wouldn't have let you stay if you hadn't promised."

"Let me break it," he coaxed.

"I won't! Just because..."

"Okay, we'll do it your way. I'm willing to wait... No, that's not true. I'm dying for you, but I'll wait until you're ready."

She bit her lip to keep from saying she *was* ready. She tried to sit up, away from him, but he wouldn't have that. "I don't mean to make you uncomfortable," she told him.

"It doesn't make any difference whether you're sitting over there or lying against me. It really doesn't even matter whether I'm *with* you. I want you, Addy. You're never out of my mind. I think I've got a really bad case of you. It's probably fatal." He sighed mournfully.

She kissed his chin, then he brought his mouth to hers, and their kiss was lovely. She sighed and cuddled against him with her head on his chest, and she felt great contentment. She'd never had that particular feeling in her whole life, this comfort she had with Sam, the contentment, the security, the belonging. She looked in the fire and wasn't conscious of any thought but the awareness of him beside her, holding her.

"If . . . you married"—Sam's voice rumbled in his chest—"would you have another child?"

"I hadn't thought about that. I haven't thought about marriage. I doubt any man would marry me. How could he take me home to his mother and say, 'This is Addy. Grendel is her child. She's never—'"

"Not that again! Good lord, Addy, let up! I've never seen anyone who carries such a needless load of guilt. Forgive yourself! *And* what's-his-name. It's *past!*"

But it wasn't past. She'd received that letter.

They talked a long time about all sorts of things, and peace returned to their companionship there by the fire. Sam said he could recognize the pitfalls in raising such a delightful child as Grendel. "It's interesting the casual way you and Miss Pru made her a part of your lives without making a big production of it. It would be easy to overdo with Grendel, since she's so adorable, but you two very carefully trod a narrow path that avoids both the role of seeming indifference and that of ruinous indulgence.

"By your judicious reaction to Grendel's behavior, you can enjoy the range of her personality without having to smother it with discipline or creating a monster child with indulgent delight in her. She's precious anyhow, and her talent of exaggeration is precocious, but what is charming at three can be a pain in the neck at seven.

"You don't make her the center of conversation either, and that has to be almost a miracle. You include her but you don't allow her to interrupt or take over. You're astounding."

"It's mostly Miss Pru," Addy said contentedly. "She's such a lady. How can anyone be tacky around her?"

"And Addy," he added indulgently.

She told him about growing up in that small town,

and all the things she'd done; and he told her stories about his childhood, and they began to know each other as they laughed and sympathized and exclaimed with one another; and they planned the St. Patrick's Day party.

They argued over food until Addy explained that whatever they decided on having, they'd get what Hedda fixed. When the food she made was what you'd asked for, you'd hit an Irish sweepstakes by *guessing* what she'd already planned to serve. And how could you argue with her when she wouldn't speak? But whatever Hedda chose to serve, it would be superb. Sam agreed.

He suggested they just ask people in their age group to this first party and expand it the following year. His words stirred a curious feeling in Addy's stomach. It sounded as if Sam was planning an extended relationship. Addy wondered if she was doomed to be his mistress and knew it would be impossible to refuse. She was only delaying the inevitable. She would eventually be his. She wanted him too badly.

Then she asked herself, Why inevitable? Didn't she have some feeling of self-worth? Why should she settle for a live-in relationship? She was capable of running her own life, and she could step off the track before the train hit her. She could do that. She was a woman, and she was strong. She sat up, straightened her hair with her fingers, and pulled down her red sweater. Red . . . she'd stop wearing red first thing.

They turned out the lights and put the screen in front of the fire before they climbed the grand stairway to the second floor. Addy was braced for the big sales pitch and prepared herself to resist, but Sam only gave her a chaste kiss and wished her a tender good-night.

Pensively she checked Grendel, who was a little warm but sleeping soundly, then went to her room. As she wandered around getting ready for bed, she heard the front door open and close, and footsteps on the stairs. Had he been out already? He couldn't have driven any-where in that time. He'd already brought in his medical bag. He'd probably been locking up his car.

She wondered if he would come to her room. Her door wasn't locked. If she was smart, she'd get up and lock it, but what if Grendel wakened in the night and came to her locked door? No, she'd just have to take her chances. It surprised her that her mouth smiled and her body stretched like a lazy cat's before she curled up and went to sleep.

She was awakened by a sound in the night. Her first thought was of Grendel. She got out of bed, dragged on her robe, and shoved her bare feet into cold slippers before going down the hall to Grendel's room. She ran into Sam coming out of it and gasped in surprise. He was dressed.

"Where're you going?" she whispered.

He smiled. "I've been and am back. So you really do wear an old flannel bathrobe."

She blushed. Caught in that tacky old thing. Then she recalled saying on the runway, the first time she'd seen him, that she was manless and the robe she was showing wasn't what she wore to bed, and her blush deepened. He'd remembered.

Sam took her down the hall and leaned her against the wall. He opened the robe and put his hands on her warm, flannel-covered body. He held her close to him and put his still-cold nose into the curve of her throat and breathed his hot breath on her skin as he groaned. He kissed her, his hands molding her to the length of him. Then he said, "If you plan to sleep in your own bed, you'd better go now."

She had to pry his hands slowly off her before she could leave him, her eyes caught by his tense, hungry ones, and then he followed her to her door and stood there as she closed it slowly, shutting out his serious stare.

She lay in bed thinking of him with longing. Then the thought intruded: he'd had on different clothes. Where had he gotten them? Had he gone to his apartment and changed? If he could get to his own place, why would he come back here? She knew why. He wanted her. And he had a better chance of getting her if he was in her house.

Then she remembered that just after they'd come up-stairs she'd heard him returning from outside. Did he have a suitcase in his car? Was he sneakily moving in? And now he had a house key! And he'd gone somewhere but he'd come back *here*. She sat up, indignant. She would not allow that! She would not! Then her heart picked up its beat. To have him here in the same house? To meet him in the hall in the middle of the night—and have him kiss her with that aching hunger? How long could she hold out against herself?

She put her head in her hands and groaned. Then she thought of when he'd come to her after that little boy had died. He'd been in rumpled clothes and unshaven. Perhaps he carried the kit and clothes in his car. That could be. Then if he needed to stay with a child, he could clean up. That sounded logical. He wasn't moving in on her. He simply carried things with him to use in an emergency. But she wasn't sure . . . and he had a key to her front door.

What was Miss Pru about, allowing Sam to become a part of the household the way she was doing? Consider tonight, for instance. Sam had dropped in at dinnertime, and both he and Miss Pru had been sure of his welcome. She'd set another place without even asking him if he would like to stay for dinner. Addy narrowed her eyes at the night-darkened ceiling of her room and asked herself, Was Miss Pru matchmaking?

Surely she wouldn't try to bring Addy and Sam together. It would only lead to a broken heart. Sam wanted her. There was no question of that. But he'd never spoken of marriage. He'd asked if *she* had ever gotten married. . . . She couldn't face being abandoned again. Not that she'd missed Paul. But she loved Sam, and if he tired of her and left her . . .

Of course, he had told her he loved her—when he'd made love to her. Love to her—how fantastic it was to be loved by Sam. To be held and to feel his hands and mouth and body on hers. What a stunning thing to be taken by him, to respond, and to be shown the wonders of love with him.

There was a haunting train whistle sounding through the night. Was the train still at a distance, or had it already passed over her? Was she lying wrecked and broken on the tracks? She didn't feel wrecked and broken. Perhaps she still had a chance. How interesting that she wasn't sure.

CHAPTER ELEVEN

WHEN ADDY GOT up the next morning, she set aside the red and white overblouse she'd made and put on a turquoise top over blue-black slacks. She'd show him she wasn't trying to please him. She looked at herself in the mirror as she braided her hair in a single tight braid, and her mirror image looked back with determined confidence and rather high color.

Dressed in a red flannel shirt, plaid pants, and woolly slippers, Grendel had put a stool under her blanket and was sitting cross-legged in front of the resulting tent, arms folded, talking to a row of dolls and animals lined up on her pillows. She looked at Addy cheerfully and invited her to join the row. Addy declined with thanks and felt her daughter's forehead.

From over by the window in the large room, Sam said, "She's fine. A little stuffy, but fine."

Addy turned in surprise and saw Sam, overwhelming one of the small, overstuffed chairs, reading from a stack of journals. "You're up early," she said.

"Early to bed, early to rise, the crafty man gets the prize." He eyed her with appreciation and breathed a soft whistle. "You look fantastic in blue. My God, you could wreck a man's restraint!"

"I thought you liked red!" Addy blurted.

His eyes gleamed. "That was before I saw you in blue."

"Turquoise," she corrected. "Have you eaten?" She had changed the subject from herself, but she felt flustered. Why could he knock her off balance so easily? She straightened her spine and lifted her chin and planted her feet a little more firmly. "Have you had breakfast?"

"Oh, yes. Grendel was lonely and came in."

Addy gasped. "You woke him up?" she asked her daughter.

"He talk in the morning." Grendel spaced the words of her long sentence.

And Sam observed, "Apparently you're not too chatty first light?"

"Are you packed?"

"Well . . . no." He smiled.

"What do you mean, 'No'?" Addy said a little belligerently.

His words permeated with laughter, he chided, "That doesn't sound like the gracious hostess of Ye Olde Inn. You must practice sounding hospitable."

"Sam." Her warning word was sharper, for she'd just realized he was wearing something yet again different: dark blue slacks with a green and blue rugby shirt. Where had they come from?

"Look outside, hostess mine. I believe I'll be around for another day or so."

Her wide eyes opening wider in trepidation, Addy searched his grinning face. Then he rose, took her arm, and led her, faltering, over to the window, where he lifted aside the lace to show her the winter wonderland of an ice-encased world. Every branch, twig, wire, and post was enclosed or covered with ice. The entire landscape was softened with fog.

The silence was the most remarkable thing. There was no traffic coming into the city. She hadn't been aware of that until now. "Listen," she said to Sam. They all stayed silent and listened to the absence of sound.

Companionably, the very large and very small early birds accompanied Addy downstairs and smacked their way avidly through her breakfast. Of course, no one else could show up for the workday, so they declared a holiday. Miss Pru went back to bed. The paperback had been such a good book she hadn't been able to stop reading and had been up very late finishing it.

Addy, Sam, and Grendel checked the birds, who were the only living things moving in that icy world. There was an electric warmer in the birdbath to keep the water from freezing, but they had to throw birdseed on top of the ice; all the rest was frozen underneath it. And since the porches and outside stairs were coated, they had to open windows and pitch the seeds from there. It didn't take long for the birds to find the seed, and they watched them chirping and quarreling and being belligerent. It was incredible to watch those hearty, feathered creatures bathe in the birdbath in that weather.

Sam was woeful. "The sun's due out this afternoon, so it'll all melt pretty fast." When Addy gave him a significant, level look, he chided, "Everyone else is friendly and likes having me around."

She sighed. "But you aren't . . ."

"I aren't what?" he prodded.

"You aren't trying to . . ." And she stopped again.

"Make love to them? What makes you think I'm trying to make love to you?"

Her eyes leaped incredulously to his face, which was so bland and innocent that she became indignant.

He continued to question her in a deadpan way. "Have I made an overt move? Have I kissed you good morning?" Suddenly he grimaced and put his hands to his hair and yelled, *"I've got to have a kiss fix!"* And he lunged at her.

Addy fled, shrieking, and Grendel, squealing, abandoned the birds and got in the way, and Sam swung Grendel up and nuzzled her neck and put her down and went after the fleeing Addy.

Attempting to escape, she ran through the rooms, but then she thought, What are you about, Adelina Mary Rose Kildaire? Men like pursuit! So she stopped and turned, standing straight, and put her hand out in a traffic-cop hand signal.

Not being a motorist, Sam simply ignored her useless gesture and gathered her into his arms and kissed her. Grendel thought that was just hilarious and stomped around and laughed, begging to be next.

Sam had been laughing, but with the kiss his face changed, and he looked at Addy with the sober onslaught of desire. She pulled back. He let her go with great reluctance. His hands lingered on her, threatening to stop their passive release and grab her back. Her fingers escaped last, and she moved away to a safer distance.

Grendel was still squealing and stomping, and without taking his eyes from Addy, Sam picked her up and held her while she wriggled and laughed. He gave the little girl a quick kiss, but his intense gaze never left Addy.

He looked at her from under his brows. He was excessively dangerous for a woman who was wavering in her determination to stay aloof from men. From one man.

With him momentarily distracted from her by the squirming Grendel, Addy turned cautiously and moved away as if from the presence of a wild, threatening beast. She walked carefully so as not to arouse the animal's instinct to pursue.

They were somewhat careful of one another for the rest of the day. Their exchanges were rather formal, as if they sat in a canoe and dared not chance moving and tipping it over. They were stiff and correct. But all in all, it was a marvelous day. Sam's beeper didn't make a sound, the telephone remained silent, and the day was glorious—first in somber, ghostly, foggy, ice-sheathed beauty and later as the magic, crystallized woods sparkled in the sun in awesome glory.

Grendel felt fine. Addy decided that her cold had been minimized by the vitamin C. They spent the day making doughnuts, cautioning Grendel not to eat too many of the "holes" as she did the sugaring. Then they watched an old movie on TV and played hide-and-seek throughout the great house. Addy and Grendel made up the opposition. It was safer that way for Addy. And they read. When Grendel napped, Sam thought he and Addy ought to take a nap too, but she turned her mouth down at the corners and shook her head at him in a reproving way. Unreproved, he grinned at her.

They continued to talk about the St. Patrick's Day party. Addy asked if the models could come. Sam said of course, they were family. She said they couldn't leave out Miss Pru; she loved parties. He agreed and said he knew a fine man who just might do for Miss Pru. She said if they had Miss Pru and the fine man, perhaps they should ask some other people that age. He said he knew a lonely doctor who'd lost his wife just before Christmas, and perhaps a St. Patrick's Day party would be the very thing for him.

Eventually they had almost three hundred people listed. "Sam, do you realize how many people we're supposed to invite?"

"They won't all come," he assured her, waving his hand nonchalantly.

He was wrong. Not only did most of the three hundred people come, but a shocking number also brought friends. Almost everyone who did said, "I *knew* you wouldn't mind."

Everyone trooped in, all in a party mood, and it was a roaring success. Hedda was canny. She apparently knew about St. Patrick's Day parties, because the food did last, but the Irish beer didn't, which would have been fortunate if some happy soul hadn't gone out and come back with a case of Irish whiskey. He denied stoutly that it was from Kentucky. In fact, he threatened to blacken the eye of any black-hearted son who said it wasn't genuine. "It's Irish!" he vowed.

After a judicious sampling, one man declared, "Yeah, I think I can taste it. It's Irish."

Another said, "Do you see any Little People?"

"Not yet."

"'Tis Kentucky," someone claimed.

"Naw, 'tis Irish, pure Irish. Taste that lilt? It's as good as kissing the Blarney stone."

"That work for Germans?" someone asked.

"For anyone with an Irish heart. The outside doesn't count."

The party lasted well into the morning. Addy told Sam, "Your friends certainly have staying power."

"I know. When you think everyone has said good night, you have to watch to be sure they leave. They tend to curl up in corners and sleep until noon, which isn't so bad, but then they want to go on partying."

"You have strange friends," she said, glancing around.

"But they're friendly."

"Yes." Her eyes came back to him. "I noticed the redhead." She gave him a sour look.

"Which one?" He stretched to look over heads.

"They all act that way?"

He gave her a curious, innocent gaze. "What way was that? Show me."

"She couldn't keep her hands off you and was leaning all over you."

"She was just a bit unsteady," he explained in a dismissive way. "High heels do that when you have too much Irish beer. Now you wouldn't for a minute believe that nice girl was being forward."

"She's forward, all right, and every bit of them is silicone!"

Sam threw his head back and laughed. "Come dance with me, my fiery colleen."

"It's too dark and crowded in there." She eyed the unlighted drawing room.

"That's when it's the most fun!" he assured her and led her through the jam of noisy people into the drawing room, where the stereo was playing party music, loud and with a strong beat. Some of it was loud and slow with a strong beat, and required close, slow dancing. Sam held Addy to him, and they swayed and moved against one another, pushed together in the mass of moving bodies. After a time she said, "I don't think we should be dancing. We should be hosting."

"Ummmm" was all he replied. His arms were around her and his hands were at the top of her bottom, pressing her closer and tighter to his hard, muscular frame, to his thighs, to his need of her.

Because his head was down and his mouth was moving on her shoulder, she could whisper in his ear. "You ought not to hold me like this."

"Ummmm. It feels good." He nuzzled her ear and whispered back, "It could feel a whole lot gooder if you'll just come up to my room for a minute or two."

"You don't have a room," she hissed.

"Let's go see if that's right."

"Sam! Cut that out!"

"I think it was that guy in back of you."

"It was *you!*"

"Now, you know I'd never do anything like that," he purred.

"Then how do you know what I'm talking about?"

And he laughed.

It was hot in the room with all those bodies moving and swaying and rubbing together. He kissed her, and she became a little faint. She thought that must be because the room's oxygen was all used up by that mass of people. After a few more kisses, she was almost ready to help him find out if he did have a room after all. That was when an orange-shirted man took umbrage over something a green-tied man said and suggested that his face was put together wrong and volunteered to rearrange it.

Their argument gathered a knot of pleasantly interested onlookers whose heads turned in tennis-tournament fashion as the insults became more intricate. When the opponents' faces became a little red and their words somewhat harsher, someone stopped the stereo and began to play "When Irish Eyes Are Smiling" on the piano. The song was taken up readily by the crowd and diverted most of the witnesses to the altercation. After that came "Mother Machree." What pseudo Son of the Old Sod could quarrel during "Mother Machree," Addy thought. It would be un-American.

When Grendel came down for a brief peek at the party, wearing her long brown flannel nightgown with a matching peaked nightcap, two people swore off Irish whiskey. An Irish-whiskey ex-doubter laid one finger to the side of his blunt nose and vowed, "I see 'em."

The recipient of that confidence scoffed, "Naw, 'tis moonshine."

"'Tis Irish whiskey," the new believer proclaimed.

"What Irish whiskey?" chimed in a disbeliever. "It's straight from Nashville! That's where this whiskey comes from. Hear the music?"

"That's from the piano," came a sober contribution.

"You don't say!"

"Cut it out, you guys," interjected a third party.

With dignity he was told, "We're having a—spirited—discussion," which brought hilarious laughter for the clever wording.

Linda, the brunette model, showed how to go-go dance and gathered an intent following and some imitators. Jeremy Tinker, Sam's friend and Grendel's doctor, flirted with all the women but was carefully formal with Addy, whom he referred to as Sam's girl.

When Addy met Diana Hunter's husband, she hid her surprise nicely. So Diana was safely married and could have no interest in Sam. Diana told Addy that Sam looked great but a little frazzled. "What are you doing to him, Addy?" she asked.

"Nothing."

Diana laughed. "He's in love with you."

"How can you tell?"

"He can't keep away from you. He has his hands or eyes on you all the time."

"That's just . . . well . . . he wants . . ."

"Sex? That too. He's never been like this with any other woman he's ever dated. He's been polite and humorous and fun, but he's never been the way he is with you. When are you going to put him out of his misery?"

"I don't want to get involved with any man."

Diana hooted. "Yeah. Sure. You're totally uninvolved!" And she laughed immoderately.

Besides the dancers, the arguers, and the serious drinkers, there were couples draped together on the stairs, against walls, on piled-up furniture, and in hidden corners. All in all it was a landmark party, and everyone had a hell of a good time.

When Sam said just that to Addy, she said pointedly, "A 'hell' of a good time?"

"They're having a good time now. Tomorrow will be hell. Headaches, upset stomachs, being tired...Only they won't remember that. They'll only remember the fun."

When they eased the last of the guests out of the house, it was almost five. The birds were starting to chirp. Alone at last, Sam and Addy gave each other weary smiles. "Whose idea was this party?" Addy wanted to know.

Sam denied any part of it. *"My* name's not Kildaire!"

"Isn't Grady an Irish name?"

"I think after tonight it'll have to be."

"Tonight was a christening of the non-Irish?"

"I'm sure of it." He nodded profoundly. "Just wait. Next February everyone who was here tonight will start saying, 'Faith, now, we'll be having our party on our day, right?'"

"It's monstrous."

He nodded gravely. "In three years we'll have to hire a hall. We'll have outgrown the house."

"We'll have..." And she stopped. "We" sounded

extremely linked. Sam and she were becoming a "we." She mustn't let that happen.

She resisted his good-night kiss in the entrance hall. She said she had to look around for burning cigarettes, and told him to go on. She went through the rooms and the kitchen, emptying the last of the cigarette stubs into the tin box there.

When she went wearily upstairs, she was startled to see Sam coming out of the bathroom, in a toweling robe that was his. He paused and smiled at her. "Want me to bathe you? I know you're tired, and you'll sleep better if you relax first with a nice bath. I'll help you, and that will hurry you into bed."

Sure he would. "No. What are you doing here?"

"I'm going to crawl into bed and, being newly Irish, I must have a personal leprechaun for a guardian angel. And I'll pray my leprechaun delivers you to me." His voice and face were serious and watchful.

She shook her head, and her eyes fell before his. She had to swallow and stiffen her backbone before she could say a reasonably steady good-night.

She stepped into the shower and found herself faced with the truth. He was spending the night. No ice or snow or sickness. They'd given a party, and he was spending the night. Why hadn't she told him to run along home? He'd just assumed he would be welcome. And he'd stayed. He couldn't do that. She yawned, so sleepy she couldn't argue with any force at the moment. She'd have to tell him about it in the morning... when they wakened later that day. He really couldn't do that. He had his own apartment and he could go on home just like everyone else. When had he brought that robe into the house? She dried herself and drooped into her room— and there he was, in her bed! He was asleep.

He was truly asleep, snoring a nice, purring snore and out cold. He was sleeping so soundly that she was tempted to climb into bed. When he wakened, she'd say, "You were fabulous," just to see his face as he tried to remember making love to her. That would be funny. The only reason she didn't do that was that she couldn't figure out a way to escape the bed if he did wake up and find her there. What if she didn't want to escape?

She toyed briefly with the idea of getting into *his* bed. He'd said he was going to see if his personal leprechaun would put her there. But again, after the joke was over, how would she get away?

So she went to bed in the room beyond Grendel's. But she dreamed of Sam the whole night long, wild erotic dreams of frustration and need. It was an exhausting sleep.

CHAPTER TWELVE

SAM WAS GRUMPY the next day. He didn't come downstairs until afternoon. He stumped around the kitchen
making his breakfast as if he were at home. Addy smiled
slyly at him. "What's so funny?" he wanted to know.

"Your leprechaun put me in your bed, and you never
did show up!" But she couldn't control her humor.

"Yeah. Sure." His tone was disbelieving.

She looked innocent. "Where *ever* were you? I went
to sleep waiting." And she sighed a long, gusty sigh.
But she was making a mistake.

He got up and went to her and grabbed her hand as
she turned in belated alarm to flee. He jerked her back
and held her against him. "It isn't a subject for teasing
me, Addy. I love you and I want you like blue murder.
I'm being very civilized about your hesitation—"

"Hesitation!"

"Yes. I'm going to get you, and the sooner you realize it the better for both of us." Then he kissed her until she was boneless. He did that deliberately, knowing what he was doing to her, she was sure, and when he'd made her realize that she wanted him just as terribly, he released her, put her from him, and sat down and ate his breakfast with every appearance of being calm.

She stood there, a shambles, and looked around the kitchen in a daze, not quite knowing what to say or do, but not wanting to walk out of the room. If she left, it would seem as if she was running away. It would be cowardly.

"Do you have a headache?" Sam asked conversationally.

"No."

"I have a bearcat."

"Take two aspirin."

He smiled. "Yes, Doctor."

"I don't have to have a medical degree to know to take two aspirin for a hangover."

He denied that. "I don't have a hangover. It's just a headache. All that cigarette smoke and all the frustration gave me a tension headache."

"Two aspirin," she advised again.

"I know a better way."

"Yes, I know. You want to tumble me and get rid of your headache, but you'd just give it to me. You'd give me all the problems, when I don't need any more problems."

"You wouldn't get pregnant," he assured her gently.

"And that makes it okay? A nice friendly tumble to rid you of your frustrations? No involvement, no . . . *side* effects? Having sex isn't that casual for me."

"It isn't casual for me either. And, Addy, I don't just want sex. I want love."

"Exclusive rights, you mean. Live-in convenience. 'Hey, I've got a headache! Come on, hurry up, hop in bed!' No, thanks."

"Hard-hearted Hannah," he accused.

"Blame me. That's typically male. Go yowl under some other woman's window."

"Like Tippy's?" He slid a cool glance at her.

"Tippy?" She gave him a still look in return.

"The redhead who was leaning on me," he elaborated.

"Her name's Tippy? How appropriate! She looks round-heeled."

"Why, Addy! What a catty thing to say. If I didn't know better, I'd think you were jealous."

"I am not!"

"Of course not," he agreed smugly. "Could I have another piece of toast?"

Automatically she took a piece of bread from the wrapper and slid it into the toaster while he watched her, his eyes gleaming. They were silent for a while. When the toast popped up, Addy buttered it and gave it to him, and nodded once to his thanks. Her eyes followed his movements as he put jam on the toast and then bit into it. Then she said, "She wouldn't have to worry about getting her hair mussed up. It's a mess anyway."

"Whose hair?"

"Tippy's."

"I think her hair's not messy so much as ... casual."

"Probably can't get a comb through it. I'll bet no man's ever managed to kiss her."

"You mean you think she's ... pure?" That obviously surprised him.

"Naw, I mean she puts her lipstick on so thick that

anybody trying to kiss her would slide right off her mouth."

Sam laughed immoderately and choked on the toast, and Addy had to pound his back, which she did with great goodwill.

They were still being a little formal when he left after supper. Grendel couldn't understand why he had to leave, why he couldn't just stay there. He told Grendel her mother was inhospitable. Grendel wasn't sure what that meant, but she gave Addy a censuring look, until Sam picked her up and kissed her and told her to behave and mind her mother, that he'd be back. He kissed Addy too, but he only leaned down and gave her a peck.

The days passed, and Sam was there more than anywhere else, but he didn't stay overnight again. He mentioned it, but Addy didn't allow it, and she didn't make up the bed under the coverlet.

Sam brought her candy, flowers, books, and gloves. With the fifth pair of gloves she told him that was enough. He said with asperity that giving presents was what courting men did and she'd have to put up with it.

"Sam, I've told and *told* you I don't want to get involved with you!" And she went on at great length repeating her reasons.

"I don't see how you think you still have the choice."

"I mean it, Sam."

But when he didn't come by one day, she called and asked if he was all right. "No, I'm not!" he replied glumly.

"What's wrong? Are you ill?" She was alarmed.

"You bloody well ought to know what's the matter with me."

"Oh, Sam . . ."

Gradually Addy forgot about Paul Morris's letter, filed under "M," which had inquired whether Grendel was his daughter. She didn't reply to it, and she assiduously didn't think about it or Paul. She mostly just thought about Sam.

Marcus told Addy he'd found Emmaline a little abandoned shop that was exactly what she needed. They all went to inspect it and consider it critically, but it really was just right. They went each day as Marcus's crew cleaned it up, and Emmaline chose the paint. Addy listened to her specify the rather startling color combination and waited for Marcus to object. He didn't, which made Addy indignant. When she got him away from Emmaline, she asked, "Why does Emmaline get to choose her colors? I wanted my house white and you didn't paint it white, you painted it blue. How come?"

Patiently, Marcus told her, "Just wait. She's exactly right. It'll be perfect."

And it was. It was eye-catching, a little wild, but it was instantly apparent that the store held unusual, high-quality, stunning goods. And it did. She named it Emmaline's, and they made a ceremony when the sign went up. It amazed Addy to observe Emmaline's slow laziness turn into élan, to see her movements take on confidence, to watch her become a stern taskmaster.

Emmaline had hired two young people. Addy met them, found them talented and cheerful, and liked them both. Marcus found two young men to help her. One maintained the books and kept track of the orders, and the other was the salesman. Both were businesslike, clear-eyed, and competent. Emmaline made them all toe the line.

"Emmaline is turning into a tyrant!" Addy told Marcus.

"She'll mellow after she's used to being boss," he soothed.

"I think we've got a black, female Hitler on our hands."
"Go wash out your mouth with soap."

Just before the middle of April a great storm threatened. Addy had been watching its approach. As tree limbs were tossed and the husks of dead leaves were strewn across the yard, she saw Sam's car turn into her driveway. She ran to the front door to let him in.

"Hurry!" she called, flinching under the onslaught of blustering winds buffeting her, plastering her clothes to her body and streaming through her hair.

He ran up on the porch, and together they looked at the inky sky to the southwest. The morning sun gave a last sweep of light, spotlighting the young, tender green leaves against the slate-black sky. The colors were breathtaking.

They pushed the door closed and stood smiling at each other as Addy combed her hair with her fingers. "The radio said severe weather and a tornado watch," Sam said, "so I came right over."

Grendel came to the landing of the grand staircase and yelled, "You're *here!*" in a most charming welcome.

"Come see what I have for you," Sam invited.

"What?" She came down the stairs one at a time, sliding her hand along the railing.

Sam held an Irish, crushable hat in one big hand. As Grendel reached the bottom of the stairs, he squatted down and held the hat low so she could see into it. He'd brought her a kitten. It was mostly ears and eyes, with an enormous purr. Addy cautioned Grendel that it was a baby cat and must be carefully held so as not to be hurt. Grendel was enchanted and watched it, amazed. Sam put it on the rug, and its eyes got bigger and its short tail stood straight up. Grendel laughed.

"Be careful of it," Addy repeated.

"She will," Sam said.

The kitten, young as it was, knew to get under the sofa or some inaccessible place when it needed to rest. And Grendel's wrists soon showed light scratches. The kitten was teaching her what was permissible. They named it Stormy to honor the day.

They played with the kitten until it had had enough and retreated under the back of a large, low sofa in the drawing room. Grendel wailed because she couldn't get to it.

"Let's play hide-and-seek or hare and hounds," Sam suggested.

"You're it!" Addy proclaimed.

The house was made for hare and hounds. Sam would almost catch Addy, but she'd reverse or dodge aside and he'd allow it. In the meantime, Grendel would flee and squeal and get in the way deliberately to get caught and kissed on the cheek and then released while Addy ran free.

After a time Grendel became tired and bored, and Sam set her up with books and the kitten in her room. Then he went back downstairs, and the game took on a different tone as he chased Addy silently. It was no longer hare and hound. It was more like cat and silent, skittering mouse.

Eventually Addy was trapped in the morning room and couldn't get out. She retreated, breathless and laughing, stepping backward, her hands up, seeking an escape and finding none. Sam advanced slowly, silently, relentlessly, his lips parted slightly to accommodate his quickened breath. His eyes were intense and serious.

"I give up," Addy said, then, at his inflamed look, she quickly changed it to "King's X" and crossed her fingers on both hands, still backing away from him. The only door available led to a huge closet they used for storage. Prolonging her freedom, she opened the door, darted inside, and closed it, holding the knob. It was dark in there, but it was refuge.

But the door opened outward, and there was no way she could hold out against him. He simply turned the knob and pulled it open. He stood in the doorway and looked at her trapped inside the closet. Then he stepped inside too, clasped her arm as he closed the door, and was there in the dark with her. His other arm swept around her to pull her strongly against him as he bent his head, searching in the dark for her mouth.

She gasped, whispering, "Sam..." in almost a plea.

"Oh, Addy," he groaned, and there was no quarter in his voice. Her mouth trembled under his fiercely demanding kiss, and she uttered little sounds as her hands fluttered around his head, her body pressed tightly against his.

His hands shook as they moved on her, molding her body. While her breath seemed caught in her throat, his was warm and close as he tugged her blouse over her head and unhooked her bra. He growled very low, "Undo your hair and *never* wear it braided like that again."

Without arguing, she fumbled to obey him. He took advantage of her body while her arms were up to her hair. When her hair was freed, he almost paused as he ran his hands gently through it, cupping her head and putting his face into the silken mass. Then he jerked off his sweat shirt and stood with his hands on her sides. He tugged her to him until her nipples touched his chest, and his palms slid up to cup the sides of her breasts, pressing them together so that the soft mounds pushed against his hairy chest.

She was becoming boneless and had to lean against him to remain erect. She heard him gasp. Her head was too heavy to hold up and it fell back; one of his hands supported its weight as he kissed her. Their mouths melded in a scorching embrace, and their bodies rubbed against each other, each of them relishing the feel of the other as they clung together in the dark closet.

There could be no denying his need of her. Hers for him was not so obvious, for she wasn't skilled or practiced. She was so amazed by the sensual thrills flooding her that her mind was turned inward, swamped by self-absorption, with no thought of giving him pleasure.

She was only able to receive sensations from him, and she did, all kinds of sensations—wild, lovely, and thrilling. She moved and squirmed and wriggled and gasped and began to reach for him to fill the growing need to hold and touch him. She was so filled with passion that she wasn't aware of how much bolder she'd become, and how she thrilled him in turn. It was inadvertent; she was concentrating on her own sensations.

Almost desperate, he laid her on the dark closet floor and allowed his tense, sweaty body to seek brief relief as he quickly took her. She moaned in disappointment as he lifted from her, but he didn't release her. He laid her back down again and began to make love to her. He showed Addy that it wasn't only sexual satisfaction he desired from her. It was her love.

He played her body like a virtuoso, and they both took pleasure in his skill. They shared the dark closet for a long time that stormy morning as he taught her many things about herself and about him. She was an impetuous student, and he had to restrain her before she learned to take her time. And in their paradise, she heard the sound of a train whistle roaring over her head as it rushed on past. She smiled in the dark and kissed him again softly, her tongue touching his lips. Then, as his penetrated into her mouth, she gently sucked it and moved under him and thought how lovely it was to walk on tracks of love. Why had she been afraid?

She put her arms around him and hugged him down to her. She moved her face over his and kissed along his shoulder and murmured to him. She heard his voice ask urgently, "Did you say you loved me?" She paused and was still, lying there naked on the closet floor with her love fused to her, and she nodded slowly. "You love me?" his harsh whisper demanded again.

In a tiny voice, she admitted, "Yes."

"Ahhhhh." He relaxed on her and made an almost purring sound into the side of her throat. "Tell me," he urged. "Let me hear you say it."

"I . . . love you." Her voice sounded uncertain and faint. Her last defenses were down. He would move in, and she'd become his mistress.

"Oh, my love," he breathed passionately, "I love you." His hands cradled her head, and he kissed her so sweetly that tears came to her eyes. He tasted them. "Tears? Honey?" And he kissed her face and her eyes and murmured of his love and his happiness that she loved him. And he said his life was complete.

Then he moved on her, coaxing her again to follow him in his desire, and he built their pleasure until they rode along the peak, balancing on the edge, hesitating, allowing it to falter, then to build again until they swept over it into that glorious explosion and on into thrilling, falling sensations. Still, it left a core of hunger in Addy that she was again eager to fill.

Later they lay for some time, limp and surfeited. "I've never before enjoyed hide-and-seek quite so much," Sam said. "I hadn't known it could be so much fun."

Addy groaned. "I imagine it will be days before I'll be able to walk."

He comforted her. "Being a doctor, I know of treatments to help you."

"I suspect exactly what you have in that busy little mind."

He laughed, filled with himself and his love for her.

He couldn't keep his hands off her, but now they were gentle and caressing. He kissed her a great deal, and she lay lax and submissive. When she asked what time it was, he put his arm near the bottom of the door so he could see his watch. It was almost noon.

Addy was appalled. "We have to get dressed right this minute and get lunch for Grendel!"

But he was in no hurry. "I'll always love rainstorms for the rest of my life."

"You're an opportunist."

"I am not either! I'm a serious lover!"

"I can vouch for that. You're fantastic!"

"Do you really think so?"

She nodded, so he had to kiss her again, and she was on her back again. "Behave!" she scolded.

"I can't possibly make love to you again, but I certainly enjoy seeing you in that position and naked."

Disbelieving, she asked, "How can you see me in the dark?"

"I'm part cat, if you recall, so I can look at your loveliness."

"You're a voyeur?"

"Oh, no. I'd never only want to look. I'm committed to total involvement."

They finally opened the door a crack so they could see to get dressed. They combed their hair with their fingers and smiled at each other foolishly. They held hands and whispered to each other as they left the closet and squinted at the sunshine that flooded from the study into the wide back hall. They stood there and laughed at each other, and Addy felt herself blushing a little, so Sam had to lean over and kiss her yet again. Then he had to put an arm around her, and they went through the back hall into the kitchen.

Of course, they were sure they looked perfectly ordinary, but Miss Pru gave them a brief, weighing glance, then shook her head. But she was smiling. Sam kissed her cheek. Then he leaned down and kissed Grendel, who jabbered about the doll Miss Pru had made for her from all sorts of scraps of material. She held it up so they could see that the doll's "flesh" was a crazy quilt and quite charming. Grendel was trying to decide on a name for it.

The lovers leaned against the counter close together, their arms loosely around each other. Addy had tried twice to move away from Sam's side, but he wouldn't have it. He yawned and yawned and grinned.

Miss Pru gave them soup and sandwiches, which they neglected. They took desultory bites as they smiled at each other and at Grendel. Finally Miss Pru insisted that they eat, and they obediently finished their sandwiches.

Miss Pru bustled around straightening up the kitchen, and Grendel said she had to have her nap and asked her dolly if she was sleepy. In a low voice Sam asked Addy if she was sleepy, and his eyes were filled with lazy laughter. They trailed Grendel and Miss Pru up the stairs and watched them disappear into Grendel's room. They were still in the hallway—and kissing—when Miss Pru went by on her way to her own room. She trailed a hand along their shoulders and said, "Nap-nappy."

They turned to watch her go down the hall, but she didn't look back, and then they were alone. Addy smiled and repeated, "Nap-nappy," as she touched Sam's face. She turned from him to go to her room, and he simply followed. She hesitated, watching him. He grinned and began quite naturally to take off his clothes. She continued to watch, admiring his muscular, powerful body as it was unsheathed. He came over to her, took off her clothes—more leisurely this time—and stood back to look down at her. He gave a shake of his head and said, "Gorgeous." Then he led her to the bathroom, and they showered and dried each other, taking a long time with each other's bodies, taking pleasure in having their hands on each other.

They went back to Addy's room and crawled into her bed. They wound their arms around each other, sighed in contentment, and fell asleep.

They didn't waken until late afternoon. Sam wanted her again, and his kisses were earnest and his hands urgent. Addy protested that he couldn't possibly! But he insisted that yes he could, she had no idea how long he'd dreamed of her, of having her in bed with him and making love with her.

Ever since he'd seen her up on that runway showing that robe... "Oh, by the way, I have something for you." He tugged her out of bed and down the hall to "his" room, and there in the closet she gasped to see two suits and three shirts!

She said, "What...?" She'd stripped the bed after the St. Patrick's Day party but hadn't checked the closet.

He reached in and took a box from the shelf. It was a Gown House box. "Here," he said to her, "I bought this for you."

She was surprised and frowned a little as she took the box over to the bed, opened it, and... it was the robe she'd modeled. She couldn't believe it. She took it out and looked at it, then turned to Sam.

He was smiling smugly, his hands on his bare hips, his interest rising. "Model it for me...so I can undo that third hook."

She continued to look at him, and her grin couldn't stay hidden. "Was it really for me?"

"I was afraid you'd sell it, and I wanted it for you so I could be the only one to see you in it and undo those hooks."

"That day, you looked as if you were going to bid on *me*."

"I can see why you thought so. I felt the same way."

"And you got me." Was her tone a bit rueful?

"I finally did," he agreed.

"That other time . . . you had me then too," she reminded him.

"That was more compassion on your part, and it was beautiful, but I wanted you to make love with me because you wanted me, not just to comfort me."

"Oh? I had a choice this morning?"

"After the first several times." He grinned at her. "I had to be sure you realized how it was with me so you'd finally be eager and willing."

"You're terrific. I had no idea it could be that way."

"Truthfully, neither did I."

"I love you, Sam."

"Come here."

"You're incredible."

"You should wait and try me when I don't have to be restrained." He looked excessively sassy.

"You're restrained?"

"Killingly."

She hooted, disbelieving, but it wasn't long before she believed. He put her down on the bed and tumbled her around and tousled her hair and squeezed and patted and kissed and mouthed her. She was astounded when he aroused her to fever pitch, and then he made her work to convince him, but he was a pushover.

He stayed for supper as naturally as if he'd lived there all along. He and Grendel set the table and chatted. But the kitten was very distracting for Grendel, and she had to keep checking on where it was. Sam chided her that when she had a job to do, she should finish it before she went on to something else. And Addy listened and thought what a good influence Sam would be on her daughter. The thought of Grendel's real father, off in the shadowy distance, tried to intrude, but Addy pushed it aside.

After Grendel and Miss Pru went upstairs, Sam and Addy sat talking. When it came time to go to bed, Sam delayed. Addy was very sleepy. "Aren't you ready to come upstairs?" she asked.

He turned his mouth down at the corners and did a lousy imitation of Addy when she had said, "I'm not a 'convenient lay' just because *you* need sex and haven't any control."

"Oh, be quiet!" Addy said. She reached out for his sleeve and pulled him up the stairs.

He feigned a great struggle—not disturbing her progress or the sleeve she held—then sighed elaborately in surrender, and in a terrible try for a high voice, he grieved, "I'll probably hate myself in the morning."

"You're perfectly safe," Addy assured him.

They debated which room they'd share. He said, "Since it's your house, I'd look like a gigolo if I crawled into your bed. It would seem more hospitable and gracious if you'd come to me."

That made her smile and, shaking her head, she went to his room. They had to make up the bed. He wanted to bathe her again, but she said, "Forget it. You're too tired, and I'd just get all excited and demand you submit and you'd cry, and I'd feel like a rat for forcing you."

"I don't think I'm that tired."

"Well, I am. You're just like a little boy with a new toy, and you should put me down and go to sleep."

"This isn't turning out quite as I'd planned."

She snored ostentatiously.

"I think a convenient headache is more ladylike than snoring," he said.

She didn't reply. He took her carefully in his arms and settled down. They were quiet for a while, then she whispered, "Aren't you glad I didn't want to?"

"You're a wretch and shut up." But he laughed, genuinely amused.

CHAPTER THIRTEEN

THEY WAKENED EARLY and grinned at each other before Sam asked, "You won't be stubborn and arbitrary and have to be married in June, will you?"

"Married?" she asked cautiously.

"Yeah."

"You want . . . to marry me?"

"What in hell did you think all this courting was all about? All those gloves and risking you getting pimples from all that candy . . ."

"Me?" She was a little breathless.

"You are Adelina Mary Rose Kildaire, aren't you?"
She nodded.

"Then you're the one," he assured her. "I want to share the rest of my life with you." He lay on his side,

169

smiling at her, then he became serious. "You're just gorgeous, lying naked in bed with your hair all messed up."

In something of a daze, she responded, "I'm all covered up, and you can't possibly see me."

"I have hands, honey, and I can feel, and you're just gorgeous."

"Sam? Do you really want to marry me?"

Very seriously he replied, "I honest to God thought you realized that."

"I just thought you wanted to get me in bed."

"Oh, you were certainly right about that! But I want exclusive rights for the rest of my life."

"You make it sound as if I'd be sleeping around if we weren't married."

"The exclusive rights include all the rest—your debts, your comfort, your protection, your cherishing. All those things too. Sex is one of the perks."

"Oh, Sam, I would love to be married to you." She flung herself at him, and their kiss quickly became ardent.

He pulled away from her a bit. "Are you just after my fabulous body?" He frowned at her suspiciously.

"So I get that too?"

And he had to show her that she did.

When they went down to breakfast, Addy had on a fiery-red sweater with red-and-black-plaid slacks, and her hair was loose around her shoulders. And her smile was tender and dewy.

Miss Pru exclaimed elaborately at their announcement and made them laugh. Addy figured that was where Grendel got her dramatics. Grendel looked intrigued by it all, though not quite clear as to what it all meant, but she exclaimed in echo to Miss Pru's comments.

Sam picked Grendel up and said he'd like it very much

if she'd call him Daddy. She tried that out and thought it sounded funny. But Sam kept coaxing her to call him Daddy.

Miss Pru opened a bottle of champagne, and they toasted the future and each other during breakfast and decided April fifteenth would be The Day. There was no need to wait. All the designs for the May show were finished, and almost all were sewn and fitted. Miss Pru could handle any other fittings. Sam and Addy could have a three-day honeymoon before they had to return to complete the line garments and for Addy to learn the narration for the fall showing the first of May.

Addy designed her wedding gown and took the material to Emmaline, who put a border of wild flowers around the bottom of the skirt in a riot of color. It was stunning.

Addy and Grendel took Sam to meet her parents, and they all survived it. Eyeing her cousins, one two years old and the other almost one, Grendel was very quiet. The kitten, Stormy, had had to stay in Indianapolis, and Addy knew Grendel was anxious to get back to it.

Addy's next younger sister was married and pregnant with her third child. Without being asked, she said she wouldn't be able to be Addy's attendant, since she was so pregnant. Then she fidgeted impatiently and finally asked, "Are you getting married because you're pregnant...again?"

Addy was stunned. So her family had speculated that she was pregnant again and that at least this time she'd get married! She said a stiff, "No."

Her sister went to the door of the living room and called, "Mama!" When she had their mother's attention, she shook her head in an exaggerated way.

They shocked Addy, and she was glad to leave.

* * *

Sam still slept at Addy's—and with her—before their marriage. One day, as he was bidding Addy good-bye prior to leaving for the hospital, he leaned over to give her a kiss, and Grendel hopped around, asking for a kiss too. A woman who was there to choose a gown laughed and said it was easy to see who was Grendel's daddy.

Grendel replied carefully, in her version of English, "April fifteenth. That's when Sam's my daddy. He and Mommy exercise, and I hear them."

The woman gave an audible gasp, flustered. Sam's dancing eyes watched Addy blush before he put in smoothly, "Aerobics." He smiled at the woman, whose turn it was to blush. Sam couldn't resist asking, "Whatever were you thinking?" and he tsked as he left, shaking his head.

Marcus's gang mended the porch for the wedding. With the weather uncertain, it might well be nice enough for the guests to sit on the porch. Addy watched them working and asked Marcus, "That wood isn't new. Where did you get it?"

Not really paying any attention to her, Marcus replied, "We tore down a house."

Addy stared at him. "Just to get wood for this porch? Did they catch you?"

Marcus turned to her and laughed out loud. "The house was due to be demolished, and we got the job. We did it by hand instead of the wrecking ball. We sell the windows, kindling, and bricks. It gives the young men something to do and a little cash. You knew that, Addy."

She looked at the planks, embarrassed. She hadn't actually accused Marcus, but she felt uncomfortable. The planks saved her. "How do I know you aren't bringing me three nests of termites?"

"Trust me."

Her eyes came up to his, and she grinned. They understood each other. Impishly she asked, "Do you know what Emmaline is charging me for her work?"

His eyes danced as he suggested, "By the piece?"

Since that was how she'd paid the slow Emmaline for sewing, she had to laugh too. "She has to be kin to you, Marcus, she's so heartless in her prices."

"She's worth it."

"I know, I know. And so are you."

"Hedda has your eats planned for the hitching. You gonna jump over a broom?"

"That's what does it? Jumping over a broom makes it legal? If that does it, why all the fuss?"

"Pearl showed me your dress—that Emmaline did."

"She did the flowers! I couldn't wait long enough for her to sew it too! I'd never get married! You coming to watch?"

"Oh, yes."

"You're really coming just to eat," Addy declared. "You don't fool me at all."

"That too. My Hedda's a supreme cook."

"Why aren't you fat?" she asked with interest.

"It isn't what she cooks as the way she does it. It all tastes so good I never realize she makes me diet."

"Does she speak to you?" Addy wanted to know.

"In many ways," he replied. Then he said, "Your Sam is a good man."

It wasn't until later, when Addy thought about it, that she realized Marcus hadn't really told her if Hedda could speak or if she simply chose not to. They were an interesting, talented pair. Finally, as she thought about them, the puzzle of Marcus suddenly fell into place. She told Sam, "Marcus is a mechanical engineer and does consulting."

Sam said, "Umm-hmm."

"How did you know?"

"You mean you just guessed?"

"That explains his absences. He's helping someone else for a change." She grinned as she gave her head a shake. "I tried to set him up in business in a repair shop in my basement." And Sam laughed with her.

The day of the wedding Hedda came up the stairs in her slow, stately way and entered the room where Addy was dressing. Addy smiled at her and was rewarded with one of Hedda's rare, marvelous smiles. Then Hedda gave a regal nod of her head and handed her a small pouch. She indicated it was to be pinned to her bra between her breasts.

Addy took it cautiously and felt it crackle delicately. Voodoo. Some sort of African witchery, that's what it was. Sam would inhale it and it would act as an aphrodisiac. She glanced at Hedda respectfully but a little fearfully. Hedda touched the red roses Addy would carry and then the small pouch. It was rose petals. Hedda gave her an extremely amused, slanting glance and left the room.

So Sam and Addy were married. Addy's mother and father both cried. Addy figured it was for joy that she was no longer an unwed mother. Sam's mother and stepfather and various relatives were courteous and pleasant to Addy's rather stiff family. They were all witness to a brief adoption ceremony that made Sam Grendel's father.

They were drinking toasts when the first of the unexpected guests arrived. Only Hedda, who had shrewdly witnessed the St. Patrick's Day party, didn't look surprised. Eventually more than two hundred people tramped in, bringing their own drinks and all sorts of gifts, but mostly plants. They were dressed in all manner of styles, all were in a party mood, and they settled down to cel-ebrate.

The crowd glanced up and cheered when Addy and Sam came down the grand staircase and went out the front door to Sam's car. Addy wore her red going-away suit. But their leaving would be only a brief interruption, they knew, and wasn't enough to disturb the course of the party.

Driving away in the car, Addy wanted to know, "Why are we leaving so soon? The party is just getting started."

"Your sister told Jeremy that Hedda gave you a voo-doo pouch with an aphrodisiac that'll drive me wild."

"It's just dried rose petals sewn into a little pouch so I'll smell nice," Addy said deprecatingly, with the wordly tolerance of a sophisticate for a small-town friend.

But Sam was certain. "It has to be an aphrodisiac because I'm affected. I can tell."

"Oh, silly, you're always that way."

"This is worse," he insisted.

"Worse?" she exclaimed incredulously.

He tried for a more accurate word. "Better?"

"Will you still want to make love with me now that it's legal?"

"Yes." He was positive about that too.

"Will you like it as well? Since it's no longer forbidden fruit?"

"I'll let you know," he promised in a way that showed he knew scientific research was vital.

"If we have a baby right away, we could get one in before you turn forty."

"I already have a daughter," he told her contentedly.

"You do?" She turned wide eyes to him.

"Grendel. We signed the papers just a while ago."

"Oh."

"Did you think . . . ?"

"Well . . ." She faltered.

"I've told you everything important that's happened to me," Sam declared sternly.

"No, you haven't! You haven't told me one single thing!"

"That's the reason. Nothing important happened to me until I met you."

Their honeymoon was the way honeymoons are supposed to be—laughter, remembering when each was attracted to the other, how they felt, what they'd thought, interspaced with lots of loving and catching up on sleep.

Lying naked on her stomach, examining Sam's face as he lay partially under her, Addy said, "I wonder if I'll ever get used to looking at you."

"Oh, sure. Pretty soon my face will be as familiar to you as your own."

"Uh . . . *my* face doesn't give me erotic feelings."

"That's strange! Your face affects *me* that way!"

It was momentous only to them. They finally returned to the big house on the north side of Indianapolis and to Grendel, who whooped and called Sam Daddy nearly every other breath. Addy could tell that Sam just loved it.

So Sam was there when Paul's next letter came. It said:

"My uncle died and I have to come to Indiana to help straighten things out. I'd like to come by to see Grendel. I had a lawyer look up her birth certificate, and I know she's mine. The way you were, I know you didn't have anyone else and, since you were pregnant when I left, she has to be my kid. I'll be there in about two weeks. Paul."

Addy sought Sam and blurted it all out. He listened. She ranted and raged, and he let it run its course. She said, "This is 'worse.'" When he looked blank, she elaborated, "'For better or for worse'? This is a worse."

"It isn't even close to worse," Sam reassured her. "You have no problem whatsoever. He can't take Grendel away from you. She's mine too. We wouldn't allow that. But, Addy, you can share her with her father."

"What?" Addy couldn't believe he'd want Grendel to even meet a man who had run from the responsibility of her, and she raged at him.

He lay back on the sofa, his hands behind his head, his face sympathetic and serious as he listened. Then he asked quietly, "Why do you feel so angry?"

She stopped, and her bosom heaved with emotion. Then she said, "I was so afraid. How could I know how it would be for a child? Would the child hate me? Be ashamed?"

Sam got up and went to her. He put his arms around her, and she clung to him. "Would you like a little swallow of brandy?"

"I need to think. I need a clear head."

"How about two vitamin C's?" he suggested. "They're good for stress."

"I need to walk."

They walked for quite a while. After they returned to the house, Addy continued to talk, to give vent to her feelings. She asked, "Why should Paul be allowed to share a child after he abandoned me and never even got in touch with me? Why should he have that privilege?"

"She's his child," Sam reminded her gently.

"Sure. All he contributed was one selfish sperm . . . and he claims she's his."

"She's a delight. She's a darling. He should know her."

"Yes. He's seen a picture of her and knows she's normal. What if Grendel had been an afflicted child?

What if her mind and body had been twisted? Would he
be beating on the door demanding his 'right' to see her?
Tracing her down and claiming her?" She turned on Sam
and demanded, "Where was *he* these last four years?"

"Remember the woman at the museum who said, 'At
least she'll know her father and be friends.' Don't you
see that Grendel has rights too? She'd always be curious.
This way she'll know him and, through him, the other
half of her family."

"How do I know they won't snub her? How do I know
he won't try to change her, give her all kinds of repres-
sions and fears? He couldn't face my being pregnant. He
couldn't face any responsibility. How can I know how
he might influence her?"

"You could lock her up, make sure she doesn't see
anyone." Then in the kindest possible way he took her
shoulders in his hands and made her look at him as he
said, "Addy, if you'll share Grendel with me, why not
with her father?"

"You're *too* understanding!"

"No. I only think how it would be if I'd been Paul."

Without hesitation, she stated, "You would never have
left me."

"No," he agreed, watching her. "Open your heart,
Addy, and give this opportunity to Grendel."

"But Paul benefits."

"Is he such a monster?"

"*Yes!*" She was positive. Then she hesitated. Then
she admitted, "No, not really. Let me think."

"Do unto others . . ." He slid that in very gently.

"That's what Miss Pru said after the first letter."

"He wrote before? You'd heard from him? How many
times?"

"Just once. It was . . . oh . . . in March? I filed it away
and forgot it."

"Did you?" Sam chided.

"No, I didn't really forget it, I tried to ignore it. He'd seen her picture in the *Journal* out in California and wrote and asked if she was his."

"Logical."

"Sam, I don't want him to see Grendel."

"Revenge?"

She admitted it. "Yes."

"You have two weeks to change your mind."

"I won't."

Ever afterward Addy recalled May's fall show as a fragmented, troubled dream. She lived through it vaguely aware of what was going on outside of herself. She knew it was a success. The word most used was "brilliant." Emmaline's scarves were snatched up almost shockingly. Two of the ladies even fought over one through clenched teeth! Addy's clients began to bring along friends to fittings so they could catch glimpses of the designs. Miss Pru said that had to stop, it led to too much confusion, but how could they stop the casual drop-ins without discouraging the business it brought?

Addy was no help. She argued with herself and at the silent Sam during the entire time before Paul's arrival. She went over and over the reasons to shun Paul, and she exhausted herself. Sam listened gravely and said little during those ten days. Then he did say, "I'm Grendel's father. Paul, being her sire, can't change that. But Paul deserves to see Grendel, and Grendel deserves to meet Paul. Even more important, you need to exorcise the bitterness you're nurturing."

"I have a right to be bitter!" she stormed.

"Yes. You did. But that's past. Don't let it eat away at you. I want all of you, and if you're harboring a lump of bitterness at another man, I'll be cheated."

"I wouldn't cheat you," she protested.

"You are now," Sam told her. "Most of your mind is taken up with this. We've only been married three weeks, but all I've heard from you is talk about another man." That startled her, so he added, "I thought I'd come first in your thinking."

"What have I been doing?" she exclaimed.

"Who's important? Paul?"

"You are!" She flung herself at him.

"And so is Grendel," he told her. Then he said again, "Allow Paul to meet her."

She leaned back in his arms to look into his face. "Do you really think I should?"

Sam didn't laugh or exclaim in exasperation; he only nodded seriously.

"All right," she said slowly. "I'll do it."

"That's great, Addy. You'll never regret it."

Paul phoned the next day. He'd counted the two weeks as including the time the letter took to get to Addy. They arranged that he would see Grendel the next day. Addy told Sam she wouldn't meet with Paul. He said she didn't have to this time, that he would.

"You be sure he doesn't kidnap her," Addy warned. "That happens . . ."

"Don't worry," Sam reassured her. "I'll be there."

"And as soon as the hour is up, run him out."

"Addy . . ."

"Well!" she retorted defensively.

"Quit worrying." He hugged her and commended, "You're being very good about this."

"No, I'm not. You're being very good about this, and I want you to think well of me."

"Whatever the reason, you're doing the right thing."

"Are you sure?" she asked worriedly.

"Umm-hmm."

"And you'll watch him every minute?"

"Addy . . ."

The next day, with her nerves twanging, Addy dressed Grendel nervously and looked at her critically—and she became very anxious. Grendel looked so darling, Paul was sure to snatch her up and run away with her. Addy frowned at a watching Sam, who shook his head slowly and smiled at her. "She looks so darling . . ." Addy began.

"Don't worry." Sam took a chattering Grendel downstairs to wait.

Addy stayed in their room upstairs, waiting. She couldn't sit still and fidgeted and paced and finally went to the front windows and peered out through the lace curtains. What would Paul look like? She had a vague memory of him as a reflection of Grendel, but since she had no picture of him, she couldn't actually remember.

He was on time. She watched him get out of a car and look up at the house and lick his lips. He was nervous. He straightened his cuffs and pulled his jacket down needlessly and fingered his tie. Then he took a deep breath and let it all out and walked purposefully up toward the porch.

It was an ordeal for him! He was scared and nervous. How strange. And he was smaller than she remembered. She'd forgotten how his beard shadowed his face blue, even as cleanly shaven as he was. She crept to the top of the stairs and squatted down behind the banister to watch from that hidden vantage point as the doorbell pealed.

Sam came into the entrance hall below and opened the front door. He introduced himself easily, and Paul exclaimed he hadn't realized Addy was married . . . the

Kildaire . . . Sam replied they'd just been married on the fifteenth. Paul shook Sam's hand nervously and congratulated him awkwardly as his eyes took in the lovely entrance hall and the grand staircase. His eyes didn't reach up to Addy's hidden site.

Then Grendel came into the hall, walking on tiptoe like a curious fairy in the woods. Her hands were up, her little neck stretched, her movements lyrical.

Paul's face suffused with color and he gasped softly, "My God," as he saw his child.

Sam turned and held out his hand as he said, "Grendel, here is someone who has come to meet you."

She smiled and walked over to Sam and took his hand as she looked up at the stranger.

"This is your father," Sam explained.

Grendel laughed. "No, silly, you are!" And with both of her hands in Sam's she swung there, off balance, playing.

Paul sank to his knees, his eyes glued to the child, and again he whispered hoarsely, "My God."

Sam was saying to Grendel, "Yes, I know. I'm your daddy, but he's your father. His name is Paul Morris."

"How do you do?" Grendel spaced out the words and swung one foot as she leaned against Sam's leg and held on to his hand.

Paul held out his hand, his face red and his eyes watery as he asked Grendel, "May I hold your hand?" His voice was unsteady.

Grendel looked all the way up to Sam's face to see if she should, and Sam nodded. Not letting go of Sam, Grendel gave her other hand to Paul, but she didn't move close to him. Her tiny hand lay in his and again he said, "My God," and his voice cracked.

"Are you crying?" Grendel asked with interest.

"Let's go into the parlor," Sam suggested kindly. And

he moved so that Paul could rise to his feet easily. Then Sam said to Grendel, "Tell him who Stormy is, Grendel."

They moved out of Addy's sight into the parlor, and she found tears on her cheeks. Still on her knees, she heard a soft sniff and turned to find Miss Pru discreetly blowing her nose. They looked at each other with all the knowledge of their times together, and Miss Pru touched Addy's head in a gentle way before she turned to go back to her room.

Filled with a strange, unknown emotion, Addy sat down, cross-legged. At a sound, she turned and saw that Sam was coming up the stairs to her. She could hear the murmur of Paul's voice, punctuated by Grendel's high-pitched, little-girl's voice coming from the parlor.

Reaching the top of the stairs, Sam stood there and smiled down at Addy before he put out his hand to help her rise to her feet. A little self-conscious, she wiped her wet cheeks and felt awkward. Would he think the tears were from seeing Paul again?

"Will you come down?" Sam whispered.

She shook her head. "Not this time." And with those words, she knew she was healed. She'd acknowledged the fact that Paul would visit Grendel again, and that she could see him. "I don't know why I'm crying."

"When you share something beautiful with another person, it touches your heart."

She looked up at Sam and saw tears in his own eyes. She knew then that he understood it all. She was at last free of her obsession, and she saw that he was proud of her. "Oh, Sam," she said. "I love you."

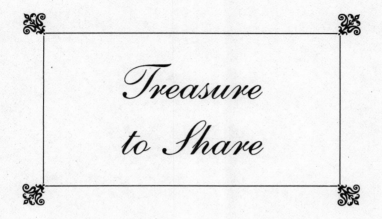

Treasure
to Share

1

AT THE ALARM'S muted buzz, Addy Grady reluctantly opened her eyes to the still-dark winter morning. She wished her day wasn't so packed with things to do, and that she could turn over in her cozy bed and go back to sleep. She closed her eyes and sighed, while next to her Sam stretched and yawned like a great big lion. A dark-haired, blue-eyed lion.

She sleepily pushed back her wheat-blond hair to look at him. It was always a pleasure. He grinned lazily and reached his strong arms out to pull her close, adjusting their bodies comfortably under the thick comforter.

"Good morning, bride." His voice rumbled deeply.

It was so lovely to lie in bed, Addy thought, relaxed and safe in Sam's arms, pressed into the heat of his

187

body on that cold January morning. She snuggled against him, slowly rubbing her cheek across the hair on his chest, and asked, "Bride? How can you call me a bride when we will have been married five years in April?"

"Five years!" he exclaimed. "Where did the time go?"

"And Grendel is eight and Bridget is four. Can you believe that?" Sam had adopted her Grendel on the day they were married, and Bridget had arrived nine months later. "Do you ever feel Grendel is Paul's child?" Addy asked, referring to the man who had made love to her and then left her.

"Never. Not since I first set eyes on her and knew I was going to marry you."

"You didn't know that on the day we met," she scoffed.

"Of course I did."

"How could you possibly have known then?"

"I was fated from birth to warm your cold feet. But there are . . . fringe benefits." He kissed her willing mouth and ran his hands down her flannel-covered back.

Sam slept in pajama bottoms or nothing. If he wore more than that, he got too hot under the blankets with Addy curled close against him. She, on the other hand, was just warm enough—especially with Sam in her bed.

"What would you have done if I'd already been married?" she asked.

"I'd have cashed in all my stocks and bonds, borrowed mother's pin money, and told your husband to get lost—made him an offer he couldn't refuse."

She laughed, and Sam kissed her again.

"Grendel actually looks more like you than she does Paul," Addy mused.

"She's absorbed my genes by osmosis," he said with the authority of a pediatric consultant, which he was.

She continued to rub her cheek slowly across his chest, relishing the sensation, and stroked his nape. "The girls have grown so. And the Gown House has expanded beyond all my expectations! Miss Pru and I thought that designing and sewing women's clothing in this house would be something like a cottage industry, a nice little business. It certainly has ballooned!"

Miss Pru was Addy's savior, the woman who had taken her in when she was pregnant with Grendel and her own family hadn't known what to do with her.

Sam scrunched his chin down against his chest to peer into his wife's face. "Are you re-evaluating your life? Examining it? Reminiscing?"

"I don't know how Miss Pru ever did it all," Addy said thoughtfully. She sorely missed her friend and mentor. Well past middle age, Miss Pru had very unexpectedly gotten married six months before and gone off to live in Tahiti, of all places.

"Miss Pru didn't do it all by herself," Sam said. "She had you to do the designs, supervise the seamstresses, and narrate the shows. Now you're trying to do two jobs. Three if you count being part of our family."

"I can handle it. Miss Pru did so much with time to spare. I can too."

"Why struggle?" Sam asked reasonably. "You need

some help. I still think you should hire my sister.
Cyn's more than qualified."

"You keep trying to order me around," Addy accused him.

"You need ordering," he declared placidly.

"I can handle my own life."

"With some help from a great and good friend."

Again she tilted her head in a slow swirl up his
hairy chest and looked into his eyes. "Have you ever
suspected ... I mean, is it at *all* possible ... that you,
always having to respond with instant authority to
desperately ill people in your work ... just might happen to have a wee tendency to be somewhat stubborn
and dictatorial at home?"

His eyebrows shot up in disbelief. "Who, me?"

"You."

"Not at all." He dismissed the idea completely and
kissed her, his hand moving over her flannel nightgown.

She broke the kiss before it deepened and pushed
him gently away. "I don't have time for fooling around
with you this morning, Dr. Grady."

"Sure you do. I set the alarm an hour early so we
could ... chat."

"A whole hour? Good grief, Sam, how could you?
We didn't get home from the Austins' last night until
after eleven."

"I wanted to talk, and you're always flying around
like the Rabbit in Alice—"

"Isn't their house beautiful? Haven't they done a
good job on it?"

"Uh-huh. Addy—"

"It was such a shame for that marvelous old house

to be all cut up into apartments that way. How nice that the Austins had the money to salvage it. Those floors? They even restored the parquetry under that leak in the dining room. Think what that must have cost!"

"Considering the size of their family, it probably would have cost them just as much to build a new house. In any case, it certainly is nice having them in the neighborhood."

"Actually, quite a number of our friends are moving back into the city. This side of Indianapolis is really changing. And with Nance and Ned buying a house only two blocks away . . . Didn't that surprise you? I thought Nance was a dyed-in-the-wool apartment type." Nance was their lawyer.

"The whole area is changing and—"

"Marty Austin told me last night that one of the town houses sold for ninety thousand dollars, and she says it hasn't even been renovated yet!"

"—and so are you, honey. You're changing too. You're too busy for everything. For me. For the kids. For fun. You've really got to get some help with the business."

"So you've said. Are you going to Houston to teach that seminar?" she asked, quickly changing the subject.

"John Mills is their first choice, but he's so dry you have to take along a glass of water just to listen to him. I'm pretty sure they'll ask me if they can edge him out tactfully." Sam's expression was smug. "John's a real graybeard."

"Old?"

"Forty-five."

Addy was amused. "Sam, *you're* forty-four. Will you be a graybeard in another year?"

"Of course not! The dividing line will then be forty-six."

"Ah! I see. I remember when we first met, and you were so indignant when I said you were forty . . . because you were only thirty-nine." She'd been twenty-seven.

"Yes." He dismissed that subject and began again. "Addy—"

"How do you like lecturing?" she interrupted again. "As much as practicing medicine?"

She succeeded in briefly distracting him. "I guess my interests are mostly academic. That's probably why I didn't mind studying so long to become a pediatric consultant in the first place. Learning has always fascinated me, you know. Lecturing gives me the opportunity to hit upon basic truths dear to my heart. I must admit I enjoy it."

"Are you going to become the complete academician? Let your hair grow and wear your cap and gown with the hood of colors to all life's events? Like touch football on the lawn? Shopping at the supermarket? To breakfast?"

"Speaking of which," he said, "Are we having pancakes again?"

"If you hadn't insisted on my having help with the cooking, the Freemans wouldn't have seized the opportunity to train another of their protégés at the expense of our stomachs." Marcus and Hedda Freeman were a black couple who lived in a huge house across the street and wielded a strong hand over the neighborhood affairs.

"You need help. Marcus's cleaning crews relieve us of the routine chores. And to give the Freemans credit, they train as many people in their house as they do in ours."

"I think we get their rejects. Sarah is a darling girl, but if she doesn't learn to make pancakes pretty soon— pancakes that meet Hedda's standards—I'll outweigh Lilabet," Addy wailed, referring to a very round Gown House seamstress.

"You're gorgeous. Just right. I like you the way you are." Giving her yet another kiss, Sam demonstrated just how nicely her body fit his hands.

"I still weigh the same as I did five years ago, but my top and bottom are bigger," Addy said fretfully.

"You're nicely round all over. Here . . . and here . . . and there. Ah, Addy . . ."

"Cut it out! I have to get up and leap aboard the treadmill." She wriggled to get free.

"Not yet." He pulled her back to him. "We need to discuss how we're going to celebrate our anniversary. Addy, I'd like us to go away for a holiday by ourselves." His voice rumbled against her body. "I need some tender loving care."

She ignored the touchy first subject—she simply didn't have any time for a trip in the foreseeable future—and addressed herself to the second. "TLC?" she teased. "Do you want me to hold you on my lap and rock you?"

He sat up and unwound her gown from around her body, then tugged it off as she made halfhearted sounds of protest. "You needn't rock me . . . on your lap, but you *could* hold me . . . and kiss me," he suggested. He grinned as if he'd stumbled onto a brilliant idea.

"There." She gave him a quick hug and a tight-lipped kiss.

"More kisses."

"More?" she exclaimed in shock. "All at once?"

"You could breathe in between them," he offered generously as they lay back in each other's arms.

She breathed in, kissed him, breathed out, kissed him, breathed in, kissed him before complaining, "That makes me a littly dizzy. You are a completely devastating man!"

"Not really," he assured her modestly. "The kisses need to be longer. You're hyperventilating."

"Oh." She slowly wrapped her arms around his head and gave him a long, hot kiss.

When she loosened her arms slightly and lifted her mouth just a little so that they could both breathe, he raised his brows and speculated, "You've kissed men before."

"Only you."

"You've certainly learned a lot in the last five years. You just made my hair stand straight up! How come I never noticed you'd gotten so good?"

"That's because you're always sneaking kisses, and you never give me the chance to initiate anything."

"Really?" He raised himself up on an elbow and frowned down at her. "I've been very stupid." He lay down on his back again and folded his hands over the covers on his chest, then said, "Go ahead."

She gazed at him blankly.

"Initiate," he commanded.

"I thought I was just supposed to kiss you."

"You have my permission to initiate."

"How kind," she replied with mock gratitude.

"Aren't initiations supposed to be done blindfolded?"

"I'll close my eyes."

She considered the idea. "I suppose that will have to do," she agreed finally. She peeked at the clock. "We haven't got much time."

With a powerful lunge he grabbed the clock, jerked its plug free from the socket, and pitched it against the wall. Then he lay down on top of her and said calmly, "Time has stopped. We have all the time we want."

"You gave me that clock for our second anniversary!" she exclaimed, no longer joking. She tried to push him away, bouncing a little to dislodge him.

"I just took it back." Sprawled across her, he kept Addy prisoner.

"You can't take gifts back!" she said sternly, falling still.

"How about the gift of love?" Something in Sam's tone made her eyes snap up to his.

She studied him for a minute then asked, "Are you talking about taking back your love? Or about giving love and receiving it in return?"

"Which do you think?"

She shifted under him restlessly, and he slowly released her. She hesitated, then moved away from him and sat up in bed, facing him. "I really liked that clock," she said solemnly.

"I'll buy you another." He lay there watching her.

"I liked that clock," she repeated stubbornly. Naked, she sat on her heels, her hands on her thighs, her mouth charmingly petulant.

"You looked at that damned clock more than you looked at me," Sam growled.

"I didn't love the clock more than I love you."

"You've made time your master."

"And *you* want to be my master?" She smiled hesitantly at him.

"I want you to think only of me."

"Do you think only of me?" she teased, her smile widening.

"Always."

"Then I'm afraid you must be neglecting your patients."

"No. While my mind is occupied with their problems, my body is remembering you." He swung a lazy hand onto her bare hip.

"Really? What part remembers me?" She grinned slyly and tilted her head, flirting with him.

Without changing expression, he raised his other hand and touched his heart. His heart remembered her.

"Oh, Sam, it's like that with me too. But April is too hectic to leave for vacation. Perhaps I can manage a day or so." She pushed her hair back with a distracted gesture.

"Get help," he told her soothingly, rubbing his palm in a circle on her hip. His hand was rough on her smooth, satiny skin, and it sent skitters of awareness radiating through her body.

With some difficulty she kept her mind on their conversation. "How could I find another Miss Pru? There she is, off in Tahiti, lying around on the beach with her new husband, and probably teaching the hula to the natives with remarkable efficiency." She sighed.

"Other people are equally capable of taking on some of the workload," Sam reminded her.

"Teaching the hula?" she asked with half a laugh.

"No. Here with your business."

"Oh, I suppose so. But right now it's all mine," she said possessively.

"You need to let some of it go."

"But I love it all."

"More than you love me?" His eyes were steady on hers.

"Never," she promised softly.

"Prove it." His hand slid over and under her thigh.

She tossed her head and batted her eyelids. "How?" she said, temptingly. "Would you like me to write you a poem?"

"Well, that wasn't *exactly* what I had in mind."

"Would you like me to fix you something other than pancakes for breakfast?"

He laughed in appreciation. "Not quite yet, but maybe later."

"Would you like me to—"

"You could initiate," he reminded her helpfully.

"Oh." Quite elaborately she put her fingers to her cheek and feigned astonishment. "I suppose I could do that. Close your eyes."

"Why?"

"The blindfold."

"Ah, yes." As he complied and his lips quirked in anticipation.

She lifted the blanket from him and lay it back. Sitting on her heels next to him, she feasted her eyes on her husband's body. He was so ruinously gorgeous. He was so beloved. Her mouth curved tenderly, and she reached out a hand to stroke his furry chest. But just then she noticed that his eyes weren't completely closed.

"You're peeking!"

"I had to know what you were doing."

"I was admiring you."

"See? When you can't look at a clock, you have the time to look at me."

"You're beautiful."

"Men aren't beautiful. They're good-looking, handsome, or well-made." It was their current running joke.

"You're all of those." She put her hand on his chest and ran it slowly over the hair-roughened skin. "And you're beautiful."

"Women are beautiful. *You* are beau—"

"Close your eyes and be quiet. You're interrupting the initiation."

"Are you sure you know how to do this? You're taking a hell of a long time."

"Be quiet." She leaned down and moved her face over his chest, turning slowly, enjoying the feel of him against her skin. She licked his flat nipples and inched her way down his body.

When he sharply drew in a long breath, she raised up to ask with all concern, "Did that seem too... personal?"

"Oh, no!" he assured her.

"Close your eyes."

"You can get as personal as you like," he said earnestly.

"Hush." Slowly, gently, she ran her hands up his thighs and around his stomach. "Maybe we should shave you all over and see what you *really* look like," she suggested. She continued to move her hands tantalizingly closer, near but not quite touching the most sensitive part of him.

"Whatever you like," he said with a gasp.

"We could buy a bear rug, and you could lie on it to see how it is for me to lie on you."

"Fine." His voice sounded hoarse.

She glanced at his face. "You're peeking again!" she scolded.

But sitting up, he grasped her under the armpits and lay back, dragging her up his body. Then he began kissing her avidly.

After a time she said in a daze, "We're not ready for the kissing part yet."

"The kissing part comes first."

"Did I get it wrong again? Darn. Now we'll have to start all over."

As he turned her over and lay mostly on top of her, she commented in a bright, friendly voice, "I'll just bet you've been through an initiation before!"

He didn't reply, and it wasn't long before she too fell speechless. Not silent, just at a loss for words.

"Umm," she elucidated a while later.

"You like that?"

"Oh," she replied nonchalantly, "a little."

"How about that?" he asked, purring.

"Aaahhh. It's . . . all right."

There was laughter in his voice as, moving purposefully, he inquired, "And this?"

"Ohh," she said in an indrawn breath. Then, "It's okay."

"Which do you like best? This . . . or this . . . or—"

"All of them," she assured him breathlessly.

"All of what?"

"All of you! Sammm."

He found other things she liked too, and as she gasped and wriggled and squirmed and shivered and clutched, his own passion was enflamed beyond containment, and they rode the wild wind together.

When they finally lay replete in a tangle of sweaty arms and legs, their heartbeats slowing, their smiles like those of cream-fed oats, Sam said, "Well, Adelina Mary Rose Kildaire Grady, can you believe that in April we will have lived in wedded bliss for five whole years?"

"As I recall, we began the bliss part a little early." She paused, then said, "Let go, Sam. I have to get up."

"We need to discuss our anniversary trip."

"Trip? Sam how can I take a trip in April when the May show comes right after that? You're mad! Do you think my Gown House runs itself? I still have the February show to get through, and then there's St. Patrick's Day. We *must* hire a hall for that, Sam. We must! That stupid party has expanded out of all bounds. The house can't hold everyone anymore." Her body tense, she gestured awkwardly within his iron embrace.

Reasonable and soothing, Sam replied, "Now that the new furnace has replaced that old monster furnace, the basement is enormous. Marcus's gang could clean it and paint it, and we could use that space too. What do you think about painting it green?"

"What about the orangies? Catholic Irish wear green but Protestant Irish wear Orange." She succeeded in prying her body free and began to crawl off the bed.

Casually Sam reached out and patted her bottom. "We could paint the attic rooms orange. With the orangies up there and the greenies in the basement, we wouldn't risk another donnybrook like the one we had last year. Remember?"

Addy remembered the fight all too well. "It was appalling! All those smashed noses and black eyes. And the language! At least you managed to herd them all outside before the fight got completely out of hand. Whatever started it all? I never did find out."

"God knows. The Irish do tend to be a little volatile," he said placidly, sliding a teasing glance at her.

"They weren't Irish!" she protested, turning at the side of the bed. "Their names were Gomez and LeTour and Schmidt and—"

"But the Irish hung off the porch, laughing and egging them on. And betting!"

"Marcus laughed out loud at that!" Addy shook her head. "And the police!" She put her hand to her forehead. "I was so embarrassed. Couldn't we just not have the party this year?"

"I seriously doubt that any of them will wait for an invitation. They will simply show up, as sure of their welcome as always, with their own brand of Irish booze and in a partying mood."

"It's monstrous."

He considered her comment soberly, then licked his lips and bit them to hold back a grin. But his eyes danced with humor as he insisted, "It's fun," before he finally laughed out loud.

She turned away with a snort of impatience, throwing up her hands in frustration, and his eyes gleamed at the sight of her naked body as she crossed the floor.

Their room was enormous, their bed king-sized to accommodate Sam's long body. The rug was an in-

tricately patterned blue Oriental, the drapes were an
equally rich blue, and the bittersweet-colored cushions
on the chaise longue added a striking accent.

Addy unlocked their hall door and headed across
the room to their bath. In midstep she stopped and
said, "Sam, I mean it. We have to hold the party
someplace else. I simply don't have enough time to
cope with the whole thing. It's become completely
unmanageable and leaves me exhausted."

"Oh, honey, you worry too much. Marcus's young
people will move all the furniture and clean, and they'll
put it all back. Hedda will take care of the food. You
won't have to do anything. All we need is a place to
hold it. And we have the room. I like having it here.
I like having everyone feel so welcome and at home."

"They certainly feel at home all right! But having
to empty out the entire first floor of this huge house
disrupts—"

There was a tap on their door and a piping voice
called, "May I come in?"

Sam flipped the sheet over his naked hips as Addy
reached around the bathroom door for her robe. "Sure,
Bridget, come on in," Sam called.

As the door opened to reveal their blond, brown-
eyed four-year-old, Addy smiled and said, "Good
morning, darling."

"What are you two kids doing?" Bridget asked,
imitating a question they'd often posed to her and her
sister. "Your door was locked."

"We were discussing our St. Patrick's Day party."
Sam held out a hand, and Bridget ran over and scrambled onto the bed beside him.

"Grendel is seeing if Stormy's going to have babies," Bridget breathlessly told her father. "He's so fat."

"Now, honey, you know—" Addy began.

"How is she deciding that?" Sam asked.

"She's sitting very still with her hands on his stomach feeling for the kittens to move like Pattycake's baby did." Pattycake was a Gown House model who was pregnant with her first child.

"Stormy can't have any babies because he's a boy cat," Sam explained.

"Well, his tummy is very fat and so is Pattycake's, and she's going to have a baby, so maybe Stormy is, too," Bridget replied with childish logic.

Addy went to take a shower, leaving them to their discussion. She stood under the spray and thought how impossible her schedule was. Everyone kept tearing off big pieces of her time, leaving her with none for herself. The St. Patrick's Day party would just have to go. But as she soaped her tender, recently-loved body, she forgot the party and thought only of Sam. Oh, Sam. And she smiled into the shower's mist.

As she dried her hair, however, Addy's thoughts turned to the problems facing her as a designer of women's clothes. It was stupid to expand her already extensive line to include maternity clothes. She knew she should concentrate just on gowns. After all, her business was called the Gown House. She shouldn't try to do anything else.

But Pattycake was so charmingly pregnant. When one had a model one cherished—and everyone loved Patty—one had to include her in the show; thus, one had to design maternity clothes.

And Addy couldn't drop Ad's Mads, the wildly different gowns carefully chosen for the select few who had the right figure to wear them. They were such fun to design. But she shook her head. She needed to condense her line. After the February show she would be ruthless and firm, and she could cut back. But where?

There just wasn't time right then to figure it out. After the February show . . . But the St. Patrick's Day party would follow, and now Sam was talking about going away for their anniversary in April, just before the May show. How could she do everything? There was no way. It was humanly impossible. There was too much to do and not enough time, not at all, at all.

She pulled on her underwear and went into their room to put on a blue V-necked pullover sweater and white slacks. Bridget had vanished, but Sam still lay in bed, his hands behind his tousled head, his chest bare. She smiled shyly at him. He still affected her in a lovely way, making her feel excessively feminine.

"Did I tell you I saw Johnny yesterday?" he asked.

"Is he all right?" she asked eagerly. He was a former patient of Sam's who had stayed with the Gradys for a while when his family was having problems and couldn't take care of him. His father had disappeared, and his mother was crippled from a car accident. Now he lived with his grandmother.

"He looks great. His grandmother is young enough to take him in stride. He's five now."

"I miss him," Addy said pensively.

"Me too."

"Little boys are different. They play differently. Their interests and reactions are so male."

"Really? Do you think so? I've found boys to be very similar. It's little girls who are different: they're so charming."

She ignored his teasing. "Those months he was here were nice. You've brought us some delightful guests," she said, remembering all the children they'd harbored over the years.

"There was Terry," Sam mused.

"Yes," she agreed soberly.

"I was so sorry she had to be institutionalized." His voice was filled with regret. The child had been self-destructive. Sam absently ran a hand through his hair.

"That was tough for you."

"There was no other way," he said, resigned. Then, "Addy, there is someone else."

She gave him a tender but wary look. "Not too young, I hope. I haven't got time for—"

"This one is an adult. Her name is Erin."

"An adult?" she said with a puzzled frown. As a pediatric consultant, Sam worked only with children.

"I thought that with Miss Pru gone, she could help out for a while. She's been through a bad time and needs to heal."

"An adult?" Addy questioned again. "Coming here for sanctuary? To this mad house?"

"It's ideal. We'll all ignore her, but she'll have people and activity around her, and gradually she'll be drawn back into life."

"What in the world is the matter with her? Sam, we can't have an unstable adult here."

"No, no, it's nothing like that. She lost her husband and two small children in a house fire just before

Thanksgiving. She's having trouble coping with her loss."

"Oh, Sam, how awful!" Addy glanced around their enormous bedroom, one of twenty-four rooms in that barn of a house. "This is a wooden house. Won't she see it as one great fire trap?"

"I don't think so. It may be wooden, but it's a solid, safe house."

"And you're sure she should come here?" Addy asked doubtfully.

"It's the only place for her."

"Now, if she could type or sew..."

"Did you get Cyn's résumé?"

The image of her cool, sophisticated sister-in-law came clearly to Addy's mind. "Résumé? Oh, yeah," she replied lamely.

Cyn was a bit older than Addy and had a polished manner that always made her feel a bit inferior—like burlap next to silk. Of course she was a superb advertisement for Addy's designs, which looked stunning on Cyn. She did sell clothes, but Addy didn't really want any help.

"Cyn qualifies, doesn't she?" Sam went on. "She could handle the business end of Gown House."

"I suppose," Addy admitted grudgingly. How could she ever explain her reservations? She couldn't. Instead she asked, "When's what's-her-name coming?"

"Erin Simmons." Sam gave her a warning look.

Addy cast a quick glance at him, then asked more kindly, "When's Erin coming?"

"Probably not for a week to ten days." Sam studied his wife. "Will that be all right?"

"Sure. She can have Miss Pru's old room."

"Want me to call the cleaning crew?"

"Great. I might forget." She went to the door and smiled back at Sam. "See you at breakfast."

His tender expression made her pause and return to his side. She leaned over and kissed him, their lips clinging sweetly. Then, following the aroma of fried bacon, she left the bedroom and walked pensively down the back stairs.

How could she make Sam understand her need to run the business by herself? All his life he'd done everything he'd ever wanted to do, achieved everything he'd set out to achieve. But so had she, to some extent, Addy suddenly realized. Her family lived contentedly in a small town and had no ambition to go anywhere else. She'd astonished her parents by being the first of the Kildares to go after a college education.

She'd gotten it too. She'd worked her way through Indiana University at a series of jobs, including file clerk, playground supervisor, short-order cook, and tutor. And she'd finished her master's degree in design after she'd gotten pregnant with Grendel and Paul had walked out on her.

She was fully capable of achieving her goals. She had Grendel. She had her degrees. And she had Sam, although she hadn't thought of him as a goal until he'd convinced her of it. She had Bridget. And she had the Gown House, which had outgrown all foreseeable bounds to become an astonishing success.

Maybe she would hire Cyn. She paused on the landing as she considered the idea, then shook her head. Although she wasn't quite sure of her own motivations, she wasn't ready to share her success yet.

It wasn't a question of money. Sam made enough

to support three families; and material goods had never been very important to her. Even now she made more than enough to provide for her needs.

Perhaps, like a mountain climber, she was trying to prove something to herself. But what? That she could do it, that she was in control? Perhaps.

2

THE KITCHEN WAS a large cheerful room with a small fireplace that a previous owner had added for comfort during the long winter months. At one end of the room, in front of the windows overlooking the south lawn, stood a round oak table that could be extended with twelve leaves. At present, only two had been added.

Along the east wall was a row of storage closets. One was for china and linens; another was for cheeses, seasonings, and breads; and the last held seldom-used pots and pans of impressive sizes. Long ago Addy had said, "I'll never in this world use those." But she had, and she'd been glad to have them.

Addy's daughter, Grendel, was seated at the table, dressed for school and almost finished with breakfast.

As expected, Sarah was making pancakes, slowly stirring the batter, preparing to spoon it onto the hot griddle. She was eighteen, tall, slender, and good-natured, and she gave Addy a friendly grin.

Smothering an inward groan at the thought of eating pancakes again, Addy returned Sarah's smile and leaned over to give her daughter a kiss.

Grendel was an earnest eight-year-old. Her black hair was plaited into one braid down her back, and her shoe-button eyes were bright, steady, and startling in her white skin. She said to her mother, "Stormy might have babies in his stomach."

"Now, Grendel, you know full well that Stormy is a male."

"But he was fixed, and the doctor just *may* have implanted a test-tube baby kitten by mistake."

"Darling, male cats don't have wombs."

"They could have fixed that too," Grendel said airily. "Doctors can do almost anything these days."

Sarah giggled and set a plate of pancakes in front of Addy as she shook her head, sighed, and straightened in her chair. All these pancakes would be her ruination. She dieted constantly, hoping her nicely rounded figure would slim down to a model's flat planes. As a designer of women's clothing she found it somewhat embarrassing to have such ample breasts and hips.

Resignedly, Addy poured maple syrup over the melted butter on her stack and dug in. "Mmm, these are really good," she told Sarah, trying not to sound too surprised. "You're doing very well."

"Thank you." Sarah's grin was wide and white in her black face. Her eyes shone with amusement.

Sarah might take a long time at things, Addy thought, but she was really very nice to have around—

extremely flexible and quite accommodating.

"Sarah, you've done so well with the pancakes, I believe you may now go on to something else."

"I'll ask Mrs. Freeman." Sarah smiled proudly.

See? Addy thought. Even in her own house she couldn't decide what she'd have for breakfast. She had no authority, no control over anything.

After Miss Pru had left almost six months ago—and what a painful and tearful leave-taking that had been—Addy had experienced a teasing excitement, the conviction that now she would finally be able to control her own life. Instead, everything was chaos. She was sure this was the fourth week she'd had pancakes for breakfast. She was thirty-two years old and still not in control of her own life, much less her own household.

"When Mrs. Freeman arrives this morning, Sarah, will you ask her to come and see me for a minute?"

"Sure. I'll be glad to," Sarah agreed.

If Addy was ever going to take control, she would have to begin in her own kitchen. Today was the day for her Declaration of Independence. She was an American, captain of her ship. She would take the helm.

Caught up in her determination, she almost shook hands with Grendel instead of kissing her good-bye. But her daughter grinned and gave her a quick peck on the cheek before running to the cavernous front closet under the grand stairs to fetch her coat and boots. The school bus was due at any moment.

Just then Bridget came clumping down the back stairs and entered the kitchen. "Pancakes!" she exclaimed brightly, earning a sour look from her mother and a grin from Sarah as she climbed into her booster chair at the table.

As Bridget ate and chatted with Sarah, Addy sat next to her daughter and sketched on a big pad. She felt it was important to spend time with her children during breakfast instead of rushing off to her studio.

"Grendel doesn't have to sit around the house all morning," Bridget complained. "She gets to go to school."

"You make your bed?" Sarah asked in her soft voice.

"Yes. But next year I'll get to go to school all day."

"Next year's pre-kindergarten, and you'll still just go afternoons," Sara reminded her.

"Again?" Bridget sighed in exasperation, propped an elbow on the table, and rested her chin in her hand.

"No elbows on the table," Sarah told her gently.

Addy was only semiconscious of the conversation and of the way Bridget shifted slightly in her seat, letting her elbow slide negligently off the table, as if the movement were made as an afterthought rather than a deliberate sign of obedience. "May I have one more pancake?" She and Sarah smiled at each other.

Moments later Sam arrived, freshly showered and shaved and looking very unlike the ardent lover he'd been in bed. "Pancakes!" he enthused. Addy jerked her head and gave him a narrow-eyed glare. Ignoring her, Sam greeted Sarah and asked for a high stack of her delicious pancakes.

Sam certainly seemed full of himself this morning. He teased Bridget and flirted with Addy. And he made Sarah laugh out loud by digging into the pile of pancakes with gusto.

Addy straightened, feeling blimpish, and realized with surprise that she'd eaten a second helping of pancakes. This had to stop.

"Don't forget to ask Mrs. Freeman to stop in to see me for just a minute, will you, Sarah?"

"I'll tell her."

"Thanks." Addy smiled slightly. "But you don't *tell* Mrs. Freeman; you ask her, please."

"I know." The girl's eyes brimmed with amusement.

Addy rose from the table, waggled her fingers at Sam to say good-bye, and walked around Bridget, who was now sitting in the middle of the floor with her hands on Stormy's stomach. The cat was lying stretched out on his back, fast asleep.

Stormy was lazy. Fat and lazy and inappropriately named. As Addy went up to her attic studio, she wondered how long it would be until the girls gave up hoping he'd have kittens. Probably when Pattycake had her baby.

Addy's Gown House operation had taken over the entire first floor of the house, with the exception of a small front parlor and the kitchen. Even the morning room was now filled with bins of fabric and drawers filled with buttons, thread, zippers, pins, and needles— all the accoutrements of her business.

Once one of the models had wanted to roll a rack of clothes into the big storage closet off the morning room, but Addy had been adamant in her refusal. "It's just empty space!" the model had protested. "Why not put it to good use? We can roll the rack out when we need something from the shelves." But Addy had still said no.

One stormy morning five years ago, when she and Sam had been playing hide and seek, Sam had followed her into that closet and made long, marvelous, delicious love to her. It was then that she'd first known they belonged together.

After they were married, she'd lured him into the closet a time or two. Once he'd picked her up in the middle of a quarrel and simply carried her in and closed the door.

How could she store a rack of clothes in there, a rack that would have to be moved out if they ever wanted to use the floor. It would be a blatant sign that someone was in the closet. So that ample space remained empty.

In the attic was her studio, where she designed her clothes, both the styles and the fabrics.

Eight seamstresses worked at the Gown House each weekday. Others sewed at home doing piecework— gussets, tab collars, and zippers. Each day customers came for fittings, and once a week Addy held private consultations for special clients.

Addy was an expert designer. Her creations hid a woman's worst features and flattered her best. She could make any woman look good and feel good.

Addy was most satisfied when customers returned to reorder favorite dresses from her past collections— those that had fit particularly well, those that made the woman feel both comfortable and well-groomed, and those that conjured up memories of a special occasion.

Since really good designs never went out of style, Addy had begun to sell her classic clothes to selected boutiques across the country. This new venture was becoming a very important part of her business.

Addy loved her work; it was a never-ending source of delight for her. The Gown House was growing bigger and better with each passing day. And she was the key to the whole operation. It was all hers.

Determinedly, Addy put all these thoughts aside and got down to business. It was several hours before she happened to glance up from her drawing board and out the window—just in time to see Hedda Freeman regally crossing the street. A magnificent, silent woman, she dressed in long, exotic quasi-African gowns and head coverings. Addy had always suspected that she might actually be skilled in voodoo.

Hedda never spoke. In all the time Addy had known the Freemans, Hedda had not uttered one single word. Addy had adjusted to the situation, but she still wondered whether Hedda really couldn't speak or simply chose not to.

Addy had once asked Marcus, "Does Hedda speak to you?"

"In many ways," he'd replied. But when Addy had thought about it, she'd realized that Marcus hadn't really told her anything.

In any event, Hedda's absolute silence gave her an undeniable aura of mystery. Perhaps, Addy speculated, she had taken a vow of silence in exchange for voodoo powers.

It was a while before Hedda entered Addy's studio. Addy rose and smiled with automatic courtesy. Hedda gave her a brief glance, then bent her head to examine the pancake she was holding in her hands. Breaking it apart, she studied Sarah's work critically.

"Oh, good," Addy began. "That's what I wanted

to see you about—the pancakes. We've had them every blessed morning for four weeks now."

Hedda raised up two fingers in a graceful gesture.

"Yes," Addy rattled on. "Peace and love."

Hedda shook her head and patiently counted the two fingers with her other hand. Apparently it had been only two weeks since they'd begun having pancakes.

"Two weeks? Is that all? I thought surely it'd been every single day since Christmas."

Hedda nodded. It was the second week after Christmas.

"Nevertheless, Hedda, we must change the breakfast menu. The pancakes are perfect. Sarah has done a superb job of them. But really, it's becoming just a bit much."

Frowning down at the pancake, Hedda didn't appear convinced.

"Couldn't we go on to something else? How about poached eggs? Eggs à la Goldenrod?"

Hedda reached into a deep pocket in her boldly patterned skirt, which probably harbored toadstools and the belly buttons of newts, Addy guessed, withdrew a piece of paper, and handed it to Addy. It was a hand-written recipe for grits.

"Grits! I hate grits!" Addy's eyes flared, her lips thinned, and she assumed a battle stance, her fists clenched. All she could see down the breakfast road to summer was . . . grits. Ugh!

Hedda made a circle with her hands, then put both hands together in a small half-moon to one side. The grits were to be a side dish.

"But I'll hurt Sarah's feelings if I don't eat them!" Addy wailed.

Hedda touched Addy's shoulder in sympathy, then turned and walked down the hall in her slow, stately way.

Good Lord, grits, Addy thought. She should have left things as they were.

Later that morning Marcus Freeman came to Addy's studio to tell her his men would be repainting the house that spring.

"Repainting it? We've painted *twice* in eight years," Addy protested, gesturing broadly.

"That first coat barely saved the house," Marcus replied. "And the second one only helped. Anyway, you'll want it all spruced up and pretty for the May shows. How about Shaker colors—dull red with blue trim?"

Addy stared at him. It was hardly a question. What he really meant was that red and blue were what she'd be getting. He'd already made up his mind.

The first time he'd painted the house, Addy had chosen white, but he'd used antique blue with French vanilla trim. The second time, Addy had again requested white, but Marcus had opted for dark blue with lime green trim. Much to her chagrin Addy had to admit that Marcus had chosen wisely both times. That was the depressing thing about Marcus: he was always right. Still, it was her house and her money.

"How about white?" she suggested without much hope.

"Too plebeian."

"Three times now I've asked for a white house, and you've refused me each time. I think you have a racial prejudice against white."

"No, we blacks are very tolerant of white people

because you're so rare, globally speaking." His eyes sparkled with laughter. "And more likely an endangered species."

Addy had to laugh.

She had first met Marcus eight years ago when she, newly-born Grendel, and Miss Pru had moved into this sprawling house on the near-north side of Indianapolis. The house had been and still was large enough to serve as both home and center of business.

They'd first named the establishment Delilah's, then used Addy's name, Kildaire's—but men mistakenly assumed she was involved in another kind of business altogether. Finally she'd settled on calling it the Gown House, but just about everyone else called it Addy's.

Without being asked, Marcus Freeman had immediately volunteered to provide her with security in that neighborhood in transition. And he'd been overseeing her relentlessly ever since. He was a large, formidable man, and his daughter Pearl was Addy's best model, six feet tall and now in her third year of medical school, thanks to Sam's influence. And then there was Hedda, Marcus's wife...

Addy was still baffled as to why the Freemans bothered with her. But she'd finally learned that Marcus wasn't actually the Godfather of the Black Mafia, as she'd suspected, but a mecanical genius, a technical engineer and consultant as well as neighborhood leader.

He gathered crews of jobless young people and set them to work at various projects. They kept the grass on her block mowed in summer and the walks shoveled in winter. They cleaned and painted her house, which stood in splendid isolation in the middle of the block, the other homes having all been demolished.

Since Marcus took everyone under his wing, and called them all his children, Addy had once teased, "Are they *all* your children?"

"Not literally," he'd replied seriously, "but God made me big and smart, and it's my responsibility to help those who are smaller and not quite as bright."

Addy had been rather touched by his paternal attitude until she remembered how much he had helped her. She tilted her head and gave him a dubious look. Did he mean to imply that she wasn't very bright? He'd just smiled.

"I would like the house white," she said now, as firmly as she could. But even to her own ears she sounded hesitant. They both knew the house was going to be Shaker red with blue trim. Addy sighed.

As Addy passed Sam on the stairs later that day, she said, "Marcus is going to paint the house Shaker red with blue trim."

"Gorgeous!" he replied. "Think of it next Christmas in the snow."

So Marcus had won again. Addy could even imagine Miss Pru writing from Tahiti, "How perfect." Addy wondered if anyone would ever do what *she* wanted.

That afternoon, when she welcomed Bridget home from nursery school, Addy said, "Wash your hands before you eat your snack."

Bridget smiled up at her and replied, "As soon as I check Stormy to see if he's had his kittens."

"Now."

"Okay," Bridget said cheerfully.

But as Addy watched, Bridget ran to the kitchen and peeked to see if Stormy was still fat before going to wash up.

Addy couldn't even make a four-year-old obey her.

That afternoon there was a delay in the arrival of a bolt of summer cotton, and Lilabet Thomas, who made up the models' gowns for the shows, became upset. "How do you expect me to sew these gowns?" she said temperamentally. "With air?"

Addy soothed the seamstress and spent the rest of the day on the phone trying to track down the missing bolt of fabric. Eventually she discovered that the material had been shipped to Indianapolis, *Missouri*.

That night in bed Addy told Sam with a long-suffering sigh, "Without me, the whole place would collapse." She didn't realize how smug she sounded. She felt proud at having managed the crisis. "My life is very intense," she claimed placidly.

"I find that you intensify my life too," Sam said.

"Intensify?"

"Come here, and I'll show you what I mean."

She moved nearer to him under the warm blankets in the frosty January night. "Is this a survey of some type?" she asked.

"Absolutely." He pulled her close and kissed her ardently.

"What type of survey?" She stroked the hair on his chest and slid a hand slowly down to his stomach.

"It's . . . a personal survey."

"What's the goal, the reason for it?"

"That's a surprise." He kissed her bare shoulder.

"Oh! Do I get a prize for participating?"

"I'm pretty sure of it, but I have to ask the key questions first, and you have to answer them honestly."

"You're questioning my honesty?"

"People have been known to do some pretty incredible things to get prizes."

"That's shocking. But how do people know if the prize is worth having.

"It is."

"What is the prize?"

"It's kind of like the Oscars, we go to great lengths to— Now, Addy, this is serious. We go to great lengths to conceal . . . Addy! . . . to conceal the prizes; otherwise the contestant might cheat."

"But is the prize worthwhile?"

"It's a fulfilling experience."

"Uplifting?" she inquired eagerly.

"Very."

"I think I know what it is!" she exclaimed jubilantly.

"What?"

"A hang-glider."

"Uhhh . . . no, I'm afraid not. I can see how you might have been misled, though. A hang-glider is uplifting certainly, and it can make you feel as if—"

The phone rang. Sam lifted the receiver and said, "Yes?" He listened. "Tell them I'm on my way."

They both erupted from the bed at once. With practiced efficiency Addy produced a clean shirt as Sam pulled on his underwear, and then she handed him his flannel trousers and a matching sweater. While he was putting those on, she ran down the front stairs, and hung his coat, woolen cap, and gloves on the newel post. Then she pulled on her own boots and coat and dashed outside to start the car.

When he pulled open the car door, she emerged to receive his quick kiss and backed up, standing in the snow as he took her place in the driver's seat. The night was crisp and cold, the plume of exhaust like white smoke as they waited impatiently for the motor to warm up. She remained standing there as he pulled slowly away, lifting a hand in farewell.

Whatever the problem, it was always serious when Sam was called out in the middle of the night. Addy gazed up at the night sky and asked God to help them. Then she thought of her own two babies and asked God to keep them safe from harm.

She went inside, into the large entrance hall with its sweeping formal staircase. Hanging down from the second-story ceiling was a silver Art Nouveau lamp, its original Edison bulb, which had never burned out, still glowing.

She removed her coat and boots and hung her hat on its peg. Then she climbed the stairs, peeked into the girls' rooms to check on them, and returned to her own very large, very empty bed.

She crawled into Sam's side and snuggled down in the warm spot he'd left. When she finally fell asleep, she had terrible dreams of the February show turning into a catastrophe.

Addy awoke in a sweat, wanting Miss Pru. Who would ever had thought that Miss Pru, her mainstay, a maiden lady who'd lived sixty-six perfectly ordinary, orderly years, would fall madly in love and fly off to Tahiti with her new husband, Jean Claude. Miss Pru's going to Tahiti astounded Addy. It wouldn't have been quite so amazing if she had simply moved to St. Louis. But Tahiti!

Addy sighed, shifted in bed, and decided she was lucky Jean Claude hadn't shown up earlier in Miss Pru's life. She didn't think she could have survived Grendel's illegitimate birth without Miss Pru. How she missed her dear friend. Yet how glad she was that Miss Pru and Jean Claude had found each other.

The next day Addy faced new pressures and problems. There simply wasn't enough time to do everything. When Sam called in the morning, she answered distractedly. "Sam? Is your patient okay?"

"So far," he replied. "Tell Sarah I was devastated to have missed her grits this morning. I'll be here at the hospital all day. But I plan to tackle my survey at the first opportunity."

"Survey?" Was he doing a medical survey?

"The one we began last night."

"Oh," she said vaguely, trying to figure out what he was talking about. "Sam, my other line's blinking. Did you want anything specific?"

"No. Miss me."

"I'll try." And she punched the button for the other call.

That evening, Addy came down the attic stairs from her studio and found Sam standing at the railing staring vacantly down at the front entrance hall, totally unaware of her. Knowing he was preoccupied with his patient, she took the opportunity to study him.

What a man! Just by looking at him, anyone would know he was in charge. He had the intellegence and the knowledge to see things through. She thought of his insistent demands that she spend more time with him. Why, if it weren't so impossible to compare him in any way to a woman, he might remind her of a neglected wife whose husband spent all day at the office.

Physically Sam was impressive. Good-looking,

well-built, he carried himself with ease and confidence. He was comfortable with himself. And he thrilled her body. Just looking at him was enough to arouse her. After five years, that hadn't changed.

Sam was twelve years older than her thirty-two years, and he had the body of a mature man. His shoulders were heavier than those of a youth, yet he was lean and fit and he moved with an athlete's grace.

Sam's concentration was such that Addy stood next to him for a full minute before he became conscious of her presence. Then his head came slowly around, and his blue eyes softened when he found her beside him. In a soft, sad voice he said, "Her name is Helen. Such an adult name for such a small child."

"Is she going to be all right?"

"There's always a chance."

It was several days before Sam was confident of that chance. During that time, it seemed he was barely going through the motions of living, without being fully aware of what he was doing. He ate and listened and walked and dressed and slept as if in a daze. And he made love to Addy without really communicating with her. He used sex as a way of releasing his frustrations. It was a measure of her love for him that she willingly gave him that solace.

In the five years of their marriage Addy had learned that husbands and wives expressed many different emotions through sex and made love for many different reasons. Sometimes sex wasn't so much an act of sharing as it was an act of giving.

At last Sam came home acting his normal self. He picked up all the threads of living that had been woven in the days he had been only half there. Stormy still hadn't produced kittens. Sarah had quickly conquered grits, much to Addy's relief, and was now struggling with popovers. It seemed they were in for a long haul with the popovers.

"We probably ought to buy some chickens," Sam suddenly suggested.

"Baby chicks!" the girls exclaimed.

Addy was dumbfounded. "Why chickens?" she asked, too busy to stop what she was doing.

"Eggs. With popovers and the inevitable soufflés that are sure to follow, plus pound cakes, it makes sense to have our own chickens."

Addy regarded him warily.

"I'll ask Marcus," he said.

"I don't want chickens wandering all over the place."

"What about a screened-in pen?"

"I'm not at all in favor of this."

"Think of it as therapy for Stormy. Maybe if he had some chickens to chase he'd lose some weight. He really does look pregnant, you know. I've considered bringing mice home, but I doubt that Stormy would know what to do with them. They'd probably get loose and breed, and then we'd be knee-deep in mice."

"Mice!" The girls chorused enthusiastically.

"Good Lord, Sam."

"I suspected you'd feel that way," he said, pleased to have accurately surmised her reaction.

Under Sarah's anxious eyes he pulled apart a popover. It looked like a toadstool that had flourished in an evil atmosphere. Placidly he spooned jelly onto an unnaturally bright yellow segment and popped it into his mouth, chewing carefully, then lifting his brows and almost nodding in tenuous approval.

"Are they awful?" Sarah asked hesitantly.

"Didn't you try one?" Sam seemed surprised.

"I thought I'd wait till you did."

"Now, Sarah, what if I gasped, put both hands to my throat and fell off my chair?"

"Better you than me." They both laughed.

"They're different," Grendel said, trying to be helpful.

"Can I have toast?" Bridget was young enough to be less tactful.

"You'd better hurry, Grendel. Your bus is due," Sarah warned.

Grendel stuffed the last bite into her mouth, scooped up her dishes and carried them to the sink, and said, "Call the principal if Stormy has her kittens before I get home. You can tell Mrs. Telford it's a family emergency."

"Stormy isn't going to have kittens," Sam said firmly.

"Bye, Grendel," Addy remembered to say, leaning over for a kiss.

Grendel took a token portion of another popover, smiled at Sarah, and yelled good-bye as she hurried out the door.

"Daddy, will I only go to school half-days again next year?" Bridget asked unhappily, knowing what the answer would be.

"Probably."

"That's what Sarah said." She sighed elaborately.

"How would you like to go some place with me this morning?"

"Okay!" she agreed, excited. "Where're you going?"

"I'm going to go ice skating with my younger daughter."

"Well." Bridget straightened as if to face the firing squad. "We can try again, I suppose." She'd already learned that ice skating was not an easily acquired skill.

"How about you, Addy? Want to come along? You haven't been skating with us since last year." Sam said.

"I can't. I'd love to, but there's something wrong with the design for one of the gowns I want Dale to wear for the show. I'm not satisfied with it."

While the others carried their plates to the sink, Bridget hurried up the back stairs to change and find her skates. Sam followed Addy into her office.

"Have you thought any more about going away for our anniversary?"

"I don't see how I can do it. I'm sorry, darling. You know I'd love to go with you."

"But not enough. I'd take you to Tahiti to see Miss Pru."

"What a perfectly wicked thing to tempt me with! You know I can't just pick up and leave."

"We went away on our honeymoon."

"For three days. And Miss Pru was here to keep everything going."

"Cyn could help. Won't you at least consider her?" Sam urged. "We need to get away together."

"Ummm," Addy replied vaguely.

Addy thought about Cyn. Besides being Sam's sister, she had everything a woman could want: good looks, élan, intelligence, and lots of money. Everything seemed to come so easily to her.

Cyn always looked poised and perfectly turned out. She wore her clothes without a thought to them, yet they behaved exactly as they should, never riding up or twisting or slipping. Addy was reluctant to invite Cyn to take part in the Gown House. She wasn't at all sure she could cope with so much perfection.

That night Sam emerged from the bathroom with a container of birth-control pills in his hand. "Addy, are you still on the pill? I thought we'd agreed..." He frowned at her.

"Well, I know we talked about it. Maybe next year."

"You might have mentioned that you were still taking them. I thought something was wrong with me."

She laughed at the ridiculous notion. "There's nothing wrong with you. You should know that. It's just that there's so much to do, I don't think I could handle another baby right now. There's not enough time as it is."

"Time! That's all you ever consider."

"You have to consider me. There's no reason for *you* to be upset."

"Well, I sure as hell am!"

"But you're always so calm."

"There are some things that make me un-calm."

"*Un*-calm?"

"I'm not in the mood for word games, Adelina."

"Adelina?" Her brows rose, along with her temper.

"Having another baby is one of the things I take very seriously. Right now I seem to favor Grendel, and you always side with Bridget. I thought we'd agreed we need another child to confuse us so we'll treat them all alike."

"That's not a good enough reason to have another baby," Abby said adamently.

"We agreed to do it."

"*You* did. I said we'd see."

"I thought you meant we wouldn't take any precautions, that we'd leave it open and see what happened."

"Leave it open?" She was incredulous. "If I didn't take the pill, I'd be pregnant tonight!"

"You have your period, and although menstruating women do get pregnant on rare occasions, it's doubtful that you'd—"

"Doubtful? That's what you said last Christmas when you wanted to make love and you didn't think I'd catch your flu. But I did."

"Addy . . ." he warned.

"I need some time to think about it."

"There's that word again."

"You don't seem to realize how much pressure I'm under right now. With the big show next month—"

"You got through the December show all right."

"Well, Miss Pru still had things lined up, or at least headed in the right direction, before she took off."

"Took off? You make it sound as if she abandoned you."

"Well, that's how I feel. I'd come to depend on her for so much."

"She was great all the way through, but she knew you needed to let go of her."

"Do you mean to tell me she got married and left

just to force me to handle things by myself?"

"No, but she must have thought you would."

"I think I can, too."

"But why struggle with it? Why not concede that this business of yours is too big to handle without more help? Why not stick to the things you do best: designing? Leave the rest of it to someone else. Cyn would love to work for you. Why not just try her? If it doesn't work out, you'll both know it. Cyn really is unusually bright."

"First I have to see if I can do it by myself," Addy muttered.

"Is this some sort of test you've set for yourself?"

"Maybe."

"Why?"

"Miss Pru helped me from the time I began my master's until six months ago. She took care of all the details, her color sense was phenomenal, and she was a perfect sounding board for me. Sam, I don't know if I can handle it all, but I need to find out."

"You've been finding out for the last half year."

"Not exactly. You see, Miss Pru was better organized than just about anyone, and she planned ahead. I got through the last two shows because of her. This time I'll be strictly on my own, though, and I feel as if the whole operation is being held together with chewing gum and baling wire."

"So Miss Pru really crippled you by making you so dependent on her?"

"No, no, no. She was wonderful. God only knows what I'd have done without her nine years ago, trying to get my degree, pregnant, and alone."

"I wish I'd found you then."

"Oh, Sam, I love you so much."

"Then come away with me."

"Is that the only way I can prove my love?"

"No, of course not. But we need to get away by ourselves for a while. These last few months I've felt as if you weren't really living with me. We're just sharing a bed. Everyone else is raising our kids. I don't like it."

"You're a special man, Sam." Her eyes held his.

"Then come away with me," he urged.

"We'll see."

"Is that the same 'We'll see' that allowed you to renege on our decision to have another baby?" His voice was grim.

"Your decision!" she corrected impatiently.

"And going away is my decision. Are you saying 'We'll see' just to put off saying no?"

"This just isn't a good time for—"

"Time!" He flung down his pajamas and strode angrily to the doorway. "I'm going out for a walk. I'm too mad to sleep."

"Don't go out now. It's not safe."

"It's perfectly safe with Marcus's people patrolling the neighborhood."

Addy knew he was right. "I'd go with you, but I'm so tired," she said apologetically.

"I know," he ground out. "I'll be back later. Good night."

The next day Sam reminded Addy about Erin Simmons, who would soon be released from the hospital. Addy decided to go see her. Erin might feel more comfortable about moving into the Grady home if she met Addy beforehand.

"How much do you know about her?" the head

nurse asked when Addy arrived at the hospital.

"Only that she's suffered a tragedy. Her house burned down and her husband and two children were killed. She was burned about the face and arms and especially her hands. She had to have some skin grafts."

"Yes." There was a pause as they walked down the hall. "Sam thinks she'll do well in your house. She has no one else to turn to since her family moved to Australia several years ago."

"She doesn't want to go there to be with them?" Addy asked.

"In time. Her parents visited right after it happened, but they finally had to go back. Sam talked to them. Right now he thinks Erin needs to learn to cope with the loss herself, before she mixes with other people who are also grieving. That's why she hasn't gone to her husband's family either. He was an only child, and his parents were devastated. So far, Erin has refused to discuss what happened or even to acknowledge that she ever had a husband and children."

"Will she be all right with us?" Addy wondered aloud, half to herself.

"I know your house. It's always bustling with lots of people around, but guests feel comfortable there. There's no pressure."

Addy, feeling frazzled, wondered to herself: no pressure?

"She'll be around people without anyone's expecting anything of her."

"Is it a good idea to see her now? Or should I go home and wait until she gets there?"

"No, I think you should stay. But be brief. Just tell her who you are and say you're looking forward to her visit."

Addy nodded thoughtfully. "It occurs to me that I don't know how Sam got involved with Erin. He's in pediatrics. Was one of her children a patient?"

"No. The Simmons' pediatrician, Dr. Eleanor Glasman, is a friend of Sam's. She was shaken by the tragedy and discussed the case with him. He offered his help."

Addy nodded. How like Sam to want to help everyone. He and Marcus were a lot alike that way.

She walked down the hall with the nurse, carrying a pink begonia plant, until they came to Erin's room.

She lay in bed staring out the window at the lightly falling snow. Or was she looking through the snowfall and contemplating her inner thoughts? Addy wondered. She was very pale and her blond hair, which had been badly singed by the fire, was beginning to grow out in soft, uneven tufts.

"Erin," the nurse said softly, "here is Addy Grady to see you."

Slowly Erin's head turned. Her eyes came to rest on Addy, but her expression remained blank. She had no eyelashes or eyebrows, and her brown eyes were like wounds in her pale face. Addy thought her healing skin must still be very sensitive and painful.

Addy set the begonia plant on a table and said, "Hello, Erin. Sam has told me all about you, and I just stopped by to tell you I'm glad you'll be staying at our house. When do you think you can come?"

With no change in her expression, no indication that she had heard and understood, Erin looked past Addy to the nurse, who answered for her, "Sam thought maybe in another day or so, if that would be all right."

Erin's eyes returned to Addy, and her lips moved almost imperceptibly as she replied, "Fine."

"Your room looks out on our woods, and there's a bird-feeder right below the window," Addy explained.

Erin gave a slow, disinterested nod.

"Well, we'll see you soon," Addy said.

After Addy and the nurse had left the room and were walking back down the hall, Addy said, "Erin will be as big a responsibility as any of the children Sam ever brought home in the past."

"I know. She's so desperately in need, so alone. Her parents mean well, but they're too anxious for her. She'll be all right once she's been with you for a while and has had time to heal."

"How can you bear being surrounded by so much pain and misery?" Addy asked, thinking of all the hurting people the nurse had to deal with each day.

"Knowing that our care makes a difference in people's lives helps us feel better, too. Besides, it's impossible not to respond to people's needs when they're so great."

"Sam . . ." Addy began.

". . . is special," the nurse finished for her.

"Yes."

The two women said good-bye, and then Addy drove home and climbed back on her treadmill.

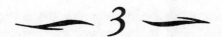

3

As THEY WERE getting ready for bed that night, Sam said, "Erin's nurse called to say you'd been up to the hospital. She was very impressed with your sensitivity. Thank you." He gave Addy a sweet, husbandly kiss.

"I thought it might make it easier for her to come here if she knew I was expecting her, that she wasn't just some stray kitten you were bringing home without warning."

"I'm touched that you took the time to be so kind to a stranger." He hugged her warmly, holding her close.

"Why should my kindness come as such a surprise?"

"It doesn't. But you weren't all that kind or wel-

235

coming to me when we first met. I had a hell of a time becoming part of the family."

"You were terrible. I had no choice; you just moved in. Nothing I did discouraged you."

"Now you even encourage people to move in. Why couldn't you have been a little more welcoming to me? I was all alone in the world, a confirmed bachelor who needed the love of a good woman, and you were mean, always telling me to leave, always thwarting me."

"When did I thwart you?"

"All the time. I was in agony, suffering untold deprivations."

"As I recall, you had your way the entire time." She loosened his grip and moved away from him.

"Your memory is faulty. That's the first sign of exhaustion from overwork. You need a holiday."

"How can we possibly go on a vacation now?"

"Not now. In April."

"We'll see."

"That again!"

Addy elaborately consulted her watch. "I have a whole three and a half minutes with nothing pressing," she said, hinting.

"I could stand some pressing."

"And if you'd like to take advantage of me, I would allow it."

"Three and a half minutes?" He looked her over and smiled as she slid him a knowing glance. His eyes dropped down her body. "Three minutes isn't very long. I'll barely get started."

"Barely? You're going to take off your clothes?"

"I thought I would, since I'm going to bed anyway,

and it would probably be quicker to take them off now, when I'm very interested in doing so, than it would be later when I'm not as interested."

"Interested? What are you interested in doing?" She moved provocatively and began to unbutton her shirt.

Apparently the unfastening of shirts fascinated him. "Um?"

"What are you interested in doing later?" she repeated.

"I've forgotten."

She opened the shirt and spread it wide as she sauntered up to him. Having captured his full attention, she took his hands, turned the palms toward her, and lay them on her breasts.

His fingers were tense and eager as he squeezed gently, then soothed and kneaded her soft flesh, rubbing his palms over the satiny nipples.

She stretched up and kissed his mouth. "You have two minutes and thirty-five seconds to—"

He interrupted her with another kiss, and then time suddenly stood still. But Sam noticed it was about forty minutes later when he held a purring Addy curled in his arms. "I've told Marcus and Hedda about Erin," he finally said, "and they've agreed to pass the word about her, so no one will blunder into saying something that might unintentionally hurt her."

"That was smart," she murmured sleepily.

"Everyone will know to treat her courteously and be as casual around her as possible."

"It scares me a little just to think of having had to go through something so terrible."

"It wasn't easy for you to have Grendel by yourself either," Sam pointed out.

"But that involved just me. It wasn't tragic, just something my family and society in general disapproved of. I felt guilty, but I had Miss Pru. I didn't lose anyone—except Paul, of course, and he wasn't really worth having anyway."

"I believe you could get along without anyone."

His remark hurt her. "How can you possibly think that?" she asked indignantly.

"You almost do now."

"That isn't true at all! How can you lie there in bed, having just finished making love to me, and say such a thing?"

"Have we just finished making love?" he asked, his voice was low and serious.

"What do you mean by that?" She pulled away from him to see his face.

"We always have great sex, but the loving part has been cut to the quick lately."

"You don't believe I love you?"

"Love is more than quick meetings in bed."

"That was hardly quick."

"I went to school all those years to specialize in pediatrics so I could chose how to spend my time, so that I wouldn't be an absentee husband. And what happens? I marry an absentee wife."

She raised herself up on one elbow and said with some defensiveness, "I was doing the very same work when you first met me. Nothing is different. I'm here all the time."

"During the last six months I seem to have lost you. We've all lost you. You sketch through breakfast. You make phone calls through dinner. Otherwise you're in your office, in your studio, or with your customers. We're living parallel lives. We pass each other in the hall or on the stairs, and we make love occasionally."

"If you call our lovemaking occasional, I wonder what you'd call often!"

"Addy, you know perfectly well what I mean. I want to share more of our lives. I want time to talk and do things together, time to have friends over."

"Are we going to hire a hall for the St. Patrick's Day party?"

"Let it be here," Sam reached out and smoothed the silken hair from her face. "Addy, it would be a completely different kind of party if we had it some other place."

"You ask too much."

"Do I? Or are you willing to give too little?"

Once again his words pricked her painfully. "Are you saying we've grown that far apart?"

"In these last six months we've become mere acquaintances."

"Why . . . *Sam!*" She was deeply offended. "How can you say that, after all we've been through together?"

"That's my point. Lately we've spent about five minutes a day in conversation."

"What about tonight?"

He looked at the new clock on the nightstand. "We've been talking for seven minutes. But we only had two minutes yesterday."

"Now, that's not true," she began to protest, but he cut her off.

"I wasn't here when you got up. We missed each other at lunch. Much later I saw you on the stairs to say hello, and you kissed me very nicely until Sarah called us to supper. During supper you got a phone call from California, and afterward you went straight back to your studio."

She didn't say anything.

"Addy?" He tilted her head up and kissed her mouth. She sniffled. "Aw, Addy." His voice was hoarse with tenderness as he cradled her and said, "Shhhh. I didn't mean to make you cry. I just wanted to explain to you how it is with me."

"I have to try to run the business by myself."

"Call Cyn," he urged gently.

"Cyn is even more efficient than Miss Pru."

"She's completely incapable of designing a handkerchief."

"But she *looks* like the person in charge. She looks just the way a designer should. *I* look like a brood mare."

"You certainly do not look like a brood mare." He chuckled. "You look like someone's naughty, well-cared-for, high-priced mistress."

"That cheap!" Addy cried, pushing him away. "Just because I have an illegitimate child and—"

"Good Lord, Addy, haven't you consigned that sorry business to oblivion *yet?*" Sam was furious. He clasped her shoulders and shook her angrily.

"You brought it up!" she accused.

"No! You deliberately misinterpreted my teasing. I will not allow you to brand Grendel with illegitimacy. If you weren't an exceptionally desirable woman, Paul would never have insisted on having you."

"He didn't love me. He just wanted sex."

"It goes against my grain to say anything good about Paul," Sam admitted, "but he must have loved you in his own way. It wouldn't help anything to say exactly what I think of his abandoning you, but for God's sake, Addy, it's done! Nine *years* ago! Leave it there. Grendel is ours now."

"You were nice to give her your name," Addy conceded.

"Nice! As in generous? Charitable? What the bloody hell are you trying to pull?" He glared down at her. "I love Grendel. She even looks like me. I adopted her five years ago on our wedding day, and *she's my daughter!* Don't contaminate my love for her with any blasted, sanctimonious mouthings about how *nice* I was to give her my name."

"Don't be mad," Addy pleaded. "I'm sorry."

"Don't be mad? I'm not mad; I'm raging!"

But Addy burst into tears, and Sam melted. "Oh, Addy, you numbskull." And he tried to gather her into his arms.

But Addy wasn't in a conciliatory mood. She felt tired and beleaguered; anything would have set her off at that moment. She pushed Sam away and scrambled out of bed.

"What are you doing?" Sam frowned at her, his voice concerned.

"Leave me alone!" she sobbed as she grabbed up a robe and left their room.

Sam lay back with his arms folded behind his head and scowled up at the ceiling. He stayed there for a long time, waiting, but Addy didn't return. Finally he got up and went in search of her. She was down the hall in another room—fast asleep.

Her hair was tousled, her cheeks moist from her tears, and even in sleep her uneven breathing told Sam that she hadn't fully recovered from a hard bout of crying.

Standing there in the cold room, Sam sighed before carefully folding back the covers and crawling in beside her. He rearranged the blanket, took her gently in his arms, and made her comfortable against his chest, maneuvering them so that his legs warmed her cold feet.

He lay wide awake in the dark night for a long time, his wife sleeping in his arms.

Grendel and Bridget were both in school when Sam brought Erin Simmons home a few days later. She carried just a few clothes in a soft bag, all her other belongings having been lost in the fire. Her lack of possessions gave Addy her first true sense of the heart-rending tragedy the young woman had suffered. Perhaps if she'd been less busy she'd have come to appreciate Erin's situation sooner.

As Addy showed Erin her room, with Sam trailing behind, she tried to think of which of the extra sample garments she had might fit Erin. She knew there were some night clothes and lingerie, but what else? Too bad Miss Pru wasn't there to help, Addy thought for the thousandth time.

They'd chosen Miss Pru's lovely, old-fashioned room for Erin. It was decorated in rich shades of brown and blue, with a light blue down comforter on the bed, a brown rug on the floor, and lemon-yellow pillows scattered on the window seat.

Erin's eyes darted nervously about, looking everywhere except at Sam and Addy. She seemed especially vulnerable to them with no eyelashes and fuzzy eyebrows. Her hair had been trimmed very short to even out the odd lengths, and the skin on her face still looked somewhat raw. Her hands were wrapped in loose dressings.

Erin turned terrified eyes to Sam. "How do I get out?"

"You just go down the hall to the stairs." Addy pointed.

Ignoring his wife, Sam gently took Erin's arm and led her to the window. Lifting back the light curtain, he said, "See? All you do is open the window, and the metal ladder is right there. If you step on the first rung, it will extend slowly to the ground." He opened the window to show her how easily she could escape from the room.

Of course, Addy realized. Erin had wanted to know in case of fire. Addy's heart turned over in sympathy as Erin glanced from the window to the bed and back again, as if measuring the distance.

Addy thanked God for the new furnace they'd recently bought. The old one had periodically clanked into life, rumbling fiercely as it fired. Then the blower would come on, whistling and roaring until the cycle ended and the contraption slumbered once again. When they were all freezing upstairs and about to go down to the basement to see if the furnace had died completely, it would suddenly labor into life again. All day and all night the old furnace would have reminded Erin of the fire it contained. The new one, however, operated silently and produced a constant supply of heat.

While Sam kept Erin company, Addy felt free to go downstairs and sort through the sample blouses, slacks, and dresses that might fit Erin.

Since the younger woman was newly widowed, it would be inappropriate for her to wear sophisticated garments, and some of the colors would be too festive, but there were quite a few clothes, including underwear, that would be fine for now. Impulsively Addy also gathered a handful of cosmetics suitable for Erin's coloring, adding a light perfume as well. She carried everything up to Erin's room, laying the clothes on the chaise longue, and the underwear on a nearby chair. She was arranging the makeup on the vanity when Sam and Erin returned from down the hall.

Feeling a little awkward, Addy gestured toward the clothes with a smile and said, "We have these samples . . . if they suit you."

"I will have the money," Erin replied, "Soon, I'll—" She stopped abruptly, and Addy realized she found it too painful to speak of the insurance money.

"Until then?"

"Thank you," Erin said softly.

Addy's eyes went nervously to Sam's. He was smiling at her with such warm approval that she wanted to cry.

When the girls came home from school, Addy realized Sam had deliberately chosen the early afternoon to bring Erin to the house. That way she could get acquainted in stages—first with Addy and the house, then with Grendel and Bridget. She'd meet Sarah at dinner.

Erin was very quiet, and Sam and Addy didn't press her to speak. They had told the girls that Erin was just like the children who had stayed with them previously. She had been sick and needed a place to live. Grendel and Bridget had had practice sharing their home with strangers and they asked no awkward questions.

However, the first thing Bridget said to Erin was, "We're waiting for Stormy to have kittens."

Addy held her breath as she waited for Erin's reaction to this reference to babies, but apparently she could handle baby kittens. So Addy added, "Stormy's male."

Erin nodded.

"Well, his stomach's fat like Pattycake's," Bridget replied, defending herself. "Pattycake's going to have a baby, so maybe Stormy is too."

Addy breathed a sigh of relief. Very simply and naturally, Bridget had prepared Erin to see Pattycake bursting with life. Sometimes things did work out right.

After the girls went to bed, Erin commented to Addy, "Grendel looks like Sam."

Addy answered carefully. "Grendel was illegitimate. Sam adopted her the day we were married, but he convinced me that I should share her with her real father, who still comes to see her every once in a while."

Erin nodded. "Sam would do that."

Addy sighed with relief again. Another hurdle had been overcome.

When they went to bed that night, Addy said to Sam, "I was worried about Erin's reaction when she met the girls. I'm so relieved that their presence doesn't seem to dredge up too much grief for her."

"She didn't have daughters," Sam replied. "That was something I considered before bringing her here."

"I see. Little boys." Absently Addy smoothed her

nightgown over her flat stomach.

"You were lovely to her. So sweet." Sam caressed her cheek.

"I didn't do anything, not really."

"You knew immediately what she needed. I saw her touching that pink thing."

"That *pink thing* is an exceptionally elegant gown," she said sternly. Pensively, she added, "I just hope being here and getting new clothes won't jar any painful memories."

"None of your clothes could. They're all so beautiful that they make memories by themselves."

"Oh, Sam."

"I love you, you wretch."

Lilabet Thomas fitted all of Erin's new clothes. Sam and Addy had discussed it and decided that mere proximity to the cheerful seamstress would be therapeutic for Erin. Lilabet's real name was Hazel, but she'd been a premature child and everyone had called her Little Bit. Since she was now five feet tall and probably five feet around as well, the name no longer seemed appropriate, so it had been corrupted into Lilabet.

Lilabet talked constantly. She never inquired into anyone's life or thoughts. She'd had so many interesting experiences of her own, and she had such fascinating insights into everything she heard or saw, that she felt compelled to share them all. When there was no one around to talk *at,* she hummed. She laughed a lot too. She was like a bee, busy and buzzing. And when she wasn't talking or laughing or humming, she was eating.

Lilabet said to Addy, "Erin needs a corduroy jacket to wear around the house. She's so skinny she's cold all the time. How about a quilted one?"

Addy agreed, and by that evening Lilabet had finished two boxy jackets with nice deep pockets. Then she made a fisherman's overblouse, a blanket robe, and a padded silk bed jacket. When Addy raised an inquiring brow and suggested that perhaps Lilabet might like to get back to work on the garments for the rapidly approaching February show, the seamstress laughed.

A few days later at breakfast, Sarah served some particularly unattractive popovers. They had overflowed the pans and looked like brown and yellow split elephant ears. Addy saw Erin try to smother a grin, but when Sarah laughed, Erin let loose the most marvelous smile. Sam and Bridget and Grendel laughed too, and Addy thought that breakfast had rarely seemed lovelier.

Sam went to Addy's office afterward and waited for her to hang up the phone before announcing, "I think I'll insist Hedda allow me to raise Sarah's wages."

"For those disastrous popovers?"

"For Erin's smile."

Addy could only nod rather tearily. Sam held her and kissed her several times. "How about coming out for a mad weekend with me?"

"Did you play hooky as a child?"

"Never. I didn't then, so I can now. But I need a playmate."

"You have two willing children."

"I want a grown-up, beautiful, sexy, willing, woman playmate."

"You mean a *Playboy* centerfold with a staple in her stomach?"

He nodded in agreement.

"No one ever offered me that position before."

"I can think of some other positions I'd like to offer you."

"Let me guess..." But the phone rang. Some of Addy's designs that had been sent to a boutique in Phoenix hadn't arrived yet, and she'd have to find out why. Sam sighed and left for work.

As the days passed, Erin kept her room clean and carried her dishes from the table to the sink, but she never participated in family activities. She stayed by herself and observed all that went on around her.

She examined the seamstresses' work, she listened to Addy practice the narration for the February show, she watched Marcus's crew clean the twenty-four rooms of the house each week. But she didn't join in the conversation or offer suggesions or ask questions. And she never mentioned her husband and children.

Nevertheless, she beamed an accepted member of the household. She wore the clothes Addy had provided, and she looked good in them. So far she had ignored the makeup, but her hair had grown a bit since the fire almost three months ago, and with each day she was looking less and less like an abandoned waif.

Addy worried because Erin didn't go anywhere with them, but Sam was satisfied with her progress.

Then one day Marcus told Addy, "You need a band for the February show, and it just so happens that I know of one."

"Somehow that doesn't particularly surprise me," she said.

When the band auditioned for her, Addy vetoed
the amplifiers and the musicians protested en masse.
"Without the amps, you can't hear the guitars!" the
lead guitarist explained.

"Then make the horn and drum softer," Addy replied with asperity.

"Softer?" The drummer was deeply offended.

"And play something that has a melody," she in-
sturcted.

"We *do* play melody!"

"What's it called? 'Garbage Day Pick-up'?"

It took Marcus *and* Sam to help establish a working
relationship.

When Marcus first brought the group to practice,
he told Addy, "They'll cost you only two hundred
dollars altogether."

"Two *hundred!*"

"For two shows."

"I thought they were playing for the experience."

"That too."

"Then why should I pay them two hundred dollars?"

"They learned two new pieces."

"Yes, the only recognizable ones they can play!"

"And they're going to perform without the amplifiers," he reminded her, as if that were a great conces-
sion.

Addy regarded Marcus suspiciously. He seemed to
enjoy their run-ins. He should; he always won.

As the band began setting up their equipment on
the wide landing halfway up the front stairway—
grumbling all the while about their wasted amplifiers—Erin came out to watch. Greeting her, Bridget
confided, "Marcus is my grandfather."

Erin looked at Marcus with some surprise. He smiled and corrected gently. *"God*father."

As the band tuned up to practice, Erin watched and listened avidly. Addy and Marcus exchanged glances. Then, to their surprise, they saw Erin go up to the band leader and ask, "May I sit in? I have a flute."

Five pairs of appalled black eyes rose to Marcus, pleading with him, but when the older man stared back impassively, the leader said lamely, "If you want."

How remarkable, thought Addy, that Marcus had managed to exert his authority without one gesture or word. How had he done that? Secretly she was pleased to see someone else bow to Marcus's will for a change. She'd certainly done it often enough.

She was also pleased to see how purposefully Erin strode upstairs to her room and returned with her flute. After a quick glance at Marcus, one young man gave up his chair to Erin and sat down on a step.

Erin played an unselfconscious trill on her flute and five pairs of eyes rolled toward the ceiling. To Addy, the trill sounded pretty good — if you liked flute music. She knew a flute could be mournfully serious. Erin's was like dappled sunshine on leaves. Flutes could be penetrating. Hers touched lightly. After the third piece of whatever it was they were playing, the five young men exchanged glances, then smiles. The flute wasn't so bad after all.

Erin's involvement in the music represented a giant step forward for her. As her flute wove and danced and tiptoed and frolicked, Addy thought how amazing life could be.

That night in bed she described the scene to Sam.

"It was just astonishing. Even Marcus was astonished! I could tell since I know him so well. He was as shaken up as I was. Sam, there's life in her. She's going to be all right!"

Of course Erin's transformation was nowhere near complete, much to Addy's disappointment. Occasionally Erin would abruptly excuse herself from the table, and there were days when she hardly emerged from her room at all. But whenever the band practiced, they let her sit in.

Addy knew that grief is natural and that Erin was grieving—but silently, carefully, so that no one witnessed it. Addy saw evidence of it in her guest's swollen eyes, and now and then she heard a muffled sound from behind Erin's closed door.

As the day of the February fashion show approached, Addy worked feverishly to complete the preparations. She finally solved the maddening problem of fitting one of the dresses Dale would wear— a gorgeous creation in shimmering sea green that made her look like a mermaid. Dale undulated like a sea creature before the room-wide mirror in what had once been the grand dining room. Addy smiled with affection, thinking what hams all her models were.

Addy had chosen the dresses they would be wearing with their individual coloring in mind. Dale's were golden, green, sand, or oatmeal to complement her red hair. Linda, with her white skin and blue-black tresses, wore dramatic hues—the primary colors, black and white—and sometimes subtler shades like heather. Pearl's warm brown skin lent itself deliciously to beige, soft yellow, and tangerine. But Pearl loved vertical stripes, which made her thin, six-foot-tall figure look ridiculous. Addy insisted on horizontal stripes, which she loved but couldn't wear herself.

Both Grendel and Bridget would model children's dresses. Addy planned to pay them, a small amount in cash but most in savings for college.

Addy also had to pay Marcus's band. Two hundred dollars!

"Pearl," she said to the striking woman who could model a potato sack and make it look great, "your father is a blackmailer."

"You can't resist a play on words, can you?"

"Only on occasion."

"Now what's he done to you?" Pearl asked, amused.

"The band—"

"Thank the Lord they're practicing here now," Pearl interrupted. "Our place is the only other house they can practice in without blowing out the windows. I've been sleeping at the hospital for two months on an examining table. Not only does the administration frown on med students camping out like that, but my poor bones don't like it either," she said, putting one long, skinny hand on her hip and limping exaggeratedly.

"If you had a little meat on your bones, they'd be cushioned," Addy observed.

"You and Hedda-mom," said Pearl, referring to her stepmother with obvious affection.

"She thinks you're too thin?" Addy asked in amazement. Could it be that she and Hedda actually agreed on something?

"Yeah. She hung up a picture of a skeleton—painted black, naturally—and labeled it 'Pearl.' No one's ever accused Hedda of being too subtle."

"Does she practice voodoo?" Addy blurted out impulsively.

"It wouldn't surprise me at all," Pearl replied calmly. "Nothing about her would. I discuss all my cases with that lady. And when she disagrees with my diagnosis, I go back and take another look at the patient and my medical books. She's usually right."

"Does she ever speak?"

"No . . ." Pearl cast a quick glance at Addy before adding, "Not that I've ever heard."

"Marcus says she talks to him in many ways."

"They're very close. So close I think they practice telepathy. I've known them to communicate from a distance, and it almost straightens my hair."

"I know. The other day I saw Marcus coerce the band into letting Erin play with them without saying a word or moving a muscle."

"Yeah. Well, I'll tell you, Addy. There are times when you know what you ought to do, but just a peek at Daddy and you know you not only *ought* to do it, but you *will*."

"He always gets his way." Addy sighed. "I would love to have this house painted white."

"It'd look like a lump of chalk, and you know it. You're just being contrary."

"I've never been contrary in my entire life!"

But Pearl just laughed.

Addy was in bed that night when Sam came home from a visit to little Helen, who was getting better. She'd reacted badly to some new medication, then suffered a flare-up that had turned out to be the beginning of an ordinary cold.

"Did you give her vitamin C?" Addy quizzed.

Sam grinned as he removed his jacket and hung it up. "In orange juice." He undid his shirt cuffs and began unfastening his shirt buttons. Addy put down the book she'd been reading and lay back to watch him.

Smiling mischievously, he began to strip, wiggling his eyebrows and looking at her with smoldering eyes as he slid his shirt off one shoulder then up again, teasing. He chuckled.

But Addy's smile was faint and her gaze intense. As she felt the first stirrings of desire for her husband, his movements became slow and earnest.

"You are so beautiful," she said breathlessly, already aroused. How she wanted him!

"Men aren't beautiful. Women are." His deep voice set off vibrations in the pit of her stomach, and she moved restlessly.

"So are men."

He reached back and pulled his undershirt slowly over his head. His eyes, shining like blue flames, never left her face. Carelessly he tossed the shirt aside and paused before her, his chest hard with muscles and soft with dark hair.

Sitting down, he took off his shoes and then his socks, twirling them in the air and tossing them away, his lips quirked in amusement. He stood to unbuckle his belt and pull it slowly from the loops, his movements fluid, his hair mussed. His sapphire eyes held her in a mesmerizing gaze.

She was lying on the bed, one arm behind her head, the long flannel sleeve of her nightgown falling back to expose the soft white underside of her arm. Her hair was spread like a halo over the pillow, and the other arm rested on top of the light cream comforter.

Addy felt her breasts swell with desire as Sam studied her. The backs of her knees tingled, and warm sensations flowed up the insides of her thighs. She smiled lazily, knowing he was going to make love to her.

Deliberately he unfastened his trousers and slowly slid down the zipper. He pulled them carefully down his hips and legs, then turned his back to her, swung the pants over a chair, and stepped out of his briefs.

His back was so marvelous! Addy's lips parted in wonder. He turned slowly toward her, knowing she couldn't get enough of looking at him.

She waited, her body anticipating him, wanting him. The pit of her belly grew hot, and prickles of desire skittered along her skin. She shivered with sensual excitement and her heart pounded, but still he didn't touch her.

Their lips parted, and their gazes met and held. He approached her side of the bed and stood looking down at her, his expression serious. She smiled again, and taking her hand from behind her head, she touched him intimately.

His body tensed slightly, and he drew his breath in sharply. Reaching down, he took hold of the covers and flung them back with a long sweep of his arm. He sat down beside her, regarded her mottled-orange, flannel-clad body, and smiled.

"You think orange flannel is funny?"

"I know what's under it." His voice was a deep, harsh rumble.

"Now, how could you know that?" she inquired breathlessly.

"I've peeked."

"How shocking!"

"You're about to be shocked a whole lot more than that."

"How many volts?" The breathiness spoiled the sassy tone she'd intended.

"Full current as soon as I plug you in."

"Oh? How do you do that?"

"I am prepared to give you a practical demonstration," he said, removing her nightgown with great haste.

But as soon as Addy was nude, Sam seemed to be in no great rush. At first Addy teased, "Now?" as he slowly moved his prickly chin down her tender flesh.

"Not yet," he growled.

His touch on her flushed skin excited her—the moist softness of his mouth surrounded by the abrasive stubble of his unshaven face; the big rough hands that probed and rubbed; the gentle fingers that sought her out. His warm breath and hot tongue felt wonderful on her cooler skin.

"Now?" she asked, a little hoarse.

He lifted his mouth infinitesimally and said thickly, "Not yet."

He drew her nipple into his mouth and pressed it against the roof, stroking the underside hard with his tongue. She gasped, and her body moved sensually against him.

His hand roamed the length of her, stroking the satin skin and following the generous contours. As his hand caressed the curve of her bottom and teased her, she shivered with desire.

They kissed, and their hands cherished each other. "Now?" she moaned.

He separated from Addy carefully and lay down beside her, his breathing coming quickly. "Pretty soon." Sweat glistened his upper lip, and he licked it away. So did she.

Their bodies grew damp from their labor of love. Sam lay back, his chest heaving, and Addy slid her hot lips down his writhing body.

He paused briefly, his eyes blazing with passion, and allowed her to take brief possession of him. Then he turned them both over and growled teasingly in her ear, "Where did you learn to do that?"

"I guessed." She panted, giggling.

But her laughter faded as their play became serious, their movements exquisitely erotic. Again and again he tasted her, then dragged himself away as she moaned and protested, trying to hold on to his slippery body.

They continued their love dance for a long time, prolonging the delicious torment, the sensual pleasure. They flirted with the flickering flames of their passion before they were finally consumed by the fire.

At last they lay shuddering with glorious aftershocks, totally sated. Sam carefully turned them on their sides and pulled up the covers without disturbing their union. Almost instantly they both fell into an exhausted sleep.

Addy woke up in the night when Sam slid a hand between her hip and the bed and clasped her to him as he grew hard inside her. They shared each other quickly, then again slept.

When she awoke the next morning, before the winter sun was up, Addy found herself lying spoon fashion with her back against Sam's chest. One of his arms held her close, and one hand cradled her breast. Her body felt stiff and surfeited. She smiled and stretched minutely to yawn. Sam's arm tightened around her, and she felt his interest grow.

She chuckled softly. "Forget it."

But he didn't. He stretched out flat before leaning over her, his mouth greedy, his hands caressing her feverishly. She pulled her mouth free and protested, "Sam!"

Without replying he made love to her again. She felt a little cross and impatient with him, and when he'd spent himself, she said, "What are you eating these days? Rhino horns, oysters, olives?"

"You."

"So I've noticed. What's made you so greedy?"

"I love you, and I want you."

"Not again!"

"No, not for a while. But I love you, and I want to make love to you."

"Sam, what is it?" She smoothed his hair back from his forehead. "You generally aren't this...uh... demanding."

"I need your attention."

"You've certainly had that since we got into bed last night. I know you sneaked another one in while I was half asleep. Very crafty, Samuel Grady."

"I've had your body, which I relish, but I want the rest of you too."

"Oh, Sam. You *know* I—"

"This is serious, Addy. Pay attention."

"Please just let me get through this February show."

"This is important, Addy."

"I love you, Sam."

"I need more."

"Okay, okay, okay! I get the message!" she said,

tossing the covers aside and climbing out of bed.

"Do you?"

"I know you want me to sit around with my hands folded, listening—"

"That's not what I want at all."

"And go on a trip with you." She flung out an arm.

"I want more than the trip."

"Sam, you have no idea how much I need this business."

"I'm not asking you to give it up. I just want you to let some of the reponsibility go."

"Oh, Sam . . ."

"I've never had a stable family."

"You've had lots of family: a mother, three sisters, heaven knows how many half-siblings and stepsiblings. Good Lord, the ramifications of parenthood are mind-boggling."

"You've said it all. I've had a lot of people around, temporarily, and they were all nice and good folks, but I've never had a real family life. Mother's had how many husbands—three or four? The family was always changing with new fathers, other mothers, and a mish-mash of other kids. I want us to have a stable family with both of us, the girls, and one more baby."

Addy stood staring at him, struggling to quell the resentment that flared hot inside her. The nerve of him, planning her life so dictatorially! Finally she said, "Let me get through this February show first."

"Pay attention, Addy."

"Damn it, I said I would!"

She snatched up some clothes and stormed into their bathroom, slamming the door behind her, shutting him out. How dare he tell her how to live!

The needle-spray shower in no way cooled her off. So he wanted *her* to pay attention, she fumed. Well, no one ever paid attention to her! So Sam was unhappy? Well, he'd survive.

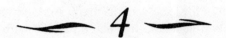

THE SUMMER FASHION shows were scheduled for the Saturday of St. Valentine's Day week. Both the afternoon and evening shows were already sold out. Addy listened to the clamor for more tickets with mixed emotions. She was thrilled that so many people wanted to see her work, but she hated having to disappoint those she couldn't accommodate.

Several years ago, in a change of policy that revealed her true brilliance, Miss Pru had decided they should charge admission to the fashion shows. The proceeds would go to the children's hospital in Indianapolis.

Addy now charged twenty-five dollars a ticket. Hedda prepared the food, as usual, and sometimes Addy wondered whether people came to see her designs or to savor Hedda's fantastic cooking.

261

Since Hedda had officially given up catering several years ago, people wondered how Addy had managed to snare her services for the fashion shows. Actually, Addy had had no choice. Marcus had "offered" Hedda's help during preparations for that first show eight years ago, and she'd been helping ever since.

Today Sam had taken Bridget ice skating again, and Erin had gone along as well. They'd all been surprised when Erin asked to join them. She had hesitated, then added, "It's been years and years since I've skated."

Was that before she was married? Addy wondered. If so, ice skating would not be connected with memories of her lost family. "I think my skates would fit you," she offered.

"It hurts when you sit down," Bridget volunteered. "Especially when you don't expect to sit down."

"Come with us for a little while," Sam coaxed Addy. "We'll rent Erin some skates. You can take your car and come home whenever you need to."

"I'm waiting for a call from Fort Wayne," Addy explained. "Another time."

"It's past time for you to get an automatic answering machine."

"I'm not waiting to hear from them, Sam. I'm waiting to talk to them."

"I'll never learn to stand up on skates," Bridget said with a great sigh.

Erin touched Bridget's head. "I'll help."

"No one has to help Daddy; he skates good."

"He skates well," Addy corrected. "Tastes good, does well."

"And he stays up on the blades. He doesn't skate on his ankles."

"It just takes practice," Erin assured the child.

"You can go faster if you're on the blades," Sam said. "Ankles don't contribute much to gliding."

"Yeah," Bridget agreed.

"Erin, slather your face with wind cream," Sam advised casually. "Wear a ski hood to protect your face, and find some thick mittens for your hands." He didn't want the cold to harm the sensitive, healing skin.

"Are you going down to the Circle?" Addy asked. The Circle, with its tall monument, was located in the center of Indianapolis. The rink was on the east side of the monument.

"It's the closest," Sam replied.

"It always gives me a giggle to think that money raised by the Midsummer Festival makes winter's ice skating possible."

Sam put his hand on the back of her neck and kissed her quite thoroughly on the lips, right in front of Erin. "You need a giggle or two now and then," he said, his voice reedy and low.

Although she liked the kiss, Addy was annoyed with Sam for being so affectionate in front of their grieving guest. As soon as Erin ran upstairs to collect her gear, Addy scolded him about it in a harsh whisper.

But Sam calmly replied, "It's okay. She needs to remember how it is between a man and a woman so she'll want it again for herself."

Addy was appalled. "How can you think of such a thing? It's too soon!"

"It's been more than three months, and it's time for her to begin again."

"She's still in mourning! She's still raw. That's torture!"

"No," he corrected softly, "it's living. Each of us is allotted only a limited amount of time on this good earth, and we shouldn't waste it. We should take delight in it."

"Not all people find the same things delightful," Addy said huffily.

"The world is a great and fascinating place, and it's lying out there waiting to be treasured."

"Are you hinting that I need to get out of the house more often?"

"How did you guess?" he said with mock amazement.

"To go out, people need *clothes*. I make the clothes. And I take delight in *that!*"

"Make yourself something and come out and play with me," he urged.

"Oh, Sam." She was about to give in when she glanced at her watch and shrieked, "The color bath! I didn't hear the timer! Oh, *rats!*" And she fled up the attic stairs, furious because she'd probably loused up her batik.

A few days later Addy brought herself a wristwatch with a built-in alarm. And she set it for everything. She would break off in the middle of a conversation, or leave the table between the soup and main course, or abruptly change direction and head down the stairs when she had been going up. Once the alarm went off after Sam had coaxed her into bed. She rose swiftly, turned off the buzzer, and smiled fleetingly as she stepped across his prone body, saying, "I'll be right back." Then, snatching up a robe, she disappeared out the door.

Sam was steaming. He became even angrier when she didn't return immediately. After some twenty minutes had gone by, he pulled on some jeans, dragged a sweater over his head, and went in search of her.

He found her sitting on a high stool in her attic studio, sketching busily. He stood watching, his hands on his hips, wondering grimly how long it would take her to notice him. Finally she glanced up and gave him a surprised "Hi." Then she turned back to her work.

"Addy . . ." he warned.

She looked back up at him. "What's the matter?"

"Let me refresh your memory. We were in our room, in our bed, and we were about to make love."

Her eyes grew wide. "Oh," she said contritely. Sitting up straight, she ran her hands down her thighs and realized with additional surprise that she was wearing her bathrobe. She'd been so intensely focused on her designs that she hadn't even realized she wasn't dressed.

Gradually it all came back to her. She'd been in bed with Sam and had left him there. She'd forgotten all about him!

Dismayed by her lapse and eager to make amends, she slid off the stool and walked barefooted to the door. Sam turned slowly to watch as she turned the lock and faced him.

Slowly she untied the sash of her robe, shrugged it off her shoulders, and let it slither down her body to the floor. Sam's lips parted, and his eyes grazed her body quickly, then more slowly. He strolled around her, observing her carefully, and she vividly remembered their first meeting more than five years ago, when she'd been modeling a scandalous robe on the runway and she'd half expected him to make a bid on her like a slave at auction.

"I'll take this one," Sam said, echoing her memory.

With controlled gestures, she moved sensuously, deliberately provocative. "I'm sorry, sir, this one's taken," she answered, tilting her head seductively.

"Right. It belongs to Samuel Grady."

"Did he tattoo that on my back?" She strained to look over her bare shoulder. "He's so blasted possessive that it wouldn't surprise me one bit."

"I've branded you all over. Anyone would know you're mine." And his hot hands claimed her.

They made love on the attic floor. It was cold, but Addy didn't realize how uncomfortable it was until they both were fully spent. "Get off you big lunk!" she teased lightly. "I'll be black and blue!"

"You locked the door, and I couldn't get out."

"Well, why didn't *you* take the bottom and let me be on top?"

"I will next time."

"Forget next time. I've got to get busy. Look how late it is!" She wiggled and squirmed, trying to be free of him. "Get up, get up, get *off!*"

"I feel as if I'm being discarded like a squeezed lemon."

She laughed, an intimate sound, before murmuring, "And the juice is sweet and sticky."

She put her robe back on and unlocked the door as he once more donned his jeans and sweater. They returned silently to their room and showered together.

Afterward, as Sam rinsed out the tub, she wiped a circle on the fogged mirror and frowned at her reflection.

"I'm getting old," she said mournfully.

"Not yet," he assured her. "You're still blooming."

"Look around my eyes. Wrinkles." She grimaced and squeezed her face up into a garish grin.

"Where?" He leaned over to see.

"See?"

"Ah, there they are! Nice. I love those laugh lines. It's the frown between your eyes that I don't like."

"That's from saying, 'Sam! Cut it out!'"

"It's settled that I'm going to Houston next week for a three-day seminar," he said. "Would you like to go along? We could delay coming back. It's coming up spring down in south Texas."

"I can't go now. Not with the show so close."

"If I let you get out of it this time, will you promise to take an anniversary trip with me?"

"Sam, you *know* that's just before the fall show. I won't be able to get away then either. How about sometime in—? No, I have to organize the winter line then."

"April's our fifth year. You've had me for five years. You ought to celebrate, brag. We need to get away."

"I've told you I'll figure something out."

"That was weeks ago."

"Don't push," she said as she hurried into her clothes and headed for her attic studio.

Several days later they were discussing Pearl. Sam grinned and said, "Pearl's going to be one hell of a great doctor."

"She told me she discusses her cases with Hedda, who either confirms or questions her diagnosis," Addy said.

"That wouldn't surprise me."

"It's too bad Marcus and Hedda never had children together. They're both so fantastic, it would be interesting to see the the child they'd produce. Do you know anything about Pearl's mother?"

"Just that she died when Pearl was a baby."

"I always wondered if Hedda might have spirited her away somehow." Addy fell silent for a minute. "Do you think Hedda could speak if she wanted to? I'm so used to her not talking, I sometimes forget how strange it really is."

"She doesn't need to speak. She's a lot like Marcus in that respect."

"You should have seen how he made the band let Erin sit in without saying a single word."

"I heard them practicing yesterday."

"I'm so sorry you missed the first sessions." She suppressed a grin.

"They're really very good. It's just that you've always been partial to elevator music."

"That's not true! Anyway, the band's music annoys Stormy."

"Probably makes the babies in his stomach dance." They exchanged smiles.

"Hedda has been teaching Erin all about the catering business."

"Is she any good? Can she substitute for Sarah and do our cooking?" Sam asked eagerly.

"How could you offend Sarah like that?"

"There has to be a niche for Sarah someplace, but

I don't think it's in the kitchen."

"She'll probably end up like Emmaline. Remember when I tried to make her into a seamstress and she turned out to be a genius of a designer? Did you know she's going to Paris this fall. Scarves by Emmaline. The other day she told me Marcus gave her some woman to train—just like he does to us! She was so disgruntled. And she said, 'She's white!' I said, 'What's wrong with white?' I was pretty indignant, you know. And she said, 'Oh, Addy, I'm sorry. I always forget you're white.'"

She and Sam chuckled. Then Addy turned serious again. "Has Erin ever had a job?"

"No. She met Jim during high school when she joined Junior Achievement. He was her advisor from the sponsoring company. They weren't allowed to date until after she graduated, but they talked on the phone all the time. There were a lot of things—company-related ones, of course—that they had to discuss."

"So she's had no experience or training for anything in particular."

"None. But Jim left her with adequate insurance."

"Cold comfort."

"Actually, it's a great help. She can use it to go back to school. She's only twenty-five, you know."

"That's true. Hedda is so wonderful with her. I wish she was as patient with Sarah." Addy paused before adding, "It does surprise me that Hedda takes so much time with Erin."

"Don't worry about it. Everything will work out."

"I don't have time to worry about it," Addy reminded herself.

*   *   *

The following week, on the day Sam was scheduled to fly to Houston, another crisis developed at Gown House when the correct lining for an important dress failed to arrive in the mail. Since Addy was tied up on the phone, trying to find the missing material, Erin volunteered to drive Sam to the airport.

Under the ever-burning Edison bulb in the front hallway, Sam held Addy tightly and whispered into her ear, "Miss me."

"I will; hurry back." She clung to him.

"Look at the time," Grendel exclaimed. "Hurry up, Daddy."

Sam lifted his head from Addy's and asked sternly, "Did you hear your eight-year-old daughter?"

She nodded.

"Hurry, hurry," Bridget echoed. "The time!"

"We've got plenty," Erin reassured them. "Don't rush."

"We always rush," Grendel explained matter-of-factly.

"Listen to our children, Addy," Sam warned her.

She raised bleak eyes to his, but her posture was defensive.

The two girls were going to the airport with Sam and Erin. Addy watched through the Tiffany glass in the front door as they piled into the car and drove away. Sam was behind the wheel, and Erin sat in the front seat with him while the two girls sat in back. They looked like a family.

As Addy thoughtfully watched the car pull out of sight, her wrist alarm began to buzz loudly. She turned reluctantly toward the stairs, only to be stopped by the sight of Hedda standing in the drawing-room door-way.

Tall and imposing in her long African dress, Hedda stared haughtily at Addy. Her pupils were jet black surrounded by white. Also black were her skin and lips, which were perfectly chiseled. Her head, which she held proudly, was wrapped in a brilliantly colored scarf.

Hedda continued to stare at Addy disapprovingly. It wasn't hard to see that she thought Addy should have gone to the airport. Addy frowned back at her, then slowly climbed the stairs under Hedda's stern gaze. At the top landing she leaned over the railing and called, "I simply couldn't go. It takes too long to drive out there and back."

Hedda didn't move. Her expression didn't change. Silently Addy disappeared into her attic studio.

The next day, much to Addy's chagrin, Marcus arrived on her doorstep with a dog. "Your kids need a dog," he said. "It will play with Bridget while Grendel's in school and Stormy's waiting to have his babies."

Addy wasn't at all eager for a new addition to the household. "There are too many dogs in the world," she protested. "Take him to the shelter."

"But this dog is interesting."

She looked down at the half-grown, dappled brown animal sitting on one hip. The dog seemed to be smiling up at her. "He's ugly and floppy," she said.

"How can you speak of him as if he can't hear?" Marcus chided. "The poor creature was thrown from a car and abandoned. Now you, too, are being unkind."

Feeling guilty, Addy leaned over and almost patted the dog's head in apology, but she caught herself in time and said firmly, "No, Marcus, you've been saddling me with misfits ever since I first met you and—"

"And look how nicely they've turned out."

"Emmaline turned out okay," Addy admitted.

"What about Sisco? Remember how disastrously careless he was," Marcus went on. "And how he'd begun to experiment with drugs? Sam made him sit in the emergency room at the hospital for a week. That straightened him out. It changed his whole life."

"Yes, I remember," Addy said with a sigh. "Have you heard from him?"

"He made the dean's list at college. He's a junior now."

"All right, Marcus, I can see that a *few* people have benefited from staying with us. But I don't want a dog."

Just then Grendel bounded up the front walkway, home from school, all red-cheeked and full of her day. "Hi!" she yelled exuberantly to the adults. Then: "Oh! Isn't he *darling!*" And she tossed her books aside and flung herself at the delighted pup.

Addy shot Marcus a withering glance, one very similar to the look Hedda had given her the day before, but Marcus just said, "He's an outdoor dog, of course," and went down the steps, leaving her standing there speechless.

She turned to separate the child from the dog, and was just in time to see them vanish through the front door. She turned back and cried, "Marcus!" But he was already gone.

The Grady household now included one bereaved woman, one falsely pregnant male cat, and one abandoned mutt. Who would join them next? Addy wondered.

Three days later, Addy was once more agonizing over the question of whether or not she should go to the airport to meet Sam. But she just couldn't spare the two hours it would take to get there and back. At the last minute she asked Erin if she'd mind picking him up. Erin said, "Of course not. I'll take the kids along."

Addy used the two hours to finish some paperwork and make several phone calls. She was beginning to realize how much she despised desk work.

She was on the phone when Sam appeared in her office doorway, his face grim. He was wearing his coat and hat, and still carrying his suitcase.

Addy gave him a big smile, then frowned into the phone and said, "What? That will never do! No."

Carefully Sam put down the suitcase, took off his hat and sailed it across the room, stripped the coat off his shoulders, circled her desk, jerked the receiver out of her hand, and slammed it into the cradle, then lifted her up from her chair.

"That was important!" she sputtered.

"And I'm not?"

He was kissing her as the telephone began to shrill. He did a very thorough job of it, then released her and said, "Your phone's ringing."

He strode from the room as Addy picked up the receiver and said, "Yes? Oh, I'm so sorry. We must have been cut off."

When she completed the call, Addy jotted down a

couple of notes, added them to a stack of papers that didn't need to be dealt with immediately, and replaced the rock that kept the pile from tumbling over. Then she went in search of Sam.

She found him in the kitchen along with Bridget and Grendel. Erin and Sarah were there too, putting the last serving dishes on the table. A circle of miniature poinsettias left over from Christmas formed a colorful cernterpiece.

Once everyone was seated, Sam served the thick, rich beef-and-vegetable stew from a heavy tureen. Apparently he'd overcome his pique, for he passed the plates around with his usual good humor. They all helped themselves to tart apple salad and hot, crusty bread, and had lemon sherbert and vanilla cookies for dessert.

As everyone ate with relish, Addy was sensitive to the fact that Sam's presence made the family whole. Even with Erin and Sarah at the table, it was still a family, thanks mostly to Sam.

Before they cleared the table, Sam produced a small pile of gaily wrapped packages. He always brought presents home from his trips. One was a large box of chocolates. "I bought it at the airport," he admitted. "There wasn't any time to shop." He gave each daughter a silver replica of the Texas state flag, and Sarah and Erin received slender silver bangles.

Erin immediately put hers on and turned it slowly around her wrist, admiring it with obvious pleasure. Addy suddenly realized that Erin had no jewelry of her own. Her fingers were still too sensitive to wear rings; in fact, the doctors had found it necessary to cut her wedding band off her finger in order to treat the burns. None of her other jewelry had been saved from the fire. Although volunteers had sifted through the ashes, not even the small diamonds from her engagement ring had been found. Addy marveled at Sam's sensitivity in choosing such a perfect gift for Erin.

They left the table and chatted in the parlor until the children's bedtime. Together Sam and Addy bathed a chattering Bridget in the girls' small bathroom, then read to her as Grendel bathed herself in her parents more luxurious tub. They all talked for a while before saying good night, and then Sam and Addy walked quietly to their room.

Sam closed the door before taking Addy into his arms and kissing her slowly, deliciously. When he finally gave her time to breathe, she said brightly, "How clever of you to think of the bracelet for Erin. Did you see her with it? She should have some earrings too. Her ears are pierced. I hadn't realized she had absolutely no jewelry. You're so sweet."

"You give her the earrings. Buy her what you think she should have."

"I don't have ti—"

"The earrings should come from you, not me."

She nodded, agreeing, then teased, "What did you get for me?"

He regarded her very seriously, smoothing her hair back gently, and said, "I brought back the greatest gift of all for you. Myself."

"I'll take it."

"You have to take my heart, my soul, and my companionship as well. I'm a package deal."

She tilted her chin up on his chest and blew on his throat. "You've hinted as much."

"Hinted?" He pulled his head back to look down

at her. "I thought I'd more than hinted."

"Loud and clear." She nodded.

"Did you miss me?"

She feigned surprise. "You've been gone?"

"Addy . . ."

And she gave a throaty, intimate chuckle before showing him just how glad she was to have him home.

The next day, Saturday, Sam met the dog. Addy watched from the landing as he walked down the hall toward the sound of giggles coming from the upstairs bathroom. Addy moved closer as Sam opened the door to find Sarah, Erin, and his two daughters bathing a pitifully skinny, forlorn-looking yellow pup, whose baleful expression almost made Addy laugh out loud.

When the dog caught sight of Sam, he let out a heart-rending yowl. Naturally Sam asked, "What in the world is that?"

Erin just smiled, but Sarah, Grendel, and Bridget laughed hilariously, "Oh, Daddy," Grendel said indulgently.

"It's a dog!" Bridget exclaimed.

"I thought it was an extremely large rat."

His daughters looked shocked, but Sarah was convulsed with laughter.

"Just wait till he's dry again, Daddy. He'll fluff up and be beautiful," Grendel assured him.

Sam remained unconvinced. The dog stared back steadily, as if hoping to be rescued, but Sam just leaned in the doorway, enjoying the spectacle of four people trying to soap and rinse one pitifully small, shivering dog.

The room and water were warm, and the two women were working with quick efficiency. There was no reason for the dog to be shivering, unless it was afraid. But it didn't appear to be fearful.

"You're good at this, Erin," Sam complimented her.

"We had dogs when I was growing up," she explained.

And none since? Addy wondered.

"What's . . . it's name?" Sam inquired.

"He's a him." Bridget piped up.

"What's *him's* name?"

"His," Grendel corrected perfectly mimicking her mother's tone of voice. Still watching unobtrusively, Addy raised her eyebrows in surprise.

"We haven't decided what to name him," Grendel said earnestly. "A name's important. You have to know first what kind he is."

"What kind of dog?" Addy said, joining the conversation. She wondered how they'd ever untangle all the strains.

"If he's a boy or a girl," Bridget explained. "He's a boy dog."

"That *would* have a bearing on the name," Sam agreed.

"Once we called a cat Lilly, and it was a boy," Sarah confessed.

Sam nodded somberly. "Think of that poor cat going around the neighborhood and the other male cats saying, 'Hi, what's your name?' and your cat having to say, 'Lilly.'" He shook his head in sympathy, while everyone laughed.

Everyone but Grendel, who said thoughtfully, "That would be tough. He *is* a boy. What name do you think, Daddy?"

Sam eyed the yellowish ragamuffin sitting grimly

in the soapy water of the laundry tub, dolefully suffering the two women's ministrations. Snapping his
fingers, he offered, "Mangy."

There were boos and protests.

"Pepsodent?"

"Pepsodent?" They were incredulous.

"Then if he got away, we could wonder where the
yellow went."

Erin and Sarah groaned as they poured clear warm
water over the subject under discussion, but the girls
looked blank so Sam sang the jingle: "You'll wonder
where the yellow went when you brush your teeth
with Pepsodent."

Grendel put her hand to her forehead in a gesture
very much like Addy's. Bridget imitated her, but she
was laughing and didn't look convincingly pained.

Then Sam offered a string of names for the dog, all
of them insulting: Rat, Whelp, Cur, Hound. The five
females rejected all his ideas. Finally Grendel said,
"Never mind, Daddy, we'll do it ourselves."

Bridget moved to her sister's side. "Then when he
goes outside, and the other dogs ask him his name,
he won't be sad."

"Fang, Revenge, Terror, Werewolf, Kill—"

"Dadddeee," Grendel protested.

This time Addy couldn't help laughing. "I can just
see the sign on the front gate listing all our names,
and at the bottom: The Killer. I'd lose all my customers."

"Call him Marshmallow," Sam suggested, full of
ideas.

His daughters giggled indulgently.

By then the dog was standing on the table they

used to sort and fold clothes, and Erin and Sarah were drying him with large faded towels from a stack of old ones that were used for household purposes. The dog patiently endured the buffeting.

Grendel patted his head. "You're going to be beautiful," she said consolingly. The dog licked her nose, and Grendel accepted that as a compliment.

"I think Grendel will be a veterinarian," Sam guessed, turning to Addy for confirmation. But she was checking her watch and already heading for their bedroom. He deserted the grooming establishment and followed.

When he reached the doorway, she was sorting through her closet and frowning.

"Going out?" he asked.

"We have that dinner next week to raise money for the museum. I'm looking for something to wear."

"Make it purple."

Surprised, she glanced over her shoulder at him, "I thought you liked red."

"I'm maturing." He stepped inside and closed the door. "I love the way purple makes your hair look like gold and your eyes like sapphires. Gorgeous!"

"Women aren't gorgeous," she scoffed. "Men are."

"No, no, no. Men are beautiful. Women are handsome and well-made."

"You're an idiot."

"There are female idiots, too."

"What time are we due at the Austins' cocktail party tonight? Is Erin still coming with us?"

"Seven-thirty and yep," Sam replied. "Do you mind the dog?"

"That Marcus!... Do you know what he had the

nerve to say? That it would be an outside dog!"

"Now we have two children, a pregnant tom cat, and a dog."

"Actually, Grendel told me yesterday she's beginning to suspect Stormy really is fat."

"I love our daughters." Sam took Addy into his arms, holding her as she leaned back and talked, needlessly fussing with his collar and smoothing his sweater just for the pleasure of touching him.

"You're a superior family man," she praised him.

"I love you, too." He gave her a friendly kiss on the mouth, then straightened up so he could enjoy looking at her. "I like living with you in this big old place. It's a little like living in a girls' boardinghouse."

"How do you know that?"

"On occasion I've been called to the nurses' quarters to take care of someone. Once I had to go to a dorm at the university."

"But you're a pediatric consultant."

"Doctors get desperate now and then and will accept just about anyone's help. Anyway, ladies aren't very different from little girls. They just have more frills." His hands eagerly explored the differences.

"If I die, you should marry again," Addy said impulsively.

"Are you planning on leaving me?"

"No. But if I did, if you were left like Erin, all alone, I'd really want you to marry again."

He kissed her cheek and studied her face, not paying much attention to her words.

She caressed his shoulders. Thinking of Erin made her feel very sentimental. "Promise me you'd marry again," she persisted.

"Not the same day," he said lightly.

"I'm really trying to tell you that I'd hate for you to be a hermit the rest of your life," she said with some asperity. She was serious about this.

"You have little yellow flecks in your eyes."

"I wouldn't want you to marry Tippy or Sherry," she said, mentioning single women they both knew.

"Not Tippy?"

"Absolutely not!" Tippy was redheaded, voluptuous, and beautiful, while Sherry was an icy blond beauty.

"But Karen would be all right," Addy went on. "She's never been married, and she would be good with the girls. She's an excellent housekeeper, and she gets along better with Marcus than I do. Of course, she just says okay and doesn't argue with him." Karen was really rather colorless, Addy decided.

"Karen?" Sam repeated, distracted.

"Yes," she said, as if the matter were resolved.

"She doesn't turn me on. I can't imagine having sex with her."

Addy jerked back in surprise. "You'd have *sex* with another woman?"

"Not casual sex; but married sex, yes."

"With another woman?" She gasped. How silly of her not to have thought of that before.

"Well, if you were dead and gone..."

"I just hadn't thought about you making love to anyone else. I thought you'd, well, be loyal."

"Did you really?" he inquired pleasantly.

"I suppose you would have to make love to her if you married her. She'd probably expect it."

"Of course, I do know someone who *does* turn me on," Sam offered.

She eyed him warily, not sure she really wanted to know, but unable to resist asking. "Who?"

"Weeelll, you do. On occasion."

"Only occasionally?" Her mouth quirked in a tiny, smug smile.

"Yeah. In the morning."

"Not at night?"

"Then, too."

They were kissing very deliciously when a knock sounded on the door, and Grendel came in to ask, "May we use your hair dryer?"

"Sure."

Sam and Addy continued kissing while Grendel got the dryer from their bathroom. Leaving the room, she said nonchalantly, "I thought two dryers would do better than one."

"Ummm," her parents replied. They separated briefly to give their daughter a vague smile as she closed the door behind her.

"I haven't got anything to wear to George and Marty's tonight." Addy gestured at her packed closet.

"Good. Go naked. You can tell them you just didn't have anything to wear, and everyone will sympathize, especially the men. Women always say they have nothing to wear, but they always turn up in something." He stood with his hands in his trouser pockets and smiled at his wife.

Then, as if a lightning bolt of inspiration had just hit him, he said eagerly, "Why don't you take off your clothes and practice now? Then I'll chase you around the room, and we can practice wrestling or something."

"I think you really would have sex with a second

wife," Addy said disconsolately.

"I'd rather not."

"Then don't."

"I mean I'd really rather keep you."

"Even if I can't go on the trip with you?"

"Addy, I've told you how I feel about that."

"I honestly don't see how I can manage it. I shouldn't even go tonight. Dale's dress for the show *still* isn't right. I ought to pitch the idea and do another gown entirely. Lilabet is going crazy ripping the seams and resewing them for me, but the blasted thing just doesn't work. And the show is in two weeks!"

Sam sighed in exasperation and demanded, "When you come to the end of your days, in another sixty or so years, what will you remember as being important to you?"

She frowned at him, disgruntled, then guessed, "You want me to say 'Being Sam's playmate of the years'?"

"Yes."

"You *are* important to me, Sam."

"How important"

"Very."

"Then go away with me."

"I just *can't*. There isn't time. And I can't spend the day running around this house naked and playing tag with you either."

That afternoon, a steady stream of shouts, squeals, and laughter floated up the stairs, and Addy finally left her drawing table and went to see what was going on. Dale's gown wouldn't even come right on paper, and Addy was more than glad to abandon it for a few minutes.

As she started down the front staircase, Grendel ran by in the hall below, laughing and yelling. Bridget, coming next, was lifted aside and carried along by Sam, who was being chased by Erin. The now clean, fluffy dog bounded up the stairs and sat down next to Addy unnoticed, to watch with her. When she rose to return to work, he followed her up the stairs and into her studio.

GEORGE AND MARTY Austin were having people over for cocktails before a smaller group went on to dinner and then to a local theater production starring their friend Gina Stephens.

"This will be a good way for Erin to start socializing again," Addy said to Sam as they got ready for the party. "We'll stay only for cocktails."

"Good."

"Oh, and I told Marty all about Erin and warned her not to light a fire in the fireplace."

"Good," he repeated.

As Addy and Sam emerged from their room, they met Erin coming shyly down the hallway, wearing a dress of soft golden-brown wool. It was perfect for her, the color warm and flattering, the sleeves long and concealing, the Mandaran collar charming. Erin was still too thin, but lately she'd been standing up straighter, as if less braced for a blow from an unknown source, and the loose cut suited her figure. Her hair was now about an inch and a half long, and it curled softly around her head. In the dress Lilabet had sewn with casual genius—Addy was continually amazed by her speed and precision—Erin looked quite lovely.

Just before Sam, Addy, and Erin left for the party, the entire Grady family, sat in the kitchen, once more discussing names for their new dog. They finally decided on Leo.

Addy winced slightly as she imagined the protesting roars of all the great lions of history and literature. Sam's eyes danced with amusement.

"He looks like a lion," Grendel said, as if trying to convince herself.

"Yes," Bridget agreed before asking seriously, "That's the one with stripes?"

"Those are zebras. Lions are like great big cats," Addy answered.

"Oh." Bridget throught about that for a while before she asked, "Will he *like* being called a cat?"

"I don't think he knows about lions," Sam assured her.

"Here, Leo," Bridget urged, trying out the new name. The dog raised his head and walked slowly, almost reluctantly, over to her. Addy wondered what he'd been called by the people who'd abandoned him.

Just then two girls from the neighborhood arrived to baby-sit for Grendel, Bridget, and Leo while Sam and Addy went to the Austins' party. The teenagers had sat for the Gradys before and were familiar with the house and rules: allow no visitors, don't open the door for anyone, write down phone numbers when people call, never tell anyone you're alone.

The sitters hung up their coats in the big closet under the front stairs and put their boots on the tray to dry, then began playing hide and seek with Bridget and Grendel. The house was a perfect place for the game.

As Addy, Sam, and Erin slipped out the front door and headed down the walkway, Leo let out a long, mournful howl. Addy chuckled and even Erin smiled, but Sam was not amused. "That's some watch dog we've got," he complained.

Since the Austins' house was only a few blocks away, they walked. Even before they reached the doorstep, the gayly lit windows and strains of music told them that the party was well under way.

The front walk had been cleared of snow and ice, and lined with candles set in sand-filled paper bags. The resulting glow added a note of warmth to the chilly scene.

As soon as they rang the bell, the door opened and a burst of sound crescendoed around them. Addy laughed. Marty must have been watching for their arrival.

"Marvelous!" their hostess exclaimed, hugging Addy and Sam. "How do you do, Erin? I'm so glad you could come." While her husband George helped Erin hang up her coat, Marty added in an appalled aside to Sam and Addy, "I'm so sorry. Before I could stop him, the caterer lit a fire in the fireplace!" The two women exchanged meaningful glances.

Pasting a smile on her face and hoping she didn't look as nervous as she felt, Addy took Erin's hand

and led her toward the back of the house. "You must see Marty's kitchen. It was featured in *House and Garden*! Marty's a super cook."

"In a minute, Addy," Sam interrupted. "I want Erin to meet our friends first." He placed his hand on Erin's back and began introducing her to some people standing at the edge of the living room.

Addy and Marty's eyes met again, and Marty shook her head in despair. Addy sympathized. The best laid plans of mice and men . . . and even the most considerate of hostesses . . . often went awry.

To Addy it was immediately apparent that Marty and George had warned most of the guests about Erin's fear of fire. Only the caterer seemed unaware of the problem. He was bustling about, oblivious to the growing tension as Sam and Erin paused to greet people farther inside the room. While Addy watched, amazed, the other guests casually arranged themselves to form a human screen between Erin and the fire. As if deliberately choreographed, the human screen shifted each time Erin moved, so that the fire always remained out of her sight. It was so brilliantly and spontaneously accomplished that Addy felt filled to overflowing with appreciation for these people whose annoying habits and irritating mannerisms she knew well but suddenly found totally insignificant. She even felt some affection for Marty's brother-in-law, who had an unfortunate tendency to pat women's bottoms.

Addy was so full of good will that she wasn't the slightest bit nonplussed when she suddenly found herself face to face with Sam's sister. The gorgeous Cyn stood surrounded by a crowd of admirers, looking absolutely smashing in one of Addy's latest designs.

She was deep in conversation with a very attractive man. After giving Cyn a quick hug and kiss and chatting about nothing in particular for a minute or two, Addy felt free to leave her sister-in-law with the handsome gentleman and catch up with Erin and Sam.

It didn't take long to introduce Erin to everyone in the living room, and Addy breathed a sign of relief when Marty led them into the dining room, where dainty hors d'oeuvres and glasses of wine awaited them. Next they inspected and praised the prize-winning kitchen, exchanging courteous nods with the busy caterer, before meandering into the library for a cozy chat with several of Erin's new acquaintances.

Instead of staying twenty minutes, as they'd intended, they stayed for over an hour, talking, snacking, and enjoying the party. They didn't return to the living room, but it was practically deserted anyway. The fire had made the room too warm.

The party began to break up as some of the guests left to keep their dinner reservations. Sam, Addy, and Erin got their coats, said their good-byes, and retraced their steps down the candlelit walkway and on toward home.

"You never have a fire at the house," Erin observed offhandedly. "How come?"

Sam and Addy exchanged uneasy glances. "Would you...like...us to have one?" Addy asked hesitantly.

"Oh, yes. We had a fireplace when I was growing up. It was so lovely."

Sam and Addy's eyes met again with ironic amusement. The Gradys had always loved using their many fireplaces, especially on bitterly cold evenings, but for the past few weeks they'd abandoned their cozy ritual in deference to Erin. And now it turned out that all the time she'd wanted a fire. Apparently she didn't equate fires in fireplaces with burning houses. Addy felt a great, thundering relief.

When they got home, Sam and the girls walked the baby-sitters back to their house—Leo declining to accompany them—and Addy and Erin changed clothes, made popcorn, and lit a fire in the parlor fireplace.

When Sam and the girls returned, red-cheeked and laughing, they all settled down to relax and play games, snug and warm before the cheerfully crackling logs. Leo lay with his head on Addy's foot; he'd clearly decided to be *her* dog. She looked down at him and shook her head in annoyance. She was the only one in the house who didn't like dogs.

When Marty called Addy the next day to ask after Erin, Addy thanked her for the splendid party and for her obvious concern.

"So you didn't have any problems?" Marty asked.

"None. And you were all brilliant. Please thank everyone, will you?"

She felt no need to tell Marty that Erin wasn't afraid of fires after all.

In the days that followed, Erin seemed to bloom. Once, unexpectedly, she laughed out loud at Leo, charming everyone with her unrestrained delight. Gradually she became more relaxed around the girls, but she still didn't mention her own children. In fact, she made no reference to her seven years of marriage, never shared an anecdote from that time. It was as if she'd stored all her memories of those years in a secret room in her mind, then locked and barricaded it.

Erin was a particularly appreciative audience of one when Addy rehearsed her narration for the February show. She seemed fascinated by the preparations for the show, which would take place the following weekend. She watched as Addy fitted clothes on the models, and applauded when they practiced posing before the huge dining-room mirrors.

Erin smiled at Pattycake, but she didn't seem as relaxed and open with her as she did with the others. Addy didn't know if that was because Pattycake was so immature—though twenty-three, she often acted like a sixteen-year-old—or because she was so pregnant.

"Are you sure you want to be in the show?" Addy asked Pattycake for the twentieth time.

"Oh, sure. I'm not due for weeks yet."

"You aren't?" Addy asked skeptically, looking at the model's blooming body.

"Now, Addy, I'm not that enormous." She laughed, not taking offense.

"It's not really a question of size; you just look ready."

Pearl interrupted them to ask, "How do you expect the three of us to show all these clothes?"

"There aren't any more clothes than usual," Addy answered.

"Sure there are. We have to show all those that Pattycake would normally model."

"I know what you want," Patty said with a long-suffering sigh. "You want me to model the white, virginal nightgown."

"I doubt it would fit," Addy replied. "But that black lace panty and bra set would look interesting on you."

"I'd look as if I was selling belly."

"Why, you're *pregnant!*" Pearl exclaimed elaborately, pretending she'd just noticed.

"No kidding."

"When was it due...yesterday? Last week?"

"I'm not due for three more weeks!" Pattycake retorted.

"Are you sure you counted right?" redheaded Dale inquired. "Is your gynecologist going to be standing by during the show?"

"Sam will," Addy offered.

"Piffle," said brunette Linda. "Sam only deals in kids. He'll sit around bored, waiting for the baby to appear, and just ignore you."

Pattycake frowned into the mirror. "Do I look that bad?"

"We're teasing you, honey; ignore us," Pearl assured her. "If you didn't look great, we wouldn't say a word."

Patty turned sideways and pulled her dress tightly around her stomach. "I can still climb up on the ramp."

"If you feel okay," Addy told her, "then it's okay. Don't worry about it. How do you like the plaid dress?"

"It's my favorite. I just love it. And it was so nice of you to put pockets in all the maternity clothes. I can keep my hands in them instead of laying my arms on top of The Bulge."

"I've given you three outfits to model," Addy explained. "Will that be too much?"

"Oh, no. I can do a robe or something else too."

"No, I think three is just right," Addy decided. "You'll bring in so many orders we might go crazy trying to fill them."

"I love your work. There isn't a whole lot you can

do to a maternity dress, but these are terrific. I feel pretty and tidy and comfortable in them."

"Thanks, honey. You look perfect. Now don't try the steps unless one of us is there to help you. And don't worry about anything. Use your head and don't do anything stupid. And remember, I don't want you on the runway; it's too dangerous without a handrail. Just turn and stand in the doorway, okay?"

"I'll be all right on the runway."

"No."

"Oh, Addy."

"No."

"Okay, okay!"

Just then Dale appeared wearing the intricately shaped dress Addy'd had so much trouble with. It still wasn't right. "This just won't work!" Dale exclaimed. "If you sell this design, you're going to go nuts with refittings and unhappy customers. Give up on it."

"But I love the idea," Addy protested. "I can't understand why it won't work."

"This seam cuts into me." Dale raised her arm and pointed.

"If I let it out or move it, the symmetry will be ruined."

"We could remove my arm instead," Dale offered sarcastically.

"Good thinking!" Addy exclaimed, frowning at the dress. She'd have to pitch the impossible thing in the trash can. Mournfully she said, "We'll just have to forget it."

"How about Pearl?" Dale suggested. "She's skinnier than I am. Try it on her."

"I'd look like I was wearing some fat little kid's cast-off," Pearl said.

"Fat? Listen, you six-foot-slat," Dale began.

"Ladies, that's enough," Addy interrupted, wistfully recalling how serene Miss Pru had always kept things.

In the midst of the confusion Erin said, "Maybe *I* could wear it."

Addy stared in surprise. Erin was volunteering to model, to go out on the runway before a hundred people? How amazing! How wonderful!

They all turned to stare at her. Her face was still discolored from the healing burns, but that could be covered by makeup. Addy's eyes flicked to Dale's dress and back to Erin.

"The color would be great on her," Dale said. She held the lovely blue-green material against Erin's chest, and they studied the effect critically.

"Try it on," Addy suggested.

Without a moment's hesitation Erin skimmed out of her sweater and slacks and pulled the gown over her head, adjusting it carefully. It fit perfectly! They all circled silently around her, looking for imperfections.

Apparently feeling a bit self-conscious beneath their intently scrutiny, Erin licked her lips nervously and ran a hand through her short hair. She peeked uneasily at the models, who all awaited Addy's decision.

"Would you like to model it?" she asked Erin. "It's perfect on you. Is it comfortable?"

Erin moved experimentally. "It's fine."

"It's your ba-zoom, honey," Pearl told Dale. "You're too busty."

Dale sent her a quelling look that made Pearl laugh.

"We'll have to be very careful about who orders

one," Addy said thoughtfully. "I wish Miss Pru were here to tactfully discourage the Dale-types. It's absolutely smashing on you, Erin, just as I imagined it. But it would be uncomfortable on anyone ten pounds heavier."

"Dale is more than ten pounds heavier," Pearl teased.

But Dale remained unperturbed. "*I* think my waist is smaller than Erin's. The weight's in my bust and hips."

"Yeah," Pearl agreed.

"Erin's a miniature, white version of you, Pearl," Addy observed.

"I've gained five pounds in three weeks," Erin put in. "And I'm probably going to gain more soon."

"Not in the next week, you won't, not if you want to be in the show," Linda advised.

Would Erin really do it? Addy wondered. She'd gotten along well at the Austins', but Sam had been by her side the entire time. Would he have to get up on the runway and hold her hand?

Suddenly, almost as if the mere thought had conjured him up, Sam's voice sounded outside the dining room. "Man on the floor," he called, using the time-honored boardinghouse cry. He gave them a chance to put on robes before entering the room. After smiling at Addy, he turned to greet everyone else, and his eyes settled on Erin.

"Have you recuited a new model?" he inquired with no show of surprise.

"If she doesn't gain any weight in the next week," Linda said.

Sam smiled and nodded at Erin, then turned his

attention to Pattycake. "How're you doing, Patty?"

"Blimpishly."

"And how's Charlie doing?"

"Great. In control."

Addy laughed out loud, and grinned as she thought of Pattycake's husband. She still couldn't figure out how those two had ever gotten together. Patty was like a spring breeze—light, flippant, and frivolous. Charlie was a rock—a practical, hardheaded accountant. People certainly were fascinating, she thought.

"Come on, Erin, let's see how you do on the runway." Addy gestured to her.

In the passage between the dining and drawing rooms three steps had been built leading to a raised runway. As everyone else mounted the steps and descended on the other side, taking seats in the drawing room and pretending to be guests watching the show, Sam and Patty went through the hallway to avoid the climb.

Addy sat down on a high stool to the left of the runway. Improvising the new narration, she began: "Erin's gown isn't for everyone. Just ask Dale. But it suits a woman with a narrow chest and small bosom."

As Addy described the gown in great detail, Erin walked down the runway, moving and turning nicely.

"Have you done this before?" Addy asked, giving her a pleased smile.

"Once, at a charity fashion show."

"Smooth out your movements, practice with the other models in the mirrors, and listen to their advice. You'll do very well," Addy said.

Erin grinned shyly and curtsied charmingly when everyone applauded. As she turned to Sam, almost as if thanking him for helping her to this point, she looked truly beautiful.

"I feel like a frump," Dale complained.

Sam eyed her with exaggerated appreciation and, kissing his fingers, said, "Delicious."

Trust Sam to know exactly how to placate Dale, Addy thought. Again she remembered the first time she'd seen him. It was at the February fashion show she'd held, and she'd been demonstrating the snaps on a daring robe, confident that there were absolutely no men anywhere on the premises. Suddenly she'd looked up and seen him. Even now, more than five years later, her body responded to the mere memory, sending a sensual wave of awareness coursing through her veins.

As her thoughts returned to the present, she heard Sam ask, "Anyone for sledding? When the girls get home, we're heading out for the hill at Butler University."

"Me!" Erin shouted.

"Bring all broken bones to Dr. Freeman," Pearl intoned.

"*I* know how to set bones!" Sam muttered.

"It'll probably be *your* old bones that get broken."

"Old?" Sam said indignantly. "I'll have you know I'm a world-class sledder," he added, looking down his nose at her.

"World-class," Pearl agreed. "Hawaii, Panama, Chad, the Mojave," she teased.

"Right," Sam agreed. "I challenged every one of them, and I won every time."

"Of course, none of those places gets snow," Pearl said with a grin.

"Oh?" Sam appeared surprised. "I thought they

were rock groups who sledded."

Pearl rolled her eyes.

"Come with us, Addy, just for half an hour," he coaxed.

"I'd love to, Sam, but the show's this coming weekend. Take Leo out from under my feet, won't you?"

Supper was ready when the sledders came bursting into the kitchen that evening with a blast of cold air. Leo flopped down on the hearth, exhausted. Grendel gleefully exclaimed, "Daddy lay on the big sled, then Erin, then me, and Bridget on top. But she fell off, and we had to start all over again."

"Leo kept getting in the way!" Bridget complained, her nose running.

"And he barks a lot," Erin commented, smiling.

The sledders ate hungrily with murmurs of plea-sure—baked ham, sweet potatoes, buttered corn and peas, crisp apple salad, and raspberry trifle. In be-tween mouthfuls, they laughed and chatted. Addy watched and smiled.

After she wearily climbed the stairs at bedtime and entered her room, she found Sam already there un-dressing. "I wish you had come with us," he said.

"You were gone almost three hours."

"You could have taken your car and stayed just a little while. You never get your blood stirred up. You need to get outside and play with me."

His words triggered a series of mental images in her head—of Erin playing with Sam, hiding and seek-ing in the big house, building a family of snow people in the side yard, lying on top of Sam on the big sled. Out of nowhere a sudden thought came to her.

"Does Erin seem attractive to you?" she asked.

"Oh, yes. She's blooming. She laughs easily now and loves to play. She's starting to enjoy life again."

"But does she . . . turn you on?" Immediately Addy wanted to kick herself for asking the impulsive question.

Sam looked surprised. "That child?"

"She's hardly a child."

"She's only twenty-five. I'm forty-four. I could be her father. She's just a girl."

"I'm only thirty-two."

"Ahhh," he said, "but you've crossed the Great Divide—that yawning abyss between childhood and adulthood that ends at thirty. Now you're old enough to pass for an adult."

"Pass?" she repeated somewhat huffily. "What do you mean, I can *pass* for an adult?"

"You really can be incredibly childish at times."

She gasped in shock and flopped down onto the bed, turning her back to him, then snapped, "Good night."

"See what I mean?" he said, and left her alone.

Addy's argument with Sam marked the beginning of an utterly ghastly week. Sam remained impatient with her. Bridget caught a bad cold. Hedda acted disapproving. Only Leo seemed eager for Addy's company—and she didn't *want* a dumb dog underfoot!

Everyone was too busy, easily distracted, and short-tempered. Marcus's crews arrived to tidy up the house and snow-covered yard. The band began practicing daily. And the models rushed around complaining about the way they looked.

When Erin told the members of the band that she

wouldn't be able to play with them durng the show
because she was going to model, they nodded solemnly, trying not to look at each other. Later, Addy
detected a marked upswing in their mood, and several
times she saw them happily clapping each other on
the back.

The more open and laughing Erin became, and the
more blithely she went off with Sam and the girls—
leaving Addy, the drudge, at home, obedient to her
wrist alarm, slaving over the myriad details involved
in producing the show—the more Addy sulked.

Her temper frayed, she snapped at people, and she
brooded because Sam seemed to be having such a
good time with his younger, thinner, more willing
playmate.

Addy reminded herself that Grendel and Bridget
always went with Sam and Erin. Several other children
often joined their lighthearted forays as well. But a
lot could go on in front of children before they'd notice
anything amiss, she thought.

Addy's impatience bred impatience in everyone
else, and tempers flared at the slightest provocation.
When she criticized Hedda's hors d'oeuvres, saying
they looked like cat food on crackers, the older woman's eyes flashed and she gave Addy a haughty glare.

Addy glared right back before bursting out, "You
never frown that way at Erin!"

Angrily Hedda pointed to Addy and held her hands
out flat. Then she indicated Erin out in the yard playing with the kids, and she twisted her fingers. Apparently Hedda considered Addy healthy and whole
and Erin temporarily crippled.

But Addy wasn't mollified. "Even we whole people need a pat on the back occasionally!" she snapped.

Hedda solemnly placed her hand on Addy's head in what Addy surmised was a voodoo blessing. But it didn't soothe her temper.

That night Addy wakened out of a sound sleep to the elusive smell of cinnamon. As she focused sleepily on the clock and saw that it was almost three in the morning, she realized Sam wasn't in bed.

On those rare occasions when he was out late at night on a case, he would come upstairs and start undressing, and she'd wake up to say, "How'd it go?" He'd tell her, and then she'd ask, "How about some cocoa and cinnamon toast?" He'd always act a little surprised before saying, "Great!" As if she'd just thought of a new and wonderful idea.

But he hadn't come upstairs tonight. He'd made his own cinnamon toast and cocoa. Maybe he had come up and she'd been sleeping so soundly that she hadn't heard him.

She dragged herself out of bed, pulled on an old flannel robe, shoved her feet into cold slippers, and went down the back stairs.

As she approached the kitchen, she heard Sam's deep, sexy chuckle. As she bent down to adjust her slipper, Addy saw Erin lean forward and murmur something that made him laugh again.

Erin had made cocoa and cinnamon toast for Sam? Addy stood still as unreasonable jealousy coursed through her veins like a parasitic beast making itself at home in her body.

She couldn't bring herself to go down to the kitchen and ask them what was going on. Instead, she watched angrily, looking for other signs of their betrayal: Sam's hand on Erin's elbow, a shared glance, light words of teasing all fed Addy's jealousy, strengthening the beast within her.

In the days that followed, everyone became less and less tolerant of Addy's outbursts and she became more and more unreasonable.

One morning Bridget came downstairs barefooted and robeless, despite her terrible cold. Addy lost her temper and swatted the child, who immediately burst into tears. Her red, stuffy nose turned redder and stuffier, and Addy felt like a rat.

Quarrels broke out among the seamstresses and models. Leo dogged Addy's footsteps so closely that one morning she tripped and almost fell over him. The pages of her narration flew out of her hands and fell all over the floor. Thinking it was some kind of great joke, Leo pounced on the scattered pages, leaving messy paw-prints all over them. When Addy shouted and pulled him angrily off the papers, he slunk away with a shocked expression.

"Everyone around here is just impossible lately," Addy complained to Sam that evening.

"Now why do you suppose that is?" he asked with mild sarcasm.

"I don't know," she answered earnestly. "I suppose it's winter and everyone is tired and waiting for spring."

"Why else?"

"Why *else?*"

"What other reason could there be?"

"The pressure of the show this weekend, and Pattycake's being pregnant and irritable."

"And?"

"I suppose it's because everyone has other jobs

too, and their time is tight, and so their tempers are short."

"Can you think of any other reason?" he persisted.

"I suppose you want me to say that I've been the most difficult of all?" she ventured.

"You got it. You took a while, but you finally stumbled onto it."

"I think it's because Erin's living here. She's having such a good time of it. She doesn't miss her family at all," Addy said defensively and was immediately ashamed of herself for being so cruel.

"Addy!" Sam thundered.

"I know, I know," she said, miserable and contrite. "That was dreadful of me. I didn't really mean it."

"I should hope not!" And he stalked out of the room.

On the morning of the show, Hedda was in the kitchen making little tea cakes assisted by Erin and Sarah. They worked peacefully until Addy came in, critical and impatient. With a puzzled expression Erin finally left the room, and Sarah suddenly stopped smiling. Finally, looking stern and serious, Hedda sent Sarah into the parlor to check on the buffet table.

As soon as they were alone, Hedda turned to confront Addy. Struggling visibly, she moved her mouth silently, awkwardly forming the word "Addy." Her face was different. She was stern. Her features showed her displeasure as her throat tensed with obvious emotion. Then, with a terrible effort, she forced a harsh sound and shaped a word with her lips: "Stupid!" She raised a trembling arm and pointed to the door through which Erin had disappeared, then mouthed "Sam" and made a sharp, chopping motion at Addy.

Addy stood stunned into immobility. Hedda had spoken! With great effort Hedda had called her stupid.

Addy's mouth fell open, and she stared blankly at Hedda, who glared back. "I'm stupid?" Addy asked.

Hedda's nod confirmed Addy's label. Then once again, with a tremendous effort, she tore a word from her throat: "Behave!" As Addy watched, the anger left Hedda, and in its place was a stern, regal expression.

Addy couldn't move. Sarah returned to the room and said something to Hedda, who received the information calmly and with fluid motions indicated what Sarah was to do next. Then Grendel ran in, chattering excitedly and stealing a freshly iced tea cake while she grinned confidently at Hedda, who smiled indulgently.

Leo scampered in, avoiding Addy with a wary glance, and eagerly accepted the piece of cake Grendel fed him. She urged him to come with her, and, with a forlorn glance at Addy standing like a piller of salt in the middle of the room, he trotted after Grendel.

Addy felt like a ghost no one could see or hear. Everyone but Leo just ignored her. She had survived Hedda's censure, but she couldn't seem to move. She stood in a daze, aware only that Hedda had spoken to her with great effort out of seemingly inexpressible anger.

After a long time, Addy left the kitchen and climbed the stairs to the attic, where she sat on the window

ledge and looked outside. A lightly falling snow softened the black tangle of branches against the winter
sky. She could hear the scrape of snow shovels against
concrete as Marcus's young men cleared the sidewalk.

Addy began to consider her recent conduct and
found it too painful to contemplate the fact that Hedda
had spoken. A very subdued Addy went back downstairs.

Preparations for the show continued. Lunch was a
hurried, stand-up affair. Hedda treated her impartially, but Addy knew she'd received a serious warning that would bear careful consideration.

After lunch, she went around the house checking
on everyone's progress. In the parlor a small fire had
been lit, one that wouldn't overheat the room. A neatly
dressed young boy from the neighborhood stood beside it, grinning. His job was to feed the fire, using
kindling from a kettle as it was needed.

"You seen the sign for the band?" the boy asked.

Addy stopped, only then realizing that the band
was already beginning to warm up. "What sign?"

"Erin put it on the front door. It says, 'Look up
when you walk in and smile at the band.'"

How dare Erin put up a sign! Addy thought furiously. Who had told her to do it? She was acting as
if this were her house. Addy stiffened, and her mouth
thinned.

"Dr. Sam put one up first, and it was awful. Couldn't
even read it," the boy went on.

"Sam did?"

"Yeah. The band was fretting because you won't
let them use the amplifiers. They thought nobody would
know they was there."

"So Sam put up a sign?"

"Yeah, and then Erin changed it so the people can read it." The boy was very amused.

"Doctors never write very well," Addy said thoughtfully, beginning to realize how stupid she'd been to blame everything on Erin.

The boy laughed at her comment, the first friendly response she'd elicited in what seemed like weeks.

Yes, she really had been stupid, borrowing trouble, being jealous of Erin for no good reason. She would have to think this out the first chance she got.

Wearily, she went up to the bedroom to dress. Sam was already there. Suddenly she felt awkward with him.

He was in the middle of tying his tie, but he turned as she entered, and examined her carefully before asking brusquely, "Are you okay?"

She nodded weakly.

"You just have to get through today to survive it all," he reassured her. "Then you can get better organized so you won't have such a load to carry."

"Stop trying to run my life for me."

"Someone ought to help you, Addy. You do recall that I have to leave for Boston in the morning? I'll be speaking at a seminar tomorrow afternoon and two on Monday."

"Yes."

"I'll be back on Tuesday."

"Yes."

"Need any help with zippers?"

"No."

"No, thank you," he corrected her.

She raised her eyes to his, feeling utterly forlorn.

Immediately Sam took her into his arms. "I love you, you wretch."

"Do you really?" she asked, unconvinced.

"You don't make it easy," he admitted. "You've been very prickly lately." He kissed her cold lips. "And extremely difficult."

"Why does everyone blame me?"

"Does everyone?" His blue eyes peered sternly into hers.

"Hedda called me stupid."

He was instantly alert. "She *called* you stupid?" he asked doubtfully.

"With the greatest of difficulty but she did say the word."

"She actually spoke?"

Addy nodded.

"Then I suggest you listen to her," he said sternly, releasing her abruptly and leaving the room.

So Sam thought she was stupid too.

Once again Addy grew hot with discomfort as she considered the terrible emotional upheaval that had forced Hedda to speak.

— 6 —

THE EXCITEMENT OF the arriving guests filtered back to the models and lifted their spirits. But nothing helped Addy. Sam's much-married mother, Elizabeth Turner Harrow, arrived, accompanied by Cyn, who looked perfect. Addy greeted them soberly and went woodenly about the tasks required of her as hostess. And wherever she went she felt Sam's speculative gaze on her.

Bridget's lingering cold meant that she had to be confined to her room, but Addy allowed her one visitor—Leo. That not only brought a smile to Bridget's wan face, it also solved the problem of how to keep their canine houseguest out of trouble. "I'll pay you to baby-sit Leo," Addy told her younger daughter, which made Bridget feel even better.

They'd arranged for one of Pearl's four-year-old cousins to model the clothes originally intended for

308

Bridget. At first Bridget had been indignant, but then
she'd said philosophically, "It sells clothes." Sam had
laughed at her obvious parroting of Addy, and Bridget,
taking his amusement as a sign of approval, now repeated, "It sells clothes," at every opportunity.

Addy was thinking about all this as she passed Sam
in the downstairs hallway.

"Remember the ice storm five years ago when you
let me stay overnight?" he asked her.

"What?"

"The ice storm."

"There's an ice storm?"

"One's expected in the next day or so."

"Will you still go to Boston?"

"Probably."

"What if you can't get back?"

"Never?" He grinned. "You mean a new ice age
might start?"

"Oh, Sam..." And she headed toward the foyer
to take up her duties as hostess narrator, feeling all
alone in the world.

When all the guests had arrived and were settled
in their seats, with much chatter and rustling, Addy
mounted the three steps between the dining room-
turned-dressing room and the drawing room-turned-
fashion salon. As she stepped through the curtains,
the women applauded her enthusiastically, and she
felt immediately comforted by the invisible wave of
approval sweeping over her. She smiled more confidently, greeted the crowd pleasantly, and seated herself on the high stool to the left of the runway.

The program went very well. Addy knew the narration perfectly and spoke slowly enough to give the

models time to effectively display the clothes. Pearl's little cousin proved to be a natural ham, happily laughing and showing off, and the women all loved her. Pattycake looked a bit pale, but she moved carefully and stayed off the runway, as Addy had insisted.

Afterward, everyone crowded around the buffet table. Hedda's cakes were perfect, as usual, and the room hummed with enthusiastic voices and an elusive excitement Addy couldn't define.

She and the models began taking orders for clothes, and as they'd anticipated, there was a rash of requests for maternity dresses. What had she gotten herself into? What had Pattycake gotten her into? Where *was* Pattycake?

Dale, Linda, and Erin were earnestly scribbling away, recording orders and scheduling preliminary fittings. But Pearl, Pattycake, and Sam were nowhere to be seen. Addy looked around the room impatiently. Where were they when she needed them?

Suddenly Pattycake's husband Charlie came flying into the front hall. Hedda grabbed the startled man and hurried him out of sight toward the back of the house. Why was he here? Addy wondered. At that moment he certainly didn't look like the staid, composed accountant she knew so well.

And then Addy realized what must be happening. The baby! Excusing herself, she hurried down the hall, following muffled sounds which she could soon distinguish as Pearl's voice saying, "Breathe, breathe . . . perfect. Now just relax. Now wait, Patty, don't hurry it. Ah, that's great."

"Well, hello there, Charlie. We've been waiting for you," came Sam's calm voice.

Charlie said something indistinguishable in a strangled voice.

Addy peered through the open doorway into the back storage room, which had once served as a bedroom and still included a marble sink. Sam was washing his hands there while Pearl unwrapped a bolt of gingham. Pattycake was leaning over the table, pressing her hands against the top, hanging her head down as her body stiffened and she moaned. She was in labor!

"Darling, are you all right!" Charlie lay his hand on the small of her back and bent to look anxiously into her face.

"Fine," she replied with a grunt.

"I *asked* you this morning!" he admonished her. "I thought The Bulge felt tight. Why didn't you say something?" He shifted automatically as Sarah removed his coat and tie and turned him toward the sink so he too could wash his hands. "You should have said something!"

"I didn't think it was serious," Pattycake said, panting. "I'm not due for another three weeks."

"I won't know how to help unless we go back and start from the beginning," Charlie protested earnestly. He and Patty had taken prenatal childbirth classes together, but he was so methodical that he could only follow the instructions in the exact sequence he'd been taught.

"No way," Patty said firmly. "You'll have to skip some and catch up."

"How could you start without me?" he scolded.

"Addy!" Dale hissed from down the hall. "Come back here! What's going on?"

Addy forced herself to focus on Dale. "Huh?"

"What are you doing back there? We need help with the orders and scheduling! Hurry up!"

"Okay, okay." Reluctantly Addy returned to the front room, refraining from telling the others that Pattycake was in labor.

When most of the guests had finally left, Sam came out and announced the news. He let them all peek through the doorway, but no one else was allowed to enter the makeshift maternity room.

Sam, Patty, and Charlie debated whether or not to go to the hospital, but Patty's labor was progressing quite quickly, and she was content to remain under Pearl's care with Sam's supervision and Charlie's support.

Addy found it interesting to watch Sarah. As a cook she had always moved slowly and functioned only tolerably well. Yet as Sam and Pearl's assistant she was proving to be surprisingly brisk and efficient.

Although drawn away by other duties, Addy checked back often. Soon Pattycake was lying on the table, draped with material from a bolt of orange checked gingham. Pearl and Sam were dressed in white butcher aprons with Emmaline's scarves covering their hair and Sam's sample examination gloves on their hands.

Addy watched, fascinated, as Patty panted and pushed, working to have her baby. Sam observed carefully as Pearl's long, gentle fingers guided Patty's baby into the world. It was a boy.

"Very nice, for a white child," Pearl said with satisfaction.

Charlie sniffled and leaned over to kiss Patty on the cheek. "Oh, darling, you were so beautiful. Thank you." Turning to Pearl he asked, "Is it really a boy?"

"A fine boy," she assured him.

"Hi, Andrew," the new parents cooed, then murmured, "Oh, darling, hello!" as Pearl placed the baby on his mother's stomach and prepared the umbilical cord for Charlie to cut.

Addy thought, How symbolic: the father separating the child from the mother, accepting his share of the child's future. How very touching.

Sam had assisted with Bridget's birth and had cut the cord too, but he was a doctor, and at the time she hadn't considered the act's emotional significance. Now her vision blurred, and she realized with surprise that her eyes were filled with tears. It was all so wondrous.

Pearl wrapped the baby in a blanket and handed him to his father. Looking down at his son, Charlie gulped and tears dripped onto the baby's soft skin. Pattycake laughed and cried. It was all very emotional.

Although she saw and heard the entire drama, Addy's attention was fixed solely on Sam through much of it. His tenderness for Patty, his delight in the fine child, his pride in Pearl, whom he called his colleague, all filled Addy with love for her husband.

Fleetingly she remembered giving birth to Grendel and mentally compared that experience with the birth she'd just witnessed. She'd had no proud, loving husband then—only Miss Pru out in the waiting room. She'd had no kind and supportive family. She'd had no one with whom to share the wonder of her tiny daughter.

When the baby was sleeping peacefully in his father's arms, Addy turned from the door and looked into

Sam's eyes. Without thinking, she went to him, straight into his arms to hold and be held. And the beast of jealousy within her withered and slunk away.

Standing with them in the hall, Linda commented, "This was a big mistake. I should never have peeked in at them. Now I'll go home and my husband Mike will say, 'What's for supper,' and I'll say, 'Let's have a baby,' and he'll say, 'Okay!' And I'm not really ready for that yet."

Dale understood. "And I might marry John, and I'm not sure we're right for each other," she said.

"Hanging around with people like Patty and Charlie, and getting all caught up in their emotional high, could make the rest of us go home and start something we're not really prepared to finish," Linda said philosophically.

Just then Hedda arrived with some unseasoned beef broth for the new mother. Pearl signaled Sarah to stay' with Pattycake while she went to the kitchen. Dale and Linda drifted away too.

Addy tilted her face up to Sam and said, "I rather like you in Emmaline's head scarf. You look like a rakish pirate."

"I shall make you my captive and sail away." He gestured dramatically.

"With some of Marcus's men for a crew?"

"No crew; just us."

Addy could hear the band playing "Happy Birthday." Someone must have told them about the new baby . . . and they'd connected the amplifiers, the better to broadcast the news. Everyone in the back hall chuckled. Patty and Charlie's laughter was soft and teary.

"Since it's so bitterly cold, how about keeping Patty, Charlie, and the baby here for a while?" Sam suggested to Addy as, arm in arm, they walked slowly toward the front of the house.

"But you'll be gone! I'd worry myself sick with them here and you in Boston."

"I'll get a nurse to come watch over them—Clara Miller. And Sarah will be here. She seems to be a natural-born nurse. You should have seen her. I really believe she could have handled the whole birth by herself. She made an excellent newspaper platter to catch the afterbirth."

"How'd she know to do that?"

"Her mother's a midwife."

Addy nodded. They paused in the deserted drawing room, observing the empty runway and scattered chairs. Sam smiled. "Little Andrew is going to be one smart kid. Sarah used copies of the *Wall Street Journal* during the delivery. He'll know instinctively how to read.

"Of course." Addy laughed. Frowning, she added, "I'd better go help Hedda."

"Kiss me," he urged, suddenly serious. "I find I really need to make love to you."

"On the runway?" she teased, pretending to back away.

"Well . . ." He kissed her, his hands moving slowly, sensuously, over her back and buttocks. He lifted his head and gazed into her eyes, then kissed her again.

"You need to call the nurse," Addy said breathlessly. "And we have to get ready for the evening show."

"Yes," he murmured absentmindedly.

"Sam, let go!"

Heaving a great sigh, he reluctantly released her. But before they could begin their chores, Leo came bounding down the stairs into the entrance hall, followed by Bridget, who burst into the drawing room, once again sans slippers and robe. "Grendel said Pattycake had a baby!" she cried.

"Yes. A little boy." Sam smiled at his younger daughter.

"Let me see!"

"Not yet." He scooped her up and carried her back to the front hall. As Addy set off toward the kitchen, he called to her, "I'll get back to you."

Pausing to watch them, she heard Sam explain to Bridget, "Your cold is almost gone, but you wouldn't want the tiny baby to catch it, would you? And have him feel as rotten as you do? We'll take some pictures of him just for you. Then when you're well, you can see him in person."

"And can I keep the pictures?"

"Absolutely."

"Is he very little?"

"He's about this big," he said, spreading out his hands as they started up the stairs.

"The whole baby?"

"The whole baby."

"I'm bigger than that."

Sam's reply was indistinct. Addy looked around the room at the chairs, all helter-skelter, knowing Marcus's crew would soon be there to restore order. Afterward they could fix up the small storage room in the back for Pattycake, Charlie, and the new baby.

Addy had arrived just outside the open kitchen door

when she heard Erin say, "We had two babies. Two little boys."

Addy froze in her tracks. Erin was talking to Hedda about her family!

Her voice continued, soft and filled with pain. "Our house burned down. John lifted me out of the high bedroom window, and then he went for the boys. I never saw them again. Just the caskets at the funeral.

"I couldn't get to my boys. People ran and held me back even though I fought them. I must have been screaming a lot because I couldn't speak for a long time afterward. My voice wouldn't work."

Hedda stood without moving, like a magnificent, mesmerizing statue, observing Erin with riveting intensity. Erin's back was to Addy. She couldn't see the younger woman's face, but she could hear the anguish in her voice.

"Oh, Hedda, I wanted to die when they did."

Hedda touched her own chest, then slowly moved her hand out toward Erin in what appeared to be a blessing, one filled with grace and compassion. Then Hedda looked up and saw Addy, but her expression didn't change. She moved her head minutely, beckoning Addy into the kitchen.

"They wouldn't let me go," Erin was explaining somberly. "I couldn't get to them."

Hesitantly Addy reached out a hand toward Erin, but Hedda shook her head almost imperceptibly and Addy let her hand drop back to her side. Oddly, she didn't cry. Neither did Erin. The tragedy was too deep for tears. And Erin had cried a river of them already.

Hedda set a half-full cake platter within Erin's reach and motioned for her to put the remaining tea cakes onto a tray. Erin's hands moved automatically as she talked.

"I remember when Billy was born . . ." Erin's voice continued, still soft but much steadier, as the memories poured out of her in a soul-mending stream. Hedda and Addy did nothing to stop them.

Finally Hedda touched the folded pad and linen cloth in front of her, signaling Addy to clear the table in the parlor to make way for the hors d'oeuvres before the evening show. Her mind on Erin, Addy did as she'd been asked. She set out candles, added pastel-colored hot-house daisies, and began laying out the silverwear and folded napkins.

She set the tray for the silver bowl that would hold the wine punch and placed the ladle next to it. She looked around the room and smiled at the boy who was tending the fire. "Why don't you go to the kitchen and have some supper?" she suggested. "Then maybe you'd like to go outside and run around awhile. You've been so good about the fire. I noticed you never let it get too big or too small. You've done very well."

"It might go out," he warned her, feeling important.

"If it does, you can build a new one."

The boy smiled in agreement, but on his way across the room he turned back twice to check the fire.

Sam strode in and said, "Clara Miller will be here in about half an hour."

"The nurse?"

He nodded, pulled Addy into his arms, and kissed her tenderly.

Resisting the irresistible, she murmured, "I don't have time for this. We have to get ready for the evening show."

"Come to Boston with me."

"And leave everyone here to cope without me?"

"They're all efficient, capable people. I need you; they don't."

"I have a sick child, a new mother and baby and father, and a bereaved widow...Sam, I almost forgot! Erin's been talking about her husband and their little boys! She told Hedda about the fire!"

As he glanced toward the kitchen a great weight seemed to fall from his shoulders. "Great. Now she'll heal." He kissed Addy again. "Boston?"

"You'll be back Tuesday. And you'll be busy the whole time you're there."

"I'm going to put Emmaline's pirate scarf back on and kidnap you," he threatened laughingly.

"A pirate with a designer scarf; you'll ruin the image of buccaneers forever. They'll all have to start dressing better."

"It's high time. I've always considered them a rather tacky lot."

"Sam, I really do need to get busy. We won't have Pattycake to model anything. The narration will have to be changed. I must go, darling." She tried to pry herself away from him.

"I'll help."

"How?"

"I'll model Pattycake's dresses. I'll grab everyone's attention and, to quote Bridget, 'It'll sell clothes.'"

"They'll put us all in the loony bin."

"When Marcus's gang comes over, they can fix up that back room for our new little family. Will that be all right?"

"Do they *want* to stay here?" Addy asked. "Have

you mentioned this at all to Charlie?"

"Of course. Every step of the way. But he still isn't making much sense of anything. He mostly says, 'My God!' or 'You've been great!' or 'Oh, Patty...' There's been an awful lot of talk about how beautiful Patty is, and how beautiful the baby is, and how beautiful Pearl is. He even told me *I* was beautiful."

"You are."

"Only women are beautiful." He looked down his nose at her. "As you certainly should know by now, I'm merely well-made, handsome, and excessively attractive."

"You admit it."

"Only to you. To others I pretend to be modest and unmoved by praise."

"I love you, Sam."

"Not enough."

"Sam..." she sighed in exasperation.

"I'm tired of only meeting you occasionally on the stairs en route to somewhere else."

"We see each other as much as any other married couple."

"I need more."

"So you've said!" Addy pushed herself free. "Let up, Sam. Please!"

They stood glaring at each other like antagonists squaring off in a boxing ring. But the bell that rang was only the front doorbell.

"Will you get that?" Addy asked, turning away.

"Of course."

Addy went to her office to edit Patty's part out of the narration. She glanced up as Sam passed the door carrying a suitcase, followed by a perfectly stunning woman dressed in a severe white nurse's uniform. *That* was Clara Miller? Didn't Sam know any dowdy women?

Despite all the emotional upheaval of the afternoon, the evening show went flawlessly. The models were on a marvelous high from all the excitement. Sharing such a wonderful experience had brought an already close group of people even closer. Now they were truly a family.

Addy announced to the guests that Pearl had delivered Pattycake's new baby. She even referred to Pearl as Dr. Freeman. Pearl loved it.

A charming, intimate quality characterized that evening show. The band played "Happy Birthday" twice more, once for the announcement, when everyone sang, and once again just before the musicians packed up their instruments. When Sam and Addy went to thank them, Sam added some cash to the checks each musician received and said, "You played magnificently."

Addy's murmurs could have meant anything, but the band took them for signs of wordless admiration. They were full of themselves. Apparently many of the guests had taken Sam's dictum one step further and looked up and smiled again on their way out.

Except for Pattycake and little Andrew, everyone pitched in to help clean up the leftover food and get the rooms reorganized. Marcus's gang removed the runway, restored the regular furniture to the drawing room, and returned the folding chairs Marcus had borrowed from his church.

Several times in the chaos of milling, laughing

people, Addy saw Hedda touch Marcus as if seeking some kind of strength from him. And each time Marcus's hand covered his wife's reassuringly. The repeated scene became fixed in Addy's mind. Hedda was invincible. Why did she need to draw strength from Marcus?

Once all the guests were gone and Marcus's gang had finished, only the extended Grady family, plus Clara, remained. They all drank a toast to the end of the show, but particularly to the new baby. Then Charlie requested a chance to make his own toast.

Looking a little frazzled, his pleasant features creased with weariness, but glowing with good will, he raised his glass and said, "To all our dear friends. How can we thank you?"

Addy glanced at Sam to share the feeling, and again she saw Hedda touch Marcus. How strange.

Much later that evening, Sam and Addy escorted Clara down the hall to her room near the back stairs and helped her settle in. Then they went to check on the children. Stormy was sprawled out on Bridget's bed, and she was feeling his stomach. "If Pattycake had her baby, it must be time for Stormy's," she said sleepily.

"I'm really pretty sure Stormy's just a fat cat," Grendel said.

Sam and Addy exchanged amused glances as their older daughter trudged down the hall to her room. Finally they went tiredly to their own bedroom.

As they got undressed Sam asked, "Have you thought any more about our having another baby?"

"No," Addy replied abruptly.

"Well, how about it?"

"I'm too tired to discuss it now."

They were silent as they finished getting ready for bed. When Addy pulled out a blue flannel nightgown, Sam took it from her hands and shook his head. "I'm cold," she protested.

"I'll get you warm." His voice rumbled in his chest like a cat's purr. He pulled her down on top of him as he settled in the middle of the bed, then covered them both with the thick down comforter. He wrapped his arms around her and kissed her passionately.

"You're lumpy," she told him, gasping from his ardent embrace.

"If you move just a little, you can adjust your body to the worst of the lumps. I'll help."

"I suspect this is some sly prelude to having your way with me."

"Now, why would you think that?"

"I've discovered in these last five years that when it comes to having your way with me, you can be incredibly innovative and sneaky."

"What a perfectly shocking thing to say to a father."

"I think maybe that's *why* you're a father."

"I love you, Adelina Mary Rose Kildaire Grady."

"Every chance you get and some chances you don't get."

"Then you've noticed how drawn to you I am?"

"You have an indicator that gives me a hint every now and then."

"Did you see little Andrew? Doesn't he make your arms ache for another child?"

"Does he yours? I'd think with all the children's problems you see every day, you'd hesitate to have another one."

"Our's would be fine."

"I'm so happy for Pattycake and Charlie." She was feeling warm and cozy lying on top of Sam, her head tucked under his chin, her breasts pressed flat against his furry chest, her hands playing in his hair.

"But not enough for us to have another?" He kissed her jawline.

"I haven't time right now.

"I may be starting menopause soon," he said sadly.

"You?" She chuckled. "You're a man."

"I'm forty-four and having a midlife crisis."

"And that can be cured by having a baby?"

"Just one more," he coaxed sweetly.

"That's what you said before we had Bridget."

"Well, we couldn't just raise poor, little, lonely Grendel all by herself. We had to have Bridget."

"Sam, I don't want to talk about this now."

"What would you like to talk about?"

"Nothing. I want to go to sleep."

"It's been an exciting day. Don't you want to talk about it? The show went well. Congratulations. Erin is finally talking about her family. She's gotten over the most crucial hurdle. Isn't it wonderful to see what strides she's made here?"

"How well do you know Clara?" Addy suddenly asked.

"Is she one of the events of the day?"

"She looks nothing like her name. Clara sounds so . . . settled. This Clara looks like a jet-setter. Are you sure she's a nurse?"

"She's a very competent nurse; she can't help the way she looks."

"I get the feeling that any minute now she'll take

off her glasses, undo her hair, and zip the neckline of her dress down to her belly button."

"She doesn't wear glasses." His tongue explored her ear.

"What about letting her hair down and unzipping her dress?"

"I'll be in Boston and miss it all," he said. "So you ought to be sweet to me and make up for it now."

"You want me to let my hair down and unzip my dress?"

"That would be nice."

"Sam, you're naked. *I'm* naked. I'm lying on top of your body, and my hair is already down."

"Yes, I noticed that. I just wanted you to notice too. What else do you notice?"

"You. You're not wearing your pajamas. I love the feel of your hairy body, and your legs rubbing on mine, and your...lumps."

"You like that, do you?"

"I'm not sure I like it so much as I'm disturbed by it."

"Where does it disturb you?"

"I'm not sure."

"Here?" He touched the top of her shoulder with his tongue.

"A little. Especially when you touch it. But other places too."

He shifted and slid her off him into the warm place his body had made in the middle of the bed. "Here?" He touched his tongue to her ear.

"Oh, my, that is nice."

He nibbled her breast.

"That's even nicer."

"So this is the place where I disturb you?"

"One of them."

"There are others?"

"Here and there."

"If I find another one, will you tell me?"

"I believe you'll figure it out for yourself."

"Hmmm. A puzzle. An enigma. How fascinating. It's like a jigsaw with various parts, and I have to fit them together."

"That sounds interesting."

"Are you going to give me any clues?" His hands moved over her body in lazy circles.

"I'm not easy, you know."

"Lord knows I know that," he said a long drawn-out sigh.

"Sam . . ." she said, indignantly.

"Shhh." He held her down. "You're going to spoil this pirate's treasure hunt." He kissed her until she purred and stretched languidly under his hands. "You are the loveliest woman alive, do you know that?"

"What about Clara and Tippy and—"

He silenced her with a kiss. "Whenever I look at you, it always thrills me to think you're finally mine."

"I'm my own woman."

"And mine."

"Partly. I'm my own."

He kissed her and ran his hand slowly from her shoulder over her breast, to her rib cage and down her stomach into the silk of hair between her thighs and then eased it gently down to the heated center of her longing.

Growling huskily, he repeated, "Mine." And he kissed her mouth, fusing them together as their tongues touched.

Wrapping her arms around him, Addy hugged Sam to her and moved her body sensuously, feeling the slight abrasiveness of his skin against her.

He let his breath out in a rush and groaned. "You're driving me crazy, you wild woman."

She breathed in his ear and licked the lobe, replying in a hot, soft whisper, "And I'm going to get wilder and wilder and wilder."

"I believe it."

Then she moved her hand exactly as he'd moved his, starting at his shoulder and smoothing her fingers down over his chest in a lazy swirl to his stomach . . . and then she made him wait.

"You terrible tease," he gasped.

"You're supposed to be coaxing me to do your will, not insulting me."

"You're a lovely, gorgeous, insidiously torturous woman who is driving me slowly mindless."

"Didn't I hear you say something earlier about warming me up?"

"Haven't I?"

"A little."

"Only a *little?*" He was appalled. Running his hands over her, he gave a triumphant cry. "Hah! Only a little warmed up? You're soaked with sweat."

"That's from you. You're aroused, as usual."

"My sweat's from being too hot under this down comforter. I'm still waiting for you to start enticing me, getting my interest up."

"Your interest is already up," she informed him smugly.

"Well, I'll be darned!"

"I wouldn't mind too awfully if you kissed me," she suggested.

"Where?"

"On my . . . mouth?"

"Right smack on your very *mouth?*" He gasped. "That would be bold."

"Try it."

He did cautiously. "Have you any communicable diseases?"

"Yes. It's called lust."

"And you let me kiss you *anyway?*"

"Sorry."

"You could have told me and at least given me the—" He snorted, and groaned and blew his breath out and gnashed his teeth and breathed rapidly. "Oh my God, I think I'm coming down with it! It's hit like lightning! Good Lord, I'm lost!" And he pretended to gobble up her body, teasing her breasts, nuzzling her belly button.

And she laughed.

He moved up her body and kissed her greedily, rubbing his face into her neck and licking her ears. His hands became more demanding, and soon she stopped laughing.

Their lovemaking became leisurely and silent except for the love murmurs between them, sounds of exclamation and of pleasure. His hands petted and teased and touched, and his mouth tasted.

"Are you mine?" Sam breathed in a low rumble.

"Almost," she whispered.

JUST THE IMMEDIATE Grady family went to the airport the next morning—Sam, Addy, and the two girls. As they chatted and laughed through brunch at one of the airport restaurants, Addy cast anxious eyes at the dark and threatening sky. She was nervous about Sam's flying in such weather and fidgeted restlessly.

"Everything will be fine," he reassured her. "Airlines are very careful with their expensive airplanes, equipment, and personnel. They won't send a plane up unless they're sure it's safe."

"I know."

"Then stop worrying. Are you going to miss me?"

"A little. With you gone, I'll have to get up in the middle of the night."

"For a cold shower?"

"No, to refill my hot-water bottle."

"You mean, all I am to you is a heating pad?"

"Pretty much. Are you good for anything else?"

"Well, I should say so!"

"What?"

"Now, Addy, you know this is a family restaurant and there are children present, but as a matter of fact my special talent is one that occasionally creates children as a by-product."

She smiled at him, but bleakly, which made him regard her tenderly. They held hands across the table while Bridget and Grendel chatted excitedly, thrilled by all the planes coming and going and the people milling about.

When it was time for Sam to board, they walked him to the gate for a last good-bye. Before he disappeared into the boarding tube, he turned and waved.

The three females watched his plane taxi down the runway, until they finally lost sight of it. As they walked out of the terminal, and headed for their car, the bitterly cold February wind penetrated their coats to chill their unsuspecting flesh. As one of the big planes took off, Bridget shouted, "There goes Daddy!" certain that it was his plane.

In the five years of their marriage there had been many times when Sam had been part of a team of doctors fighting to save a child's life, and he'd stayed at the hospital for several days and nights. During those times he always called Addy regularly.

When he went to another city, the situation was no different. They were still apart and he still called every day. But the realization that he was hundreds of miles away made Addy miss him all the more.

That afternoon she took the girls to the children's

museum and wandered after them as they rode the merry-go-round and peeked in the windows of the colonial American general store to see the old tools. Addy remembered the many times Sam had brought them here. If anything ever happend to him, how would she live without him?

She drove home in a thoughtful mood, the girls quiet in the backseat. As they pulled into the driveway, Addy admired their house — dark blue with lime-green trim, set against soft white snow and black tree branches. They hurried inside to the cozy fire Erin had built in the parlor.

Pearl and Clara were sitting with Erin. Addy sensed that she'd interrupted a serious discussion, but they didn't hesitate to welcome her and the girls, immediately moving over to make room on the sofa.

Leo rose from his place beside Erin and poked his wet nose against Addy's hand, trying to get her attention. But she ignored him, and he returned to Erin, flopping down wearily. Erin patted him absently.

Just then Charlie tiptoed into the room and said in a hushed voice, "They're sleeping."

"Honey," Pearl chided him, "you're five rooms away from them. You don't have to whisper clear out here." She went on to explain to Addy that Patty and the baby had had a long day with a stream of visitors. Charlie's clothes were askew, and he looked tired. It had been a rough twenty-four hours for him too.

"Have you seen Andrew today?" Charlie asked Addy.

"*I* haven't," Bridget said, pulling her mouth down and looking for sympathy. "Daddy says not before Tuesday."

Charlie sneezed. He froze, appalled. "I sneezed!" he exclaimed.

"Go take some Vitamin C," Addy ordered. "Right now! We have some in the kitchen."

"I sneezed!" he repeated in stunned amazement.

"Gesundheit!" Pearl intoned.

Charlie gave her a steely glare. "I won't be able to go back in their room."

"No need, honey. You've done did your bit," she answered, amused.

"But they need me!"

"You do have some back-up," she assured him, grinning. "No need to panic."

"We can put a rollaway in the storage room," Addy offered.

"Put you on hold, so's to speak," Pearl added.

Charlie became indignant. "You're treating this very lightly."

"No, no, no," Addy corrected. "We're simply taking it in stride. There's no reason to be upset. You can wave from the door and see them every day. But keep your distance until we're sure you won't give them colds."

"I've . . . let Patty down."

"No you haven't." Pearl smiled encouragingly. She understood how he felt.

"I was late getting here yesterday, and she could have given birth without me." He sounded forlorn.

"No," Pearl insisted, "she needed you, and you did very well. You were vital to her well-being." Pearl stood up. "And you still are. You know that. Daddies tend to feel a little useless and neglected just about now, but don't you worry. They both need you. You can do everything Patty can, except nurse the kid. And she'll be feeling a little blue by tomorrow, a little sore and weary, so she'll particularly need you to tell her she's lovely and that you still love her."

"Sam used to come home late at night and sneak the baby out of her basket and hold her and talk to her until she woke up," Addy put in. "Then I would wake up, and he'd say, 'Oh, she was awake so I thought I'd take care of her and just let you sleep.'"

"I did that last night," Charlie confessed. "Babies are just amazing, aren't they?"

The women all chorused, 'Yes,' in loving voices. Then, to everyone's surprise, Erin added, "And it's all worth it. Even if things don't work out right." And again everyone murmured their agreement.

"Come on," Addy said to Charlie, "let's go get you some vitamin C."

They found Marcus and Hedda in the kitchen just taking off their coats. They'd brought several dishes of food which covered the table. They nodded at Charlie, who woefully announced, "I sneezed."

Hedda's lips curved in one of her fabulous, rare smiles, and Marcus said soothingly, "It'll be all right."

Charlie held his forehead. "I feel a little weird."

"Being a new father gives all men odd feelings of one kind or another. Sit here," Marcus said. "Hedda, you got any of that new-father brew?"

Hedda looked at her husband with sloe-eyes and reached into a cupboard for a mottled green stone bottle.

Addy opened her mouth to speak, but the words died on her lips when she received one quick glance from Hedda's magical eyes. Almost shyly Addy gave

the black woman a tiny smile and received one in
return. The bottle contained a voodoo cure-all. Hedda
had used it on Addy once or twice.

Hedda took the bottle over to Marcus and set down
two crystal shot glasses. Then she touched Addy's
arm, and the two women went to the other side of the
big kitchen, leaving the men alone at the small round
table next to the fireplace.

Some coals still burned from the morning's fire,
and Marcus stirred them up and added some twigs,
kindling, and several large split logs.

Supplying wood and kindling was another service
Marcus's young men provided for Addy. They removed dead trees from neighbors' property and split
the wood, stacking it in neat piles to season at one
end of her block. Then they sold it to her. With all
the fireplaces in that old house, she was their best
customer.

As Marcus continued fiddling with the fire, Addy
realized he was trying to divert Charlie's thoughts
from the responsibilities of new fatherhood and help
him relax. He was also giving Charlie plenty of time
to size up that strange stone bottle. Marcus too was
a healer.

Marcus and Hedda had brought over a roast turkey
with a bowl of spicy dressing and another of cranberry
sauce. Addy leaned down to sniff the seasonings of
the hot dishes and then smiled at Hedda again. She
still felt a little awkward around the woman, having
forced her to speak, and now she said shyly, "That
was a nice thing for you to do—cooking dinner for
us."

Hedda touched Addy's shoulder and pointed a

graceful finger toward the back of the house. Briefly she cupped her arms as if to hold a baby. Since the Grady's were sheltering the new baby and his parents, Hedda wanted to help out.

Then Hedda's gaze shifted from Addy to Charlie and back again. She tilted her head imperceptibly, indicating that Addy was to take a discreet glance at Charlie.

He was warily eyeing the bottle, which looked valuable and mysterious, as if it had been burried for centuries. It had to contain something wonderful, perhaps a rare elixir whose formula had been long-forgotten.

Charlie took a quick look at Marcus and one at Hedda, and Addy knew he knew the bottle contained a voodoo cure. It would take reckless courage to sip from that bottle, and Charlie was now a family man. He couldn't afford to be careless.

So when Charlie's questioning eye came to rest on her, Addy smiled slightly and gave a tiny nod, just like Hedda's. Charlie visibly relaxed.

Marcus seemed to relax too. If he'd been any other man he might have guffawed, but being Marcus, he maintained his dignity.

Gravely he picked up the stone bottle, lifted it to his ear, and shook it slightly. Charlie's body tensed. He looked as if it wouldn't surprise him to see the bottle explode just then.

When Marcus removed the stopper, no vapor rolled out from the opening. He poured about half a jigger of an unidentifiable dark liquid into each small glass, put the ancient bottle carefully aside, and raised his great, black, wise eyes to Charlie's. Then he lifted the glass, saluted the new father, and wet his lips with the liquid before setting the small glass back on the table.

Charlie, being a cautious man, noted that Marcus hadn't actually drunk the potion. He too lifted the small glass and gingerly wet his lips before replacing the glass on the table and looking up at Marcus. A surprised expression came over his face. His tongue darted out to lick his lips.

He raised astonished eyes to Marcus, then burst out laughing. Of course, as Addy knew, it was grape juice. Homemade grape juice that Hedda had canned. It was rich, purple, and delicious. Charlie slugged down the rest in his glass and laughed louder. And Addy wondered for the first time how many of the Freemans' voodoo rituals were done for their own amusement. People really were so gullible.

With a grand gesture Marcus poured them each another shot, and Charlie began to catalogue the wonders of his new son. Marcus listened with calm interest and twinkling eyes.

Addy's daughters came in. Bridget climbed up on Marcus's lap, and Grendel, holding Stormy, went to sit in another chair. They also took small tastes of the beautifully bottled grape juice.

The fire crackled. After a while Pearl, Clara, and Erin joined them, adding to the warm hum of conversation. It was very cozy in the kitchen on that cold winter night. Addy and Hedda finished preparing the meal, Pearl took a tray of food to Pattycake, and Erin and Grendel set the table. Then they all sat down to eat, still talking, happy to be together.

* * *

After dinner the others helped with the clearing up and putting away, and Addy and Marcus went down to the basement. "Sam thinks the basement should be scrubbed and painted," Marcus said. "It would make a good meeting or game room."

"You can't fool me," Addy replied. "You mean it would make a good place for our St. Patrick's Day party. You're just like Sam. I want to hire a hall."

"This house was made for parties," Marcus said, unperturbed.

"But *I'm* not especially made for parties. They're a lot of work and make for a lot of confusion."

"You have more fun than anyone."

"But the whole downstairs has to be emptied out. The party has gotten completely out of hand. It's outgrown the house. And having to move everything disrupts our whole routine." She gestured wildly and frowned.

Marcus remained unconvinced. "It's good for all of us to be disrupted and shaken up occasionally. And it gives the crew time for a good spring cleaning."

"What you really mean is you think we should have the party here—just like Sam. How old are you, Marcus?"

He raised his eyebrows at her sudden change of subject. "How old do you think?"

"You could be Sam's age or you could be a hundred, you're so wise." She contemplated him, pushing out her lower lip. "Sam wants me to go off on a trip with him for our anniversary. There's no way I can do that."

"You need to take a good, hard look at your life and decide what's really necessary and what you can do without," Marcus advised.

"I've worked so hard for this business."

"Have I said anything about your business? How interesting that you immediately brought it up. Does that tell you anything?"

"You and Sam have been talking!" she accused him.

"Has Sam been talking to you about the business?"

"He wants me to hire his sister, Cyn, to help me out."

"Why don't you?"

"I worked awfully hard to build this business with Miss Pru. Now I want to see if I can do it all on my own."

"No one can control all the aspects of a big business."

"This isn't big business."

"Yes, it is. It requires a lot of people and a lot of time. And no one has more than twenty-four hours a day. No one has more than one lifetime. How do you intend to spend yours?"

"The next thing you're going to say is: When you come to the end of your life, will you have any regrets? Will you wish you'd done things differently?"

"Will you?"

"Die? More than likely."

"Have regrets?"

"How come everyone thinks they can tell me how to run my life?"

"Who besides Sam?"

"Marcus, Hedda spoke to me."

His eyes flashed, and his nostrils flared, and he reached out and briefly grasped her arm. His whole body tensed instantly. "What did she say?"

"She called me stupid, and it wrung something terrible from her to say it."

"Then listen to her!" Marcus thundered.

"What happened to her, Marcus? Can't you tell me? I saw her give Erin a voodoo blessing."

"What are you talking about?" He regarded her impatiently.

"After Pattycake's baby was born, Erin went to Hedda in the kitchen and started talking about her children. She told Hedda all about losing them and her husband in the fire. And Hedda touched her chest and held up two fingers to bless Erin."

Addy watched in shock as Marcus's face crumpled momentarily before he regained control of himself. Did he think she was criticizing Hedda? "It was a lovely thing for Hedda to have done," she added to reassure him.

He turned abruptly away, and she saw with alarm that his right fist was clenched and that he was battling an overwhelming emotion.

"Erin *is* going to be all right," she hastened to say. How strange that he should be so upset about Erin. He'd never paid much attention to her.

Addy watched with concern as with great difficulty, Marcus finally began to speak. "I've known Hedda since she was a child. Even then, she carried herself like a queen. She was always tall, and she was always beautiful. I loved her."

In all the years Addy had known Marcus, he'd never really shared any of his feelings with her. Now she didn't move, afraid that she would stop him.

He stood with his back to her, and in his deep,

deep voice he went on: "But she loved Joe Diamond, and she married him. I'm big, but he was bigger. He was a big, mean man," Marcus said scornfully. "He was no good. But she loved him anyway." He moved his shoulders in helpless rejection and began to pace the room restlessly.

Addy dared not even move her head, but her eyes turned to follow him, and she breathed silently through parted lips.

"Hedda was glorious and serene in her love for him. Three times I watched her body bloom with his seed." The last words were wrenched from him, as if they still tasted bitter. "I married someone else and had a child of my own—Pearl—but I never stopped loving Hedda.

"From the windows of my room I could see across the street and down the block to her house, especially in the winter, when the leaves were gone from the trees. One night I saw a strange light flickering in her downstairs windows. At first I thought it was their television set, but it spread quickly to all the downstairs windows. Then I realized that her house was on fire.

"The snow was deep, but I ran to her. I was still three houses away when I saw Joe Diamond silhouetted in the upstairs window. With his bare fist he smashed out the glass, taking the frame with it. Then he turned back into the room and appeared again with Hedda in his arms. She was struggling to get away from him, struggling to go save her babies. But he was stronger than she was, and he threw her out the window into a snowbank. She screamed the whole way down."

He turned to face Addy, but she knew he was still seeing only Hedda, falling into the snowbank.

"Her clothes were on fire. And her hair. She dragged herself to the front door and tried to open it," he continued. "When I ran up to her and tried to put my coat around her to smother the flames, she tore out of my arms. She was desperate to go back for her babies, but the door wouldn't budge. She punched her fists through a window pane and had almost climbed through before I could stop her and roll her in the snow to put out the fire."

He was silent. So was Addy, seeing it all in her mind's eye, stunned by Marcus's revelation. That was no voodoo blessing Hedda had given Erin. She'd been saying, 'Me too.'

"Miraculously, Hedda's face and upper body were spared," Marcus continued. "All the rest of her is scarred from the fire and broken glass. That's why she wears long skirts and Emmaline's scarves around her head."

And Addy had thought Hedda was simply expressing pride in her African ancestry.

"Her eyelashes and eyebrows never grew back, and she can't speak, except occasionally and with the greatest of agony.

"My first wife had died when Pearl was just a baby, so I was free to offer myself to Hedda. Several months after the tragedy she accepted and married me, but she was a shell of the woman I'd first loved." He took a deep, slow breath. "Still, every day I thank God for giving me this much of her, and for making Joe Diamond love her enough to save her life—even at the expense of his own.

"Hedda had always done some catering to support her family. Joe rarely had a job. After the fire she worked obsessively, exhausting herself so she'd have no time to think. Then you moved in here. You and Grendel and Miss Pru.

"You fascinated her. She made me look out for you. You gave her an interest outside of herself. She wanted desperately to cater your shows. For a while I thought I'd have to bribe you to let her."

Marcus looked intently at Addy. "So she struggled and suffered to speak to you? Please have the courage to listen!"

Beyond him, at the top of the stairs, a slight movement caught Addy's attention—the hem of Hedda's skirt grazing the doorway and moving out of sight. Had she heard? How much?

After a silence which Addy couldn't break, Marcus said, "She made me come over here and see what you were doing and go back and tell her. When you were looking for models, she insisted that Pearl try out. You should have seen Hedda's face when Pearl came home and said you'd hired her.

"As soon as Sam showed up, she made me check him out. He's lucky he's flawless."

"You checked out *Sam?*" Addy was amazed.

"Hedda didn't approve of his mother's many marriages, but everything was okay after she actually met Elizabeth."

However shakily, Addy had to laugh. For years she had thought Marcus was the one interfering in her life, but it had been Hedda all along. "Does she practice voodoo?" Addy asked. It seemed a good time to find out.

Marcus shot her an indecipherable glance and said, "She has many talents."

"How about a simple yes or no?"

"I am unable to reply with any certainty."

"You mean *you* aren't sure?" That startled Addy.

He shrugged, but his eyes grew soft. "She is a good woman who would do no harm to anyone. Listen to her."

"People make it very difficult to lead an independent life," Addy observed.

"A dependent life is the only way. Sam is equally dependent on you."

"That isn't true. I have no say in his life at all."

"If you wanted to be a beachcomber, he'd throw up everything and become one too." He paused, then added, "Of course, he'd have a clinic hidden in the bushes somewhere, but he'd do things as much your way as he could. He's living here in your house."

"He paid off the mortgage, and it's closer to the hospitals."

"It's your house. Give him credit."

"I know."

"And Addy, listen to Hedda. Don't be stupid."

"I'll try."

"You've got a good man."

"I know."

"And Addy, you're a good woman."

Her lips parted in surprise, but Marcus had already turned away. Clearly he'd said all he intended to say on the subject. "We'll start cleaning out this basement in two weeks," he stated matter-of-factly. "It's a good time of year for the men to have a big project to complete."

Suddenly Addy felt uncomfortable with Marcus because of all that he had shared with her. There was an awkward moment of silence, and to fill the gap Addy asked, "Do you miss the old furnace?"

"Not at all." He grinned back at her.

"You have no sense of adventure, of challenge."

"None."

"Balderdash."

Again they grinned at each other. But he spoiled the special moment by saying, "Have the St. Patrick's Day party here."

"Marcus, let up!"

"Have you been pushed too hard?" he asked with feigned concern.

She waved her arms around and let out a soft, controlled, "Eeeeeee!"

"I suspect you have." He turned again and went up the stairs.

After Marcus and Hedda had said their good nights and were on their way, Addy watched them cross the yard. Threatening clouds hung low in the sky, but their figures were sharply silhouetted against the clean snow.

Halfway home, they stopped. Hedda stood facing Marcus. She moved her hands to her chest and mimed opening her coat. Then she seemed to reach inside and remove something that she held for a minute in her gracefully raised hand. Slowly she extended her hand toward Marcus and offered him the gift.

Their shadows merged, and Marcus lifted his face to the sky before bending his head over Hedda, holding her close to him. After a time they turned, his arm still tightly around her, and walked slowly home.

All at once Addy understood. It wasn't her coat

that Hedda had mimed opening; it was her chest. She'd removed her heart and given it to Marcus.

Feeling lonely in her bed that night, Addy lay awake thinking about Hedda and Marcus, and tears slowly filled her eyes. Marcus had said he could see Hedda's house from his windows. Addy imagined him standing there in the night, yearning for her love but knowing he could never have it. What exquisite torment!

And Addy considered how Hedda had been touched and changed when she and Grendel and Miss Pru had moved into the neighborhood. People never know how they affected others. But she had touched Hedda . . . and had helped her. With no conscious effort, they'd helped Hedda.

And Hedda had given Marcus her heart. Addy remembered all the times she'd seen Hedda touch Marcus, as if to draw strength from him. A woman didn't turn to a man like that unless she loved him. Marcus had had her love for a long time. He simply hadn't known it. But now he did. Hedda loved Marcus.

And Addy loved Sam.

She lay staring into the cold, dark February night and asked herself what was really important to her. People were. No question about that. Sam mostly, but other people too. And, of course, her business.

Her work was almost as important to her as Sam was. Designing clothes and seeing them become a reality fulfilled a deep creature need in her. She couldn't give it up. She wouldn't. But what if . . . what if she had to choose between Sam and her business? She'd choose Sam. She could give up her business and devote her time to him, their children, and the community. She would lead a reasonably contented life, though there would still be a part of her that craved something more.

But Sam hadn't asked her to *give up* her business. He just wanted her to set some limits on her involvement in it. And suddenly she felt perfectly willing to admit that she couldn't handle it all by herself. She'd need some help. She would hire Cyn.

Marcus had said Sam would give up everything if Addy wanted to be a beachcomber, but he'd have a clinic tucked away in the jungle. Well, next door to the clinic she'd have a dress shop. Sarongs and raincoats. It rained a lot in the tropics.

Addy called Cyn the next morning, and Sam's sister came right over. She was ecstatic.

"I've been wild, hoping you'd hire me!" She laughed without restraint, looking quite perfect with her cheeks flushed and her hair smooth. "I can't tell you what it will do for me to be part of the Gown House. I love detail work." Cyn's bright eyes darted around the disaster area that was Addy's office.

"This madness?" Addy couldn't understand Cyn's enthusiasm.

"The satisfaction," Cyn extolled. "The being a part of a whole, something greater than myself. The adventure of it. I can't wait. Uh... would you mind if I started now? If you'd just give me a general idea of what pile is what, I could get right to work. How are the files?"

"Not too well organized," Addy admitted reluctantly.

"Don't worry for a minute. No problem. I'll get it all straightened out." She took off her sleek jacket and, to Addy's surprise, rolled up her sleeves, instantly destroying the perfect line of her outfit. "In a

week I'll have a pretty good idea of who you deal
with and why. Then it will be easier for me to help
you with all this paperwork. Oh, Addy, this is so
exciting for me. Thank you!"

Addy felt a little strange, now that she had finally
allowed someone else up on her mountain. Of course,
this mountain was built of unfiled papers, back orders,
unpaid customer bills, unbalanced ledgers . . .

"I could never do what you do, Addy," Cyn enthused. "I'm awed by your designs. You can't imagine
how much you used to intimidate me. Then I took a
long, hard look at myself and realized how good I am
at what *I* do. After all, without my kind of organizational skills, you geniuses would have to waste a
lot of valuable time. We free you. But, Addy, I love
organizing things as much as you love designing."

With another start of surprise Addy realized that
Cyn had gone through the same process of soul-
searching that she herself had experienced. Curious,
Addy asked, "And just before you die and your life
is flashing across your mind, will your work have
been enough?"

"Well, at least I'll have the satisfaction of knowing
that I've left things tidy." Cyn laughed lightly. "Obviously Sam has been at you."

"He gave you the Last Thoughts lecture too?" Addy
asked.

"I was feeling . . . inadequate after one of your shows.
You do such a fantastic job of it. You could make a
real name for yourself if you went east."

"Inadequate? You?"

"Oh, yes." She shook her lovely head ruefully.
"Is it possible you don't realize how formidable your
talent is? You really are intimidating."

"But all along I've been so envious of you," Addy burst out. "I knew I needed you, but I put off asking for your help, and kept putting it off, because I thought you'd be the one everyone would think was in control. You look so serene and in charge."

Cyn laughed again. "It's all a façade."

They hugged each other impulsively, warmly.

8

THE ICE STORM began on the Monday night after Sam left for Boston. Addy heard the pinging against the windows and shivered. Not surprisingly, when she awakened in the middle of the night she found Bridget curled up on Sam's side of the bed. Bridget often slept there when her daddy wasn't home. Even when he was there she occasionally cuddled down between him and Addy. Grendel did too whenever she had one of her rare nightmares.

Addy got up to refill her cold hot-water bottle. She paused by the window and gazed outside at the white curtain of ice, controlling an impulse to call the airlines and warn them not to fly in such weather.

When would Sam get home? she wondered. He wouldn't fly the next day—not with such ice.

She wrapped the hot-water bottle in one of Sam's old undershirts and crawled back into bed. Nudging

349

the water bottle with her toes to make it slosh, she thought about her husband. Even when she was being somewhat difficult, he had a way of looking at her and touching her that made Addy feel treasured. And when she'd truly angered him, he didn't condemn or reject *her*, only the specific behavior that displeased him. He was really quite mature. But could she say the same thing about herself?

What a perfectly embarrassing thing to wonder about!

She'd grown up thinking she was the center of the universe. Then as a teenager she'd seen a stunningly beautiful one-minute film of a woman sitting in her back yard. The camera had focused on the woman, then drawn back, higher and higher until she was just a dot in a tiny green square. Then the camera had shown the whole block, then the city, then the state on a map, then the country on a globe, then the hemisphere from far out in space, then the world. The camera had continued to travel out of the galaxy until the sun was just a tiny speck and the Earth had totally disappeared.

After viewing that film, Addy had begun to see herself from a new perspective. Then her family's censure and her own humiliation over Grendel's birth had taken away all her confidence. She was not the center of the universe; she was just an inferior, insignificant part of it.

In the years that followed she had gradually regained a sense of self-worth. Sam had helped. His love had made her see that she wasn't such a terrible person. She had sound instincts for what was right and what was wrong. And so she had survived.

The ice kept tapping on her window, as if begging to be let in, but Addy fell asleep. She slept late and woke up just before Bridget. They lay in bed talking and laughing. Soon they were joined by a giggling Grendel. Then Stormy arrived, and Leo bounded in, slobbering all over them. It was getting pretty crowded by then, so the Grady girls got up and dressed.

Considering the icy, gloomy day, Addy thought they should all wear something cheerful. "How about some sunshine colors?" she suggested.

"No school!" Grendel exclaimed. "We'll have a holiday! With fires in the fireplaces.

"And popcorn," Bridget contributed.

"Daddy will miss it." Grendel's expression turned sad.

"Poor Daddy," Bridget said, equally sad. Then she brightened. "Let's have pancakes!"

Addy gave her a shocked glare; she still hadn't recovered from Sarah's pancake period.

"With blueberries and powdered sugar!" Grendel shouted.

The two girls bounced past an appalled Addy and down to the kitchen.

With a sigh Addy tried to make the bed, but Stormy was still in it. And despite the buffeting she gave him, the cat wouldn't budge. Addy finally admitted defeat and put on a snug red jumpsuit and ski socks before going downstairs.

A houseful of people had gathered around the kitchen table. In addition to Charlie, Clara, Sarah, and Erin, there were Pearl and Cyn.

"Well, hello!" Addy exclaimed.

"Morning, lazybones," Pearl greeted her, grinning.

"Cyn, how did you get here?" Outside, nothing was moving in the ice-coated world.

"Well..." She let out an embarrassed laugh. "As soon as it started sleeting, I got dressed and came over. I didn't want to be iced in at the apartment when I could be here digging into the fascinating treasure in your office."

Addy's eyes grew wide in disbelief. "You got up in the middle of the night to come to work?"

"I know, it's ridiculous." Cyn shrugged, looking absolutely charming.

"You're a workaholic!" Addy declared.

"That's what my second husband said just before the divorce."

"And Pearl? What's your excuse?"

"I know nothing's going to happen," the twenty-five-year-old third-year medical student replied, "but when I heard the sleet, I came over to help Clara here—her being responsible for the new mother and baby and all by herself."

Clara, the forty-year-old nurse with seventeen years of on-the-job experience, licked her lip and looked so pleasantly deadpan that everyone laughed.

"Poor old Sam isn't going to make it home today," Cyn said.

"Did he call?" Addy asked anxiously.

"No. As a matter of fact, we're being asked to stay off the phones and to use as little electricity as possible, because some lines have fallen and the others are weighted down with ice. It's been five years since we had an ice storm like this one."

"If you have to stay tonight, you two, there's certainly plenty of room," Addy offered automatically, instantly remembering the storm more than five years ago that had forced Sam to stay overnight. He'd tempted her almost mindlessly. He'd been wickedly unfair.

Since Charlie hadn't developed a cold after all, he ushered Pattycake and their son out to the kitchen for a midmorning visit. Patty walked carefully and sat down gingerly.

Bridget squealed with delight at the sight of the baby. "It's the *baby!*" she cried ecstatically. "Today is Tuesday and I can see him!"

"Not so loud," Addy cautioned.

So Bridget hissed in steam-blasting whispers, "Can I see him?"

"*May* I?" at least three voices chorused.

"Yesss!" Bridget hissed exuberantly.

Pattycake unwrapped the squirming bundle with the scrunched-up face and showed Bridget the baby's tiny fingers and toes.

"He's so little!" Bridget laughed.

"But he'll grow." Charlie beamed.

"Only if you'll unwrap him now and then and give him a little room," Pearl said.

"But it's cold," Pattycake protested.

"I'll bet five maraschino cherries he's sweating."

"He is!" the new parents exclaimed, astonished.

"A sweater is what a child wears when the mother is cold," Pearl quoted. "If his feet and hands are warm, he doesn't need a blanket too."

The conversation continued as Addy toyed with the blueberry pancakes on her plate. She was gazing out the windows trying to decide whether or not the storm had lessened. Would Sam be safe coming home?

In a daze she rose from the table and wandered through the house, touching random objects without paying much attention to them. She was aware that Cyn had disappeared into the office. Addy went upstairs to her attic studio and spent the day there, thinking of Sam and rehearsing what she would say to him when they were finally reunited. If only he would get home safe—and soon. She listened to the radio for news of the storm and learned that it had swept east— toward Boston. It might be days before he could return.

Shaking her head, she realized how silly she was being. Sam was perfectly all right in Boston. He was a grown man fully capable of taking care of himself. He didn't need anyone to hold his hand.

The ice stopped falling at about noon, just when the front edge of the storm was approaching the East Coast. Sam wouldn't be able to fly out. He'd be stuck there when Addy so wanted him home. She couldn't wait to tell him she'd hired Cyn and that she was now ready to admit she couldn't handle the business all by herself. He'd been right. She wasn't invincible after all. She was only human.

Not everyone succeeded in accomplishing what they set out to do, Addy finally realized. But, she told herself with some pride, she'd at least tried. Actually, she had accomplished a great deal in her life so far.

Once again she went to the window. Outside, heavy trucks were inching along, spreading a mixture of salt and sand on the streets.

Oh, Sam. She missed him so awfully, more this time than any other. Why was that? Maybe because of Erin and Hedda, two women who had lost beloved husbands. Thinking about their tragic experiences had made Addy more keenly aware of how very precious Sam really was.

Or maybe it was just that for the first time in months she didn't feel weighted down and distracted by mind-boggling, anxiety-provoking details concerning the Gown House. She'd momentarily dumped everything into Cyn's eager hands.

Fancy *enjoying* that kind of work! It was amazing that Cyn considered the sorting out of the business an adventure. People certainly were strange.

In the middle of the afternoon Addy received a telegram by phone. A man's voice said, "For Mrs. Samuel Grady: 'My love'—I'm quoting—'My love, I am flying south to try to get around the storm.' Signed, 'Superman.' That's what it says, 'Superman.'"

"Thank you." Addy slowly hung up the phone. That idiot husband of hers. Why didn't he just wait safely in Boston?

They were all seated around the kitchen table that evening, enjoying a hearty supper, when the radio news reported a plane down over Louisiana. Letting out a gasp, Addy sat up ramrod straight and her eyes flew wide open. Could Sam be on that plane?

"Louisiana's nowhere near Boston, Addy," Pearl chided.

"No," Addy said softly. She looked down at her plate and bit the inside of her mouth, tasting blood. She couldn't possibly tell them Sam had flown south to avoid the storm. He might not be on that particular plane. She couldn't upset the entire household with worry until she knew whether there was anything to worry about.

At ten they received the full report. The plane had

been hit by a freak downdraft on landing, and there were no survivors. None.

Sam couldn't possibly have been on that plane, Addy told herself. But then she realized that everyone who'd known someone on it was probably having the same thought. It couldn't be. It wasn't possible. Oh, my God.

Addy stood up, not knowing what to do. She'd have to wait. But she couldn't just sit there. She smoothed her long red quilted skirt and folded her arms across the fitted jacket that matched. She walked aimlessly through the downstairs rooms, feeling thoroughly chilled.

It was just nerves. Her mind didn't feel him dead. He couldn't be.

Cyn too left the parlor and came to find her. "Do you think Sam was on that plane?" she asked quietly.

Addy's eyes flew to Cyn's, and she began to shake her head, denying it, but Cyn had seen her eyes. "He probably wasn't on that plane," she said. "Don't let him die in your mind until you hear. Wait."

Addy nodded stiffly, and Cyn helped her to lock up and turn off the lights. Before they separated in the upstairs hall to go to their rooms, Cyn lightly touched her shoulder in sympathy and encouragement.

Oh, Sam, Addy's soul wailed in silent torment as she undressed and crawled into bed, shivering with fear. She got up and filled three hot-water bottles, her mind repeating Sam's name like a litany, then went miserably back to bed, placing one hot-water bottle on each of her frozen feet and holding the third against her chest.

Don't borrow trouble, she admonished herself.

Wait. That was the only intelligent thing to do. There were hundreds of planes in the southern sky. Sam could be on any one of them. He was all right. He had to be.

Why was she behaving this way? It had to be because of Erin and Hedda. They had lost their beloved husbands. If it had happened to them, it could happen to her.

It would be a terrible thing if Sam never knew that she really did place him first in her life. If he never knew that she was capable of sorting out what was important to her. If he never knew that she had finally acknowledged her limitations.

Getting out of bed, she put on soft slippers and a thick robe, and with Leo at her heels she began to pace across the front of the house, where she wouldn't disturb any of the people sleeping. She maintained a lonely vigil for Sam, looking out the windows, counting her footsteps across the cold floor. Leo followed silently and sat down beside her each time she paused. For once she found his presence comforting.

Outside, nothing moved on the frozen landscape. And then, to her astonishment, she saw a cab creeping down the road. She wondered what kind of fool would venture out on such dangerous streets. Only an idiot would risk his neck driving on a night like this. It was so stupid, so—

The cab turned into their driveway.

Could it be . . . ? Wait. Just wait. Don't think. Watch. Oh, my God. Please.

The cab slithered to a stop, as if in slow motion, and Sam's tall form emerged in a perfectly normal, everyday, unmiraculous way. He reached into the back seat for his suitcase, bent to say something to the cabdriver, and lifted his hand in farewell as the vehicle slowly backed away.

In shock, half afraid she was only hallucinating, Addy watched Sam come up the walkway as the cab carefully turned and began creeping back down the street. Sam reached the door, his key ready — the same key he'd tricked her into giving him during the ice storm five years ago — and opened the door with sure movement. He looked up to see her standing in the light of the ever-glowing Edison lamp.

"Well, hello, you angel! Waited up for me, I see. How did you know I was coming home?"

"Sam!" She flung herself at him, gulping and gasping.

"Ah. So you heard about the downed plane." He engulfed her in his arms, and pressed his cold face against her flushed cheek.

"I was hoping you hadn't," he told her. "I didn't know what flight I'd be on. I'm fine, darling. Look at me." He pried her away so she could see his face. Hers was stark and white.

"I'm fine," he repeated earnestly. "Hug me." She did, clutching him tightly. "See?" he said. "I'm solid." He hugged her even closer. "I'd have come back if I had to drag my dead bones to do it," he murmured. "Don't you know that?"

"Oh, Sam."

"I'm here, baby, I'm here."

"Sam."

"I'm all right. Our ninety-nine-year contract isn't up, and you can't get out of it so easily."

But she just clung to him wordlessly.

"You'd better be careful," he cautioned, "or I'll think you have a yen for me."

At last they kissed, with tender emotion. When they parted minutely, Addy gently said, "Come here." She took his hand and tugged for him to follow.

"Let me get my coat off." As he moved to do so, he glanced up the stairs and smiled. "Hi, Cyn. You get trapped here?"

And Addy realized that Cyn too had been wakeful with worry.

"Nice to see you home, Sam," Cyn said in a completely normal voice. "Good night." And her footsteps whispered down the hallway.

"Good night," Sam called as he flung his coat untidily over the newel post and whispered to Addy, "Where do you want me? In front of the fire? How about the morning-room closet? We haven't tried that for a long time. Here on the floor?" He grinned arrogantly seductively down at her.

"In the kitchen."

"In the *kitchen?* Well, that doesn't seem very cozy, but I'm willing to try anything once."

When they arrived in the kitchen. Sam tried to take her into his arms again, but she put a restraining hand on his chest, holding him off. Then she unfastened her wristwatch, held it up dramatically, and dropped it into the waste basket.

"Ah," he said, immediately becoming serious.

"We'll have the St. Patrick's Day party here," she began, trying to steady her shaky voice. "Marcus and his gang—"

"We'll have it here?" Sam interrupted, astonished.

She nodded emphatically. "And I've hired Cyn.

She looks on that disaster in the office as a treasure hunt!"

"But—"

"And this summer we'll go to the Tetons and camp out . . ." He didn't react at all, and her words trailed off weakly. "Sam? You *do* still want to go away with me, don't you?"

"Of course. I suspect your guilty conscience is making you realize how you've neglected me, and you're trying to assuage it in a rush of catching up, and I'm trying to remember what else I'd like so I can ride this wave."

"Anything," she promised, flinging out her arm.

"Well, there *is* one immediate pleasure I can think of." He grinned wickedly and hugged her marvelously, warming her near-frozen body. Then he smoothed her hair back from her face and decided, "We'll go to Tahiti for our anniversary." Together they headed toward the front stairs.

"I'm not absolutely sure about the April holiday," she said reluctantly. "The show—"

"Cyn can do it."

Addy stiffened and pulled slightly away as they reached the foot of the stairs. "Cyn?"

"Certainly. With her here, and the Freemans, we can leave the kids without a qualm. We'll have a—"

"Do you think Cyn's some sort of genius who can get this whole mess all whipped into shape?" She was fighting the last remnants of envy.

"Yes. Just the way your genius allows you to come up with a whole new line for every season." Sam's arm tightened around her, and they started climbing the stairs—he with purpose, she letting him lead the way.

Not quite mollified, Addy said, "Cyn is so smooth and elegant. That office defeated me, but she's conquering it with no trouble at all. She gave herself a week to get it in shape, but I think she'll do it in three days. Three days! She's been digging in like a terrier at a rabbit hole."

"She was a business major, it's her field. She's efficient and she knows what she's doing, but she couldn't design clothes if her life depended on it."

"It's just that she's so darned elegant..." Addy sighed, not quite comforted. "Do you think I'm human?"

"Extremely." Laughter laced that word as Sam hugged her at the top of the stairs. They saw Leo trot past them into Erin's room. Neither had noticed him standing beside them, patiently waiting for attention.

"And you?" She looked earnestly up at him. "You signed the telegram 'Superman.'"

"Yes to both counts. I too am merely human... except when it comes to you. Then I'm a superman."

Grendel drifted out of her room and came to them to be lifted and hugged by Sam. "We missed you," she said sleepily.

"Me, too, but I'm home, darling. Now let's get you back to bed." Sam carried her into her room, and he and Addy tucked her in. As they turned to go, they met Bridget standing in Grendel's doorway.

"All of my ladies to greet me!" Sam exclaimed in his deep voice as he lifted Bridget high into the air.

After they'd tucked Bridget back into her bed, Sam and Addy went on to their own room. Again they stood in each other's arms.

"What caused your great reformation?" Sam asked as he reluctantly released Addy so he could take off his suit coat and hang it on the walnut valet. "Did my being away from home do it? I went to Houston, but that didn't budge you. What happened?"

Addy unknotted his tie as he unbuttoned his shirt cuffs, and then she turned up his collar and slid the tie from his neck. She looked so vulnerable that he took advantage and held her against him to kiss her mouth and smooth his hands down her spine.

Her fingers were so weakened by the onslaught of desire that she had trouble holding on to the tie. As she placed it on the valet, she said softly, "Marcus told me about Hedda."

She turned to look at her husband, who'd pulled the shirt loose from his trouser band and was unbuttoned it. He was so thrillingly handsome as he stood there watching her that she felt an almost overwhelming agony of love.

"Tell me," Sam urged in his deep voice.

So she told him Hedda's story, just as Marcus had told it to her, her voice trembling. Such ordinary words, strung into sentences, to communicate such a tumultuous event in their lives. Tears filled her eyes and flowed down her cheeks as the poignancy of Sam's safe homecoming returned to her with fresh awareness. She could reach out her hand and touch him. And she did.

He gathered her softness to him, comforting her against his strong, hard, male body. He kissed her sweetly and combed his fingers through her long hair. "I try not to dwell on the horrendous ordeals that people manage to survive," he said solemnly.

"Erin talks very easily now about her family. Almost too much. It's as if she needs to talk about them in order to make them stay real for her."

"She'll be all right. There are various stages involved in overcoming grief. It all takes time." He kissed her again and stepped back a bit to put his shirt on the valet before slipping off his undershirt.

Addy filled her eyes with the sight of him, and again she reached out to touch him. Which delayed his getting undressed. His kisses became deeper as he opened her robe and moved his hands over her flannel gown, feeling the shape of her body beneath it. She clutched at him to reassure herself that this was no dream, that he was truly there with her.

"So you missed me?" he said playfully.

"A little." She managed to make the expected reply, but she gulped in the middle of 'little.'

He gave her bottom a soft swat and left his hand there to cup the sweet contour. Pulling her closer, he kissed her again, then lifted his head and asked with a smile, "Is my hair all standing up on end?"

She reached up languidly to check, plastering her stretched-out body along his. Taking advantage, he pushed her back to the wall and pressed against her, fusing their mouths with a passionate kiss. His tongue flicked lightly across her lips before plunging inside.

When she could, she gasped, "I don't think it's your *hair* that's standing up."

He murmured inarticulately between ardent kisses, purring, coaxing.

"Sam," she whispered urgently, her fingers working along his shoulders.

"I need to get my shoes off." He held her away from him, then sat down on the chaise longue, and bent to untie his shoes with rough jerks on the laces.

Readily, she knelt down to help. They each peeled off one sock. He rose, but she still knelt there, watching as he unbuckled his belt and removed it from the loops, then unhooked the band of his trousers and unzipped them.

From her convenient position point she took firm hold of the sides and helpfully tugged down his pants. When they were halfway down his thighs, she placed her hands on top of them against his hairy legs and pushed them all the way to his ankles.

Being the athlete he was, he could stand on one foot while she removed first one pant leg and then the other, without holding onto anything. When she reached up and slid her thumbs under the legs of his briefs at his hips, she hesitated, her eyes locked with his. Smiling just a little, she tugged teasingly before pulling them down—with some difficulty.

He stepped out of them and squatted down in front of her to peel off her robe and toss it aside. He lifted the hem of her nightgown and swept it from her body, flinging it away.

Still kneeling in front of each other, they gazed into each others eyes with a hot intense look that expressed all of their pent up longing and desire. And then Sam lifted Addy in his arms and carried her to their bed.

"I love you," she breathed passionately.

"I suspected."

"When?"

"When you were so charmingly uncomfortable about my coming to the showing five years ago." He was concentrating earnestly on her earlobe, his mouth moist and hot against the sensitive tissue, his teeth nipping the soft skin.

"Now, why would you remember that?"

"Because I was so mesmerized by you that I could count your heartbeats from across the room, and I knew how many times you blinked, and exactly where you were every second. Also how many glances you sneaked at me. I knew right then that I was going to marry you."

"Just from seeing me up on that runway, making a complete spectacle of myself?"

"You were graceful, talented, and sexy as all hell, and I wanted you so much it's amazing I didn't storm that runway and carry you off right then and there."

"Hah! And if I hadn't been interested?"

"I only needed to see how nervous you were around me to know I had your attention. You did offer some stimulating resistance, I must admit, but I knew I'd win you eventually." His breath fanned across her flat tummy before he caressed the area with his palm.

"Shall we begin practicing the technique required to fill you up with a baby?" His voice was low and growly.

"How about waiting until we go to Tahiti?"

"You'll go?" He pulled back to look into her eyes.

"I can't give up the entire business. I need it."

"I understand that."

"Marcus said you'd be a beachcomber if that was what I wanted—"

"Which beach?" he asked, as if he were already considering it.

"But that you'd have a clinic in the jungle."

Sam lay back and laughed. "He certainly does know me."

"Well, next to the clinic I'd have to have a dress shop."

"Done."

"I had so hoped I'd be able to handle the Gown House all by myself after Miss Pru left. I can't help feeling something of a failure." There, it was out.

"How can you possibly?" He was astonished, then indignant as he raised himself up on one elbow. "Miss Pru was an organizational wizard, but even she couldn't do the designs you did. No one can do everything. We all need someone to help sometimes."

Having made his point as well as it could be made, Sam lay half on top of her and began earnestly nibbling her shoulder. He gathered her close to him, his body heat almost scorching her where their skin touched.

"You are unique," he said. "Wondrous, a genius. You continually astound me. Besides being a perfect wife and mother, you have a fantastic gift of design that you fulfill with such earnest dedication. I admire you enormously. I'm proud of you, Adelina Mary Rose Kildaire Grady. And I love you."

"Oh, Sam. And if you had it to do over, would you marry me again?"

"In a flash." He kissed her deeply, eagerly, discouraging further conversation. "You're mine," he couldn't resist saying, his voice possessive.

"Almost entirely," she whispered, pressing herself against him and sliding her hands down his hot, strong torso. When he lifted his head to shift their bodies, she said, "I—" but he kissed her again, and although she did make one or two more attempts to speak, she eventually forgot what else she'd intended to say.

She trembled with wanting him, and their passion blazed, almost consuming them in its heat. While they made sizzling love under the down comforter, outside the February winds moaned and the frozen limbs of trees creaked in protest. The house groaned as it shifted against the wind's buffeting. And all the while Sam and Addy moaned and groaned with the passion of their desire.

Briefly they paused in exquisitely erotic torment, balanced precariously on the fine edge between need and fulfillment. And then demand overwhelmed control, and they came together in the ultimate union.

It was a night filled with love.

Afterward, as Sam lay sleeping, Addy stared at his precious face and marveled at how truly and completely she loved this man. At last her priorities were clear. Her children were jewels beyond compare, and the Gown House had greatly enriched her existence. But she'd come to realize that her love for Sam was the greatest treasure she'd ever have—and, best of all, it was one that could be shared.

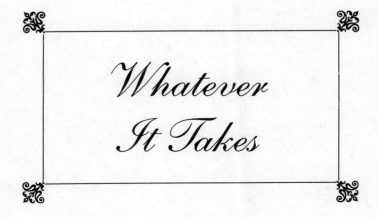

Whatever
It Takes

1

To Marcie Foster, the house on the north side of Indianapolis that had been given to her and Thad had only one redeeming feature—it was on the bus route. The house was huge and impossible to keep clean, and when he got his first pay raise, Thad said Marcie could have part-time help. But finding someone willing to take on the job was impossible.

One woman told Marcie, "It's just too big."

"But you wouldn't have to do it all at once," she protested. "Just one room a week."

"But I'd never be done! By the time I got the last room clean, the first one would need it again. It's just too big."

Marcie changed the ad each time she ran it so no one would realize it was for the same job and wonder if something was wrong with her or the house.

Marcie was proud of the latest ad. She felt sure her clever wording would fool everyone. But no one had called and no one had come by.

She had listened for the bus all day and had run to the living room window to watch whenever it came speeding down the road. But it had rumbled on past the bus stop every time.

Those periodic trips to the window punctuated what was fast becoming a frantic day. Both kids were in bed with chicken pox, so between soothing them and trying to tidy the house, Marcie more than had her hands full. From time to time, she caught her image in the mirror and eyed herself critically, as if she were the one who had to make a good impression.

By late afternoon Marcie was frazzled and tired. She told her mirrored image, "Chin up, Marcie. Somewhere out there is someone who'll look on cleaning this house as a challenge." But the blue eyes that gazed back at her weren't convinced.

Her hair was being quirky that day, so she pulled out the pins and brushed it with impatient strokes, then re-coiled it in a loose knot at the back of her head in a fruitless effort to look old enough to be the lady of the house . . . and in charge. It was so discouraging. At twenty-three, she was still carded in bars. She'd learned to keep her driver's license readily available.

It had been a grueling week. No week was easy, but that week chicken pox had broken out in the kids' nursery school, and both Gina and Kelly had come down with it. Marcie knew they felt rotten. They were despondent and cranky. At four, Gina was small for her age and usually made up for that with her feistiness. (She had no trouble informing people that her name was pronounced Gin-ah, not Jeen-ah, as everyone tended to say it.) But today she was sad-eyed and certain she'd never feel well again.

Although a year younger, Kelly was already taller

than his sister, to Gina's dismay. She kept reminding him and everyone else that she was older and therefore the boss. Kelly was reasonably tolerant of her.

Although no cleaning lady came that day, Marcie was cheered when Thaddeus skipped his weekly racquet-ball game and arrived like a weary, darkly handsome knight on a fagged red horse (his vintage Ford Mustang) to help Marcie cope. He was almost a foot taller than her five feet two inches. He was nice looking, clean-cut, with intelligent dark eyes and unruly dark hair.

He gave Marcie a tired smile before he was attacked by the two speckled kids. He touched their heads in sympathy as he leaned his briefcase against the newel post and sat down on the bottom step of the front stair-case. The kids crowded close and began to list all their problems.

He said, "Aw. Is that right?" and took them on his knees and hugged them tenderly as they vied with each other to be the more pitiful.

Gina raised tne back of her hand to her forehead and told her daddy, "I don't feel very well." She managed to squeeze out a tear as she lifted her eyes to him. "I look terrible." Her mouth pulled down at the corners.

"You're the most beautiful daughter I have," Thad assured her, and she was somewhat mollified. "Don't scratch," he cautioned Kelly.

Kelly heaved a big sigh and said, "It itches."

"We'll find something to put on it to help," Thad told him and leaned his son's head against his chest.

Marcie and Thad didn't say much as they coaxed the children to sample their suppers, put soothing ointment on their chicken pox, and finally settled them into bed. That accomplished, Thad set their own places in the dining room as Marcie carried in a casserole and salad. They sat across from each other at either end of the monstrously large table, which Thad's mother had found for them the previous month.

On first viewing the table, Thad had remarked, "Found? That implies it was lost."

Archly his mother had suggested, "Discovered?"

"I suspect it was abandoned one dark night," Thad replied, laughing. Beatrice Foster had become huffy.

In the continuing silence, Thad and Marcie finished eating, cleared the table, and carried coffee cups into the solarium.

"Would you like to watch TV?" Thad inquired politely.

Marcie shook her head.

"Listen to music?"

She declined.

They sat in silence, sipping their coffee, not speaking. Finally Marcie said, "It's time to check on the kids. Want to flip me for it?"

She really thought he'd volunteer to go up and see to them, but he dug out a quarter and flipped it. He won the toss.

When Marcie came back downstairs, Thad said, "We should have waited."

She frowned, trying to figure out what he meant, then asked, "Huh?"

"To get married," he elaborated.

"Yeah," she said vaguely.

"We're not old enough to be so settled down." He watched her somberly.

"We've only been married for five years. We have two more to go before the seven-year itch sets in."

Running a weary hand through his thick, rumpled hair, he said gloomily, "We were too young."

"That's what everyone said at the time. But you argued that we weren't."

"I was wrong."

She looked up, surprised. "I thought you were never wrong."

"I'm not generally, but I was about that. We could

have had an affair if you'd been more flexible."

"Well, it's too late. I don't think we can send the kids back."

"No," he acknowledged with a great sigh. "We're stuck."

"That's a depressing attitude."

"I never had a chance to run around. And I never did have an affair."

"Running around? An affair?" She frowned.

"I'm twenty-six years old, married five years, with two kids, a barn of a house . . ." He gestured to indicate the surrounding walls, which were obviously closing in on him.

"I'm twenty-three," she offered.

"We're too young."

She smiled. "New girl at the office?"

That annoyed him. "No."

"Then who?"

"No one!" he replied, getting cross. "It's just that we're so . . . *married.*"

"I thought this sort of thing hit men at forty."

"Can't you be serious?"

She turned up her hands. "This is serious?"

"Yes."

"Oh."

He frowned at her, and she smiled at him. The sight of him rarely failed to capture her awareness of how handsome and well made he was. Apparently he was also restless and discontented. She lifted her brows and inquired, "Is the thrill gone?"

"Marcie, you know damned good and well you're fabulous . . ."

"But you're not in the mood for an old married woman?"

He didn't reply.

It seemed her heart stopped beating as she asked quietly, "Are you telling me you want to be free of me . . . of us?" She waited for him to protest how silly that was. Or to laugh.

"It's something to talk about."

She stared at him, shocked. In disbelief she asked cautiously, "Talk about?"

"Yes," he replied firmly.

"You're kidding!"

He shook his head. "I wish we'd had an affair. Or could meet for the first time now. Or better yet, could meet four or five years from now."

"In four years Gina will be eight and Kelly seven."

"And if they marry as young as we did, Marcie, we could be grandparents while we're still in our thirties!"

"That would be shocking." The words were right, but amusement had crept into her voice.

"Marcie!"

Perfectly matching his tone, she exclaimed, "Thaddeus!"

"If you can't be serious, we might as well not try to discuss this until you can control your tongue."

She was tired and by that time almost as irritable as he was, so she stuck out her tongue and tried to see it by crossing her eyes. He made an exasperated sound and stomped out of the room—and out of the house.

That annoyed Marcie. Why could he always leave the house when they quarreled and go for a walk or drive or whatever, while she had to stay with the kids? So he was tired of being married? Big deal. Didn't he think she got fed up now and then, too?

She'd had no intention of getting married at eighteen. She'd been headed for a career. Numbers fascinated her, computers promised opportunities that boggled her mind. She'd planned to finish college, get a job, and have her own slick apartment, designer clothes, a neat sports car... Sure, sure. And old Silver Tongue had convinced her that what she *really* wanted was to marry him, work as a clerk-typist for three years, helping to support them while he got his MBA, and have two unplanned babies.

She carried their cups into the kitchen and thumped them down on the counter, resisting the temptation to put the chain on the door so Thad couldn't get back inside. She was more mature than that. But she considered it.

She went upstairs and checked the kids. She studied each impartially and decided she wasn't tempted to return them. They were as stuck with her as she was with them.

She took a long shower, hearing but not listening to the old pipes thump and rattle and groan as they reluctantly delivered the water. If she and Thad separated, they could sell the house before they had to replace the plumbing. Some good came with everything. She'd let the house go with great goodwill. So Thad wanted out? Good-bye, Thaddeus!

She didn't see much of him as it was. Each semester she still took a class one night a week—she'd be about eighty when she finally graduated. And he had his racquet-ball night, Saturday golf, Jaycees, business travel, and weekly Spanish class because his company was expanding southward.

She was a housekeeper. She kept the kids and the house. She wasn't a companion or a lover, just a friendly housekeeper . . . unpaid, of course. The more she thought about it, the angrier she became.

There was no way she'd wrap her arms around one of Thad's legs and allow herself to be dragged along, begging him to stick around. If he wanted to get out of their marriage, he could just take off!

But it was his house; it had been a gift from his parents. And like all of the gifts, it had cost them in some way—more than they wanted to spend for something they didn't want in the first place.

The house was a big, formal structure with double front doors leading into a central hallway, two living rooms—rugless and scantily furnished—a solarium, den, a dining room and kitchen, and one and a half baths. Upstairs there were five bedrooms and two baths, and on the third floor were empty maids' rooms.

The whole place was impossible to maintain, and it was all Thad's. Beatrice Foster had explained that at length. "The house is Thad's," she'd said, "because, you see, it's a gift from us." A gift to their only child.

Thad had immediately teased Marcie, "I'll never actually charge you rent."

"How kind."

"We'll think of some exchange to justify your living here."

"How big of you."

He'd leered at her and promised, "You might work on it."

They'd spent the first weeks making love in a different room each night. Thad insisted it was the only proper way to warm a house.

"I thought a housewarming was a party with all your friends," Marcie had said.

"Where did you ever get a silly idea like that? Why on earth would you want to make love in front of other people?"

She'd ignored him and continued, "And the friends bring gifts for the house."

"Take off your clothes. I have a great gift for you."

"Oh, no, not that again."

"You're totally spoiled by my indulgence of your lusts. I'll have to be more withholding so you'll appreciate your opportunities."

She had laughed.

If they did get a divorce, where would she and her homeless babies live? In her mind she saw herself standing in the driving snow on an Indianapolis street with a child huddled on either side of her, clinging to her skirts as she clutched a shawl around her head with one chapped hand.

She sighed. She didn't own a shawl, and it was April. Tulips, jonquils, and hyacinths were blooming; and the forsythia was golden, like captured sunshine.

Of course, she and the kids could be bag people and live in cardboard boxes. "It's time for Daddy to drive by in his limousine," she'd say. "Watch closely, children. Perhaps he'll toss a dime out the window for you."

Thad wouldn't do that. He wouldn't allow his children to go without support. Some men divorced their families and forgot them and didn't do anything to help. And there were wives who took revenge for being discarded by taking their ex-husbands for every cent they were worth. But she and Thad weren't like that.

Still, she became absorbed by the idea of living in cardboard boxes. Her family would have a fit! Her dad would appreciate the melodrama but her mother would never understand. Marcie wondered how her father and mother had ever married each other; they were so different. Sex. It trapped everyone.

If it weren't for sex, would she have married Thad? Yes. No question. He was so funny. At least he had been funny. It had been a long time since he had been really amusing. He was now very serious, somber, and brooding. Was there another woman? Marcie didn't think he had time.

'They' said men did it at lunch. But Thad wasn't in the two-hour lunch bracket yet, and if he had a choice, would he choose sex instead of lunch? No. Although he would probably try to manage to have both.

She imagined a tawdry motel room with a naked Thad atop a writhing woman. Spread out on a napkin by the woman's shoulder was his lunch—from which he selected bites with divided interest. Marcie sighed again. He'd never had any trouble doing two things at once.

Finished with her shower, she dried her body, pulled on one of Thad's discarded T-shirts, which came down to her thighs, and an old pair of cotton underwear. She plaited her hair in one thick braid and regarded herself critically in the mirror.

Her body hadn't changed much during her marriage, despite two babies. Her breasts were fuller, making her look thirteen instead of ten. She had inherited her dad's eyelashes, which were so black and long that they didn't need mascara. She had five freckles, a full lower lip, and dark brows that had to be plucked or they became eccentric. Her eyes were dark blue. Her face was a nice oval, she decided, and her thick dark hair was okay. She couldn't complain about her appearance, but she did wish she were a little taller. At five feet two, she had to look up a lot.

Briefly she wondered if she should get out her black lace nightgown and seduce Thad. She hadn't worn it much because as soon as he saw her in it, he took it off again. He'd never been able to wait long enough for her to seduce him.

But she wouldn't bind Thad to her with sex. It wouldn't be fair. They had to figure out a way to live without either of them feeling trapped.

How would it feel to be unmarried? She'd gone from family to marriage, and Thad was the only man she'd known sexually. She tilted her head thoughtfully and asked her image, would she ever be interested in marrying another man? Would she ever want to entice another man? Without doubt, the answers were no.

In their five years of married life, she'd had several opportunities to be unfaithful. At first she hadn't even realized men made overtures to married women. The discovery had shocked her. She still couldn't quite accept it.

She'd never yet met another man who interested her that way. She'd always felt sorry for the wives of men with wandering eyes, and she'd felt lucky she had Thad. Was he now out looking?

Aggressive women often made blatant plays for Thad's

attention. He never appeared to notice. Or did he? Did he now regret those lost opportunities?

She checked her two sleeping children, then crawled into her side of the bed. She lay there considering whether she could do anything to change Thad's mind.

Without quite reaching sainthood, she'd been a pretty good wife. She'd worked uncomplainingly for three years until Thad had gotten his MBA. She'd never campaigned against or competed with his mother's possessiveness. Beatrice had seen no reason to financially help out a marriage she didn't approve of, so although the senior Fosters had continued to give Thad an allowance, it hadn't been enough for them to live on while he was in school—especially with two kids. True, Thad had cheerfully worked at two campus jobs, one in the library and one at a hamburger drive-in. Still, it had taken every nickel they could scrape up to pay the bills, and the first years had been a very frugal time.

Marcie would have preferred to live in a smaller town than Indianapolis, but she'd realized that Thad needed to be near his job, and she had endured the house with amused tolerance. She invited people in, dressed in an attractive if limited wardrobe, and made love with enthusiastic delight ninety-two percent of the time.

If Thad was discontented in their marriage, there really wasn't anything she could do about it. Her time, energy, and ingenuity were limited. If anything, he was the one who needed to share more of his time with her. He thought *he* was discontented, but he'd only made her aware that there were great unfulfilled needs in her own life, too.

2

WHEN MARCIE WOKE the next morning, she was snuggled as usual against Thad, who slept with his arms loosely around her. If they split up, she'd miss sleeping with him. One of the nicest things about him was the way he tolerated her burrowing against him and warming her cold feet on him. He gasped when she edged her icy toes against his warm calves but he never objected or complained.

Pensively she lay awake, conscious of his hair-roughened skin along her smooth back. She was naked. Gradually she remembered him coming into bed and seducing her, peeling off the T-shirt and making love to her. He hadn't said anything. His lovemaking had been hot, intense, and silent.

How many times had they made love in the last five

years? And in so many different ways—from loving to rollicking to sensual to erotic to hilarious. But lately it had become rather perfunctory. Last night had been different yet again. It hadn't been sex between lovers, but . . . a mating between old acquaintances?

He yawned, so she knew he was awake, but he didn't say anything. Gently she rose up on one elbow to squint at the digital clock. It was almost time to get up. Feeling unusually self-conscious at being naked, she crawled across the bed and got out on her side. Still Thad said nothing.

She stood next to the bed and looked down at him. He lay naked, lax, his eyes closed, discouraging conversation. She took a pale orange flannel robe from a hook in her closet and pulled it on as she tucked her toes into brown scuffs. Then she quietly left the room. How strange that neither of them had spoken.

Her speckled children were still sleeping in their separate bedrooms, sprawled in twisted covers. It was the first night they'd slept well, so she didn't disturb them, though she did cover Kelly's bare foot before she went back into the upstairs hallway.

Bordering the stairwell was a heavy waist-high railing, which, like the rest of the woodwork and the bare floors, had been varnished black. The stairs were eight-feet wide with a landing twenty-one feet long on which was a wide casement window with a deep window seat.

The house was best suited to a large family, Marcie thought again as she went down the stairs. And the youngest should be at least ten—or better yet, twelve. Turning at the landing and continuing to the first floor, Marcie wondered when Gina would try sliding down the banister. She rolled her eyes in a silent plea for help.

As she started breakfast, she heard the water pipes complaining and knew Thad was up. She stacked plates and utensils on the tea cart and thought for the thousandth time how inconvenient it was to have a kitchen without room in which to eat a quick meal. When the house had been built, it had been fashionable to have a cook and a serving maid. Now there was only Marcie. And Thad . . . for at least another day.

He was really very good about wheeling the cart into the dining room and setting their places at one end of the monstrous table. He also helped clear while she stacked the dishes in the dishwasher.

Gina's small voice floated down the great stairwell. "Can we come down?"

"May . . . Put on slippers and ask Daddy to get your cotton robes. Is Kelly coming down, too?"

"I told him to put on slippers," Gina replied virtuously.

"Kelly?" Silence. "Kelly!"

"I got them!" he declared impatiently.

"Put them on," Marcie instructed.

"Oh."

Marcie was making toast fingers when Thad came down with the kids. "Morning," he said.

She watched him, not replying. He spoke as if this were their first meeting of the day, that she hadn't moved out of his arms not half an hour ago.

"It's my turn to push the cart," Kelly declared.

"No, it isn't, it's mine!" Gina was equally determined.

Thad solved it. "You may both help me push it."

Marcie's dad had made each child a booster seat to be placed on a dining room chair so that they could sit easily at the table, using the front of the chair seat as a foot rest. Thad helped the kids up on their seats and turned to the tea cart for their eggs.

"I get the duck!" Kelly crowed.

"*I* get the duck!" Gina snapped.

Thad held closed fists in front of him and said, "Pick a hand." They each picked one, and Thad gave the duck to Gina, the rooster to Kelly.

Marcie's mother had painted the eggcups in a ceramics

class. When she'd given the cups to Marcie, she had commented how strange it was that a rooster held the eggs instead of a hen.

As they all ate breakfast, Marcie thought they looked a quiet family group. Yesterday's spring bouquet of flowers from the yard stood on the big black table. The two children looked healthy and beautiful, even with chicken pox. They were concentrating on dunking toast fingers into the soft-boiled eggs and digging out the rest with demitasse spoons.

The freshly shaven daddy was wearing his suit and tie, ready to leave for the office, and the mommy was sleepy-eyed in a robe. They didn't look as if they were considering a separation. Thad's comment of the night before probably meant he was just restless. Maybe he had spring fever.

For a month the Fosters had been planning a cocktail party for sixty people, to be held on the next day. Marcie had sent postcards to all those invited, warning them that the kids had chicken pox and letting the guests decide whether or not to come anyway. Several couples had cancelled. One woman said her mother couldn't remember if she'd had chicken pox or not, and another said her baby book had been lost in a move some time or other, and she hadn't the foggiest idea about childhood illnesses.

Marcie was in the kitchen later that morning when Phyllis came over to watch. She'd been one of the first neighbors to visit after Marcie and Thad had moved, and she came very close to making a pest of herself. She was green-eyed with raven black hair and a sleek figure. She was divorced. Her husband hadn't left just her; he'd left the country. Marcie thought that was extreme.

Phyllis's green eyes had sparked with interest when she'd first met Thad. But Marcie considered her too old to be a serious threat. Good Lord, she had to be at least thirty-five.

Thad grumbled occasionally about Phyl always being underfoot, but Marcie didn't mind, for she knew the woman was lonely. It did occur to her, however, that, considering Phyl was a native of Indianapolis, it was strange she didn't have friends of her own.

It was never difficult for Phyl to learn their plans because she always asked. Then she would volunteer to contribute to them in some slight way and thereby manage to be included. For the Saturday cocktail party, she'd loaned Marcie a big blue jar to be filled with blooming forsythia branches and set in the curve of the dark stairwell. It would be lovely.

When they'd first moved in, the senior Mrs. Foster had told Marcie she should strip the varnish from the floors and woodwork. Marcie had refrained from replying, "It's not *my* house," and said, "I'll put that on the list of 'Things to Do.'"

Late on Friday afternoon, the day before the cocktail party, Phyllis was hanging around, waiting for Thad to come home, when Beatrice arrived with another surprise gift.

Beatrice always pulled the great brass chain, which tolled a big brass doorbell. Marcie had padded the bell so the sound was a thud instead of the original reverberating clang.

Wiping her hands on a towel, she went into the entranceway and opened the front door—and found not only Beatrice but several men burdened with rolls of what appeared to be carpeting.

Marcie raised questioning eyebrows as her mother-in-law hastily entered, flung wide both sides of the double doors, and directed the men, "Put that one in *that* room and put the smaller one down here."

The men silently obeyed. Beatrice Foster was forty-

seven, small, dark, pretty, hipless, bosomy, and busy.
She told Marcie, "All you have to pay for is the cleaning
and repair."

Faintly Marcie asked, "Cleaning and repair?"

At that particularly dramatic moment, Thad ventured
through the open doors into the hall and joined the spec-
tators, who now included the children and Phyllis.

His mother bubbled with enthusiasm. "Do you know
that old theater that's being torn down? Old theaters have
carpeting! One man had a hooked knife, and he ripped
out the good parts, and several of them loaded it on the
back of the station wagon for me." She stood back and
gestured like a magician.

The rug was red, in a way—blotchy and unevenly
worn. Phyl made a disparaging sound, and Thad said,
"It looks as if it soaked up the results of the St. Valentine's Day Massacre." He paused. "What's this going to
cost me?"

"Well, of course it was *very* dirty," his mother began.
"But I had taken the measurements some time back,
thinking if I ever found a real bargain—"

"How much?" Thad repeated.

"They had to clean it all first and then sew it together
and bind it." She shot a glance at him and added, "Under
two hundred dollars."

"How far under?"

"Well, I believe it's just about . . . one hundred, ninety-
nine dollars. And ninety-five cents."

Marcie spoke up firmly. "It's smashing." When no
one said anything she added, "And you went to a great
deal of trouble over it."

"It was free," Beatrice said again.

"Free?" Thad echoed with some amusement.

"I think it's . . . stunning," Marcie said.

"I am stunned," Thad agreed.

Moving a hand to indicate the entire entrance hall,
Marcie said, "Look at the colors. The shining black of

the varnished floor and woodwork, the cream of the plaster walls, Phyl's blue vase, and that red rug. It's marvelous." If one looked at the strange rug as part of a whole, it *was* marvelous.

Beatrice said, "I would have checked it with you, Thad, but I did so want to surprise you."

"I am surprised," he acknowledged.

Two years before, when they'd moved into the house, Beatrice had presented them with a gift of two long, solid oak church pews. They'd been at the front of the church and, therefore, were as good as new. The two benches had given the unused, otherwise unfurnished living room the look of a carelessly abandoned meeting hall. Now the rug, with its strange shading and mottling, made the room seem warm and rich.

Beatrice fussed, directing the carpet men to arrange the pews in such a way that one mended edge of the rug, which was inclined to cup, was flattened by the weight of one end of a pew. "There!" she said, pleased. "It's all wool," she announced into the critical silence.

The carpet men discreetly handed Thad a bill, accepted a tip, and slipped quietly away.

"Now Mar-she-ah," Beatrice said, "remember you're to needlepoint cushions for the pews. They should be in red, brown, and mustard with a touch of light blue."

"Oh, yes."

"You've been a long time getting that done," Beatrice reminded her.

"Yes."

"Isn't it perfect?" Beatrice demanded and Marcie agreed.

"It's beautiful!" Gina's little voice exclaimed from the French doors leading into the hall.

Thad picked up Gina and touched Kelly affectionately on the head.

"Can we have supper in here?" Kelly asked. Gina thought that was a good idea.

"May . . ." Marcie reminded her younger child. "You might spill—" Beatrice hesitated.

"How could you tell if something was spilled?" Thad chuckled, earning a cool glance from Beatrice. "Staying for supper, Mother?" he asked.

"No, dear, I—"

"Then would you drop off Phyl? It's just around the corner."

"Glad to. Ready?" Beatrice Forster inquired briskly. "I must rush." But she couldn't resist saying, "Do you like the rugs, Thad?"

He simply kissed her on the cheek, which she took as an affirmative, then she bustled out calling to Phyl, who lagged behind, saying, "I'd be glad to help with the canapés."

"Thanks, anyway," Thad replied, and urged her out the door, closing it on her heels.

"I wouldn't have minded," Marcie chided. "Phyl's lonely."

"I didn't want to have to be pleasant," he explained.

"Bad day?"

"Not especially." He surveyed the rugs. "Do you mind them?"

"I honestly think they're great."

Gina agreed as Kelly appeared with a box of his treasures, which he dumped in the exact middle of the rug. He looked up at his father and pointed to the fireplace. "Just a little fire," he suggested.

"Please," Thad reminded him.

Kelly nodded.

"Then we will have a picnic?" Gina inquired, her tiny body poised and her slight brows raised in inquiry.

"Okay?" Marcie asked Thad, who shrugged, indifferent.

Gina climbed up on a pew to watch her father build the fire. She stuck her thumb in her mouth, then pulled it out and said, "Since I'm sick, I won't fetch and carry. Do we get hot dogs?"

Her mother smiled. "How's the tummy feel?"

"A little weezie."

"Queasy," Marcie corrected.

"Ummm," Gina agreed.

"How about soup and crackers?"

"Just right," her daughter decided.

Marcie went to the kitchen and put together supper thinking all the while how Thad had said he didn't want Phyl there because he didn't want to have to be pleasant. Did that mean he was going to be unpleasant?

But he wasn't. He was just very quiet and . . . pensive. Melancholy? She left him alone. The kids, having passed the peak of their illness, were also quiet, tired, and willing to go to bed. They would sleep better—and did.

FIRMLY BELIEVING THAT one *can* control oneself if one sets one's mind to it, Marcie crawled into bed that night determined to stay on her side. It was too bad they had no other bed. It might be less strained if they could occasionally sleep apart. Sleeping together made them seem so friendly.

Having strictly admonished herself not to intrude on Thad's territory, she nevertheless awoke the next morning crammed against him as usual, with his arms around her and his body clinging to the edge of the bed.

She listened to his slow, deep breathing and wondered how he managed to stay asleep. Habit. He'd said he was so used to it that when he was traveling and had a whole bed to himself, he still slept on the edge. Maybe that's what was the matter with him. He never really rested.

He didn't rest, so he was tired and therefore unhappy.

Very carefully Marcie eased away from him, but unconsciously his arms tightened, and he gathered her back against him. He usually slept naked. His upper leg slid over hers, and she felt the texture of his muscular thigh on the smooth skin of her hip. It was so warm and cozy.

Her cheek lay against the wiry hair of his chest, which moved with his slow, steady breathing. She looked down his body, admiring his beauty, and felt a familiar squiggle of desire.

What she *ought* to do was get out of bed and check on the kids. That's what she ought to do, all right. She turned her head infinitesimally and touched her hot, wet tongue to the hard wart of his nipple. Just a tiny flick. There was a pause in his breathing, then it continued, but it wasn't as deep.

She didn't move. Neither did he. Was he awake?

They lay silently. Her breath bent several hairs on his chest. She sighed as if in sleep and watched the hair move next to her cheek.

Her family had once had a lazy cat who could sleep through almost anything—except a stealthy fingertip barely touching the outer hairs along his side. The cat would twitch a couple of times, then jerk out of sleep to bite and lick at the place where he thought a flea had been traveling through his fur.

She lifted a fingertip and barely touched the hair near Thad's navel. His breathing skipped a beat, then, as she paused, it went on in the same measured rhythm. Very carefully her finger continued its sneaky path around his navel, then ventured cautiously down below. A blast of hot air ruffled her hair, and she heard his swift intake of breath.

Her fingertip hesitated, and so did his breath. His chest still rose with silent, shallow movements, but she knew he was awake. He was already aroused, and she watched him grow tense with increasing interest.

It was clinically interesting to Marcie to see how quickly he'd gone from relaxed sleep to full, hot arousal. She wondered if the transformation had ever been timed or studied in a laboratory.

A sound rumbled from his chest under her ear. "Are you flirting with me?" He pulled his head back to try to see her face hidden against his chest.

"Oh, no," she assured him.

"Then just what *are* you doing?" He was about as interested as he could get.

"We had an old tomcat once, and when he slept, we'd touch his side and he thought he had fleas. And he'd go after them..." She tilted her face up to him.

"You think I'm an old tom."

"Well..." She smoothed the hair on his taut stomach. "There's all this fur..."

"I'll have to show you how we human toms go after rash little fleas."

"Oh, I already know that. You'll just scratch and wiggle."

"That's a...fairly...accurate description." His hands were on her, and his mouth snaked down, his head pushing hers back so he could find her laughing mouth. His unshaven beard was harsh against her smooth skin.

His kiss was hungry and demanding, his hands equally so. He peeled off the old T-shirt she was wearing and quickly tossed her old, faded panties to the floor. He pinned her flat to the bed and loomed over her in the early morning light. Then he paused.

His smoldering eyes raked over her nakedness. His right hand moved where he wanted it to, to caress and excite and possess her. His lips parted with his accelerated breathing, and his muscles knotted with his movements. He was tense, rigid.

She took pleasure in running her hands over his upper arms and shoulders, cupping his head, feeling his rough cheeks, moving her touch down his chest and around his ribs to his back . . . the sweetly familiar trails.

He watched avidly as her body flexed and relaxed with her movements. She felt boneless and flaccid. Her eyes were lazy and teasing, and her lips soft and inviting.

With practiced ease his mouth went to hers to sip and taste. His right hand trailed tickles over her body, and his tongue licked and nibbled like a cat after a flea. He could make her respond so wildly, and she held back nothing. When she began to moan, he took her almost violently and with great mutual satisfaction. Their flight was thrilling and wonderful as their pleasure intensified to a sensual peak of fulfillment.

Finally, still coupled, they lay panting, their hearts pounding and his weight lovely on her. Gradually they calmed and slowly separated. It had been quick and delicious.

But . . . but . . . something was missing. There had been a deliberateness about it. As they lay sprawled, sweaty, physically replete, Marcie felt a vague, intangible hunger for something more. She still needed . . . what? Love? Was that what was missing? A bleak sadness settled on Marcie's heart. Even without love, their encounter had been marvelous. Thad was a practiced, skilled, considerate partner. But without love it was incomplete.

Love, commitment, and responsibility fulfilled the act. Otherwise they were being subtly cheated. It became participation in a sexual act instead of a sharing of sexual love. Distracted by her thoughts, Marcie left the bed, aware that her husband's eyes were following her, studying her.

She showered, put on her orange robe and brown scuffs, and peeked in at the kids before going downstairs to start breakfast. It was Saturday, the day of the party.

Since their friends were mostly their age and also beginning to set up their own households, the sparsely furnished house didn't bother Thad or Marcie. They felt

no qualms about asking their guests to bring their own
bottle of whatever they wanted to drink. Thad bought a
case of Chablis for the people who would inevitably
forget.

Over several days Marcie had made and frozen
hundreds of bite-size pastry puffs, which, once thawed,
would hold a variety of filling. She'd hardboiled several
dozen of the smallest grade eggs, which she'd later put
in a red bowl lined with parsley. She'd fried a mound
of chicken wings and refrigerated them, and she'd cut
up and sliced vegetables to be eaten with dip.

On Saturday all she really had to do was mix the
fillings, prepare the dips, cut the flowers, and put the
food on the table. It was really relatively painless.

Thad spent most of the day watching her. He studied
her efficient hands, the way she turned her head, and the
way her body moved. He helped, too — getting extra ice,
sorting dishes, trundling the filled tea cart, dispensing
serving spoons and forks, and spending time with the
recuperating children. But during that whole day Marcie
was aware that he was studying her. Was he judging her?
Testing her? Comparing her? Balancing her good and
poor qualities? How was she measuring up? Against
whom? What right had he to scrutinize her so?

That evening, knowing their guests' garb would range
widely from remarkably casual attire to suits and dressy
dresses, Thad put on dove gray trousers, a white shirt,
and red tie, with a soft navy-blue V-neck sweater.

Marcie had made herself an evening pajama outfit
modeled gently on overalls. It had wide legs and the top
of the bib barely came to the middle of her breasts. The
soft fabric was printed with wild pinks and reds on a
white background and the full-sleeved blouse was in white
gauze with a recklessly plunging neckline.

As the kids watched her critically, she brushed her
dark hair so that it swirled around her shoulders. She

applied more eye makeup than she usually wore and red-red lipstick to match her freshly polished nails. Then she fitted long, thin red hoops into her ears and slipped on pink sandals. When she asked her offspring if she looked all right, they nodded in sober seriousness.

Marcie had hired a neighborhood teenager who'd already had chicken pox to spend the several hours before bedtime with the children.

Phyl arrived, too early as usual. "I've come to help," she announced, but Marcie knew by then that Phyl wouldn't do much but stand in the way, talking to Thad as they worked around her.

Marcie made a last-minute check of the list she'd posted of what was to be served—she knew from experience that it was the only way to stay cool in the heat of entertaining—and, sure enough, she'd forgotten the chicken wings. Just as the first guests began arriving, she hurried the chicken into the roaster to reheat.

The house was well suited to entertaining. All the downstairs rooms opened into each other with double French doors, so crowd flow was no problem. With spring flowers in great bunches and the newly acquired rugs, the house looked cheerful and inviting. So did the host and hostess, who appeared perfectly normal and untroubled.

As with any gathering, they'd invited the people they wanted to see and grudgingly included a few have-to-haves, Phyl chief among them. Then they'd added some new faces. Betty and Max were a middle-aged, childless couple who'd recently moved in down the block. They were cheerful and friendly. Max was a builder who'd made a bundle before the housing slump and was now making another bundle in house repair and expansion. He arrived with a cigar clamped between his teeth. Marcie said, "Don't light it," which made Betty laugh in understanding and agreement.

"I never do," Max promised. "It's my security blan-ket." He added that he'd managed to buy Cuban cigars when they were in Europe.

"I always planned to have a summer's holiday in Eur-ope with Marcie," Thad said thoughtfully.

Marcie considered his words. Did that mean he no longer planned to make such a trip with her?

She looked around at all their friends and wondered how they would react to news of a Foster divorce. Would they choose sides or would they divide their loyalties? Would it be awkward? She looked at Thad as his eyes caught hers. His expression was serious and thoughtful. What was he thinking?

He was thinking she was beautiful. She mixed so well with all sorts of people. And he could tell she was having a good time. She was whole. She didn't really need him. She was competent, efficient, and did it all so casually. She could survive without him. But could he survive without her?

He watched as she moved through the crowd, making sure everyone had someone to talk with, was eating his or her share of food, and was comfortable. She should have married a politician. He saw her find Betty and stop to talk to her, and he moved over to eavesdrop.

"Max's tie is beautiful. Did you buy it when you were in Paris?"

"I made it." Betty grinned.

"Did you!" Marcie was impressed.

"It's easy. If you want to learn how, I'll show you."

"Our friend, Lisa, has a crafts gallery, and she invites people to teach there. Would you be interested in teaching a class in tie-making?" I could make one for Thad as a going-away present, Marcie thought to herself.

"Sure," Betty agreed, "It'd be fun."

The downstairs was filled with the hum of voices as people gathered and chatted and separated and ate and refilled their glasses. In the hubbub Nance arrived with her friend Ned.

The Fosters' friend as well as their lawyer, Nance was a beautiful woman, and she wore clothes well. Her thick, wheat-colored hair was arranged in a French twist, showing off her long neck and stunning, subtly Nordic face. She greeted Marcie with sparkling blue eyes, and Marcie introduced her and Ned to Betty. "Oh, I know Nance. She's done legal work for us," Betty said.

"Hi, Betty." Nance smiled at her. "Have you seen the table yet? I've heard of nothing else since they got it."

As they moved through the noisy crowd to the dining room, Marcie made the others laugh by describing Beatrice's arrival with the rugs and Thad's cautious reaction. Thad joined them in the dining room as Nance viewed the table. "That table and the sideboard are nothing short of magnificent!" she declared.

"I thought of you as soon as the movers wrestled them into the house," Marcie said. "I thought to myself, 'Nance will think they're remarkable.'" She shook her head.

"Magnificent," Nance corrected. "What kind of wood is it?"

"Very heavy," Ned guessed, and they all laughed.

"You ought to strip off the varnish," Nance suggested.

Marcie clutched her hair dramatically and protested that she didn't have time. Thad smiled at her.

Nance said, "You know, you must admit this table looks better than that postage-stamp-sized card table you used to have."

Ned agreed. "It does suit the room."

"I believe the delivery men charged by the pound," Marcie said. "They advised us quite seriously that, if we ever move, we should stipulate that the table and sideboard go with the house. We should insist on it."

Nance stooped down to examine the surface of the supporting trestle. "There's a face on it," she exclaimed.

The rest of them bent to look, too, and Ned ran his

hand over the dark surface. "It may be Bacchus. Feel," he told Thad.

"Grapes? Leaves," Thad said, feeling. "And a laughing face!"

"That's it, all right." Betty was down on her hands and knees, half under the table. "A table for a feast with the god of wine."

Gradually other guests heard of the discovery and had to look, too, and the Fosters were repeatedly advised to strip off the dark varnish.

Almost last to arrive at the party were Lisa and Russ. Marcie thought if Botticelli had been Dutch, he would have painted all his goddesses and angels with Lisa's face. She was beautiful. It always caused something of a jolt to see her eat ordinary food and hear her speaking in a down-to-earth manner.

At Marcie's urging, Lisa examined Max's handmade tie and asked Betty, "Would you be willing to teach tie-making at my crafts gallery?"

"Sure," Betty said. "I don't have anything to do, and I'm going nuts."

Russ and Max agreed that the table was oak, hand-carved, and that the carving on the hall end was of Bacchus. Then they discovered nymphs and satyrs running through strategically placed leaves on the other end of the table, and Marcie chortled to Nance, "Wait till Beatrice finds out!"

Soon after that, Marcie was standing with a group of people not far from Thad and Nance. She overheard him saying, "How do young couples manage financially when they split? There's generally not enough income for two households."

Marcie went into shock. He was serious about getting a divorce! She talked, smiled, and moved, but she did it in a fog. She felt numb. The party surged on with an animated hum, punctuated by laughter, until well past midnight. There were still stragglers left at two A.M.

As the remaining guests helped clear away the food, Lisa set up times for Betty's gallery sessions. Phyl hung around with the men, drinking another glass of wine. She'd asked Thad to walk her home, but Betty had said she and Max would.

Eventually everyone left. Marcie sneaked troubled peeks at Thad as they turned out lights, banked the fires, and set the fire screens in place. Thad seemed perfectly normal to her.

As they checked for smoldering butts left in the ashtrays, Thad said, "It was a good party."

"Yes," she replied, but her voice sounded wooden. She sighed sadly and headed for the stairs. She couldn't possibly ask him about his comment to Nance. She couldn't handle anything else right then.

"I'll be along in a while," he said. "I'm not very sleepy."

Her heart twisted. He didn't want to go upstairs with her. "Good night," she said softly.

"Good night, Marcie." He followed her to the bottom of the stairs and stood watching as she climbed them.

As she undressed and washed her face and brushed her teeth, she again heard Thad quietly ask Nance, "How do young couples manage financially when they split?" And in her mind Marcie again witnessed Nance's serious, concerned expression.

DURING THE NEXT several days, their lives continued in a strange, sealed-off way. Thad looked dejected and unhappy, and Marcie, unable to sort out her own feelings, didn't know what to say to him. She still felt angry with him for putting them in this uncomfortable limbo.

Since she kept the books, she was fully aware of how much money there was and how it was spent. They didn't spend recklessly. Their only unnecessary expenditures were those required by the "gifts" from the senior Fosters. Two hundred dollars just that month for the cleaning and binding of the rugs. And, though they managed well, there wasn't enough to support two households.

People separated and divorced every day. One out of three marriages ended in divorce. How did those people manage? Marcie refused to consider going home to her mother and father. She would not saddle them with her responsibilities. And she needed to control her own life, she couldn't go back to being a dependent again.

Besides, she wanted to stay in Indianapolis. She'd made many good friends there. There must be some way to handle the situation. She considered the problem logically. She and the kids would need a place to live and she would have to find a job. But that could be done: Indianapolis was a big city with many opportunities for employment, and she had some work experience, having been a clerk-typist to help put Thad through school.

How much would she need to earn to support herself and the two children? What was the very rock-bottom she had to make? What work was available to her?

She began scouring the want ads and making telephone calls. There were several clerical positions open in small offices that she could easily handle. As supplemental income, any one of them would have been fine, but she couldn't support herself and two kids on the wages they were offering. What should she do?

She would have to train for a higher-paying position. Therefore, she had to go back to school. And the solution came: She'd helped support Thad during his last three years in school. Why couldn't he support her until she could complete her own training? She had two years to go for a degree.

If Thad didn't remarry right away, they could split the house. He could have the den and one bath, and she and the kids could take the upstairs. She'd go to school, and he'd pay her to keep house and take care of the children. From that income she would have money for tuition and food. But she'd have to hire a sitter for a good part of the day. Where would she get the money for that?

For several days she mentally reviewed and refined her solutions. If she dropped dead, Thad would have to solve a good many problems. Keeping her as an efficient live-in housekeeper would be much cheaper and easier.

Was she efficient? She was devoted, conscientious, and she had the children's best interests at heart. You couldn't buy that kind of help. Thad was getting a jewel . . . cheaply.

Being practical, she knew she couldn't go to school full time. She figured it would take four years. She'd be twenty-seven when she graduated; Thad would be thirty. Both kids would be in grade school by then. Maybe she could do it in three years.

Not long after she'd settled on her plan, Thad dragged home from work, ate glumly, sighed dispiritedly, and slumped in a chair in the solarium to watch the television news. Marcie suspected he would bring up The Subject. She was certain when he clicked off the news in mid-sentence.

In the adjoining room Gina and Kelly were pretending to be bears whose cave was under two old Indian blankets draped over the pew and two dining room chairs. Their laughter was so infectious that, hearing it, even Thad smiled. "I like them, you know," he said.

"Great."

"Don't be sarcastic."

"Was I?" Marcie cocked her head. "I thought 'great' was positive. I could have said, 'Are you only now discovering it?' or 'So you're not going to give them away?'"

"Marcia!"

"Thaddeus!"

He glared at her. She gave him a patient look that wasn't especially friendly. He finally looked away and heaved a great, melancholy sigh. "What it comes down to is we're trapped," he said in a low, sad voice.

Although she'd been expecting something like this, a terrible pain shot through Marcie. She swallowed, then said, "I think I've figured out a solution."

He regarded her warily. "What?"

"If I dropped dead—"

Alarmed, he sat straight up and leaned forward. "Are you sick?" he snapped.

"No. If I droppped dead, you—"

"What's the matter?" He stood up swiftly and came toward her, frowning.

"Nothing! Just listen, won't you?" She glared at him.

"You're feeling okay?"

"Yes! Will you listen? Sit down *and just listen!*"

"Marcie, you would tell me if there was something wrong, wouldn't you?"

Something wrong? She stared at him as if he'd grown a second head. Something *wrong?* Where had he been? She took a deep, steadying breath and began again, "If I dropped dead, you'd have to find someone to stay with the kids. If we're to be divorced, there are problems we have to solve. I have to get my degree. In exchange for my tuition and sitter fees, housing and food, I could be your housekeeper. If you'd let us stay here, we could have the upstairs and you could sleep in the den and use the bathroom down here. That way we could survive financially, and I could get my degree in four years, going part time. I might even be able to do it in three."

There was a long silence as Thad leaned slowly back in his chair and simply stared at her. Finally he said, "You've been thinking about this for a long time."

"Only since you mentioned how you feel trapped, how you haven't gotten running around out of your system, how you don't want to be so settled down, how you wish we'd had an affair instead of getting married."

"Well, you certainly took up the idea quickly enough!"

She shrugged nervously and replied, "It seemed smarter to figure it out than to suddenly be out on the street in the snow, trying to think where to take my babies." The pitiful picture filled her mind again.

"You'd stay here," he growled.

"It's your house."

Very cross, he replied, "I put it in both of our names right away."

"You did?" She looked up at him, surprised. "Does Beatrice know?"

"I haven't made a point of mentioning it." He paused, then asked, "What does my mother have to do with this?"

"When we divide things up, you get the table. I'm going to keep your father, but you can have your mother back."

He watched her from under frowning brows. "You've put a lot of thought and planning into this."

She ignored him. "If we did stay here, what would happen if you remarried?"

"Hell!" he exclaimed in irritation. "If I wanted to be married, I'd keep you!"

"Would you?" It was a challenge—she was daring him to convince her—but he took it as a plea.

"Oh, Marcie..." He turned toward her helplessly, but she'd left the room, not seeing his expression.

To Marcie, the surface of their lives appeared unruffled, yet there was a distance between them. They spoke tersely but courteously, and they still shared the same bed, having no other. They discussed their children, they entertained, and they made love.

It was very strange to make such love, to feel the compatability of their bodies while their hearts and minds were estranged. It was all very unsettling.

Occasionally Thad introduced The Subject in sentences that began, "What would happen..." or "If..." So she knew he was still toying with the idea of getting a divorce. But he seemed to be watching her expectantly, waiting for her to say something. She sensed an almost palpable urging for her to speak, but she didn't know what more he wanted her to say.

As time went on, Marcie became impatient with the

limbo into which Thad had forced them. She felt restless
and irritable. And as she considered the possibility of a
split, she began to prepare for it, hoping to force Thad
to choose one way or the other.

She signed up for summer school and arranged for a
college student who was studying behavorial problems
in children to stay with Gina and Kelly. She hired her
on the condition that she allow the Foster children to
grow without the benefit of clinical guidance.

Cassie was a honey blonde with big blue eyes and a
nice figure; her appearance was at odds with her professional approach. Being a neighbor, she knew Gina and
Kelly and said they were really very dull, being normal,
but she'd take the job because she needed the money.

It was the first step toward a divorce.

The night Marcie hired Cassie, Thad made fierce and
urgent love to Marcie several times, but he didn't speak.
It was strange, probably because they didn't speak. They
hadn't chatted or teased through their lovemaking since
Thad had first brought up the subject of separation. And
the next morning Marcie again awoke in his arms, having
pushed him to the edge of the bed.

Several weeks later, in a desperate attempt to solve
the stalemate, Marcie made an appointment for them both
to see Nance. Thad went along warily. It was Marcie
who asked Nance how to go about such an involved
separation. Nance frowned at them and told them to seek
counseling.

Again Thad waited, as if expecting Marcie to speak,
and when she didn't, he said, "I doubt that would do any
good."

So she concluded Thad had chosen divorce over rec-
onciliation.

Nance said, "It will be sixty days before you can file
for divorce. Many people decide to get divorced impulsively, in an angry moment, and lots of them change
their minds. It's the law in Indiana that a couple can't

file until sixty days after meeting with their lawyer."

It was the second step.

After leaving Nance's office, Marcie steered them to a furniture store, where they bought a sofa bed for Thad to sleep on in the den. It was delivered two days later. Marcie hung his suits in the den closet and found a chest for his other clothes. The room looked tidy and comfortable.

When Thad came home from the office that evening, Marcie was in the kitchen as usual. The kids bounced around Thad, begging to be picked up and held. He stopped casually in the kitchen doorway and said, "Hi."

She replied with a smile, wondering if to him the smile looked weak? Strained? Nervous? Slight? Polite? She said, "The furniture store delivered the sofa this morning. I put your things down here."

A great stillness came over him. He didn't move. Then he said, "I see," and turned toward the den.

They were not comfortable together. Marcie thought they were extremely lucky to have children around to make it less awkward. Of course, if they hadn't had the kids, they'd have simply separated.

Thad waited until the kids were alseep before he opened the sleeper and inspected it. Marcie showed him which drawers held what and helped him to make up the bed.

"Want to help me become acclimated?" he asked. "You could sleep down here with me tonight."

"Better not." She avoided looking at him.

"We have fifty-eight days left."

"I don't think you'll change your mind."

"Perhaps not. But the privileges of our marriage continue until we file."

"I don't believe that's a good idea."

"But fun," he teased her, coaxing.

She looked up at him then, and he smiled beguilingly, but she shook her head and fled up the stairs. He stood in the doorway, and as she reached the top of the stairs, he called just loud enough for her to hear, "Coward."

She looked down at him but didn't reply.

It was the third step.

Marcie was very conscious of their separation, that Thad wouldn't be getting into bed with her. She put on one of his T-shirts and smoothed it gently down her body with sad hands. She slid into an old pair of underwear, braided her hair, and climbed into bed. And, silently, she wept.

Who would ever have believed their marriage would come to this? The tears wet her cheeks, and she began to get a headache. She got up, took two aspirin, and went back to bed, deliberately focusing her thoughts on the final exams coming up for her present class. Finally she fell asleep.

The next thing she knew, she had fallen out of bed. Searching for Thad, as usual, she wiggled clear across the big bed and fell off his side, crashing to the floor, hitting her temple, and making a hell of a racket on the bare floor with her knees and elbows. It hurt. She sat stunned, wanting to bawl alone there in the dark; then the hall light came on and Thad, naked as usual, ran up the stairs. He stopped at the kids' rooms before coming to her door.

"Marcie?" His expression of concern changed to one of amusement as understanding dawned. He went to her and squatted down, smoothed back her hair, and said, "So... you need me for a bumper pad." His voice was low and husky and very pleased.

She shook her head in denial and gulped down a sob.

"Hey," he exclaimed softly, "are you all right?" His gentle concern was her undoing.

"I hit my head and elbow and knee and my bottom."

"How'd you manage to do all that?"

"I forgot the pillows."

"Pillows?"

"When you're gone, I put pillows along your side."
Her breath caught. "It hurts."

"Poor baby . . ." He reached out to comfort her.

She scrambled backward, away from him, leaving him
squatting on his heels, his back to the hall light, his naked
flesh backlighted, his face and the front of his body in
shadow. He looked supremely primitive, dangerously
male — and thrilling.

As she stood up, her breasts lifted under the thin shirt,
her lips parted, and her eyes became enormous. Since
she faced the light, he could see her. The tears had clotted
her eyelashes and were smeared over her cheeks. She
took a jerky, weepy breath, and he rose effortlessly and
peered into her face, his big hands coming up to grasp
her shoulders.

She said, "No," but the sound was very faint and easy
to ignore. She backed away; he followed. "Thad . . ."
She was still backing slowly away.

"Shhh . . ." He moved quietly, almost as if he were
stalking her. His back still to the light, his face in shadow,
he looked a little frightening.

"Thad . . ." She came up against the wall and held out
her hands to stop him, but he simply trapped them between their bodies.

Miserable, she shook her head. "Thad . . ."

He kissed her soft mouth, pushing her head up and
back, drinking thrilling sensations from her lips as his
hands moved on her. She squirmed, trying to get away,
but her movements only excited him further.

He reached for the bottom of her T-shirt and stepped
back just enough to tug it over her head, moving her
elbows and hands to force her to release the cloth and
allow him his way. As they tussled briefly over her panties, her breasts swung against him, and he pushed her
against the wall, holding her captive.

It was extremely exciting for him. For her, too. They *had* decided to part. It was a firm decision, but it didn't count for much. Not that night.

Even wanting him, she was determined not to allow him to take her. She struggled and strained and pushed and turned...and he did as he chose. Sensually, he rubbed his hot hands and body wherever he wanted, and he kissed her however he wanted. He followed her down the wall, squatting over her as she writhed, and he lifted her, turning her, tasting her with his mouth until her resistance took on the movements of an erotic dance, which he followed.

She was breathing unsteadily. He kissed her long and thoroughly. She gasped and submitted. Then he sat back on his heels, his elbows on his knees, his hands hanging loosely between his widely spread knees. His own breathing had grown harsh.

He rose to his feet in a single, fluid movement, then reached down and helped her to stand. He led her across the room, guiding her faltering steps. When she would have gone to the bed, he moved her around it. She followed in dazed obedience until they reached the door. There she halted. "Thad?"

He bent, lifted her nude body into his arms, and carried her across the hall and down the stairs. She didn't struggle. She put her arms around his shoulders and clung to him. He entered the den, placed a knee on the open sofa bed and lay her in the middle of it.

He moved beside her, pulled the covers over them, and with leisurely relish he began to make long, erotic love to her. Eventually he took her, and it was thrilling. Was it exciting because now it was somehow forbidden? She slept as if drugged.

He wakened her in the morning, holding her clamped against him, his hands on her, his expression intense, and his eyes brooding. She was sure he wouldn't want her again and began to leave the bed, but he pulled her back and began to make almost harsh love to her.

Lying under him, not moving, she said crossly, "You haven't been this greedy in a long time."

"You're still mine for fifty...seven more days."

"I am not!"

"For fifty-seven more nights."

"No."

He lay still on her, not moving. "Yes."

"If you plan fifty-seven nights like last night, it'll kill you."

"Then you'll be a widow."

She was impatient. "This is ridiculous."

There was a pause as he moved slightly on her then, sounding sentimental, he said, "Yours is going to be a tough act to follow."

"You're going out looking?"

"Naturally."

"Oh, yes," she said as if she'd only just remembered, "the running around." Brightly she added, "That's an idea!"

He rose up on his elbows and stared down at her. "What do you mean by that?"

"Oh...nothing." She shrugged.

"Marcia!"

"Thaddeus!"

"You behave yourself!" he commanded.

"I'll follow your lead," she promised, with some malice.

"What do you mean, my lead?"

"Since you seem to want freedom so much," she replied, "perhaps I'd be missing something not to experience the same thing."

"Why, you little—"

"And what are you?" she retorted.

"Your husband!"

"Only fifty-seven days," she reminded him.

"And nights." He held her and started moving on her.

She pretended to yawn and looked around for the clock. There wasn't one in sight. She reached for a book on the end table she'd placed by the side of the sofa, but he tore it from her hands and threw it across the room before kissing her deeply, his hands rough. A wild passion built in him, and he very deliberately built an answering one in her. She was moaning and her hands were moving on his shoulders and back when he demanded, "What do you want?"

"More."

"More what?"

She opened her eyes, and they regarded each other antagonistically. "I want you."

"You get me . . . for fifty-seven more nights."

And he took her on a wild, turbulent ride to a release that was not satisfying.

THREE DAYS LATER Marcie bought a gray shawl. She took it to Nance's office. Nance couldn't understand why she'd bought it.

"It was seventy-five percent off," Marcie explained listlessly. The shock of the impending divorce was wearing off, and the pain was beginning. She was just starting to realize that she might actually lose Thad.

"I can see why they cut the price. That shawl is gloomy."

"Yes," Marcie said glumly, "I think it's just right."

"You'll never wear it. Mark my words." Nance quickly tidied stacks of papers on her desk.

"Want to have lunch at the market?"

"Okay," Nance replied, "but how about a quick swim

at the club first? I've been in court all morning, and I'm
wound up."

"I didn't bring a suit."

"I have an extra in my locker. We're nearly the same
size. Okay?"

"All right," Marcie agreed without enthusiasm.

Nance caught up her purse. "How'd your final go?"

"I aced it."

"Brilliant."

As they left the office, Marcie added, "I signed up
for summer school."

Nance gave her a casually penetrating glance. "Oh?"

"I found a sitter for the kids. She's a psychology major
studying the behavior of disturbed children. Hiring her
is the first step toward a divorce."

"That still on?" Nance frowned.

"Oh, yes." They left the building.

"You should go for counseling," Nance said firmly.

"Thad won't. He says we don't need it."

"Then you go alone," Nance urged as they headed
toward the club.

"Oh, Nance, if he doesn't want to be married, it'd be
wrong to try to make him stay. I wouldn't want him
under those circumstances."

"This whole thing is total idiocy."

"We were very young," Marcie explained.

"That's no excuse. If you do file, how are you going
to handle telling your family and friends?"

"Quietly?"

"It's going to be awkward," Nance warned. "Divorced
but still living together."

"Not living together. It's called sharing a house."

"It will be more awkward than a usual divorce."

"Maybe, but at least I won't have to deal with Beatrice
anymore."

"I'm not sure she means to be so possessive," Nance

ventured thoughtfully. She opened the door, and they entered the club.

"Well, I no longer have to struggle to adjust to her whims or slights. I'm sure Thad's next wife will be someone she approves of."

"Has she been that awful?"

"Yes," Marcie confirmed. "Only Thad's handling of her made her tolerable."

"That ought to tell you something."

"That he's fair," Marcie agreed.

"Idiocy . . ."

Once in the women's locker room, Marcie started to undress while Nance fiddled with the combination lock, then flipped open her locker. She turned back to Marcie with the extra suit in her hands and gasped at the sight of the purple bruises on Marcie's winter-white body.

Thinking a man must have wandered into the locker room, Marcie spun around, then looked questioningly at Nance, whose face was a mask of grim anger. "Did Thad do that to you?" she asked rigidly.

"What? Oh, no. I fell out of bed!"

"Of course." Clearly Nance didn't believe her.

Marcie laughed. "Really, Nance. Honest! We bought a sofa bed for the den, and Thad's been sleeping downstairs. I usually put pillows along his side when he's not there, because I always crowd him in bed, but this time I forgot and fell off. I honestly did. Aren't they beautiful colors?"

"Has he ever harmed you?"

"Oh, no! Not Thad. He's very sweet."

Convinced at last, Nance shook her head. "Idiocy."

"Do you always discourage your clients this way?"

"Only the idiots."

At the pool they separated to swim laps, then dressed and pulled their hair into damp buns before walking to the brick market building. They strolled down the aisles, selecting goodies from the wide variety of booths. They shared a slice of quiche, ate sausages hot off the grill, crunched on apples, and enjoyed hot, fresh-baked and sugared doughnuts for dessert. They bought sacks of fresh vegetables and homemade bread and rolls to take home.

As they headed away from the market, Nance asked, "Where are you going now?"

"I'm meeting Betty at Lisa's gallery. She's giving a lesson in tie-making."

"A tie for Thad?" Nance asked.

"No. I decided to make one for my dad for Christmas."

As they parted, Nance said, "Let me hear how it goes." They both knew she wasn't talking about ties.

"I will, Nance, and thanks. The swim and the visit were great. Just what I needed."

"Can I mention counseling again?"

"No."

"Then I won't." They exchanged a fond look and parted.

Marcie was late getting home. Thad was already there. He had paid the sitter and sent her home. The two kids were sparkly-eyed and laughing and wouldn't hold still. As Marcie put away her purchases, she found a pizza all made and ready to be heated for supper. She eyed the kids as she asked, "Okay, you wiggling little bunnies, what's the joke?"

They squirmed in her arms and cried, "Now, Daddy?"

Thad was waiting at the stairs with one elbow on the curving banister. Gina and Kelly bounced into the entrance hall and clutched his knees and hands and coaxed, *"Now?"*

Thad glanced at Marcie, then down at his children, and said, "Yes."

"Come upstairs!" they shouted. "Now! Wait till you

see what Daddy got you. *Hurry!*" And they giggled.

Marcie turned puzzled eyes to Thad, but he kept his face expressionless.

"What is it?" she asked, but the kids just shrieked and urged her upstairs. She went, drawn impatiently, turning to see that Thad was following.

They tugged her into her room, and there on the bed was an enormous stuffed tiger.

The kids flew to the bed and struggled up onto it and fell over the tiger and laughed and babbled and shrieked and questioned, but for a minute Marcie could only stare. The tiger was beautiful. It lay on its stomach, its head turned toward the door, its fake eyes alert and watchful.

She glanced back at Thad, who was leaning in the doorway. Watching her, he explained briefly, "A bumper pad."

He almost made her cry. Quickly she turned back to the bed. It would no longer be Thad in her bed but a toy tiger. A stuffed tiger was a depressing substitute.

Thad was silent, still watching her. She struggled to control her emotions.

Gina was attempting to tie a knot in its tail, and Kelly had fetched his magnifying glass and was examining the tiger's eyes. Marcie stopped Gina, protesting that it was *her* tiger.

"When *I'm* twenty-three, *I'll* have a tiger, too!" Gina told her mother. Marcie pitied the tiger as Gina flung herself on top of it and laughed. Kelly was looking in its ear.

"Do you like it?" Gina demanded.

"It's beautiful," Marcie replied.

"You'd better kiss Daddy or he might take it back," Gina advised.

And suddenly Thad was right next to her shoulder. When had he moved?

Marcie turned and stretched to kiss his cheek, but he

shifted his mouth to meet hers. Excitement flared inside her. His mouth unexpectedly touching hers still did that to her.

"You didn't hug his neck," Gina criticized.

But Marcie distracted her by saying, "We need to go heat the pizza."

"Pizza!" Kelly was energized.

"Do we get Cokes?" Gina wheedled. "To celebrate the new tiger?"

When they were sitting at the large table chewing pizza, Gina swallowed, licked her lips, and said loudly, "I know why Daddy's sleeping in the den on that new bed that opens out that way."

"When did you see that?" Thad asked.

"I had a bad dream, and I couldn't find you." She made her eyes sad and dramatic. "So I . . . searched." She nodded over finding the right word. "And you were sleeping down here." She pointed toward the den.

"Why didn't you say something to me?" he asked.

Gina shrugged elaborately and told him, "I got in bed and you cuddled me and never did wake up." She bit off another bite and chewed it busily. After she'd swallowed, she repeated, "I know why you sleep down here."

Marcie and Thad exchanged fleeting glances. Did the kids know about their plans? Cautiously Marcie asked, "Why?"

"Because you always push Daddy over, and he never gets to sleep. He spends the whole night hanging on the side of the bed."

Thad laughed, but Marcie asked, "Who told you that?"

"I heard him complain," Gina replied.

"I see." Marcie avoided Thad's eyes.

"And"—Gina shrugged and raised tiny, silken brows in an adult way—"I watched and I saw you do it."

"When?" In spite of herself, Marcie exchanged a look with her amused husband.

"Lots of times." Gina examined the last bite of her

pizza. "And once I saw him working and fighting, trying to get you to move over. He was on top of you and making noises." She regarded her mother with censure. "You should give him more room so he doesn't have to be on top of you!"

Marcie blushed furiously and thought she detected a bit of Beatrice in her child.

"Once I saw *her* on top of him," Kelly informed Gina. He pointed to his mother and father.

Thad looked serious and added, "Often."

Gina sighed. "Poor Daddy."

"I really don't mind." Amusement threaded his words.

His daughter considered him seriously. "You're very kind."

Thad nodded and sent Marcie an eloquent glance, but she only blushed and lowered her eyes to her plate.

"Poor tiger," Gina said sadly.

Thad couldn't resist. "Why is it a poor tiger?"

"Mommy will push against him just like she did you."

"I suppose so," Thad replied. "Poor tiger."

"I wouldn't mind having a tiger, too," Gina decided.

"Me, too," Kelly said with his mouth full.

"Don't speak with your mouth full," Marcie automatically chided.

"Muuump uh."

"I don't see why Mommy gets a tiger," Gina continued, "and I'm only a little girl, and *I* don't have one."

"How about a bear?" Thad suggested.

"I'd have to see it first." Gina turned cautious. "There was a big one on TV that growled and showed its teeth."

"I want a big, big lion," Kelly decided.

"*You're* not old enough," Gina directed. "You have to be twenty-three."

"What about the bear?" her daddy asked.

"Well, a bear is all right when you're four." She gave him a direct, communicating look.

"I see." He watched her for a minute as he chewed.

"What about the teddy bear you have now?"

"No." She shook her head so that her hair fanned out and hit her cheeks. "Teddy isn't nearly big enough."

"Your mommy had to wait until she was twenty-three," Thad reminded his daughter.

"But before that she had you," Gina countered. "And Kelly and me sleep in our rooms all alone by ourselves."

"Yes, you're very brave about that," Thad reminded her.

"Well, yes. But if Mommy doesn't have to sleep alone, and she gets a tiger, maybe we should, too."

"You could ask Santa," Thad suggested.

Gina sighed. "That's a long, long, long, long way away."

Kelly nodded, still chewing.

The subject changed, and the kids forgot about that campaign, or at least they didn't bring it up again.

In the middle of the night, naked in the reflected light of the full moon, mounting the dark steps two at a time with sinuous ease, Thad went to Marcie's door and looked in on her. The tiger's eyes caught the light and seemed oddly real, protecting the woman whose dark hair spilled under the tiger's chin and whose arm and leg were flung over the stuffed body, crowding it.

Newly mindful of prying children's eyes, Thad silently closed the bedroom door almost all the way and placed the covered-brick doorstop to hold it there. He went to the side of the bed and looked down on his wife...of fifty-four more nights. He eased the stuffed animal out from under her arm and leg and set it on the floor. Then he lay down in the tiger's place, breathing stealthily through parted lips, his heard thudding in his chest. His eyes glinted in the dim light.

It didn't take long. Marcie sighed in her sleep, turned her head, and moved toward him. Her groping hand found his shoulder, and she inched over automatically.

He made it easy, raising one arm so that his shoulder formed a natural harbor for her head, which slid into place with practiced ease. His other hand covered her breast.

She breathed sensuously against his throat and wiggled in contentment, nuzzling closer. Her hand went over his chest, petting it, and he knew exactly when she wakened.

She raised her head to orient herself, and he heard the sharp intake of her breath. He made an amused rumble of contentment in his chest just before he kissed her.

6

THE RADIO WAS playing a cheerful tune when Marcie felt the bed bounce as Gina and Kelly jumped in. Gina laughed. "Did you fall out of bed last night? Did the tiger save you?"

Marcie realized that the bulk in back of her wasn't Thad after all. It was the other tiger. When had he replaced it? Or had he? Had it been only a vivid, erotic dream that he had come to her?

She moved sleepily and realized she was naked. No stuffed tiger had ripped off her T-shirt and panties. She yawned and stretched.

"Daddy didn't even have any breakfast," Gina informed her.

"He didn't?"

"No. He just blew us a kiss and ran down the stairs."

He'd run down the stairs. So he hadn't left her in the middle of the night. And even though he'd been late, he'd taken the time to replace the tiger so she wouldn't fall out of bed. She smiled, pleased, but after that hopeful beginning, the day went downhill.

Phyl came early, before they finished breakfast. Marcie and the kids were still in robes. Marcie said, "You didn't make the tie class. There was a mob."

"So you went?

"Yes. I made a tie."

"Was it difficult?"

"Not the way Betty teaches."

"Can I see it?"

Marcie went upstairs to her room and searched for the tie, but she couldn't find it. Puzzled, she tried to remember where she'd put it. Finally she decided she'd left it at the gallery.

She glanced at the clock and, seeing how late it was getting, pulled on jeans and a shirt, wiggled her toes into loafers, and hurried back downstairs. Phyl was just emerging from the den with the kids. "I didn't know you bought a sleep sofa." Her smile was inscrutable.

How was Marcie to reply? "Yeah."

"It appears to be . . . very comfortable."

"We like it. I can't find the tie. I must have left it at the gallery." Wanting to get rid of Phyl, she added, "Cassie is due here in forty-five minutes. I've signed up for summer school."

"How silly," Phyl said. "You grimly keep going to school. When will you ever use an education?"

"One never knows." Marcie held open the front door. "'Bye for now."

Marcie was taking only one course, but since a semester's work was concentrated into so short a time, she had classes all day Monday, afternoons on Tuesday and Wednesday, and all day Saturday.

Damn. She hated being away so much, especially in the summer, but, she told herself, she could handle anything for a limited time.

On the first day of class she bought the books she'd need and stopped by the computer room to dally with her beloved machines, then drove home. Beatrice was there, her mouth pinched, and a rebellious Gina stood in the doorway watching her mother with a mutinous glare.

"Hi, darling." Marcie smiled at her daughter and greeted her mother-in-law with weary forebearance.

"I told her she could not get up on the table," Beatrice said.

"Why were you up there?" Marcie asked the child.

"I had to see if there were any more ladies and goat-men," Gina replied reasonably.

Marcie nodded.

"I *told* her ladies never get on tables," Beatrice snapped.

"She wasn't dancing, she was looking," Marcie explained.

"Mar-she-ah, you really shock me. Your mother should have raised you better."

"Better?" she said with quiet anger. "She did a superb job. I've been corrupted by your son these last five years."

"This is *no* time to be frivolous, Mar-she-ah!"

Ignoring her, Marcie turned to Gina. "Did you find any ladies and goat-men?"

Gina shook her head.

"Then you won't have to get up on the table anymore, will you."

Gina grinned.

"Run along, darling." Marcie let her go.

Her mother-in-law huffed and accused, "You did not scold her!"

"There's no need," Marcie replied with great patience.

"*I* bought that table! I cannot approve of the manner in which you care for it."

"Then take it back," Marcie replied calmly.

"Why, Marcia!" Beatrice exclaimed, shocked.

"Yes, Mother Foster?"

They stared at each other in the silliest manner. Then Beatrice folded her gloved hands under her ample chest and announced in lofty tones, "I shall have to speak to Thaddeus about this."

"Do that."

The older woman marched to the front door and slammed it shut behind her.

Marcie felt nothing at all except relief that she was gone. The woman needed more to do, more to think about. She was a pain. It was almost worth losing Thad in order to get rid of Beatrice.

When Thad came home after work, Marcie was in the kitchen organizing supper. The tea cart was loaded and ready, and the kids began bounding around in their usual frisky, noisy, welcome home Daddy way.

"Mother called," Thad informed her.

"Did she?" Marcie asked in a flat voice.

"She was crying."

"Naturally," she agreed.

"What the hell went on?"

Marcie sighed. "I can only testify to what I witnessed."

"Run it by me—reasonably fast and condensed as much as possible but still coherent."

Marcie did.

"That's all?" Thad frowned.

"All," she promised.

"She said you told her to take the table back," Thad said.

"She didn't approve of the way I was caring for it, so I figured she must cherish it. I don't."

"Could you have been a bit kinder?" he chided.

"Could she?"

"Impasse." He eyed her. "I had to listen to three minutes and forty-seven seconds of how fortunate we are that she found that table."

"How patient of you," she commented with asperity.

"You're sassy today," he observed with some amusement.

She slammed several pots around with more force than was necessary.

After a moment he said, "Russ came by the office with the tie you made for me. You'd left it at the gallery."

She whirled around to face him. He was wearing her father's Christmas tie, and he thought she'd made it for him!

Fingering it and looking down at it on his chest, seeming very pleased, he said, "It's beautiful."

"I'm ... glad you like it." What else could she say?

"I could become used to handmade ties," he suggested huskily.

She didn't say anything. What was he doing to her?

Finally he asked slyly, "How did you like the tiger?"

"Which one?" she retorted.

And he laughed.

Later on, when they were clearing the table and stacking the dishes in the dishwasher, he asked, "Why did you tell Mother I'd ruined you?"

"Corrupted," she corrected.

"Oh." He raised his eyebrows and pulled down his mouth as he digested the new word. "I can understand *corrupted*. *Ruined* puzzled me." He waited, then added, "Why corrupted?"

"She said my mother should have done a better job raising me, and I replied that Mother had done a superb job, but that in the last five years Beatrice Foster's little boy, Thaddeus, had corrupted my mother's good work."

"Ahhh. That must have rankled."

"Apparently."

Curiosity forced him to ask, "Did you actually say,

"Beatrice Foster's little boy, Thaddeus?'"

"No. But since she altered words for you, I felt free to embellish my own."

He smiled. "There are times," he said, "when I'm tempted to keep you."

She didn't look up or reply.

"When we're divorced, will you go out with me now and then?"

"No."

"No?" He sounded surprised.

"No."

"Why not?" He was a little annoyed.

"Why beat a dead horse?"

"You equate me with a...dead horse?" He wasn't sure whether to be offended or amazed.

"The marriage."

He frowned. "You feel it's dead?"

"You convinced me."

"You still...respond well enough," he pointed out slyly.

"That's finished." She turned to face him. "I mean it. No more. No more sneaking up the stairs, no more dragging me down them, no more hanky-panky at all."

"We'll see," he said smugly.

"Try it and I move out."

"How would you go to school if you moved out?"

"I'd borrow the money," she snapped.

"No."

"Then keep away from me," she warned. "Starting now."

"You're not starting anything; you're talking about finishing."

"Starting my new life without you."

"Without...?" He gestured to indicate that they'd be sharing the house.

"Without you in my bed or me in yours. We're not playing around."

Just then Phyl walked in. "Hi, you two. What's up?" Her green eyes were eager, and a sly smile curved her lips. How much had she heard? Marcie wondered.

Thad looked at Phyl and asked, "Doorbell not working?" He strode past her into the hall where he called to the kids to bathe.

"Did you want something, Phyl?" Marcie asked.

"Just wandering around." She set her rump on the hip-high stool and flipped back her long hair.

But Marcie was fresh out of patience. "It's been a long day. I'm sure you'll excuse us."

"Oh." Phyl's eyes widened in surprise. She scooted back off the stool, smiled, said, "See you," and left with an airy wave.

Once classes started, it seemed to Marcie that she had hopped onto a treadmill that was already running but wasn't geared to her stride. She was hectically busy. She loved the classes, excelled in the work and gloried in the computers. But the housework and laundry piled up, and she had to struggle to find enough time to study. Each day when she came home, the kids were lined up with scores to be settled.

Cassie shrugged. "It's perfectly natural. Sibling rivalry."

"Why can't you solve these disputes?" Marcie complained.

"I have," Cassie said tolerantly. "You're the Court of Appeals."

Sourly Marcie exclaimed, "Goody."

"Motherhood is fulfilling."

"How would you know?"

"The book says so." Cassie grinned.

She had put a casserole in the oven for supper. She'd also sliced strawberries and tossed a salad, and the kids had set the table.

"You didn't have to do all that, Cassie, but it's lovely

to come home and have it done."

"It gave the kids and me something to do, and it was a constructive learning experience."

Marcie flinched at Cassie's use of jargon and Cassie grinned again, then told the kids, "See you brats tomorrow."

"Bye-eee."

"Bye, Cassie!"

"Professor Younger," Cassie corrected, but that made them giggle.

At supper Thad asked Marcie how her day had gone, and she bubbled over with enthusiasm. He shook his head in amazement. "I'd never have taken you for a career woman."

The kids had finished eating and been excused from the table. "You never asked me what I wanted," she said, regarding him seriously, giving him an opportunity to ask more.

He smiled. "All I could think of was how to get you into bed."

The moment passed, she looked down at her plate. "You made that obvious."

"It would have been much better if we'd simply had an affair."

"You may not remember this," Marcie said, "but the offspring were not on the appointment book."

"I know." He sighed.

"So an affair wouldn't have changed anything. What would you have done about a pregnant Marcie?"

"There's that to consider," he agreed.

"You'd have taken off for the hills," she accused.

"No!" he protested indignantly. "I would have married you."

"You did," she reminded him.

"Maybe if we hadn't been married, we'd have been more careful," he speculated.

"I'm glad they're here."

He shook his head. "It isn't convenient."

"Children never are," she told him.

"Never?"

"Never."

"How do you know? Some of them have to be. That's only logical."

"Cassie said so."

"How the hell would *she* know?"

"It's in the book."

"Good Lord."

After they got the kids to bed, Thad said he felt restless and was going for a walk.

From the darkened landing, Marcie watched his marvelous male form as he moved down the street. He paused. A woman's figure joined his. They apparently spoke, then turned and walked away slowly together. The woman was Phyl.

MARCIE'S BIRTHDAY WAS June second, and she was twenty-four. "And next year you'll be a quarter of a century!" her father said, laughing over the phone.

"I'm ready for it."

He chuckled. "Feeling aged?"

Marcie sighed. "I've lived enough to be older than that."

"One of these days, you'll finish school," he promised. "The kids will be in school, and you can coast, become a lady of leisure."

He meant to comfort her, but she thought: Yeah, she'd be a divorced, working mother juggling two kids. Her stomach clenched, and a chill went down her spine.

Her mother said Marcie must have been adopted because she wasn't old enough to have a child that age.

She wasn't old enough, her mother declared — ignoring Marcie's older siblings — to even remember back twenty-four years, much less have a child that age.

Beatrice gave Marcie a beautiful Spanish shawl made of fragile black lace with a long fringe that almost touched the floor in the back. It was new! Marcie decided it was a good thing she had the gray woolen shawl because the black lace held around her head in the snow would look seductive, not pitiful.

Harold Foster gave his daughter-in-law a check for five hundred dollars. That was stunning. She studied his face intently, but he only smiled and winked. Then he got down on his hands and knees to investigate the elaborate caves made from empty appliance boxes that Cassie and the kids had constructed in the second, still-empty living room.

Thad gave Marcie a computer with lots of extra features and a disc drive. She cried and said it was too expensive. Thad told her he'd been saving for some time in order to buy her a personal computer.

The kids gave her cake-smeared kisses, bunches of yard flowers with stems of widely assorted lenghts, and a video game cassette. "Who bought the game cassette?" she asked with interest.

"I can't remember," Thad replied thoughtfully, as if straining to recall. "I believe I must have. I'm sure I must have. I don't think the kids realized I'm hooked on this game." And he grinned at her, very amused.

A light dawned. "So that's where you spend your evenings — at the arcade."

"It beats bar hopping." His eyes seemed to burn into her.

He'd been out most nights since she'd started summer school. He'd help get the kids into bed, and then, while she studied, he was off to racquet-ball or Spanish lessons or just out. He went every night. He'd stretch and say he thought he'd be in early, then he'd look at her and wait, as if expecting her to ask him where he was going, but she never did.

Instead, she wondered. She agonized over it. And a painful, hideous emotion twisted through her, making her groan and gasp, but she refused to name it.

Marcie found an old, scarred conference table with one broken leg, sanded it and replaced the leg, and set it up in one of the empty bedrooms upstairs. The room had been rapidly collecting odds and ends that no one wanted to make a decision about, so she did that, pitching ninety-eight percent of it. Using her birthday check, she bought another disc drive for her computer, a good comfortable chair, and she was in business, writing programs and feeding in information. Soon she was lost in another world. To her, it was fascinating.

Since Thad had made no move to alter the progress of the divorce, Marcie asked him one evening after the kids were in bed, "When should we tell our families?"

He scrutinized her and didn't reply.

Impatiently, she said, "Shall we wait until just before we file? That should save some of the hassle."

"All right," he agreed solemnly.

Marcie knew he would be divorcing only her. He liked the kids and didn't mind at all that they'd be sharing the same house. He didn't want to be separated from them; he just didn't want to be married to her. She stared in the mirror at her sad face and nice body. He wanted to be free of her.

"Are you . . . seeing anyone?" she blurted out one night as she waited for him to leave.

"Why?" he asked quickly.

"Well, one of my schoolmates has asked me for a date." It was true, but she'd said she was married.

Thad scowled. "Who?"

"Just someone I met on campus."

"What did you tell him?"

"That I had a class on Saturday."

He frowned thoughtfully, watching her, but he didn't say anything.

"*Are* you seeing anyone?" she repeated.

"No."

"I thought you wanted to . . . run around."

"We haven't filed yet," he reminded her, as if he needed to.

"Lots of people see other people while they're still technically married to other people."

"I know," he replied. "But that's not the way I do things."

"Who do you have lined up . . . waiting?" Why couldn't she shut up?

"No one in particular." He rocked casually on his feet, eyeing her.

"Would you tell me if you did?"

"Why?"

"Is it . . . Phyl?"

His head snapped up. "Phyl?" His voice rose in disbelief.

"Is it?"

"Why Phyl?" He lifted his head and studied her from under half-lowered lids.

"I've only recently realized that she's been hanging around just to attract your attention."

"You never realized that before?" he asked, surprised again.

That surprised *her*. "You did?"

"She was fairly obvious."

"Are you attracted to her?"

"Why do you ask?" His lashes screened his eyes.

She blushed. What business was it of hers anyway? "I . . . well . . . I would hate for her to ever have anything to do with my babies."

"They're mine, too," he reminded her.

"I know, but..."

"Would I have any say in what happened to the kids if you remarried? Would you marry another man?" He studied her intently.

She shook her head.

"You wouldn't?"

Keeping her head down, she bit her lip and shrugged. She didn't see his slight smile.

"Promise me..." he began.

"What?"

"That we have dinner together the day our divorce becomes final. Just us."

His request amazed her. "To celebrate?"

"Dinner," he repeated.

She hesitated. Should she? She wasn't sure she could handle something like that. But she said, "All right."

He smiled, pleased, and asked, "Want to fool around?"

She raised bleak, hostile eyes to him. "No."

He reached out and cupped her chin in his hand, but she pulled away from him. Softly, silkily, he teased, "I can prove you're lying, and anyway, we ought to have one for the road..."

She turned and went up the stairs, and he laughed low and deep. She knew he was standing there watching her, but she didn't look back. That's all she'd ever been to him: a bedmate. Even now he wanted "one for the road." No sentiment or love involved, only another "one."

She also knew he'd given her no information at all. He had answered none of her questions. She knew nothing more about the women he might be seeing.

Wherever it was he went, his nightly forays didn't seem to cheer him. Marcie realized she hadn't heard him whistle in a long, long time. He had a true whistle. He also had a good, piercing whistle. He wasn't using either at home. Where would he be whistling tonight? Where was her wandering boy going tonight? With whom? But she avoided speculating.

To their closest friends Thad and Marcie said their marriage wasn't going smoothly. No one took them seriously. A tiff, they surmised. Everyone had them.

Being a coward, or simply not wanting the hassle, Marcie told Thad he could be the one to tell his parents about the divorce. Beatrice would immediately assume it was Marcie's fault, and she'd probably be secretly pleased.

Marcie took the two kids and went to see her parents on a Thursday and returned on Friday afternoon. Her parents reacted to the news of the impending divorce just like everyone else. They assumed that Marcie and Thad's problem arose from a brief quarrel that would resolve itself. However, they did ask if Thad had abused her or the kids—and received a shocked, indignant denial. They said they were very fond of Thad, listed all his good qualities, and expressed the hope it would all work out. They didn't believe Marcie when she said her marriage was beyond repair.

Marcie's birthday marked the beginning of a parade of special occasions. Gina's fifth birthday was next. Two days after that came Kelly's fourth. And after that, Marcie and Thad's sixth wedding anniversary.

How does one handle a wedding anniversary two days before filing for divorce? Checking their appointment book, Marcie noted that the anniversary fell on the evening of the Midsummer Night's Festival. They had promised to go with several other couples. Maybe they could just ignore the anniversary. How awkward.

Marcie had attended several Midsummer Night's Festivals. They were put on by the Cathedral Arts Foundation and sponsored by the Episcopal Church, which was located on the Circle in downtown Indianapolis.

The purpose of the foundation was to bring the arts

downtown. The foundation supported mens' and boys' choruses, the Christmas carolers on the Circle, and the ice-skating rink. Its newest project was an international violin competition, to be held every four years in September.

The festival was very popular and, since Thad was a native of Indy, he recognized a great many people as he and Marcie strolled down the streets, side by side.

Once, as a surge of people pressed them together, Thad's arms went around her protectively, and he kissed her. "Happy anniversary, darling," he murmured.

How ironic. "Happy?" she asked.

"Live for the day." He grinned into her solemn face and pressed her head against his chest; and she stood there, listening to his heartbeat and waiting for a path to clear in the crowd. Two days. He was right. Why not live for this day, this night? She slid her arms around his waist and clasped her hands behind his back. He kissed her as one hand slid around her ribs, his wrist briefly caressing her breast before sliding down her side to her hip.

Both of them seemed to forget about tomorrow and the day after. Soon they were acting as casually intense as a couple on a date. They exchanged comments, looks, touches, and laughter.

They strolled along, sharing bites of food, calling out to passersby, waving, stopping to chat, moving on, staying separate from the others until it was time to meet their friends.

It was after one A.M. when they finally returned home. Thad walked the sitter the three houses down to her house and returned as Marcie was about to go up to bed.

"I have a bottle of champagne." He took her arm and tugged her into the kitchen. He opened the refrigerator, took out the bottle, and grinned at her.

"What are we drinking to?" Marcie asked, her expression guarded.

"Another day?" He gave her a penetrating look.

"Yes." One more day. She went into the dining room to the sideboard where she kept five champagne glasses. She took two back to the kitchen and watched as Thad popped the cork. She felt a little disoriented standing in their kitchen drinking to the end of their marriage on its anniversary. Or were they drinking to their divorce?

He poured the champagne. They raised their glasses and toasted each other silently. What could they possibly say? Then he picked up the bottle and indicated that she should follow him into the den. The Tiger's Den.

She could stop it now. She could get up and say good night, and go up to the other tiger and go to sleep. But she didn't. She sat on the innocent-looking sofa, which so easily opened into his bed, and she sipped the champagne and glanced at the man who was still her husband, this attractive stranger whom she no longer knew. Her heart fluttered. She felt like a fly caught in a spider's web.

He told her about a trip he'd made one summer with some friends to the quarry by Bloomington to swim. It was probably a funny story, and he must have told it well, but she was only half listening as she anticipated its finish, when Thad would begin seducing her.

What an odd situation. It was as if they had just met and were irresistibly attracted but awkward together, as if they didn't know quite how to conduct themselves.

Thad was plying her with champagne. She could tell he thought he was being subtle. He kept topping her glass while barely sipping his. He would add a drop in his nearly full glass, but he replaced every sip she took.

It amused her. She pretended not to be aware of what he was doing and refrained from looking at him.

He probably had it all plotted out. He would open up that sofa and—guess what? She slid out of her shoes and took off her jacket. He assisted her with alacrity. His hand brushed across her breast.

As if not thinking, she pulled out the pins in her hair and let it tumble down her back. She combed her fingers leisurely through it. With slow, sensuous movements, she played with her hair, idly drawing a handful across her mouth, twisting it around her fingers, pushing it aside, gathering it in back of her head, then leaning forward to pick up her replenished glass, allowing the silken mass to slither forward again.

Thad's eyes burned on her, and tiny flares of excitement shot from her stomach to her breasts. She leaned back against the sofa and waited for his next move. He didn't make one. Instead, he got up and yawned. The sight of his powerful body sent thrills licking through her.

"Good Lord!" he exclaimed. "Look at the time. Up, woman, get to bed." He tugged her to her feet, swatted her bottom, and pushed her out of the room. In shock, she stumbled toward the stairs.

"Wait!" he called. She turned, expecting him to grab her, but he handed her the discarded shoes and jacket. He grinned. "See you." And he turned away, loosening his tie. He was dismissing her!

Numb, she turned and, with stern control, climbed the stairs, her back stiff. She was determined not to cry. She scrubbed her teeth with unnecessary force, washed her face with savage vigor, and returned naked to her room in search of a clean T-shirt and panties.

"What are you doing?"

She whipped around, her hair flying, and there he was—gorgeously naked, and holding two filled glasses of champagne. She gasped.

"Don't put on that damned T-shirt," he ordered.

It fell from her nerveless fingers to become a cloth puddle on the bare wooden floor.

"Get in bed." He nodded to indicate the bed . . . as if there were more than one. "We're having one for the road," he explained.

"I—"

"It's already one forty-five A.M. We've wasted most of the night, you know."

"But—"

"If I have to put these glasses down in order to convince you, the first time is going to be wild."

She got into bed. First time? Flares and skyrockets and prickles and thrills surged inside her.

He sat down on the edge of the bed and looked over at the tiger, who was turned discreetly away, watching the door. Thad grinned down at her. "Are you going to give me any trouble?"

She shook her head solemnly no.

"Just as well. I'm spoiling for a good tussle."

In a wink she had jumped over the tiger and was running for the door. Since he had to put down the glasses, she got all the way down to the entrance hall before he caught her. He laughed as she struggled. "You never have been able to resist a challenge, have you? You little tease! Now you're going to get it." He lay her down on the red rug and quickly took her.

When he rose, she followed, hiding her disappointment. She turned away and started back up the stairs, but he came, too. She looked down at him over her shoulder. He grinned and slid a hand over her bare rump, and she knew he wasn't finished with her. She put her nose up in the air and sassily slapped his hand away as she walked haughtily toward her room.

At the door she turned and raised her hands to either side of the doorway to block his entrance. "This is my room. Yours is down there."

He put his hands under her armpits, the wrists squeezing her breasts together, and lifted her backward. He kissed her mouth with slow, probing sensuality, his tongue moving, searching, teasing.

She hung from his supporting hands, soft, pliant,

unresisting. He pulled her to him, bending backward to mold her body to his. Taking his time, he kissed her again, long and thoroughly. She raised her hands to his neck and pressed her breasts against his chest. She thrilled him until he gasped and shuddered.

The texture of his hot, damp, hairy chest against her smooth, soft skin made her toes curl. Finally he carried her to the bed and lay her down and began to make long, sensual love to her.

He offered her a sip from one wineglass, then poured champagne into her navel and licked it clean, with slow tiger laps. He sprinkled drops on her nipples and suckled them. He smoothed the wine on her lips, and his tongue tasted it slowly.

She, too, sprinkled wine on him and took it from him with her mouth and tongue. And her hands moved and teased to pleasure him. It was a bacchanalian night, and it occurred to Marcie that they should be down on the table in the dining room with the nymphs and satyrs and the laughing wine god. But they did well enough upstairs on a bed with a silent, watchful tiger.

At last, as the ticking clock recorded the first hours of their final day together as man and wife, they slept.

Thad made love to Marcie again in the early morning. She had no interest at all, so he just pleased himself. His need wasn't urgent by then so he took his time before he took her.

8

MARCIE THOUGHT HOW appropriate it was that, on the day they filed for divorce, it rained. As often happens in Indiana, it was a cold summer rain that made Marcie want to huddle next to a fire in the fireplace. But she suspected she'd be shivering even if the sun were out. What was happening to them?

They wore rain hats and slickers and ran through a downpour that was whipped along by a gusting wind.

Nance was waiting for them. Marcie had supposed they would have to sign a couple of papers. But Nance also had a list of financial responsibilities to be divided up and decided upon even before the divorce became final—credit cards, Marcie's car and the gas, medical and dental bills, allowance, tuition and expenses, nights off...

Marcie expected Thad to call a halt to this madness at any moment, but he didn't speak, and neither did she. To have shared so much so intimately for six years and now to be so isolated and estranged was deeply painful to her.

"Nights off? I get nights off?" Marcie's voice faltered.

Nance regarded her sternly and replied, "Of course. On Saturday, in order to free Thad that day, you should use the sitter service provided by the university." Nance gave Marcie the number to call.

Marcie hadn't realized there was so much to decide. In a small whisper, she said, "I would never have thought about those things."

Nance was patient. "That's why you came to me. It's my job to know about them."

"The allowance for Marcie isn't enough," Thad said stiffly.

"But she has few personal expenses," Nance pointed out. When he frowned, she added, "Well, see how it goes. You're both adult and fair, and if you disagree, I'm here to help. Are you sure you don't want to call in a second lawyer?"

"No," Thad said firmly, "we can work things out." But he became very quiet.

When they'd signed all the papers they needed to, they told Nance good-bye and headed back through the rain to Thad's car. "It's almost lunchtime," he said. "Why don't we go to the Columbia Club or the Hilton and have lunch?"

"I can't," Marcie said stiffly. "I'll barely make it to class on time as it is. I had no idea all this would be so complicated. Do you want me to catch the bus? I've got to get home and change and grab my books. Cassie can make me a quick sandwich."

"You mean"—he seemed startled—"it's business as usual? You don't think we should...talk."

"Oh, no. Not anymore."

"But I thought we'd take the afternoon off and have a long lunch and reminisce and discuss all this. Maybe go somewhere for dinner."

She stood in the rain and thought: Yeah, and go back home and have another one for the road. "Sorry." She turned toward the street.

"Where the hell are you going?"

"To catch the bus," she yelled back through the pelting rain.

"Marcia!" Furiously he ran after her and grabbed her arm. "I'll take you home. What do you mean, running off that way?"

She stopped and calmly removed her arm from his grip. "You may not grab me. I am not your wife. If you want to drive me, you may ask me courteously."

"Courteously!"

"No. You say: 'Marcie, may I drive you?'"

"May I?" he snarled.

"Why, thank you, Thaddeus."

He eyed her with hostility as he unlocked his car and opened the door for her. She slipped in, then reached over to unlock his door as he stormed around the car. Lightning flashed and thunder rolled, and the rain came down harder. Why was Thad so angry?

"Do you have to have your books? I could just take you over to the school."

"Thank you," she replied politely, "but I do need them, and I'll need my car to get home."

"I could pick you up."

"There's no need."

"We could go out for a late dinner."

"I'll have to study. These summer sessions are so condensed that you have to scramble. I know one girl who did *The Iliad* and *The Odyssey* in two days. She just stumbled around reading. And finals are next week."

"I hate to see you work so hard," he objected.

"I love it."

"But not me."

She turned to look at him. "That's never entered into it."

"You've never loved me?" He was shocked.

"You're not through running around," she reminded him.

"Why don't you skip school today and run around with me?"

"Sorry." She really was sorry. "Each day is equal to about a week of regular classes."

"Are you managing?"

"Barely," she admitted. "This summer I'll complete my sophomore requirements. I'll start my junior year next fall."

"You don't have to do this, Marcie. I'll support you and the kids."

"There isn't enough money for two households."

"There will be in a couple of years."

"But what if you remarry and have other kids?" She found it hurt to voice the possibility because it was more likely now.

"It isn't marriage I want," he said. "I told you that. If I wanted to be married, I'd keep you."

"Would you?"

"Of course," he reassured her. "You know that."

"How do you know I'd want to stay?"

"Why, Marcie!" He was astounded.

"Yes, Thad?"

"Do you mean you *want* this divorce?" He'd parked the car in their driveway.

"Good Lord!" she exclaimed, thoroughly exasperated, and slammed the door shut behind her.

He followed her slowly into the house. Cassie was supervising the kids as they glued large daisy petals to a long strip of paper. They would hang it with masking tape on the wall of the living room, which they'd taken over as a playroom. Hardly greeting their parents, the kids continued their work with busy concentration. They were using rubber cement. A great deal of rubber cement.

Cassie hurried to the kitchen to slap together a bologna sandwich for Marcie, who ran upstairs, reappearing in a moment dressed in jeans and her slicker and carrying a plastic sack for her books. She grabbed the sandwich, yelled good-bye to the kids, and left, racing through the pouring rain.

It wasn't until she was in the car and on her way that the scene registered in her mind, like an instant replay on television. Cassie had strolled over to Thad, tucking her shirt into her jeans so that her breasts were outlined by the taut cloth. She'd looked up at him, her big blue eyes wide, and asked, "Papers all signed?"

Cassie?

Marcie chewed off all her lipstick before she got to class. Could she fire a perfectly good babysitter because she was eyeing her almost ex-husband? What were the rules about that? Who could she get to replace Cassie?

She had a hard time concentrating in class that day.

Two days later, the fact that they had filed for divorce appeared, as requested by law, in the public notices printed in the *Journal*.

Soon the telephone calls began: "I can't believe it!" their friends exclaimed. And, "I never in the world would have thought you two..." And, "I've never heard of anything so stupid! You're not serious, are you?" How was she supposed to answer all those questions?

Her parents called. "So you did it. How foolish! Where are you planning to live and how?" So she had to explain, and they were disgusted. "Now, that's just plain weird."

Then there were female callers who asked for Thad without saying who they were. Marcie jotted down phone numbers on slips of paper and left them in the den. A strange feeling crept over her, and her muscles seemed to tense, almost as if she were mentally preparing for battle.

Her father-in-law, a big man, came over and stood awkwardly in the entryway. "My heart is very sad," he said, and he sat down with a great sigh. The children scrambled into his lap. He patted them but didn't seem to hear their chatter. He looked very gloomy. Finally he asked mournfully, "Won't you change your mind and stay with Thad?"

"We're staying here until I get my degree," she replied.

He shook his head, put the children down, and walked distractedly through the empty rooms before he finally left.

Marcie didn't see Beatrice, but Thad reported, "Mother is astonished you actually did it."

"I?"

"Well, she can't understand why you'd let me go. I have no faults, you must realize."

"Right."

"So it has to be you."

"You're all heart."

"A lover," he agreed, giving her an inscrutable look.

A lover? Who was he loving?

Both kids got the flu, and Marcie was trying to cope when their senior preacher, Mr. Jamison, came over to remonstrate. "Why didn't you come for counseling?" he demanded.

"Ask Thad," she suggested.

"I shall, but why didn't *you* come to us?" he scolded.

"I don't have time," she replied, which was true.

"No time for God!" He was appalled.

"I talk to God all the time!"

"Petitioning..."

"No, being thankful."

"Thankful?" That puzzled him.

"Thanking Him because a truck hasn't hit me, or because a cop wasn't around to see me sneak through a stop sign, or because Gina hasn't tried to slide down the banister..."

"Mommy!" Kelly yelled in distress.

She ran up the stairs, and they made it to the bathroom in time to hold Kelly's head.

Mr. Jamison's hand appeared from nowhere and handed her a wet cloth, then his voice said, "What God hath joined together let no man put asunder." He was very cross. He took the cloth from her, washed it, wrung it out, and gave it back as he lectured, "Cleave only unto..."

Thad came to the doorway and asked pleasantly, "Having a party?"

Marcie's angry expression should have blasted him back into the hall. He gave her an understanding grin, took the preacher's arm, and led him away, soothing him.

Soon it was Gina's turn to throw up. Finally, when both kids were feeling more comfortable, Marcie washed up and drooped downstairs. Mr. Jamison gave them a stern lecture, blessed them, and left.

Thad took Marcie's limp hand and smiled. "I suppose now you want to chicken out of the divorce."

She groaned. "I had no idea how exhausting friends could be."

"We're lovable," he explained.

She gave him a skeptical look. "You are, anyway. I've put lists of phone numbers for you in the den."

"Who called?" He was frowning but he sounded interested.

"Women."

He brightened. "Who?"

"Phyl for one."

His interest faded. "Oh."

"Good night."

He held out a restraining hand. "Why don't you sleep down here, and I'll take first watch? You've had a hard day."

She hesitated, considering his offer.

He patted her shoulder. "Go ahead. Take a shower. My T-shirts are in the top drawer. I'll wake you if I need your help."

"Okay." She dragged herself off, showered, and crawled into the sleep sofa, set pillows along the edge, and went to sleep at once.

The next morning she woke, stretched, and looked at the clock—and where she'd slept—in surprise. She pulled on Thad's robe and went upstairs to find him in his underwear asleep in her bed, one arm draped companionably over the stuffed tiger, both kids curled at his side.

She looked down at him, feeling as mournful as her father-in-law, then ordered herself not to think about it. If she ever really thought about never seeing Thad again, she was sure she'd come unglued. It was all very well to decide that if he didn't want to be married to her, then she didn't want to be married to him. But the reality was that she couldn't imagine life without him.

The kids were pink-cheeked and sleeping deeply so she tiptoed downstairs and made popovers for breakfast, studying furiously while they baked.

At the last possible moment she crept upstairs and gently wakened Thad. His eyes opened at once, and he smiled at her. His glance traveled down his robe, which looked enormous on her slight figure, and he lifted the sheet and whispered, "Room for one more..." He pushed over the stuffed tiger until it teetered on the edge of the bed.

Marcie steadied the tiger and gave a slight, self-conscious shake of her head.

He grinned and shrugged. "Well, I tried." He rose
from the bed with an effortless flow of perfectly coor-
dinated muscles and walked past her, patting her bottom
in a familiar way.

Exhausted from the previous day, the kids slept on,
and Marcie didn't disturb them. Divorcing husband and
wife shared breakfast alone at the huge table in the dining
room. Wearing a suit, Thad looked slick, well dressed,
and civilized. He was marvelous. Exciting.

Marcie bit her lip and turned her thoughts to breakfast.

Thad mmmed over the popovers and ate with relish.
Was he deliberately making the sounds sexual, as if he
were in bed with her and enjoying her? Or was eating
simply another sensual delight for him? She'd never considered it before. She couldn't remember him ever making those sounds before. They seldom ate alone. When
they went out... but that was always at a public place,
usually with friends. This was the first time they'd had
breakfast alone in... how long? She couldn't remember.
But his sounds stirred her desires.

He picked up his briefcase and, ready to leave for the
office, made his daily request. "I need a kiss to get me
there."

She replied at once, "And who's at the office to start
your day?" Her stomach writhed as she wondered if there
was, indeed, someone waiting for him there. While her
thoughts were thus occupied, he gave her the kiss he
wanted to, pressing her buttocks hard against the edge
of the table with his hips and holding her there, making
her fully aware of his body. His kiss was delicious. His
voice husky, he offered, "I could take the next train..."
It was their joke; there were no trains to the city, and
anyway, he drove.

But instead of replying, "There are seven trains..."
she only gazed bleakly up at him.

He kissed her again, putting aside his briefcase and
using his body and hands and, in return, getting his hair

messed up and his tie a little askew. It was the tie she'd made for her father.

He left soon after that, smoothing his hair and straightening the tie and grinning back at her, looking very pleased with himself.

What was he up to? Did he assume that she'd be easy to get into bed? That she'd be there for him to make love to whenever he felt like it? Her body, her arms, her whole being longed for him. It wasn't fair. He wanted to be free, but he also wanted to sleep with her. Never! She could not.

She loved him. And if he simply kept her around as a sexual convenience, it would tear her apart. She had to guard herself and be firm, for it was obvious he would give her no quarter.

 *9*

DURING ONE OF the Saturday coffee breaks she occasionally shared with Professor John Brown, the tall, gentle, rather fragile man commented, "I understand you're getting a divorce." His moustache and beard were on the wispy side, his brown hair thinning, his eyes magnified by his glasses. His mind was sharp, his long hands nervous and expressive.

Marcie's mind had been elsewhere. "Ummm?" she replied. Then, realizing what he'd said, she agreed, "Oh. Yes."

"My wife and I were divorced three years ago."

Marcie nodded.

"She's remarried." He made wet interlocking circles

457

on the table top with his coffee cup. "She's going to
have a baby."

Marcie sensed the pain behind his words and couldn't
think of anything to say.

And he poured out his story: how his wife had wanted
a career, and how she'd attended college free where he
was teaching. When she'd gotten her masters, she'd found
she no longer wanted to be married to him. He felt she'd
slept with him for five years in exchange for free tuition.
She hadn't really wanted him, only the degree. He'd
been used. Now she was married to another man and
having his baby. Three years had passed since the divorce, but he was still raw.

Marcie felt great sympathy for him, but she didn't
express it. She couldn't get entangled in anyone else's
problems; she had too many of her own. She wondered
if he would ever break free from his hurt, and from the
past, and build some kind of future for himself. When
she got her own life under some semblance of control,
she would try to find a woman who would like John.

Soon after that, one of Marcie's woman professors
from the year before stopped her in the parking lot and
told her she'd been divorced for five years. "I was devastated when Jack said he wanted out. I felt he was
abandoning me on a desert island. I felt helpless. There
I was, alone, with two little boys. How would I ever
manage to survive?"

Marcie didn't say anything. That was exactly how she
felt.

"I knew I wouldn't get any help from him. He's like
sixty percent of all exes. Right after the divorce it was
'Good-bye', then 'Who are you?' But I'd always worked.
I took care of the house, the repairs, the kids, the sitters,
the laundry, the cars, and any sickness. A couple of
months after he walked out it suddenly dawned on me
that he hadn't contributed one damned thing to our lives.

He was a taker. I didn't need him.

"With him gone, it was so peaceful. No hassles. He'd always complained that I hadn't done something, or why hadn't I done something else, and I'd always felt guilty. It had never occurred to me to ask why he hadn't done it himself. So in a way, I must have contributed to his being so worthless. He was a drag! I'd been handling everything all along, but since he was so critical of me, I hadn't even realized it. I had never needed him.

"A couple of months later, he started coming around and said he wanted to move back in. No way! The divorce has been an emancipation for me. The kids are easier to deal with; we're so companionable and relaxed without Jack. I'm still amazed by how marvelous it is without him. Cheer up. You'll love it!" And she strode off, strong and free.

But into Marcie's mind came the image of Thad sleeping in her bed with two flu-stricken children; and Thad assuring Gina that she'd recover and that she was beautiful even with chicken pox; and how the kids exploded in noisy delight when Thad came home . . . and how she did, too.

Thad wasn't like Jack. Marcie would never love being without Thad. She would be like a floating island in the middle of a sea of people—adrift, bereft, lost.

Another woman told her, "The first one is always hard. After that it isn't nearly so bad. You should have an affair immediately. It'll distract you, you'll see."

But Marcie didn't want an affair.

Then someone else said, "For God's sake, don't jump into an affair. It's disastrous. Affairs are like little marriages: You're totally committed to an uncommitted man, giving him all the privileges and conveniences of marriage without any security. You risk being casually dumped or parting in a hellish emotional storm that's worse than divorce because you've been used. And you don't even have a divorce to make it a clean separation, one you can grieve over properly. He just walks out, and you're left there, alone."

It seemed to Marcie that people whose lives had been knocked about and changed by divorce were very similar to people who had experienced other disruptions or disasters. They felt they'd shared a common experience with Marcie and were anxious to share all the details with her. They spoke openly and freely of their indignation, sorrow, guilt, and self-pity—and they all gave a great deal of unsolicited advice.

Apparently Thad's friends and acquaintances were confiding in him, too, because he complained, "Everybody's putting in his two-cents' worth, and that's about what it's worth. It's our divorce. They all ought to butt out."

By actual count there couldn't have been more than thirty-five people who were quarreling with them over the divorce, but it seemed as if everyone in Indianapolis had some comment to make. At the end of the first week Thad and Marcie were both thoroughly tired of the whole subject—of listening, explaining, defending, or struggling to keep control of their own lives. The situation was complicated by the fact that neither to them had moved out of the house.

"If you're still going to live together, why get a divorce?"

That was a tricky question to answer, and Marcie struggled to find a reply. Finally she said, "We're not."

"Not what?"

"Uh . . . living together."

The knowing looks that followed made her blush every time.

Her mother thoroughly disapproved of the whole setup and didn't hesitate to expound on all its aspects at any time and at great length. At one point Marcie told her mother, "If you don't let up, Mom, I'm going to recall my ambassador."

Her mother gave her a puzzled, exasperated look and walked away, but her father, who was reading the newspaper in his favorite easy chair, chuckled appreciatively.

"Are you threatening to break off diplomatic relations with the family, Marcie?" he asked.

"I'll never break off relations with you," she assured him with a hug.

Despite these complications, Marcie and Thad agreed not to tell the children about the divorce.

"Since the only change in their lives is that you're sleeping downstairs, why bother them with explanations?" said Marcie.

"Their lives won't be affected for years," Thad agreed.

"If they have any questions, we'll answer them as we go along, okay?"

"I agree."

As time went on, Marcie found that she and Thad had become the butt of some crude jokes.

People said Thad was having his cake and eating it, too. The speculative stares made Marcie furious. She told Thad, "If we were living together without ever having been married there wouldn't be this much static!"

"Does it bother you?"

She took a deep breath and said with false sweetness, "Perhaps people aren't as rude to you."

She received several invitations to assuage the emptiness of her sex life. She turned them all down. No other man attracted her. "Why not?" people said, and, laughing, one added, "What's sauce for the gander is sauce for the goose." She didn't think that was funny. What sort of sauce was Thad getting?

He was certainly getting enough calls. Every night he received at least one. Marcie thought the women shockingly bold. She grimly took numbers and didn't care that she sounded abrupt and disapproving.

"Sylvia told me you were very rude to her on the phone," Thad chided, but his mock seriousness was betrayed by his dancing eyes.

"Get your own phone number and an answering service!" Marcie snapped back.

He laughed.

He still helped set the table and clear it, and he still bathed the kids while she finished cleaning up the kitchen. He still said, "I'll be back early," as he left every night; and she still tried to study, wondering where he was.

If possible, the second summer session was even more intense than the first, but perhaps it only seemed that way because of the heat, and because of the emotional turmoil in her life. She worked furiously as June became July.

After some debate Marcie's mother invited Thad to the family's Fourth of July picnic in Columbia City. Marcie's parents always hosted the celebration because their house and yard were enormous. Marcie was reluctant to go, but went anyway. It was a mistake. They were subjected to lectures, sly comments, and flirting. Marcie barely restrained herself from throttling one female cousin who couldn't seem to keep her hands off Thad. He loved it . . . or appeared to as his laughing eyes caught Marcie's stormy ones.

It was a long, hot, noisy, tiring day. Kelly felt insecure in the crush of relatives, and Marcie ended up sitting on a bench under a big, old tree at the edge of the large yard. She had placed a dish towel on her lap to keep Kelly's head from sweating as he slept, worn out. From that vantage point she could watch Thad.

A baseball game was in progress. The players had devised all sorts of handicaps so they would be equally pitted against each other. Thad had to throw left-handed, bat with one hand, and hop to the bases on one foot.

As Marcie watched him, she wondered when he had become a man. She'd married a youth, and he'd grown into a man. When had he taken those first steps into maturity? His shoulders had filled out, his body was more graceful, his confidence in himself was more evident. He was a beautiful, powerful male. He would be breathtaking when he was forty. Where would she be then? Would she have a chance to witness the fulfillment of all that he promised?

As the afternoon wore on, Gina refused to take a nap and became cross. Without ceremony, Thad picked her up and carried her around as he talked to one person or another. Gina went to sleep draped securely on her daddy's shoulder, not waking even when he occasionally shifted her slight weight.

How could the children be without their daddy? Why would he want to be free of them? Then Marcie reminded herself yet again that it wasn't the kids he was divorcing—only her.

Would he want custody? What if he married some witch—like Phyl—and won custody of the kids? Phyl would ship them right off to boarding school. Her babies. That mustn't happen. Nance would have to see to it that Marcie got custody. But then she looked at Gina, her head lolling on her father's shoulder, secure and sound asleep. How could she deprive the kids of the easy care he gave them—their evening bath, his gentle chaffing, his teasing, and his concern? How could she deprive *him* of that relationship?

Thad said he didn't want to be married, but he'd meet some barracuda and never know what hit him. He'd be married and swept away from his children and never see them again. Or maybe he'd see them occasionally for lunch. She imagined the conversation:

"How are you?"

"Fine."

"How's school?"

"Okay."

"What have you been doing lately?"

"Nothing."

They'd be strangers. How awful.

She got a terrible headache. Her cousin Janet came over and said she looked ghastly, which didn't help Marcie feel any better. But Janet brought her two aspirin and a glass of water. Kelly slept on, and Janet sat down. Marcie realized that she and Janet looked very similar. Janet just had a bit more of everything—she was taller, rounder, her hair was thicker, and she looked somewhat exotic. She had a dead-level practicality and a good sense of humor.

Janet asked Marcie a lot of personal questions that not even her nosiest aunt would have dared ask. By that time, however, Marcie had learned to field unwanted questions and ask some of her own. "When did you lose your virginity? Are you sleeping with anyone now? What are—"

Janet gasped. "Marcie, how could you ask that?"

"Well, you asked me if Thad and I were still sleeping together."

"I was just curious!" Janet protested.

"So'm I." Marcie grinned.

Janet laughed, then said, "He certainly is a gorgeous man. How can you let him go?"

"I was surprised Mother invited him—under the circumstances." Since her mother was Janet's aunt, they were free to discuss her. "I would think she'd feel a little hostile toward Thad. Actually, though, I suspect she's feeling more hostile toward me."

"Well," her cousin said, "you're not nearly as good-looking."

"Don't tell me you have a yen for him, too."

"I wouldn't dare!"

"That reminds me. Would you go find Chas for me?"

"Your brother? Why?"

"Because I want to set him up with our sitter, Cassie. Cassie and Chas." Marcie nodded to herself. "They were meant for each other."

"If you're going to start matchmaking, do me. Who the hell cares about this Cassie?"

"She's rolling her eyes at Thad," Marcie explained. "But she's too good with the kids to fire her."

"You're jealous of Thad?" Janet frowned. "Why are you divorcing him?"

"I'm not." Marcie gave her a level, soul-bruised look that struck her cousin to the heart. "He's divorcing me."

"Oh, good Lord . . ." And Janet flung herself away.

In time she returned with Chas, who took his awakening nephew from Marcie's lap and made Kelly comfortable on his own. Chas took Marcie's hand and held it tenderly. He listened as she described Cassie. She was careful not to gush. "You were made for each other" is guaranteed to alienate any two people before they even meet.

The picnic was a big success. There was too much food, and it was all delicious. The corn in the fields was the required 'knee high by the Fourth of July' so they'd bought fresh corn elsewhere. They slathered the cobs with melted butter, using small paint brushes, and no one minded if the butter dripped on the ground.

Thad ate his full share and commented to Marcie that she came from a tribe of good cooks. No wonder the meals she prepared were always so tasty. Her food? She had trouble accepting his compliment. Why would he tell her she was a good cook when she was awful? If not awful, at least indifferent. As she tried to puzzle him out, he smiled at her with great charm. He was baffling.

All the usual American dishes were served—hot dogs, hamburgers, pizza, cole slaw, potato salad, baked beans, potato chips, Fritos, tacos, lemonade, Cokes, beer, and coffee with hot cherry and apple pies. Then ice cream, watermelon . . . and misery.

They all lay in the shade and rubbed their bellies and burped and groaned . . . and complained. Finally they were able to move around slowly, and then they found they could do easy things like play horseshoes, throw frisbees, and fly kites.

Marcie was intensely aware that Thad had stayed at her side. He helped with the children and frequently touched her in a tender, loving manner. How could he?

By the time it was dark enough to set off the fireworks, everyone was ready to sit quietly and watch. Some of the kids went back to sleep, but Gina in Thad's arms and Kelly on Marcie's lap stayed awake to watch with wide eyes. It was marvelous to see the magic colors.

One of the older uncles said that, in the South Pacific during World War II, the bombardments of the islands had looked just like fireworks. If you could forget that people were being killed and whole towns were being destroyed, then it was beautiful. There was always something good in whatever happened.

How strange life is, Marcie mused.

She wondered what would be good about the divorce.

 *10*

MARCIE WASN'T SURPRISED when Chas drove the one hundred miles from his farm to Indianapolis to meet Cassie. Being sneaky, as most men over sixteen are, he didn't drive to the house but came to the university and was waiting next to Marcie's car when she emerged from class. He left his car in the parking lot and rode home with her, arriving amidst the usual flurry of the kids' greetings and their demands that Marcie settle the day's disputes. Marcie watched Chas covertly size up Cassie. If his reaction was negative, he would casually take off, grab a bus back to his car, and vanish.

Being equally sneaky, Marcie had undersold Cassie, and poor old Chas had trouble keeping his eyes in their sockets. Marcie whispered that his mouth was hanging open though it wasn't really. Actually he was acting cool and mature. But his heart rate must have accelerated because he moved restlessly.

Chas was thirty, tall, broad-shouldered, and had dark hair like most of Marcie's family. Being a farmer, he was in the sun so much that his unruly hair was streaked with shades of almost burnt orange. His eyebrows were thick and shaggy. His eyes held humor, and his jaw held purpose. How he'd escaped marriage baffled their mother, who was annoyed with him most of the time. He was his father's child so he was amused by his mother's vexation.

When Gina and Kelly had calmed down, Chas casually asked Cassie, "Psychology?"

Squinting just a little, as if she couldn't believe he was that good-looking, Cassie said, "That's right," adding, "Abnormal."

"Well I wrote all the case histories in the sex manual. Under different names, of course. You can have a field day figuring me out."

"A maniac sex fantasist?" Cassie tilted her head back as if to study him through the bottoms of bifocals.

Nodding, he said earnestly, "A loving, gentle, *caring*—"

"I only do children."

He dropped to his knees. "I'll walk on my knees, and we'll pretend... What age do you specialize in?"

Worried that the undercurrents of the scene were quickly becoming sexual, Marcie shooed the children into the kitchen.

Chas rose to his feet in a lithe, easy movement and said, "Cassie and I are going to take the bus downtown to my car."

Cassie nodded vaguely and they walked hand in hand to the bus stop.

Watching them, Marcie knew the meeting had taken. She was rid of Cassie as a threat.

Since distracting Cassie from Thad had worked so well, Marcie spent the next few days mentally reviewing all the men she knew who might get Phyl off his trail. Finally she asked Betty, "Do you happen to know a man for Phyl?"

"Why?"

"She's been sniffing after Thad like a she-wolf after the dominant male." Then Marcie told her what she'd done about Cassie. "But I've only got one brother left, and he's twenty-eight—too young for Phyl—and I really would rather not have her in the family."

Betty laughed. "You have to admit Phyl has good taste."

"I feel as if I'm on a sled in Russia in the middle of the winter, fleeing a pack of ravenous wolves. I have to throw someone off the sled every time the wolves get too close. Chas was the first. Who will I heave over the side next?"

"You've read Willa Cather?" Betty said.

"Why do you ask?" Marcie blinked as she returned from her fantasy on the Russian steppes.

"She was the writer who told that story and she wrecked wolves' reputation. There's never been an authenticated attack on people by wolves."

"I suppose you're going to say Count Dracula is a fable, too?" Marcie asked, disappointed.

"No, he was real all right, and murderous, but he wasn't a vampire."

"I hesitate to inquire about Santa Claus."

Betty laughed again, then admitted, "Well, I agree Phyl is predatory, and you need to throw her a bone. Dog packs have attacked humans, and Phyl's...uh... uh...a female canine?"

"Nicely said."

"Let me think about Phyl for a while. I just might find someone who'd benefit from knowing her."

"Benefit!" Marcie exploded.

"That'll kind of narrow it down, won't it?" Betty grinned.

On the following Saturday, at about seven-thirty in the evening, Chas arrived with a large bouquet of pink carnations and baby's breath. He gave it to Marcie with a flourish, and Thad commented, "It's not her birthday. What's up?"

"Pink is for girls." Chas grinned at his brother-in-law and asked if he could bring Cassie to dinner the following evening.

"Sure," Marcie said. "If you find someone for Janet."

"Janet?" Chas asked blankly.

"Janet, our cousin."

"Oh," he said. "Okay." And he lifted a hand in farewell.

"Someone decent!" Marcie yelled after him.

His deep voice floated back, "That's the only kind of man I know."

Thad was still confused and said, "Pink is for girls. Marcie . . . are you pregnant?" His voice was hoarse, and his body was tense and still.

"No."

"Oh." Did she hear disappointment in his voice? Why would he be disappointed? They were getting a divorce. Then Thad asked, "What's the deal with the flowers?"

"I introduced Chas to Cassie."

"Cassie and Chas?" He considered that. "They'll fit," he decided.

Immediately she imagined them together physically and pictured Chas smothering Cassie—he was so much larger. "I'm not sure," she mused.

"He's very patient, and she's so busy and off on tangents." Then she realized Thad had been considering their personalities.

"What made you think to introduce them?" he inquired.

"One throws off the surplus from the sled to the ravenous wolves."

That really confused him. "Huh?"

Ignoring him, Marcie asked instead, "Do you have plans for dinner tomorrow?"

"I'm invited, too?"

"Yes." She was a bit irritated. Did he want an engraved invitation?

"I'd be delighted."

Without replying, she went to the freezer and took out a large beef roast. Thad carried it back to the kitchen.

"I'm glad you're free for dinner," she said impulsively. "It would be strange to have dinner with Chas and not you."

"I find it strange that you felt you had to invite me."

"Well . . ." Marcie felt a little awkward. "I don't want to intrude on your time."

His eyes narrowed as he studied her. "If I wanted to invite someone to dinner, would you cook it for me and get flowers for the table?"

He wanted to bring some woman to their home and serve her dinner there! Marcie kept her head down as she prepared the meat, concentrating on what she was doing. "I'm your housekeeper," she said.

"So you would?" he asked tightly.

"Of course. Give me a day's notice." She continued to work with the meat, waiting for him to say something else, but he didn't. He just leaned in the doorway with his hands in his pockets and watched her.

Marcie wondered about the woman Thad was bringing to dinner and what it would take to get rid of her. His women were becoming a burden. Grimly she vowed to fight to the bitter end, until the last available man was pitched off the racing sled.

She put the roast in the microwave oven and set it to brown and bake. She'd serve it sliced cold the next day. Thad was standing around, moody and silent. She glanced at him a couple of times, wondering what he was thinking. Finally he said, "It's your night out. Where are you going?"

She blinked in surprise, then suggested, "You go ahead."

"You have no plans?"

She hadn't used a free night yet. "No."

"Then how about going to a movie with me?"

"Thanks"—she concealed her surprise—"but I have to study."

"Oh." He continued to lean in the doorway watching her as she planned what they would have for dinner the next day. Neither of them spoke. When she finished, she set the timer so she'd know when the meat was done, then she headed out the door. He moved too slowly out of the way, forcing her to hesitate. She looked up at him. He was studying her very seriously. "Are you going upstairs now?"

"Yes. I have to study," she repeated.

"Well . . . good night." He leaned forward and kissed her very sweetly. He lifted his mouth and looked soberly down at her.

She had to swallow before she said, "You're not supposed to do that any more."

"Not even as old friends?" he asked.

She looked away. "Well . . ." Unable to think of anything to say, she went slowly past him and up the stairs.

She did study, but she also looked out the window without seeing what was there.

As they walked home from church the next morning, with the kids running ahead, then lagging behind, Thad asked Marcie, "Have you noticed that in the last several sermons Mr. Jamison has been harping on the sanctity of marriage and how divorce is wicked, and he looks at me the whole time?"

"You mistake the direction of his gaze. He's looking at me," Marcie corrected him.

"Do you suppose he's trying to say something to us?"

She nodded. "There is that possibility."

"My friend Russ told me every man gets at least one opportunity in his life to make a bald-assed fool of himself, and he thinks I'm using up more than my share of chances. He's afraid I'll intrude on his share."

"Subtle." Marcie took his arm in order to slow his steps to match the kids' progress.

"My dad was telling me how brilliant you are and what a clever, pretty woman you are and I said . . . you know, a little bragging . . . that I'd taught you all you know."

She laughed.

"And the next thing I knew he was discussing Brueghel's painting, 'The Blind Leading the Blind'—the use of colors, the emotional impact . . ." Thad waved a hand in circles to illustrate.

"Now he *is* subtle."

"Am I really blind?"

"Only mentally," she replied readily.

"Why?"

But just then Betty came out on her porch as they passed her house and called to them, so they stopped to chat. Max stood chewing on his unlit cigar and discussed his yard with Thad. Max had plowed up the entire south lawn and planted his first vegetable garden. He'd planted four fifty-foot rows of radishes. He tried to coerce Thad into accepting a bushel of them.

Betty took Marcie into the house to give Gina and Kelly a cookie each—and told Marcie she thought she'd found just the man to distract Phyl: Sidney Adams.

"What a quick worker you are!" Marcie praised her, pleased.

"Sidney is more our age. His wife is dead. No children. He has a bundle of money and is very generous. He needs a hostess. He likes sultry women. He'd spoil Phyl rotten and never be too emotionally involved. She'd travel and lead an exotic life. I think he'd be perfect for her, and she for him. I haven't mentioned her to him."

"When can she meet him?" Marcie was eager to deal with this last threat.

"He's coming over tonight for supper. How about joining us?"

"Why don't you and Max bring him to our house instead," Marcie countered. "My brother and Cassie are coming to dinner... and I'll ask Phyl."

"Sure," Betty said. "I have an apple-and-lime Jello salad and a turkey roll."

"I have a cold beef roast, cole slaw, and key lime pie."

Betty grinned. "A ball and a banquet!"

"Be casual," Marcie suggested for dress.

"What time?"

"Sevenish?" Marcie asked.

"We'll be there." And they grinned at each other.

When they emerged from the house, Betty told Max they'd take Sidney to the Fosters for supper and combine their meals. Max nodded, removed his cigar, and said, "We'll bring radishes."

Phyl, of course, accepted the invitation. Marcie didn't mention the extra male guest.

"Phyl's coming?" Thad asked. "Why Phyl?"

Blandly Marcie looked at her almost-ex husband and lied, "I haven't seen her for a while, and I've missed her." No lightning came through the roof, and she didn't turn to stone or anything.

Thad snorted in disgust. "She calls here every single night, the exact moment I walk in the door."

"Oh?"

He gave her a sour look.

The victim, Sidney Adams, was a man of medium height who looked like a shrewd-eyed bear. He met Phyl with a slight smile. She gave him a startled look, recognizing his name as a mover and shaper. She became aloof and made him work to get her attention—which amused him. Betty and Marcie exchanged knowing glances.

Chas and Cassie burst into the house laughing, and as a surprise, were followed by Marcie's pregnant sister, Carol, and her husband, Jack. Cousin Janet came, too, plus Mark Williams, the young man Chas had promised to find.

The three couples had spent the afternoon picking blackberries in one of Chas's back lots on his farm, and they were windblown, thristy, and so tired that they were all a little silly. It was fun. There was plenty of food, and Chas nodded judiciously over Max's radishes and sampled them with the narrow-eyed concentration of a professional. He pronounced them superior. Nearly bursting with pride, Max told Chas how to grow radishes.

It was readily apparent that no sparks were flying between Janet and her date. He was a nice guy but blah, and they just weren't meant for each other. On the other hand, anyone with two brain cells could feel the heat of the attraction between Cassie and Chas. Marcie's envious eyes were drawn to them again and again. They laughed and teased each other like lovers of long standing who genuinely liked and felt comfortable with each other.

The evening progressed very satisfactorily, everyone enjoying the food and each other's company. They talked and laughed, ate and drank, until quite late.

After everyone finally went home, Marcie grew pensive. She finished straightening up and, deep in thought, headed toward the stairs and bed.

Thad met her at the bottom of the stairs, and before she knew what was happening, he took her in his arms and kissed her. She lay her head against his shoulder, filled with sadness, enjoying the ache of nostalgia his kiss stirred. She kissed him back. Finally he raised his mouth from her soft lips and said, "Good night . . . old friend." He smiled at her, and damned if he didn't release her!

She went upstairs, mesmerized by his kiss. At the landing she looked down. He was still standing there watching her.

She crawled into bed and absently petted the alert tiger. She thought about Thad and the fact that two of the ravenous wolves had been flung distracting bait. Perhaps she and Betty should set themselves up as matchmakers and charge a nominal fee. Figuring out how much to charge, expenses, sources, and so on put her to sleep. In her dreams she was hired to choose a new bride for Thad. But every single candidate was unsuitable.

11

As Marcie was driving home from school several days later, the car radiator hose broke. She'd studied how to make minor car repairs and had tape with her as well as a gallon of water, a can of oil, rags, a fan belt, and the other recommended items.

She was under the hood, repairing the hose, when a Mercedes-Benz 380 SEC pulled up next to her. A man got out and came toward her. "Why, Nick! How nice!"

It was Nick Santini, an old friend she and Thad had made in college. He wasn't quite as tall as Thad, his hair was light brown, he had laughing green eyes, and he was very good-looking. He was a successful man whose luck was hard work and a good brain. "I thought that was your car," he said. "I pass you on this road several times a week."

Marcie was glad to see him. Laughing, she asked, "How've you been?"

"Fine. I just heard you and Thad split."

She sobered a little and said, "Yeah," then turned back to finish taping the hose.

Nick leaned over to watch. "Where are you living?"

"At the house."

"How's Gina?"

"Fine. She's five!"

"No! Not already." He watched her instead of her hands, and she wondered if she'd changed much in the last three years. Then he asked, "Are you working?"

"No. I'm still getting my degree."

"You're still in school?"

"Mmmm. Computers. Accounting. That's why I travel this road."

"They ought to check your hoses when you get gas," Nick said critically.

"I go to the self-serve pump."

"Then you ought to do it," he lectured. "You're doing a pretty good job there, but be sure to replace the hose. Don't count on the tape."

"Yes, sir."

"A liberated lady saying, 'Yes, sir'? I never thought I'd live to see the day." He had a nice low, husky voice. Very masculine. Marcie remembered that women went a little wild around him, which he enjoyed.

"I always say, 'Yes, sir,' when I'm ordered to do something," Marcie said.

"Oh?" He was amused. "Was I out of line?"

She wiped her grimy hands on a rag and turned to him. "Never," she assured him with only a bit of sass. "Oh," she added as she looked past him at the Mercedes. "What a nice little car!" She knew it had cost a bundle.

"I'll give you a ride one of these days," he promised.

She smiled, noncommittal, wondering if there was a double meaning to his words. But why should she feel wary with good old Nick? "Still with the family business?" she asked.

"I wish my parents had had more sons. Ron, Walt, and I are run ragged."

"My, how sad." She grinned at him. "How is Walt?"

"I think he's going to father the next generation all by himself. His wife—did you ever meet Dora?"—Marcie nodded—"she's about to have their fourth. No sweat. Just a slender, designer-clad, brood mare, and she's content with it. Incredible."

"And you're not married yet?"

"Still running."

"One of these days you'll stop," Marcie predicted.

"That...could...well be." He spaced the words deliberately.

Marcie wondered fleetingly if she and Betty could produce a candidate for him. At a fee, of course—and with his resources he could afford a nice, fat fee.

He took out his handkerchief and steadied her head with one hand as he carefully wiped her cheek with the other. Her eyes darted uneasily. It was a little strange to have a man almost flirting with her. He folded the handkerchief and replaced it so she couldn't see if there was a smudge left on it. He could have handed her his handkerchief and directed her to wipe off the smudge, if there even was one. Doing it himself that way made the gesture provocative and not quite appropriate for a married woman. Of course, she and Thad were getting a divorce. But she still felt married. Awkwardly, she mumbled something about getting on and how nice it was to see him and take care. She got in the car and was surprised when he closed the door for her, smiling down at her.

"Good-bye," she said for lack of anything better.

His smile turned into a grin, and he called, "Good-bye." He stepped out of the way, and she barely remembered to watch the traffic before pulling onto the main road. She drove home as if by instinct.

She remembered when Nick and Thad had been frater-
nity brothers, rather wild and rollicking. When she and
Thad had first dated, Nick had made it a threesome until
Thad had objected. After that Nick had begun turning
up sometime during the evening and hanging around for
a while. Then he'd begun bringing along one girl or
another and double-dating with them. Thad had been
annoyed because he'd wanted to be alone with Marcie,
and Marcie hadn't paid a lot of attention to Nick because
Thad had dazzled her.

After they'd married, Nick had continued to hang
around. He'd find reasons to help Marcie, or kiss her on
birthdays and holidays, or bring her flowers, or take them
out to dinner.

When Gina was being born, he'd shown up at the
hospital and sat with Thad. Afterward, he'd claimed Gina
was partly his own. Then, after Kelly was born, Nick's
attention had waned, and he'd drifted gradually away
from his involvement with them. Their lives were so full
and busy that he was gone long before they actually
noticed.

Like Thad, Nick had matured in the intervening years.
His build had changed, and he walked differently. He
was eye-catching. Marcie considered all her famale acquaintances, trying to find one worthy of such a prize.
There was her cousin Janet, but then ... Maybe she should
put Nick on hold just in case more ravenous wolves
chased after Thad. She would save Nick for a formidable
opponent and throw him from the sled into the jaws of
the most threatening wolf.

Although that plan seemed a little heartless and selfish, Marcie decided that one did what one had to do to
save ... Save? What did she have to save? And she pon-
dered deeply the rest of the way home.

When she arrived and the kids began stating their cases
to the Court of Appeals, Cassie told them to be quiet and

run along. She wanted to talk to their mother. She tagged along after a bemused Marcie, relating all the clever things Chas had said and done. She asked about the women he'd gone out with. Marcie tolerated Cassie with good nature.

But Marcie was puzzled over Cassie's attitude. She'd never seemed to be the star-struck, impulsive, giggling type. And now that Cassie had stopped panting after Thad, Marcie wasn't particularly interested in Cassie's love life.

But Cassie seemed to think Marcie deserved to know everything and that she was hanging on every word. So Cassie expounded in great detail. How boring. Cassie told her Chas had found another candidate for Janet.

After the kids were in bed that evening, Marcie took a light out to the cavernous garage and replaced the radiator hose on her car. While she was working, Thad strolled over to watch.

He complimented her and told her about his day. "Sidney called, and we're going to have lunch next week."

"Oh?"

"He wants our company to handle some of his business, and he's asked specifically for me."

"Terrific!"

"Yeah." He looked pleased with himself. "The guys at the office were impressed."

"I'm so glad for you." She straightened to smile at him, then bent back under the raised hood.

After a time, Thad continued, "Max tried to donate the radishes to an old people's home, then to an orphanage, but nobody wanted them. They're too strong. But he found someone at the farmer's market who was delighted to take not only the radishes but also any other vegetables he grows. Max is exuberant. He's going to donate the money to the civic theater."

Marcie thought: Their conversation was so ordinary, so domestic. It was as if everything was fine between them, as if a cloud of disaster weren't looming over them. It was very strange.

Several times she thought to tell Thad about seeing Nick, but she forgot about it in the turnings of their desultory conversation.

The next day Marcie ran into Professor John Brown. He stopped to tell her he'd seen the announcement in Sunday's paper for the play competition, and he had decided to write about his divorce. Even if he didn't win the competition, writing it might act as a catharsis.

Marcie listened, nodding. She was surprised by his straighter, more purposeful bearing. He smiled and took himself off. She watched him walk away. How fascinating that he had found a way to heal himself.

Then one day Beatrice came by. She hadn't been to the Foster home in a month, though Marcie hadn't realized it until just then.

"Well, hello," Marcie said neutrally. "Won't you come in?"

With a hint of a challenge in her voice, Beatrice asked, "Am I welcome?"

"You're always welcome in Thad's house, Beatrice."

"Beatrice?" She bristled at the use of her first name.

"Since Thad and I are almost divorced, I can hardly continue to call you Mother Foster. Would you prefer Mrs. Foster? I feel we've shared too much to be that formal. Will you allow Beatrice?"

"So you're going ahead with the divorce? I thought you might have changed your mind." She paused, then blurted out, "How can you divorce Thaddeus?"

"I'm not divorcing him, Beatrice. He's the one who no longer wants to be married to me. Take heart. He's a loving man, and he'll find someone else." She ushered Beatrice into the dining room and offered, "Tea? Lemonade? Iced coffee? It must be going to rain, it's so muggy."

Beatrice narrowed her eyes and demanded, "Are you running around with other men?"

Marcie looked her mother-in-law in the eye and said, "Not yet."

"Not yet?"

"I've been too busy."

"You'd live here in my son's house and go out with other men?"

"Thad is free," Marcie reminded her.

"You could do that?" she persisted.

"Tea, coffee, or lemonade? Which will you have?"

"Where are the children?"

"Building canals in the sand." Marcie gestured out the window to where they were playing in the backyard.

Beatrice went to the window and watched them, then said critically, "They're wasting water."

"It grows children." Marcie poured two glasses of lemonade from a pitcher on the table and added ice from a bucket.

"I'll have coffee," Beatrice decided.

"Try the lemonade."

"It doesn't agree with me." She followed Marcie into the kitchen. "I cannot tolerate your living here with my son and his children and you running around with other men doing God knows what."

"How nice you won't have to worry about that."

"You're moving out?" Beatrice's eyes flashed.

"No."

"Then . . ."

Thad came in the front door, his jacket dangling from one finger, his tie undone. "Hi." He left his briefcase and hung his jacket in the hall closet. "You girls having a nice chat?"

Marcie avoided a reply. "How about some lemonade?"

"With a little gin," he suggested. "Where are the kids?"

"Out building canals."

Thad went to the window and observed his offspring, then said, "Look how green the grass is around the sand. That's done by dissolving money and running it through the hose."

"Your mother's coffee is almost done. Excuse me. I have to go..."

But as Marcie started past, Thad took her arm in an iron grip and smiled through clenched teeth. "Stick around and tell me what we're having for supper." He unfastened several buttons on his shirt and reached around to unstick it from his back. "Lord it's hot."

She smiled at him through her teeth, mimicking him, and replied in a sweet voice, "All the goodies. Hot dogs, potato chips, green Jello, bananas, and Twinkies."

Beatrice sniffed. "That's a dreadful meal to feed a grown man."

Marcie regarded Beatrice placidly and said, "He could eat out."

"Not dreadful," Thad corrected his mother. "It's an interesting menu, filled with meaning. Let me guess...it's a bribe."

Marcie cheered. "Right the first time! Give that man a silver dollar!"

He tapped his temple, pretending to think. "Was it a quarrel? Or naps again?"

"Both."

He sighed elaborately, but he was grinning. "These dog days can get desperate."

"I had to study," she explained.

"May I have onions on my hot dogs?" he requested.

Marcie grinned. "You got it."

Just then they became aware that the doorbell had clanked several times. Marcie pried her arm free of Thad's fingers and went to answer it.

There on their doorstep stood Nick Santini, holding a bouquet of flowers and a box of fried chicken, and wearing a big grin. He also wore shorts and a summer knit shirt, but she especially noticed the grin. He looked so friendly and uncomplicated. She grinned back and exclaimed, "Nick!"

12

To Marcie's surprise Nick leaned forward and kissed her on the mouth. "Am I in time for supper? A picnic? Remember when—"

"Nick!" Thad was standing just behind them, but Marcie was sure he hadn't seen the kiss. He had heard Marcie's exclamation of Nick's name.

Nick's head jerked up and his nostrils flared briefly in annoyance. He looked astonished to see Thad. He forced his voice to be cordial. "Hello, Foster." But when Thad thrust out a welcoming hand, Nick indicated that his were full.

"Hello, Nicholas," Beatrice said, having followed them into the foyer.

Nick frowned as his eyes went past Thad and found

her. He returned her greeting with a slight bow of his head.

"Here, give me those." Cordially, Thad removed the box of chicken from Nick's hands. "It's been a hundred years since you fed us last. Where the hell have you been?"

"Are you visiting?" Nick asked. He'd kept his hold on the flowers and was still standing in the doorway.

But Thad was saying, "Come on inside," acting the perfect host. "It's great to see you." He carried the box of chicken into the kitchen.

Nick looked searchingly at Marcie. "He's visiting the kids?"

"No, he lives here."

Nick scowled. "I thought—"

"We split the house."

"It's Thaddeus's house," Beatrice interjected.

"The bottom half." Marcie gave Nick a minute shrug. It was all extremely awkward.

Only gradually did it dawn on Thad that Nick had dropped in to see Marcie, not him. From the kitchen his strong, deep voice called in amusement, "There's only enough chicken here for two people and two finicky kids."

"Yes," Nick replied.

Coming back into the hall, Thad asked, "Aren't you staying?"

Trying to soothe Nick's ruffled feelings, Marcie repeated the invitation. "There are hot dogs and Jello and Twinkies..."

"If you ask me, I prefer the chicken," Thad said, grinning.

"Nobody asked you," Nick said.

Thad chuckled, but his eyes turned thoughtful and his laughter faded. He became watchful and pensive.

Turning slightly away from Thad and his mother, and effectively shutting them out, Nick handed Marcie the flowers. "These are for the table." His husky voice was caressing, his eyes warm.

Thad took a sharp, almost inaudible breath as Marcie gave Nick a perfectly natural smile and said, "You've always had marvelous taste in flowers." Thad stiffened.

Beatrice moved over to her son. "Do you want me to stay?"

Thad frowned at the implication that he needed protection. "Oh, no. Tell Dad hello," he replied, distracted, his attention riveted on Marcie and Nick.

"You're sure?" Beatrice was ready to do battle for her only chick. She raised her chin and frowned at her tense, tight-lipped son. Marcie saw all that and thought they were both too silly for words. Thad, who didn't want to be married, was staring at his old friend Nick as if he wanted to blast him to perdition.

Trying to defuse the situation, Marcie moved with Nick into the kitchen, talking casually. Thad's eyes followed them.

"Thaddeus . . ." Beatrice began.

He snapped his head around, startled to find her still there, and said, "Good-bye, Mother." He opened the door and held it, but his attention wasn't on her. She hesitated, then left, patting his shoulder as if to say, "Mother's on your side." It irritated him.

In the kitchen, chatting easily about old times and friends, Nick and Marcie laid out the food and dishes for supper. Thad stood angrily in the doorway, not wanting to be left out but not wanting to contribute to a cozy gathering. Neither Nick nor Marcie seemed to notice him.

Marcie called the children inside to wash, and Nick said all the nice things about them that a man who is interested in a woman will say about her children. Thad's eyes narrowed.

Squatting down beside Gina, Nick told her that he'd been at the hospital when she was born and he'd always considered himself her uncle. Kelly watched. Gina grinned and hugged Nick's neck, then allowed him to lift her so that she could be carried about on his arm. She looked very smug.

Kelly looped a friendly arm around his father's leg and leaned there, smiling at Gina without envy. Thad thought that Gina was like all women: Her head was easily turned by male attention. Sons, on the other hand, were loyal.

But when Nick sat down in the dining room with Gina on his lap and began taking quarters out of her ears, Kelly went over to laugh and have a quarter taken out of his ear, too. Thad's expression became grim. He felt abandoned ... like a ghost returned to the family table to find everyone there happy, laughing, chatting, all of them having forgotten him.

"Have you seen any of the old gang?" Marcie asked Nick.

"I saw Jake just last week," Nick replied.

"Jake? Did he marry Ann?"

"No, Connie."

"Connie! I thought they hated each other!"

"They did. They're divorced."

"It happens." Marcie looked down and was silent.

Then Nick asked, "Did you get your radiator hose replaced?"

Thad glowered at him. Nick sounded just like a husband ... and a chill shivered across his shoulders and crept down his spine.

"*I* replaced it." Marcie raised her nose in the air and grinned in what a somber Thad thought was an unpardonably flirtatious manner. Her shirt was too tight, too.

"Well, after we eat, we'll just have to check it out," Nick said with a grin.

"I already did," Thad snapped.

Marcie and Nick turned to look at him with amazement. Kelly said complacently, "Daddy's good at cars."

Not to be outdone, Gina added, "He put my dolly's head back on. It was very hard, but he did."

"It must have been extremely difficult to take it off in the first place," Marcie ventured.

"I almost couldn't," Gina agreed. She was chewing on a drumstick. Marcie noticed that she and Nick were the only ones eating the hot dogs.

Referring to the headless doll, Nick said, "Like mother, like daughter. Fixing things."

Placidly Gina replied, "I don't fix things yet. I still just take them apart."

"Can you fix things?" Kelly inquired of Nick.

"Why?" he asked cautiously.

"Daddies always fix things."

"I'm not a daddy...yet." He sneaked a glance at Marcie, who wasn't looking his way and missed it. But Thad saw. His eyes darted back to Marcie, who was licking her lip. To Thad, the gesture seemed erotically sensual. He glowered because her hair lay around her shoulders in a lovely cloud of dark silk, and her eyes shone like precious jewels, the lids offering teasing glimpses of blue as she raised and lowered them. Everything she did looked to him like it was slow motion, heightening the erotic effect. She looked down at her plate, then glanced up to see if Kelly was handling the chicken leg all right.

Thad stared at her mouth. Even without lipstick, it was pink and softly inviting. His eyes dropped to her shirt, and his fingers itched to fasten the top button. Nick could very easily see two whole inches below her collarbone—and he'd ache to slide his hand in to explore that satin skin.

Thad glared at Nick, who was slathering another hot dog with mustard and chatting with Gina, who smiled and giggled and confided that she thought she *finally* had a loose tooth. Nick said, "No kidding?" Gina nodded her head all the way down and all the way back up, very

importantly, and wiggled in her booster seat, sitting taller
to appear older.

Thad watched sourly as his erstwhile friend smiled,
sharing an amused glance with Marcie. How dare Nick
share amused glances with another man's wife.

"My wife . . ." Thad blurted out, and the others looked
at him. He wasn't sure what he'd started to say other
than that he'd been thinking Nick should leave his wife
alone. Instead he said, "My wife makes better chicken
than this."

"Your . . . wife?" Nick raised his eyebrows in a snide
manner.

Thad's eyes met Marcie's. Nick's words seemed to
echo in an endless silence before Thad amended, "Marcie's chicken is better than . . . any . . ."

"I told her that when I opted for hot dogs," Nick said
disparagingly. Dismissing Thad, he turned back to Marcie.
"Remember . . ."

Thad fell silent. He sat there silently. The others
laughed and chatted, and no one paid him any attention.
He flexed his powerful body to reassure himself that he
wasn't made of mist, and he lost his appetite and sat
back in his chair and sulked.

After a while he heard Nick say, "Saturday . . ." and
". . . on Saturday . . ."

After they'd all cleaned up the kitchen, with the kids
underfoot, Nick expressed great interest in seeing Marcie's
computer. Everyone but Thad trooped upstairs. Thad
watched, trying to control an impulse to commit may-
hem, forcing himself not to follow. He paced the hall,
straining to hear what they said.

He caught the murmur of indistinguishable words
coming from Marcie's study, then their voices floated
back into the upper hall. The kids shrieked that Nick
should see Mommy's tiger. Thad gnashed his teeth and
continued to pace as he heard Nick ask with intimate
laughter, "Your . . . tiger?"

Thad paused, but he heard no reply from Marcie. However, Gina offered, "Mommy always crowded Daddy, and he had to move downstairs so's he could get some sleep. But when he did that, Mommy fell out of bed! So Daddy got her the tiger."

And Thad distinctly heard Nick purr . . .

Evenutally Nick left. Marcie chatted gaily at the door and laughed far too much. Thad didn't hear Nick say anything funny enough to warrant such gales of mirth. She had a good laugh that made a man feel very clever, and Thad didn't see any reason for her to make Nick think he was that funny.

Thad's good-bye to his old acquaintance was cool and formal, but Nick didn't seem to mind.

When Marcie finally closed the door, she turned, still smiling and found Thad regarding her soberly from under heavy eyebrows. Her smile faded, and she blinked as she tried to figure out why he was looking so serious. "It was great to see Nick, wasn't it?" she said.

"Do I have marvelous taste in flowers?"

"What?" she asked, confused.

"You said he did."

"I did?" Then she smiled and agreed, "He always did." She called the kids to take their bath. "Remember how he'd show up with flowers and supper?" She chuckled and turned away from her silent, glowering husband.

The kids fought over who would go up the stairs first. Gina tried to block Kelly, but he went right on past her. Gina stamped her foot and yelled with great indignation, "Mommy! Did you see that?"

Marcie said she needed Gina to hold her hand going up the stairs, and Gina shot a haughty expression to a triumphant Kelly, who was standing on the landing. He then waited for his mother and generously offered to take her other hand. She thanked him for his additional escort, and they went the rest of the way up to the second floor.

Thad joined them. He teased the kids to elaborately underline how hilarious his children found him.

"You're getting them over-stimulated," Marcie cautioned. She studied him, puzzled because he normally never overindulged them. He was smarter than that. She grew impatient with his odd behavior.

It was some time before the kids wound down. Finally Marcie left Thad to cope with them by himself. He sat in a chair, holding the kids on his lap, and told them a very dull story. By the time he put them to bed they were grateful to be there.

Marcie was in her study, engrossed in her books, when Thad entered. She didn't look up, so he wandered around, picking things up and putting them down until she was forced to notice him.

With carelessly concealed irritation, she put down her book and asked, "What's the matter?"

He affected great surprise. "Nothing. Why?"

"You're acting strange. You've been acting strange all evening. Did Beatrice say something to upset you?"

"Why would you think that?"

"Well..."

He waited, but she seemed reluctant to continue. "Well?" he echoed.

"I can't think of anything else that could have set you off, and you've been impossible all evening. I supposed it started because your mother chose today to visit."

He wasn't stupid. "Did she say anything to you?"

"She objected to my living in her son's house, carrying on, dating men, and doing heaven knows what all." She gestured angrily.

"She wasn't as lucky as we've been. She had only me."

"I wish she'd just quit trying to run my life."

"You run your own life."

"I resent her interference." Marcie sighed, then added, "Time will take care of it all."

He frowned. "Time?"

"Our divorce will be final next month."

He was taken by surprise. He narrowed his eyes and watched her. She sat there, beautiful in the light from her study lamp, her expression inscrutable. The divorce didn't seem to affect her one way or the other. Could she really be as aloof and unconcerned as she seemed?

He strolled thoughtfully to the doorway and turned back to remind her, "Don't forget. You promised to have dinner with me the night the divorce is final."

She nodded soberly.

He searched for a reaction, but she turned back to her book. Finally he said, "Good night," and left.

13

ON SATURDAY MORNING, as they passed each other in the hall, each intent on different errands, Thad said, "That film you wanted to see is playing tonight at the dollar cinema. Want to go?"

"It's my free evening. I'm going out."

He stopped dead in his tracks, and his head whipped around. "You're what?"

"I'm going out," she said over her shoulder.

"Going out? With Lisa?" he asked cautiously as he turned and followed her.

"No. Nick."

"Nick?" he roared, then immediately recalled hearing Nick say something about Saturday night.

Marcie looked back at him in puzzled surprise. "Yeah. Why?"

He couldn't answer. Finally he replied, carefully casual, "We'll double date."

She dismissed the idea with a snort of laughter and went about her chores.

During lunch Thad asked, elaborately offhanded, "Where are you and Nick going?"

"To dinner." She shrugged, denoting vague plans.

Thad nodded, but his eyes were alert. "What are you going to wear?"

"My white cotton suit, black blouse, black sandals and, if it's more casual than that, I can take off the jacket."

That had better be all she took off, he thought. He clenched his teeth and stared at his plate, trying to think of something to say that wasn't idiotic or revealing. The kids' chatter filled the conversational gap, and his contribution wasn't missed.

For the rest of the day Thad didn't mention her date with Nick again. After they'd fed the kids supper and while Marcie was dressing, he offered to go get the sitter. For the first time she noticed that he, too, was dressed to go out. She wondered where. When Nick arrived, they had to wait until Thad returned with the sitter. He pulled up behind Nick's Mercedes.

With a sinking feeling Marcie watched not only Thad and the sitter emerge from the car, but also a strange, nicely dressed, attractive woman who was obviously Thad's date. Marcie felt like sitting down on the curb and throwing up.

The situation got worse. The sitter went into the house to be greeted with exuberance by the children, and the front door closed. Those left outside made introductions all around. The woman's name was Sue Bond.

Thad was heartily friendly with Nick. Too heartily

friendly. Taking Sue by the arm, he approached Nick's car, seemed to admire it, then opened the door and helped Sue into the back seat!

"Hey..." Nick called and flung out a hand as he glanced at Marcie for a clue. She felt as if she were in a trance.

Like a cheery host, Thad then took Marcie's arm and said brightly, "Why don't you sit in back with Sue. I'll sit in front and talk to Nick." And he ushered a zombielike Marcie into the back seat of the car.

"Just a damn minute..." Nick protested.

"He said you're his wife?" Sue asked. Indignantly she protested, "Thad! I didn't come out with you at the last minute this way to sit in the back seat with your wife!"

"Almost ex," Marcie supplied woodenly.

"I'm not going to," Sue went on determinedly. She scrambled over Marcie's feet and out of the car, where she gestured angrily, arguing with Thad, who tried to placate her.

Meanwhile, Nick reached in and pried Marcie's inert body out of the back seat. Ignoring the others, he helped her into the front seat, pushed down the lock, and slammed the door. As Thad banged on the door and ordered Marcie to open it, Nick went around to his side, got in, and drove away. Thad yelled after them, and Sue stalked off toward the bus stop.

Nick drove rather fast for a while before he calmed down enough to inquire, "What the hell was that all about?"

"He's dating a woman," Marcie replied.

Nick shot her a glance. "He's been dating men?"

"Pac-Man."

"Huh?"

"He's been going to the arcades."

Looking a little confused until he realized that she

wasn't functioning on full charge, Nick asked, "What the hell's going on?"

"He's dating a woman," she repeated in a hollow voice.

"Well," he snapped impatiently, "you're going out with a man!"

"But it's just *you.*"

Offended, his eyes flared, and he shot an indignant look at her. Why was he so angry? She couldn't think. When he asked where she wanted to go, she said she wasn't hungry. She slumped down in her seat and looked mournfully out of the window.

They went to a dim bar, where Nick found a stool for her while he stood beside her. He ordered their drinks, and she sipped hers dispiritedly as an occasional tear fell down her cheeks. Nick ate several trays of fried potato skins, cheese cubes, and various sliced fruits that the sympathetic bartender placed before him.

Marcie sat drooping on the stool and was uncommunicative amidst the noise of music, talk, and laughter. Nick was restless and impatient. Half of her first drink was still left after he'd had several. Finally he growled, "Let's get out of here."

He took her to his apartment. It was as neat and stylish as he was, and, being air-conditioned, it was very inviting. He turned on only a light or two, took off her jacket, and led her to the sofa. He squatted down and removed her sandals, grinning up at her. "You okay?" She gave him a watery smile. Then he mixed her another drink and sat down beside her.

He put his arm around her and kissed her temple. She lay her head on his shoulder and sighed sadly. He kissed her cheek. She nestled her head against him and shifted to fit better against the comfort of his side. He took her drink and placed it on the table, then leaned his head around and kissed her mouth.

Grateful for his understanding sympathy, she kissed

her old friend Nick and put her arm across his chest, laying her head in the hollow of his handy shoulder.

Then she noticed that his heart was thudding at an accelerated rate, his breath was coming quick and shallow. Her eyes opened wide as the realization struck her. He was aroused. Nick? Good old Nick? He wanted sex with her? Old married woman, mother of two children, abandoned by her husband . . . her? He couldn't *possibly* be that desperate.

But Nick's breath began to come in hot gusts. He slid his mouth down to hers and pressed her head over his arm exposing her throat. His hands began to move. One went to her soft breast, and the other traced slow, sensual circles on her stomach. How lovely it was!

Then with a jolt her conscience came awake, and she struggled to push his hands aside, free her mouth, and sit erect. He was not easily put off. She squirmed and poked him with her elbows and became tight-lipped and determined. But he didn't really give up until she began to cry. She cried so seldomly that she always made an unsightly mess of it.

He sat back, ticked-off. "Am I that revolting?" he asked angrily.

"What? Oh, Nick, don't be dumb. He's going out with a woman!"

Nick looked at Marcie with great disgust and snarled, "So what?"

Her face crumpled up, and she wailed.

"The neighbors will think I'm beating you!" he muttered. Then he sat silent and disgruntled, watching her. It wasn't long before her sincere distress aroused his sympathy. "Good Lord," he said, and again he took her into his arms. Even in her misery, Marcie could tell the difference, in the way he held her. "You need to get out of that house," he said reasonably.

She hiccuped and blew her nose before replying, "There isn't enough money for two households, and I've got to finish school. It's the only way."

"I'll *give* you the money! I've got more than enough. Let me do that so you can get away from him. You'll be miserable if you go on living there. You won't realize it's finished. Or . . . come live here."

"You're sweet, Nick, but I couldn't do that. I still love Thad."

"I've never understood why you chose Foster."

"That's because you're a man. If you'd been a woman, you'd understand. Women go mad for Thad." And she told him about the ravenous wolves.

"If you come and live with me, you'll forget Foster," he promised.

"Why do you keep calling him Foster as if he were a stranger?"

"I've hated his guts ever since he first dated you."

"That doesn't make any sense at all. We've been the best of friends!" She frowned up at him.

He looked at her as if he'd overestimated her intelligence and remained silent.

She went on and on about all the things they'd done together and how he'd been there when Gina was born . . . and he grew impatient with her lack of perception. Finally he said, "I love you, Marcie."

"I know that, and we love you, too. There aren't many friends we could count on. But Nick, you always headed the list."

He regarded her grimly, then said, "We need to talk about this some other time. Come on, I'll take you . . . back. Will you be all right?"

"I have to get used to it."

"Come live with me," he urged. "When the divorce is final, I'll marry you."

"Oh, Nick, how nice of you! But you don't have to do that. Just because I'm upset doesn't mean you have to ruin your life. There *is* a limit to what is expected of a dear friend." She touched his cheek and gave him a sweet, teary smile.

He rubbed his forehead very hard and replied, "We'll talk another time."

Thad waited up for Marcie. He paced and worried and sweated. After Marcie and Nick had roared off in the Mercedes, Thad had chased after Sue. He'd caught up with her, but he'd had a hell of a time coaxing her to let him drive her home instead of taking the bus. She'd told him just what she thought of him and his wife and their idea of a double date.

He hadn't heard a whole lot of her tirade because he'd been preoccupied with wondering where Nick was taking Marcie and what he might be doing with her. He'd always suspected Nick had a yearning for Marcie. Now his old "friend" saw the opportunity to do something about it.

After he saw Sue to her door, Thad drove around town looking for Nick's car. He never found it. Finally he drove home to be there in case Marcie had to fend off the lecherous Nick and called Thad for a ride home. But she didn't call. Why didn't she? She must be enjoying it! She was wrapped in Nick's arms and . . . Thad continued to pace and run his hands through his hair.

Nick walked Marcie to the front door and gently kissed her. She thanked him for being so kind and understanding—such a good friend. He grunted a harsh word and unlocked the door, handed her back the key, kissed her again, and went down the steps to his car.

She lifted a hand to him, shut the door, and relocked it, then she turned and gasped. Thad was standing right there, scowling furiously. "Where have you been?" he demanded.

He looked so threatening that she took a half-step back. "With Nick."

"Do you know what time it is?" He pointed to his watch.

She peeked and said, "Five after ten?" Frowning, she started to ask him what was the matter.

His lips parted in a shocked gas   and he accused, "You've been crying!" and he reached out and grabbed her upper arms with hard hands.

"Yes . . . well . . ."

"Did he hurt you? What did he do? That bloody bastard! I suppose he tried to rape you! Did he? I'll kill him." And Thad shook her, then released her so abruptly that she staggered.

"No!" she protested. "Thad! Stop this! Nick didn't do anything. Stop. Wait!" And she caught his arm to keep him from storming out of the house.

"Why are you protecting him? He's been after you all along, and he forced you, didn't he!"

"Don't be silly. Nick's our friend . . ."

"Friend! Hah!" He shook off her hand and strode toward the door.

"Thad!" She wrapped her arms around his waist, locked her hands together, and clung like a leech. Without hurting her, there was little he could do to quickly dislodge her. "I had a ghastly headache," she said, "and Nick was a total gentleman. I didn't want anything to eat so we just talked."

"What about?" Thad snapped.

"Oh"—she raised large, woeful eyes to him—"just old times and—"

"Where'd you park?"

"We didn't . . . park." She was irritated. "We're too old for that. You're being completely unreasonable, Thad. I can't for the life of me figure out what's gotten into you lately. You're acting so strange." She put a limp hand to her throbbing head.

"Does your head really hurt?" He put an arm around

her and cupped her head gently in his large hand.

"It's a bearcat." Her voice was faint.

"You ought to know better than to drink without eating. Come on, I'll make you an eggnog and some toast. Marcie, he didn't hurt you or try anything, did he? Tell me the truth."

"He's a good friend. He wouldn't do anything like that."

"Then why did you cry?"

"I don't know." She flung out her hand. "I suppose it was a combination of an empty stomach, a drink, and talking about old times."

"And he didn't try to make love to you?"

"Of course not."

Thad got out the milk and an egg and vanilla and nutmeg and dumped them together in the blender. He put some bread in the toaster. "What was it about old times that made you so sad?" He studied her woeful expression, still not understanding.

"I don't know. I guess the realization that... things...change." She almost swallowed the last word, and again tears threatened to spill.

Thad wasn't stupid enough not to understand the ramifications of that statement. So change—the divorce— *had* touched her emotions. She wasn't as cool and removed from it all as she seemed. Did she feel regret? He felt very tender toward her. He sat her on the stool until he'd prepared her snack, then poured the eggnog into a glass and buttered the hot toast and arranged it on a tray. He added two aspirin and escorted her into the den.

He sat next to her on the sofa bed. She protested that she'd get crumbs on it. He said she could put crumbs into his bed any time. He grinned as he squatted down and took off her sandals. She was suddenly intensely aware of the déjà vu with Thad in place of Nick. Would

Thad comfort her as Nick had? Would he kiss her and become aroused? She sipped the eggnog slowly and waited.

Thad resumed his seat next to her and put his arm along the back of the couch. Nick had been like the toy tiger, there to comfort her. But she was intensely aware of Thad as a desirable man. She felt self-conscious. She was perspiring in the heat of the late July evening.

If the house wasn't so big, they could air-condition it. She found herself saying, "Nick's lucky. His place is small enough to be air-conditioned." The sentence seemed to explode in the sudden silence like steel balls dropped onto a wooden floor.

"Nick's . . . place?" Thad repeated carefully. "You were at Nick's apartment?" His body went stiff.

"Well, the bar was so smoky and crowded."

"So you went to see his etchings?" he guessed harshly.

"Oh, Thad," she protested, "it wasn't like that at all."

"And why didn't you mention before that you went to his apartment? You said you hadn't parked, that you were too old for that. I assumed you meant you were too mature for cheap necking." His tone was acid.

"You are deliberately reading something nasty into my visit with an old friend."

"Old friend." He sneered.

"Yes!" She got up and thumped the glass down on a side table and raged at him. "You accuse *me* of doing what *you* do. Sue Bond!" She pronounced the name as though she were saying "Mata Hari."

"Now, Marcia . . ."

"Now, Thaddeus! You can just go jump off a bridge."

"Sure, sure. The best defense is a good offense. Go on. Accuse me of all sorts of things."

She sputtered furiously. Then she turned blindly, stumbled over her sandals, picked them up, stood still a minute until her head stopped throbbing, carefully took the aspirin from the tray, and went up the stairs—all under his angry, unsympathetic gaze.

She swallowed the aspirin, then crawled carefully into bed, swearing she'd rid her mind of any disturbing thoughts. Eventually she fell asleep.

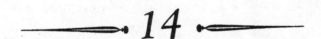

14

SHE AWAKENED THE next morning feeling dull and exhausted. She dragged herself through the humid heat, to sit in church next to Thad and the kids, fanning herself with the church bulletin. The sermon was on the responsibilities of marriage. All the smart people had gone to their summer cottages on the lake and the church service was sparsely attended, so preacher Jamison took the irresistible opportunity to hit on a few home truths. He also mentioned skipping church and the light collection plate.

August came, and the fans whirled twenty-four hours a day, but they moved the hot, humid, air through the house without cooling it.

Nick dropped by several times after that emotion-packed Saturday. The first time he arrived, Thad told him Marcie wasn't home. The second time he said she was studying and didn't have time to talk, so what did he want? After Nick phoned to tell Marcie what had happened, she confronted Thad with baffled irritation. Thad snapped, "Oh, I didn't realize Nick was so privileged that he can interrupt your studying when no one else can."

"That's not true! Why would you say something like that when the kids interrupt me all the time?"

"You don't love them."

She pulled her hair and bared her teeth and gave a frustrated "Augh!" but he simply regarded her with calm reason. Then he asked, "Will you prepare dinner on Friday? I've invited Debra Speaker to dinner."

Marcie had been expecting such an announcement for some time, but she was still shocked when it came. She felt like a tree that had just received the final blow of the ax.

Stiff-faced, she replied, "Of course." Who was Debra Speaker? She'd never called for Thad when Marcie had answered the phone. Maybe she was one of the women who had refused to leave a name. But Marcie didn't ask Thad who she was.

When she got home from school the next day, Cassie met her at the door and followed her around complaining about Chas, who she said had grown aloof and quarrelsome and difficult to deal with.

"Do you know what he eats? Meat and potatoes!" Cassie gestured uncomprehendingly. "I prepared a perfectly beautiful quiche with a fruit salad and cloverleaf rolls, and *he* went out and bought *hamburgers!*" She paused for effect. "And ate them!" She glared at Marcie, who didn't react. "After eating three quarters of the quiche!"

"He works hard," Marcie mumbled.

"Ughgle!" said Cassie, and she stormed out of the house.

The next day she was cool to Marcie and spoke in monosyllables.

Once summer school finished, Marcie spent two days in a stupor recovering. She swore she would never go to summer school again.

Nance called to remind her that the hearing for the divorce was the next Tuesday. She wouldn't be needed in court since it was Thad who'd filed, but there was still time to stop this foolishness.

"Have you contacted Thad, or do you want me to remind him?" Marcie asked.

"I told him, too."

"Well. You don't need me in court?"

"No. Marcie . . ."

"School's out so I may come anyway. It's an important step. Thad and I are going out for dinner afterward.

Grimly Nance commented, "Idiocy."

Thursday, as she arrived home from shopping for Thad· and his friend's dinner, the phone was ringing. Cassie answered it, then said with prim formality, "Your sister is here." She thrust the phone at Marcie and busied herself within earshot.

Marcie said, "Hello?" Chas's exasperated voice asked, "Why the hell am I talking to you?"

"I don't know."

"Well, tell Cassie I'm going to be there at seven tomorrow night, and she'd better be there, too."

"Just a minute." She put her hand over the mouthpiece and said to the lingering Cassie, "It's Chas."

Cassie raised cool brows and asked icily, "Who?"

In that moment Marcie swore off matchmaking for all time. "My brother, Charles."

"Oh. Him."

"He's going to be here at seven tomorrow night, and he would like you to be here."

"Why?" Cassie inquired indifferently.

"Why? she asks," Marcie said into the phone.

"Because I said so!" Chas replied furiously.

Marcie eyed Cassie patiently and reported, "Because he says so."

"I may." Cassie looked out the window, then back at Marcie, and added, "And I may not." She turned on her heels and walked toward the door.

"She may or she may not," Marcie reported to Chas.

"She sure as hell better be, or I'll fan her tail."

Marcie interpreted that to Cassie. "He asks you, please."

"I didn't say that!" he yelled into the receiver.

Marcie sighed. "That's how I understood it."

"Let me talk to her," he demanded.

"Cassie." Marcie held out the receiver.

The younger woman eyed it warily and moved her body slightly, taking her time deciding whether or not to accept the phone. Finally she heaved a big sigh into the mouthpiece, as if she was being very patient, and asked in a pouting, unfriendly way, "What do you want?"

Later, Cassie trailed upstairs and stood in the doorway of the study. "We won't be here for supper tomorrow night after all."

"You were going to eat here?"

"Thad asked us."

"Do you know if he asked anyone else?"

Cassie shook her head. "I'm going to drive up and spend the weekend with Chas."

"No, Cassie . . ." Marcie warned.

"At your parents' house." Cassie lifted a proud chin.
"Oh."

"I'm not stupid, you know."

At supper Marcie asked Thad, "Anyone else for dinner tomorrow? Chas called, but Cassie tells me she's driving up there, so they won't be here."

"Yeah, Chas called me, too. No, just us."

He already referred to *her* as *us*. Marcie reeled under

the onslaught. How could she ever survive in that house with Thad dating other women. What was she going to do?

The dinner was a nightmare. She made cold cumcumber soup, chicken Florentine, lemon tea rolls, and sliced melon and cookies for dessert. Thad brought home a bouquet of flowers for the table and smiled, waiting for Marcie to say something. She took them without a word and exchanged them for the zinnias she'd picked from the yard. He mentioned how pretty the table looked, then said in surprise, "You've only set two places."

"I ate with the kids."

"Well, you'll just have to eat again."

"She's your guest," Marcie pointed out.

"So? Cassie and Chas and all the rest were *your* guests, but *I* stayed around."

"You were my guest, too." This was getting silly.

"There! So you'll be my guest!" He'd solved that.

"This is *silly*. Anyway, I didn't know you'd invited me."

"Set another place."

"Oh, Thad . . ." She was thoroughly exasperated with him.

"Marcia!"

"Thaddeus!"

"I mean it!"

Grimly she obeyed. She went upstairs and put on a simple, sleeveless cotton dress of blue and green that made her blue eyes appear almost purple. She twisted her hair on top of her head and clipped blue button earrings in her ears. She glared at her reflection. She looked mutinous and sulky. She stretched her mouth into a false smile that made her laugh at how ludicrous the situation was.

What would it be like for the other woman, Debra Speaker, who'd been invited to Thad's house for dinner and would soon discover that his soon-to-be-ex-wife would be serving the meal? Would she eat it? Would she eye the wine suspiciously? Would her back tingle when Marcie moved behind her chair? Would she be able to handle it all with aplomb?

Curious, Marcie went downstairs to find Thad, who eyed her critically, then smiled in approval. Now, why did how she was dressed concern him? Had he expected her to appear a slattern in a loosely tied robe, flapping slippers, and tousled hair?

Debra arrived. She was perfectly charming, at ease, and pleasant. She smiled at the children as they said good night, and she didn't gush or coo at them. She was new to Indianapolis, found the city a delight, was looking forward to living there, and she ate the food Marcie had prepared without any hesitation.

She commented on Marcie and Thad's living arrangements and commended them for being adult enough to solve their problems reasonably. When she complimented Marcie on the flowers, Thad smiled smugly. Debra also complimented the meal as she ate it with relish. She said the lemon rolls showed a stroke of genius. Debra was a nice-looking, curvaceous, poised, mature, twenty-eight-year-old woman, and Marcie didn't like her at all.

Thad outdid his hospitable self and relentlessly—but with great tact—included Marcie in the conversation. She responded the way Gina did when she was out of sorts. Marcie knew she was being immature and struggled against it, but she couldn't help acting like a balking child.

She had lied about eating with the children. Still, she had no appetite and picked at the delicious food as she scolded herself for acting so boorish. It didn't do any good. Without her presence, Debra and Thad would have had a delightful time. Even with her there they still had a merry, interesting discussion punctuated with laughter.

Marcie quickly learned that Debra worked in Thad's office. Marcie was unpardonably unresponsive. She sighed. Well, maybe the next time he wouldn't insist that she join them. Next time...

She cleared the dinner plates and returned with bowls of fruit and a plate of cookies. Then she excused herself, telling Debra that she had a headache, that she knew she'd been a lackluster hostess and that she hoped to be forgiven.

Debra graciously replied, "I realize you must not feel well—you've been so quiet—but thank you for your company and for the lovely dinner."

Thad escorted Marcie to the bottom of the stairs and said he hoped aspirin would help her headache. But they both knew she didn't have a headache.

She lifted clear, pain-free eyes to his and said solemnly that she was sure it would. She knew he was furious with her, but why? Why did he insist that she sit there with his new date? Why was he determined to rub her nose in the fact that he was interested in another woman? Would he expect her to be hostess to all his women?

Her head did feel strange, and she would have liked a glass of milk, but she couldn't possibly go traipsing down there now. She put on a T-shirt and panties and climbed into bed. The sheets felt clammy against her hot skin. It was only nine o'clock. How was she ever to sleep all night in that ghastly hot room?

She didn't dare fill the bathtub. The pipes were so loud and intrusive. She turned over and sighed. Then she turned on the lamp, which added more heat, and studied a page in a book for a long time. What were they doing down there? She raised her eyes to the digital clock. It was only nine seventeen. Good Lord.

She got up and swallowed the two aspirin, then turned off the lamp and grimly lay down. She strained to hear what was going on downstairs. Were they finished with dessert yet? He'd probably hurried Debra along and was enticing her into the den.

She groaned aloud in anguish. Downstairs she heard Debra's faint, pleasant laughter, muted by the big house. Marcie lay still, her thoughts a kaleidoscope of images of Thad. Tears blurred what she could see of the dimly lit room, but she was determined not to cry.

The front door opened. They were leaving! Why was he taking her somewhere else? Perhaps he had some compunction about seducing a woman in the house while she and the children were there. Thad had never shown such consideration when he was with *her*. She'd never forget the first time they'd visited her family...

Then from outside she heard a car pull away. Only one? Was Thad driving Debra home and taking a cab back? Then the front door opened and closed again. Hadn't Thad gone? She lay in the dark room, rejecting sad thoughts, trying to relax into sleep. A few minutes later she heard a stair creak and turned her head to see Thad emerge on the landing, his naked body silhouetted against the moonlight.

Before her incredulous eyes, he came into the room and shoved the stuffed tiger to the floor. Without saying a word, he got into bed with her. What was he doing? She sat up. "Now, just—"

"Oh, shut up!"

She gasped. He had never spoken to her so harshly. She lay back down, her indignation rising. She sat up again and took a deep breath, ready to pour out angry words, then changed her mind and lay down without saying anything. "If you're going to do sit-ups, get on the floor," Thad growled. "You're rocking the bed."

It was *her* bed! She lay there sorting out a scathing, devastating... What was he doing up here? "Wouldn't Debra give in?" she snapped.

"Why should she?"

"Well, what was she doing here?"

He spoke with grim patience and through gritted teeth. "She's the new head of personnel, and each department head is having her to dinner."

"Oh. Why didn't you tell me?"

"I did! When Joe Peterson left, I told you who we were interviewing for the position. I explained everything."

Her second "Oh" was very faint. As she considered this new information, she turned her head and stared at his back. His naked back. Her eyes trailed down his length, blurred in the night. She felt very bad that she had so misjudged him. Poor Thad. She'd been awful to him. And he was there in her bed. Why had he come upstairs? It had been a long time since they'd been together in bed.

She'd missed him terribly. Why shouldn't she have him as long as he was willing? Although he didn't seem very willing just then, silent and with his back turned to her. What was he doing there?

She remembered the first time they'd been in bed and how scared she'd been. He'd been so kindly loving. He was a marvelous lover. She remembered the touch of his hands and mouth. She moved over stealthily until she was close to his back.

"Get away from me!" he said sharply.

She recoiled in surprise and hurt. He'd never rebuffed her before. As she drew away, he continued to lie there, rigid. If he really didn't want her near him, what was he doing in her bed? She thought about it and remembered all the years she'd slept unconsciously jammed against him. He had never complained.

Slowly she curled up against his back, put her arm gently over his side, and pressed her lips to his hot, sweaty shoulder. She flicked her tongue to taste the salt of his sweat. He didn't move or speak. His body was like a furnace. His skin under her cheek and against her breast and hip was scorching and slick with perspiration in that miserable night.

They lay there silently, and passion awakened in her. She pressed her body deliberately against him, and slid her hand down his side to his hip. He stirred and she froze, expecting rejection. But he moved slowly and carefully until he'd turned in that limited space and was facing her. He took her in his hard, hot arms, and his mouth came down on hers in a kiss that sent thrills ricocheting through her.

Passion flared quickly out of control as they feverishly fed on their need of each other. His hands were demanding and her nails lightly scratched his back and shoulders as she tried to draw him even closer. She tightened her restless, grasping hands in his hair, and their breaths came in fiery gusts as they moaned with desire.

He took her quickly, and she received him in a violent rocking that tore sounds from their throats. Their rigid, convulsing bodies jerked in a brief wild, torrid mating dance like none they'd ever experienced.

They collapsed against each other, panting for breath. Their hearts still thundered in clamorous unison, and the hot night's humid breath felt cool on their damp bodies.

As their breathing calmed, Thad lifted his weight from Marcie's chest and rested on his elbows. He looked down at her, turned aside, and shifted to take her face between his hands. His touch was not gentle. He looked deeply into her eyes, his expression harsh and somber. Then he leaned over, opening his mouth, and again he kissed her. He didn't hurt her, but his kiss was demanding . . . as though he was staking a claim.

Still coupled with her, he moved minutely, rubbing his hot chest across her tender breasts. He kissed her cheek, then grazed his stubbled chin against it, licked her ear and buried his face in the side of her throat, where he suckled her earlobe.

As he moved, she made small noises of near-protest.

She was so sated and tender that she wanted only gentle murmurings, featherlight caresses, and sleep. But he tenderly coaxed her into a renewed response, and they made love again, long sweet love. Then they changed the damp sheets before curling together in sleep.

But when Marcie awakened the next morning, it was the stuffed tiger that guarded her fall.

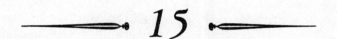

15

THE WEEKEND PRECEDING the hearing, all of their friends and relatives—except Beatrice—tried to get the Foster marriage straightened out. The constant questions and advice, and resulting emotional exhaustion were almost more than Marcie could endure.

On Sunday, Mr. Jamison asked the congregation to pray for special intension. Although he bowed his head, he glared at the Fosters from under his eyebrows.

On Monday, Marcie drifted around the house like a ghost. Thad remained serious and quiet, ever watchful. The children went their exuberant way, unaware. Innocence was a great protector, Marcie thought.

She asked her husband, "Are you sure?"

"Are you?" he countered.

"You're the one who started this."

"Yes."

Marcie wondered if he meant yes, he was the one who'd started it, or yes, he was sure. Either way, it made no difference.

Various members of her family called to ask if she needed help. She was touched by their concern, but she couldn't handle any more displays of emotion so she said she was all right.

By Tuesday, Marcie was a little strung out. The hearing was scheduled for that afternoon. Nance had invited them to lunch beforehand, but they'd declined.

Marcie had warned Thad, "Nance wants one more crack at mending us." She watched to see his reaction.

Thad blinked and asked, "How could you use a crack to mend anything?"

Marcie refused to reply. How could he make jokes about something as serious as a divorce?

She wore her white suit to the hearing. Her marriage had begun in white, and it would end in white. Anyway, the Chinese wore white to mourn the death of loved ones. Marcie felt she was going into mourning. She wore sunglasses because her eyes were bloodshot from unshed tears. She stood up straight, determined not to think. If she did, she'd lose control and disgrace them all.

She witnessed the hearing as if it were a silent film, while in a corner of her mind a voice repeated over and over again, "It's happening. It's really happening. Can you believe this?"

Nance conducted herself formally in the courtroom, and when the hearing was over, her lips were thin and her expression stern. She shook hands with Marcie and Thad then brusquely leaned over and kissed Marcie's cheek. The kiss almost destroyed her control, and she took an uneven breath, but Nance turned and strode away.

Silently Thad took Marcie's arm and led her from the courthouse. She was grateful for his support. Otherwise she might have wandered blindly through the city. If she found herself in the police station, lost and without money, who would claim her? She told herself to stop being maudlin, but it was a maudlin occasion. If she couldn't allow herself to be torn apart by a divorce, when could she?

Still silent, they walked to the Hyatt Hotel and took the elevator to the Eagle's Roost on the top floor. They found a table next to a bank of windows overlooking the city. It was early, and there were no other customers.

They sat down, and Thad ordered champagne cocktails. Marcie found it difficult to swallow. Her eyes darted everywhere but at Thad, and she still wore sunglasses. She wondered why in God's name she'd ever consented to anything so incredibly stupid as to have dinner with Thad on this of all days? She couldn't handle it.

Her left hand lay lifeless on the table. Thad reached for it—and removed her wedding and engagement rings!

She watched in stony silence. How could he? Of course, he'd put them there, so she supposed he could take them off. But at least the diamond engagement ring should be hers. The diamond was so small that it couldn't be seen clearly from a distance of more than three inches. But it was infinitely precious to her. When she could speak again, she'd ask for it back.

Thad didn't release her hand. He took a box from his inside pocket, opened it, and removed a small gold ring. Two clasped hands were engraved on it: a friendship ring. She wasn't sure if she was touched or offended. Was he offering her friendship after all they'd meant to each other? Finally she looked at him.

He smiled and said, "We're the best of good friends." He put the ring on her right hand, then kissed it. Her face frozen, she retrieved her hand and bent to examine the ring through sunglass-covered, tear-filled eyes. She couldn't see it at all.

"Will you have an affair with me?" he asked as he slid her wedding and engagement rings into his side pocket.

She blinked. "W—what?"

"An affair." He took up her left hand again and kissed the palm. His eyes held hers intently.

"What are you talking about?"

"I want to have an affair with you," Thad said, "because I love making love with you." His thumb caressed her palm.

"I thought you weren't through running around."

"I'm not. I'm going to have a mad, passionate affair. With you." To Thad, that said it all. It was what he'd always wanted. And now she knew he wanted it with her. Only with her. He shifted confidently in his chair, leaned back, and continued, "I'm going to meet you after school and carry your books. On my lunch hour we're going to meet at a motel and have a loving nooner. And we're going to Uncle Pete's lake cottage and spend the night and go skinny-dipping and make love in the reeds."

If he'd deliberately planned to distract her, he was being extremely successful. "You're mad." She was astonished she'd never realized it before. He took after Beatrice.

"You don't want to make love in the reeds?" He considered that, then shrugged and said, "Okay. We'll scratch the reeds." He chuckled. "Got that? Reeds. Scratch. I'd imagine they would scratch."

She glared at him. "I thought you didn't like married women."

He gave her a sly, lazy smile. "You're no longer married."

"Yes," she said bleakly. It was true. How amazing.

"A sexy, gay divorcée, ripe for an affair." He moved his chair closer to hers and quickly kissed her mouth—a hard, possessive kiss.

She gasped in surprise, for he'd always been reasonably circumspect in public, and darted her eyes around the empty tables. He laughed deep in his throat, very pleased with himself. But she was struggling out of an emotional fog that held her in an insidious grip. "No," she said.

Surprised, he frowned at her. For the first time he appeared uncertain. "No? Why not?"

"Maybe you thrive on emotional turmoil, but I can't handle it."

"What do you mean?"

The back of her throat was dry as she said, "The ending of anything causes some sort of reaction."

"Lost love?" His voice was a little hoarse.

"Or relief." She was thinking of peace coming after a war.

His uncertainty deepened. "You feel...relief?"

"At least it's solved. It's over."

If he told her then that he loved her, she would over-react. Probably with self-pity. "No, it isn't over," he said huskily. "Not yet. Martial privileges continue until midnight. We get to have one for the road, for one last legal time."

"I don't believe..." She hesitated.

"Oh, yes. In everything I've ever read about divorce, the couple always does that the last day. It's traditional. You start out that way, so you have to end up that way, if you'll forgive the expression."

"I think it'd be better if we just had dinner and then forgot it. If we go to bed, you'll feel you can hop upstairs any time you want to."

"Only when invited." he smiled.

She raised her eyes to him. Even through sunglasses he was devastating. But the numbness was wearing off, and a physical pain was beginning to throb through her entire body. She needed to take care of herself.

He took her lifeless hand and raised it to his lips. "Remember our wedding night?"

At first she couldn't reply. Then lovely memories eased the pain and sent her back into the emotional fog. How dreadful of him to do this to her. "You were so sweet," she said.

"So were you." He chuckled tenderly. "My dad told me to leave you alone in the room so you wouldn't be embarrassed about undressing. He knew you'd never gotten undressed for me. I paced the lobby of the hotel with rice falling off my clothes, and I thought how friendly people were because everyone was smiling at me. After an endless time I finally went upstairs, all tingly and restless, and what did I find? My bride in lace, languishing in bed? No. You'd unpacked everything, hung it up, and organized the drawers. And there you were, in jeans and a T-shirt, watching TV."

"I thought you'd turned shy."

"You thought I was shy?"

"Well, a lot of men are all talk."

He laughed, genuinely amused.

"You know," she said, "I never did find out how that movie ended. You had me out of those jeans so fast, I'm amazed we made it to the bed."

"Now, now. Your memory is faulty." At her protest, he held up a hand. "Yes, it is. I was very slow and patient and gentle."

"It may have seemed so to you."

"I love making love to you." He kissed her on the mouth again.

"Then why . . ." she began but stopped.

"Why?" Again he insisted that she continue.

"Why the divorce?"

"I've told you all along that we should have had an affair. Let's have one now," he urged, his voice husky and coaxing.

"I just can't. It's like jumping out of the frying pan and into the fire. And I don't understand why you want to. You know me completely. Why have an affair with me, of all people?"

"I . . ." He almost said it then but stopped himself. "I want you," he amended. "I want to have an affair with *you.*" Surely he was making himself clear.

"No. No, it wouldn't work. Let's go eat and get this over with."

He frowned at her as they rose, but from dismay, not irritation. Then he raised his jaw and squared his shoulders and followed her from the room with a determined walk.

Throughout dinner he entertained her, with sentimental reminiscences and funny stories. "Remember when . . ." he'd begin. He talked about their courtship and when the kids were babies. He was unscrupulous as he coaxed her into surrender. Marcie was flooded with a wash of memories, all tender, all dear, all involving Thad.

When he said at last, "Are you ready to go home?" she knew they'd make love one last, legal time.

And when Thad kissed her in the parking lot, he knew it, too. He held her close as a wave of tender passion washed over them, then he kissed her again, controlling his ardor as he hadn't had to in six years.

He would have to be very careful with her, or his plan might fail and he might lose her.

He helped her into the car and went around to his side. He glanced at her as he started the engine. She was watching him warily. He smiled gently, and fear swept through him at the thought of the tremendous risk he was taking with their lives. He would have to be very, very careful.

He would have given anything to know what she was thinking.

Inside Marcie, a calm, clear voice said, "Why not?" She gazed at the night lights scattered like diamonds across the land, and the voice said again, "Why not?

Why not have an affair with him? It would prolong having him."

But hadn't she experienced enough upheaval? Wouldn't a clean break be better? Living in the same house, seeing each other every day, would be unendurable if they made love again. How had she ever gotten herself into this tangle? But she tingled with excitement at the possibility of having him for a little longer.

They were silent as they drove home.

When Thad returned from taking the sitter home, Marcie met him at the front door wearing the black lace nightgown she'd never had on long enough for him to notice. He stopped dead in his tracks and regarded her with hungry eyes that gleamed with appreciation.

She moved and turned for him. Then she lifted her free-flowing hair and allowed it to fall around her shoulders again. She walked slowly toward him, her breasts moving gently beneath the sheer fabric, her hips swaying provocatively. He watched, mesmerized.

There, in the downstairs hall, she displayed herself for him as she'd never done before. Breathing through parted lips, he watched, enthralled. He stood as still as a statue, only his eyes moving over her, and his expression seemed to say he thought she was a dream.

She stood in front of him and removed his jacket. She kissed him on the mouth as she undid his tie and unbuttoned his shirt, pulling it free from his pants. She had to undo the cuffs before she could draw his shirt from his body. His heart beat furiously beneath her fingers, but he gave her no help.

She unbuckled his belt, unzipped his trousers, and slid them off his lean hips, down his muscular thighs. She had to take off his shoes before she could remove the pants from around his ankles. Her movements were purposeful, her expression earnest. He didn't laugh at her ineptness.

She knelt before him as he stood in just his socks. She looked up his body to his face, and their eyes locked in an intense gaze. He waited, hoping she'd speak. But instead she placed tentative hands on his knees and looked up at him as a tiny smile curved her lips.

She looked like a wanton woman, kneeling there in the black lace nightgown, with her dark tousled hair, her red lips parted, and her blue eyes sparkling like jewels.

Very slowly she ran her hands up his hair-roughened thighs and caressed him. He gasped, and all his muscles became rock hard.

"Oh, Marcie," he groaned. He lifted her to him, and they kissed, their mouths soft and yielding.

After a time, their mouths parted minutely, and she breathed against his lips, "Octopi."

"Or octopuses."

"Ummm."

"Do you like that?" he asked hoarsely.

"Ummm."

"Let go of me for a minute until I calm down."

"Aren't you calm?" she inquired languidly.

"Not very."

"I'm so relaxed, I seem to have no bones. I don't believe I can stand up by myself." She began to sink toward the stairs, but he picked her up and carried her into the kitchen. He directed her to open the refrigerator and remove the bottle of champagne inside. She complied. He carried her into the dining room, where she collected two glasses, then he carried her up the stairs and into her bedroom. He lay her down on the bed and shoved the tiger to the floor, saying, "Get lost. I'm taking over."

She lay back watching him, her arms above her head, one knee slightly raised. He stood looking down at her, his interest obvious. She smiled slightly and rolled slowly over, then over again.

"I thought I told you to let me calm down."

She slid her wrists up under her hair and spread it out on the pillow. "I haven't touched you. You only told me to let go of you."

He gave her a puzzled grin and asked, "Where did you learn to act this way? I've never seen you so . . . enticing, so deliberately asking for it."

"You never gave me the chance."

"Didn't I?" He tried to think, but she was extremely distracting. He put a hand over his eyes and said, "Whew!" and shook his head as if to clear it.

She laughed low in her throat, which made his toes curl. He gave her a rueful grin and told her again to behave, then he carefully worked the cork loose from the champagne bottle and poured them each a glass of the bubbly liquid. They drank, silently toasting each other.

"I like your outfit," he said. "Is it new?"

"I've had it for years, but you never allowed me to wear it long enough to make any impression on you."

"You've worn it?" he asked, surprised as he tried to remember. He sat down on the bed and leaned over to kiss her, pressing her back against the pillows.

Then he took the glass from her fingers and placed it with his own on the bedside table before he loosened her straps and pulled her gown down below her breasts. "I think I like this outfit even better." He grinned at her and very adroitly pulled the gown down her hips and legs and threw it onto the floor.

"That's what happened every time I wore it."

"It is pretty, but this outfit is beautiful." He put his hands on her naked body. "The other one served its purpose: It attracted my attention." He kissed her breasts. "But just look at the colors of this outfit. Pink,"—he touched her nipple—"and black"—he ruffled the fluff between her legs—"and white and tan. Lovely." He indicated the areas where the sun hadn't been allowed to reach. He trailed his fingers over her, touching, feeling, squeezing.

They sipped champagne as they made love. He excited her until she gasped and mounted him, but when she became too aroused, he parted from her grasping hands and curling body and lay beside her until she calmed down. Then he began again.

He turned the clock around so she couldn't see what time it was. "As long as it's dark out," he told her, "it isn't yet midnight."

"Dawn doesn't come at midnight."

"Until daylight comes," he insisted, "it's still our last legal time."

At his words she grew sad and quiet, and he had to work to revive her passion. Then it was frenzied, almost desperate, and he was awed.

At last their passion flamed beyond control, and they were swept into convulsions of sweet surrender, their bodies writhing wildly. Afterward, they floated in euphoric disorientation until they realized they were tangled in damp sheets. It was still dark outside.

Thad tried to speak twice before he managed, "We might need to rest for a little while before we begin again."

Marcie couldn't think of anything she needed less right then than another session of lovemaking. It seemed so impossible that she felt a bubble of rising laughter at the very idea. She grinned, and the laugh escaped. She couldn't control it.

"What's so funny?" Thad raised himself on wobbly elbows and smiled down at her.

"We're both helpless with sexual exhaustion, and you say we *might* need to rest a little before we do it again. *Might?*"

"Well, we still need to have one for the road." When her eyes turned sad, he hurried to add, "Tomorrow begins our affair."

"I haven't agreed to an affair."

"Oh, you needn't agree," he assured her. "It's all been

decided." He smiled tenderly, and his voice was rough with emotion. Then, to distract her, he suggested, "Let's call the sitter back and go to a motel."

By this time nothing he did surprised her. Nevertheless, she protested indignantly, "When one invites a lady to indulge in an affair, one never hustles her immediately off to a motel."

"Sure he does."

"Never! One courts the lady and makes an affair appear desirable." She thinned her lips and attempted to appear prim, which was rather difficult lying in bed half under a naked man. "One of the things I've read recently about divorce is that one must never rush right into an affair," she lectured.

"I'm sure it's perfectly acceptable."

"You're premature in stating your purpose so boldly. You should be suave and patient, in a manner that allows me to subtly refuse you."

He frowned. "But you accepted."

She gave him a cool glance. "I haven't yet given my reply." But in her heart she knew what it would be.

"Tonight we're having one for the road, and tomorrow we begin our affair," he firmly reiterated.

"Tomorrow we *consider* an affair," she corrected.

"I've already considered it. We're going to have an affair and make mad passionate love."

She sighed with exaggerated patience. "A man," she instructed, "makes the woman think crass sex is not foremost in his mind."

"No?"

"No. He pretends he finds her mind fascinating, her conversation delightful, her company indispensable. He concentrates all his attention on her words and invites her opinions and he listens."

"Then he jumps her."

"Then he kisses her."

"And jumps her."

"Thad! I'm trying to explain!"

"I'm listening!" He held up both hands and assumed an innocent expression.

"Then he tells her how sweet she is and holds her and trembles with desire, but he doesn't mention it."

"He *doesn't?*" He rolled his eyes and gasped in disbelief of such foolishness.

"Of course not," Marcie said firmly. "He wants her to know he's controlling his baser impulses."

"*Im*-pulses?" He was becoming amused. "There are also out-pulses."

She ignored the remark. "Then he holds her hand against his chest so that she can feel how wildly she makes his heart thump."

"His . . . heart?" he asked.

She shot him a quelling glance. "Yes."

Thad's shoulders shook with restrained laughter. Laughter spilled from his dancing eyes.

Only by gesturing to show her impatient aggravation did she manage not to be carried along by his hilarity. "And he sends her flowers and finds meaningful gifts for her," she continued.

"I have a gift for you." He was enjoying her.

She knew he was and pretended to be indifferent to him. "Then he tells her he can't survive without her. His kisses become fevered and frantic."

"Now we're getting someplace."

"And that's when he asks her."

Suddenly he was curious. "How do you know all this?"

"That's what you did to me."

"I did all that?" When she nodded, he added thoughtfully, "I couldn't get you out of my mind. You were terrible. You'd put your hand on my knee and just about paralyze me."

"I never did that! My mother forbade me ever to do that!"

"Believe me. It was my knee, and you did."

"I can't believe it. I wouldn't ever have done that. Mother said it wasn't fair."

"And you'd smile and look up at me, and you'd look down and then look up at me again, and it was like I'd touched a million volt wire. Only my native brilliance kept me from flunking out of school. And then, you damned holdout, you wouldn't sleep with me. Not that you'd have ever gotten to sleep, but you wouldn't make love with me."

"That's when I learned that your evolutionary forebears were octopi."

"Octopuses is also acceptable."

"And I knew if I ever did give in, I'd turn into a Thaddeus Foster groupie, panting after you, begging for more. So I held out to save myself."

"I dreamed such erotic dreams of you. I wanted an affair with you so badly."

"You saw me as a convenient lay," she corrected cynically.

"No. It was great, unbridled love. All romance and castles and white horses and dragons. Your mother qualified as a dragon." He slanted a grin at her.

"I wonder if I'll be dragonish with Gina." She yawned, a lengthy, tired yawn. "It's time we went to sleep. I'm finished."

"Not already!"

"Zapped."

"Well, I suppose I could let you catnap for a spell."

"Ummm."

He kissed her, reached over and turned off the light, and made her comfortable against him. But in doing so he became aroused, and he made lovely, languid love to her.

When morning came she wakened with her head on the pillow and her body curled around the toy tiger. Next to her was a rose from the garden with a note that said. "You are beautiful and a charming conversationalist."

Around the tiger's neck was a twisted rope of tiger lilies, the black dust of which stained the sheets, and hanging from his ear with a paper clip was an invitation to lunch.

Naked, Marcie sat up in bed and stretched. She glanced at the clock. Nine-thirty. *Nine*-thirty! Where were the kids?

Hearing water running, she got out of bed and hurried to the window. Gina and Kelly were playing in the sand-pile, engrossed in an adventure.

Marcie yawned and stretched again and went to the bathroom to shower. On the showerhead was another note: "I wish I were bathing you." On the mirror was still another: "I wish I were looking back at you."

At ten o'clock Thad called and said, "Cassie will be there at eleven-thirty to sit with the kids. You're to come have lunch with me."

Slowly she replied, "All right." And she knew she'd committed herself to having an affair with him.

Speaking as if by rote, he added, "You're an intriguing personality and I can hardly wait to listen to what you have to say."

She had to laugh.

At noon she met him at the restaurant. He handed her a nosegay of rosebuds and baby's breath. He told her rapidly, "You're clever, and I've always wanted to know a woman with a mind like yours. You're concise in your evaluations, succinct in your observations, and astute in your character analyses."

"I haven't said more than hello."

"Your manner in saying that was what tipped me off." He then handed her a book, explaining, "I know how intensely interested you are in the subject."

Naturally she expected it to be a dissertation on the future of computers, but she unwrapped *The Joy of Sex.*

He fastened a small diamond pendant on a gold chain around her neck, watching it slide down between her breasts. "I got a long chain because I think a valuable jewel should be protected in that magic hollow—and anyway, your jiggling will keep it polished."

She looked at him with patient tolerance. "You're strange." And he agreed.

When they'd finished eating, he led her toward the elevator, then took her instead into the stairwell. He stood her against the wall and kissed her. "I can't tell you how sweet you are. Would you like to feel my heart thump?"

Her laughter became a gasp as he placed her hand on his chest.

He hurried on, saying, "You're gorgeous, and I can't live without you, and now that I've fulfilled all the requirements, how about going to a motel?"

"But you're not supposed to complete all the preliminaries in one day!" she protested. "Actually, in one lunch hour! You're supposed to spread them out!"

"What I'd like to do is spread you out. That's what I'd like to do all right."

"How can you possibly think of sex after last night?"

"Is there anything else?"

A security man came along and eyed them pointedly. Thad grinned and explained, "She's stubborn."

The security man wasn't amused. He remained standing there, so they left.

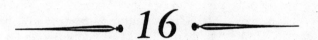

16

THAD CALLED FOR their car and pleaded his case. "Let's go to a motel. I've taken the afternoon off, and if you won't go with me, it'll be wasted. I've completed all of the preliminaries," he coaxed. "I sent you notes, flowers, gave you a book and—candy! I forgot candy!" He was so appalled, and looked at her in such elaborate shock, that she couldn't help but be charmed by him.

He snapped his fingers. "There has to be some at the drugstore. You drive, and I'll hop out and get you a candy bar. Will that do for now?"

What could she say? His approach was unique, funny, perhap not the most romantic, but he was determined. She smiled and gave up. "Okay," she said, shaking her head at her capitulation.

He kissed her and straightened his tie. It was the

handmade one. Their car arrived and he escorted her to the driver's side. After getting in himself, he directed her to the nearest drugstore, where he hurried out into traffic and dashed away.

She had to drive around the block three times before he returned. The sober part of her brain told her how stupid she was. being. Then came the strident words of her friend saying, "Affairs are like little marriages, and all of them are disastrous." Next a voice said, "What will Mother say? Beatrice will have kittens and . . . poor Mr. Jamison. He'll be very upset." Such thoughts tended to dampen the thrill of adventure that was spreading through her.

Thad was waiting impatiently when she drove up the third time. He opened the door and swung quickly into the car, holding up a candy bar. "There were only two vanilla ones left," he said smugly. "I bought you both of them." He patted his pocket. "I'm keeping one for an emergency."

"You're too kind. Flowers, a diamond, a book, and a candy bar."

"You're worth the price."

"Thad . . ." she began, then hesitated.

"What?" He was quickly alert, his face sobering.

"Would you mind driving? I know no one is going to notice who's driving when we get to the motel, but I'll know. And it seems so . . . bold for me to be driving the car. It's as if I'm dragging you there, forcing you."

The tension drained from him, leaving him sagging with relief. He thought she'd changed her mind. Triumph surged into him, and he said with teasing earnestness, "There's nothing wrong with your forcing me. I might struggle, but I'd never scream." Nevertheless, he watched the traffic and suggested she turn off onto a side street.

They changed seats, and Thad drove off again, giving her a wide grin.

They parked in the motel lot and entered the lobby, where a discreet sign announced a meeting of area businessmen who were there to view an advanced computer system. Groups of men were already milling about, having just eaten lunch in the dining room.

Thad left Marcie standing to one side, telling her, "Don't try to get away." He approached the registration desk.

She stood self-consciously, dressed in a sleeveless white dress, holding her purse, the nosegay of flowers and ribbons, a book, a candy bar, and wearing a blush. She felt as if there were a sign above her head reading "shady lady" in six languages.

Several men glanced her way, and her blush deepened. She kept her eyes on the floor, shifting nervously from foot to foot. Then, to her mortification, a familiar voice reached her ears. Nick! She looked up quickly to see him standing in the middle of the lobby surrounded by businessmen. At that moment their eyes met across the room, and his face broke out in a smile of delight. "Marcie!" As she stared in horror, he pushed his way eagerly through the crowd, drawing further attention to them. He reached out and clasped her hands in his. "So you're single again! What are you doing here?" He kissed her cheek and stood back, his face lit up with a great big smile.

"Uh...I...we..." and she went scarlet, which she felt was appropriate, but she could have died.

"Are you with the computer people?" he asked loudly, his voice booming across the room.

She shook her head. "I have to go..."

Just then Thad arrived. He put his arm around her, preventing her escape, and smiled smugly at Nick. "Hullo, Nick."

"What the *hell* are you doing here?" Nick barked.

Marcie tried to help. "Uh...I...we..."

But Thad replied smoothly, "We're having an affair."

"What?" Nick thundered, and Marcie heard several unmistakable gasps, barks of sudden laughter, exclamations of surprise, and whispered explanations. Everyone in the room seemed to be staring at them. Nick and Thad were oblivious, but Marcie trembled with painful awareness.

In a low voice she said to Thad, "I would like to speak to you outside."

But Thad and Nick were nose to nose, exchanging angry words in low growls. "I'll wait in the car," Marcie said, but Thad held her with an iron hand. She stood as if frozen, fighting down hysteria.

A kindhearted gentleman announced that the meeting room was free and why didn't they move to their seats. Gradually Marcie realized that the lobby was emptying. An older man took Nick's arm and gently urged him away from Thad, who was acting outrageously triumphant. Marcie could have kicked him.

Very low, she whispered, "Let's go home."

Nick turned back toward them and growled, "I'll call you, Marcie!"

She shot him a quelling look and, keeping her face averted from the registration desk, whispered desperately to Thad, "We have to leave."

He stared at her vaguely, as if in a trance, then his eyes focused. "Let's go to the bar," he suggested.

"No."

"Aw, honey, come on." Without waiting for her to agree, he took her elbow in a strong grip and urged her resisting body toward the bar.

It was dark in there. By not blinking, swallowing, or breathing, she fought off rising hysteria. Everyone there knew she was a newly single woman who had registered with a man at the motel . . . and that *another* man had been angrily shocked by her indiscretion.

Thad ordered two grasshoppers. He talked to her

cheerily, assuring her, "Everyone thinks you're a new bride with that white dress and the nosegay, and your blush is perfect."

"Nick . . ." she began.

"He's the discarded rival." Thad laughed quietly.

Maybe, just maybe, Thad was right, she decided. She ordered herself to swallow and found that her body obeyed the command. She breathed carefully in and out. She blinked.

Thad led her down long hallways to their room at the back of the motel near the pool. He set his wristwatch alarm so that they'd be certain to leave on time.

Marcie said, "I believe I'll just take a shower. I'm a little tense and wound up."

"I'll unwind you," Thad promised.

"I want a shower anyway."

He kissed her and rubbed his hands in hard strokes down her back and over her buttocks, crushing her to him. She gave him only stiff, shallow kisses in return and said, "I'll only be a minute."

It wasn't much more than that when she emerged from the bathroom. Thad was in bed, naked and asleep. Very soundly asleep. He'd pulled all the buds off the nosegay and scattered the petals across the sheets. She looked down at him, sleeping deeply, and her heart squeezed in pain. How could she bear to lose him?

She crawled into her side of the bed and lay there quietly. She computed how much each minute was costing them to lie in that strange bed and was appalled. She sat up and put her hand on Thad's shoulder. "Thad . . ." He snorggled and buzzed—and remained soundly asleep. As she lay down again, he automatically put his arms around her and adjusted his body to hers. She lay there pensively, closed her eyes, and slept.

The alarm awakened them. Thad stretched, tousled her hair, and grinned at her. All at once his grin faded

and he exclaimed, "We never did it!" He sat up indignantly. "We paid to take a nap!" He was so put out that
Marcie laughed.

He grinned back at her and lay deliberately on top of
her and roughed her up with bold hands. "Do you realize
what the night will be like, as rested up as we are?" he
demanded. "We'll have the whole night, lying awake in
bed, with nothing else to do."

They got dressed, and their good humor lasted until
they were standing at the door, about to leave. Marcie
balked.. "I'm not going to walk through that lobby."

"No one will be there!" he argued. But the gleam in
his eyes told her he hoped there *would* be someone so
that he could strut by him. Marcie refused to budge.
"Okay, okay," he said. "Wait here and I'll meet you at
the back door with the car in exactly ten minutes." They
synchronized their watches.

It was not an auspicious beginning for an affair. Thad
couldn't carry Marcie's books because her classes didn't
start for another week, and when they drove to Uncle
Pete's cabin for a weekend, it rained.

With optimistic determination, Thad insisted they go
skinny-dipping, but Marcie said he was nuts. Thad de-
fended himself voluably, but still Marcie refused to frolic
in the reeds. She ran back to the cabin in the cold,
dripping darkness, stubbing a toe on an exposed tree root
and scraping her shin on the cabin steps.

Thad got thoroughly chilled and went to bed shivering.
Marcie got in with him to warm him up and succeeded
only in getting cold herself. Before dawn they rose,
straightened the cabin, and drove home. Thad had a
splitting headache and was beginning to sneeze. He came
down with a terrible cold.

Word that Marcie and Thad were having an affair
reached their friends and families. The reactions were

all predictable. Her mother wouldn't speak to her at all. Even Marcie's dad didn't understand. Nance deliberately refrained from talking to them about it.

Beatrice brought over the needlepoint canvas and all the yarn for the pew cushions. "You have to buy it all from the same dye lot so that the colors will match," she informed Marcie. "And the only cost to you will be for the pattern and yarn. It will give you something to do evenings," Beatrice added with thin lips.

Betty was the only one who didn't censure and scold. In fact, she and Max set Beatrice to finding stage props, and soon Marcie rarely saw Mrs. Foster.

When Mr. Jamison heard of their affair—and Marcie wondered how he had—he came over to see her. Afterward she complained to Thad, "He called me a scarlet woman, and his eyes had tears in them."

Thad sighed. "Think what his sermons will be like now." He coughed and took another vitamin C pill.

"I guess we'd better split."

"No."

"Everybody is upset."

"Are you?"

"A little," she admitted.

"Are the kids?"

She shook her head. "They're oblivious."

"I like our affair."

"It's really a strain. Nothing is going right."

"Oh, I wouldn't say that." He grinned and nuzzled her neck. "Do you like me?"

"Oh, yes."

"What do you like about me?"

"You're sexy."

"Yeah. What else?"

"Humorous. You have flair. You're alert."

"A lert. Yeah. The Lert strain is from my father's side. There aren't many of us Lerts left."

"My mother thinks we're crazy."

"She would."

"Lisa asked me, 'What *are* you doing?' and I couldn't think how to answer her."

"What does she think people do when they have an affair?"

Despite all the hassle, Thad possessed an air of satisfaction that baffled Marcie. Their lives never had been so disorganized and disrupted, yet Thad was serene and pleased. He had taken to whistling.

He whistled in the shower, he whistled going off to work, and he was whistling when he came home. It was incredible. Their sex wasn't *that* fantastic. In fact, it was at best harried.

The kids came down with Thad's cold, and after that she and Thad tried another motel nooner. Marcie refused to return to the same place, choosing a bargain motel instead. She stopped at a hamburger stand and bought their lunch, picked up Thad, and drove to the motel.

There, they undressed and crawled into bed right away. They didn't have a whole lot of time. The mattress smelled of stale smoke, but soon that was overcome by the smell of the hamburgers.

They had barely begun to make love, and were seemingly engrossed in the act, when Thad paused and looked down at Marcie under him and said, "I'm going crazy."

"I agree." She'd thought so all along.

"Let's eat first and get back to this. That pickle smell is driving me wild."

She burst into laughter. She laughed until she was gasping for breath. Thad chuckled companionably with her. She was remembering her fantasy of some months before: Thad making love to a woman and eating lunch at the same time. It just proved she knew him pretty well.

He sat naked on the edge of the bed and chomped noisily on a hamburger and french fries and took sips of a chocolate shake. Marcie watched, grinning, then she ate, too. They never did get back to making love. They left soon after so Thad wouldn't be late getting back to work. It was really a very strange affair.

When Marcie's fall classes began, their relative leisure ended. Thad had moved back upstairs when the kids caught his cold so he could help during wakeful, fretful nights, but he and Marcie didn't make love so much as they had couplings.

In mid-September there was a period of cold, nature's warning of what was to come. As the Fosters lay snugly in bed, Marcie observed, "I really don't think an affair means you're supposed to move in. I think it just means we're supposed to be extra friendly on dates and not go out with anyone else."

"Do you want me to move back downstairs?"

"Ummm, not especially." She curled up next to him under the blanket.

"Do you want me to sleep up here?"

"Well . . . all right."

"Why?"

"That other tiger doesn't put his arms around me." She wiggled a little, getting closer to him.

"And you like that?"

"Weeelll, it keeps me from falling out of bed."

"What else do you like?" His voice had grown rough.

"I like you." She loved him.

"I don't believe we've established the ground rules for this affair. You're not supposed to go to bed in a T-shirt and panties." He sat her up and took them off her.

"The black nightgown?" she guessed.

"Nothing."

"Nothing at all?"

He clenched his fist and pulled up his arm so that she could see his bunched arm muscles. "See that? It's from taking off that T-shirt and those panties so often."

"I thought you lifted weights."

"I only lift you. So no T-shirts and no panties in bed. Understand?"

"You'll get flabby," she warned.

"I'll think of another way to keep in shape." He raised himself and leaned over her to kiss her mouth. She responded eagerly. He rubbed his face over hers and then down over her soft, bare breasts and up under them, pushing them.

His beard prickled her tender skin and sent waves of erotic sensation zinging along her nerves. He moved his big, hard hands over her stomach, around her navel, and between her hipbones. She murmured sighs of contentment.

But he surprised her. He lay back and said, "Make love to me."

She had on occasion initiated their lovemaking, but he'd always taken over and guided them. He'd dominated the variations of their love themes. She'd cooperated, as he'd instructed and with great enjoyment, but she'd never orchestrated their movements.

Hesitantly she began by kissing him more fully. He responded tentatively and waited. She kissed him again, her tongue caressing his lips. His parted then, allowing her tongue entrance. Her reactions, her enjoyment, became fevered.

She brushed her breasts against his hot, hairy chest and relaxed, relishing the texture of his maleness against her smooth, tender skin. She kissed him as she stroked him.

Moving to her hands and knees, she bent over him and teased him with her mouth and breasts until her own need heightened. She became wild and bold and innovative. She coiled herself around him, this way and that, stroking and smoothing, nibbling and touching, kissing and licking.

He managed to hold out for a remarkable length of time, considering how enflaming she became. She was groaning with need, but he made her wait. "Do you want me?" he demanded.

She laughed huskily. "Yes."

"Mindlessly?" He pressed for her reply.

"Can there be any doubt?"

"Would you take another man right now? Wanting it as you do, would any man do?"

In the dimly lit room, she sat up, mind-bendingly erotic to him. Naked, her hair in disarray, her mouth beginning to pout with anger, her breasts swollen with desire, she stared at him. "What nonsense are you talking about?"

"You want me to make love to you, right?"

"Yes." But she sounded uncertain because his strange mood perplexed her.

"Would you take another man if he made love to you now?"

"Are you mad?" She was deeply offended.

"Would you?"

"No!"

"Why not?" His eyes narrowed as he waited for her reply.

"This is silly." She gestured angrily.

"No. Tell me. Why not?"

Furiously, she snapped, "I don't *want* another man. I want you."

"Do you love me?"

"Yes!"

"That's what I wanted to hear." He reached for her, laughing deep in his throat, very pleased. He tried to cuddle her, but his questions had put her off. He turned on the bedside lamp. "Look at the ring."

She blinked and raised her hand to shield her eyes from the bright light. When her eyes had adjusted, she could finally look at the ring. "It's a friendship ring," she stated flatly.

"Look closer. I had it made especially for you. See? The man's hand is holding the woman's. See the difference in size? It's his right hand and her left hand. They aren't shaking hands; he's holding hers. He's holding her so she can't get away. I meant it for us. Although we're divorced, I'm not letting you go."

"Why not?"

"Because I love you, and you're mine."

She stared at him, flabbergasted.

"Then why...?"

"Why the divorce?"

She nodded, lying in the lamplight, her hair a dark cloud around her head, her blue eyes filled with hurt and confusion.

"I've always wanted to have an affair with you. I told you that. No other woman attracts me."

"Do you mean...?" She struggled to sit up, but he pushed her back down.

"I didn't do anything about the divorce because I wanted to know what you would do, how far you'd let it go. I needed to find out if you married me because you loved me or if you'd married me to sleep with me legally or if you loved me enough for us to survive all this."

"You're insane."

"You love me," he stated serenely. "Without all this, how was I to know? When I talked about a divorce, you didn't object at all. I had to know. You seemed to take up the divorce idea so fast," he continued, "and you never appeared to question it. I had to see if you'd stop us. But you didn't. You didn't tell me you loved me or that you wanted me to stay or even that you'd miss me. But you did make love with me so sweetly, and there was the tie. If it hadn't been for the tie you made for me, I'd have been scared."

A shiver went through her. "How could you have done this to us?" she demanded. "I've been sick to my soul over you. I thought you didn't love me, that you were tired of me."

"How could you have thought that?" he asked, astonished. "Why didn't you say something?"

"Why didn't *you?* Why didn't you ask me? Or tell me what was bothering you?"

He reached out and turned off the lamp. Then he said in a low voice that made her toes curl, "I love you with all my heart and soul. Without you, I would die. I look at you and all of life is worthwhile. But I didn't think you were paying any attention to me. I had to shake us up. I didn't think you cared. I thought I was just a habit."

"Oh, Thad, you're my *life.*"

They kissed a long, lovely kiss. Later, he raised his head and pulled her gently close and said, "Will you marry me?"

"I don't believe you," she whispered.

"Will you?"

"Thad, what have you been doing to us?"

"That's what you should have asked five months ago."

"I was waiting for you to say something."

He rose up on his elbows to peer into her face. "We need to promise to tell each other what's wrong, what hurts, how we feel about things."

"If you'd done that, it would have saved me a lot of heartache."

"I'm sorry, darling. I never meant to hurt you. I only wanted to know if you loved me enough."

"After all I've done and put up with and coped with? How could any man doubt it after all that?"

"But you didn't say so."

"I do love you."

"Would you do it all again? Say, in fifteen years? I understand the forties are tough on a man, and I might need more reassurance. Will you have an affair with me then?"

"Oh, Thad, you stupid man. I'll do whatever it takes."

"Me, too."

They kissed tenderly, cherishing each other for a long time before they finally curled up close together and went to sleep.